THE BOWLING WAS SUPERFINE

THE BOWLING WAS SUPERFINE

WEST INDIAN WRITING AND WEST INDIAN CRICKET

EDITED BY STEWART BROWN AND IAN MCDONALD

PEEPAL TREE

First published in Great Britain in 2012
Peepal Tree Press Ltd
17 King's Avenue
Leeds LS6 1QS
UK

ISBN: 978 1 84523 054 8

Supported by
ARTS COUNCIL
ENGLAND

CONTENTS

Ian McDonald   Foreword: Cricket: A Hunger in the West
      Indian Soul   9
Stewart Brown   Introduction   17

POETRY

John Agard   The Devil at Lords   37
    Prospero Caliban Cricket   37
    Professor David Dabydeen at the Crease   39
Joan Anim-Addo   Thoughts from a Cricket Orphan   40
    Take a Peep at the Crowd   41
    She Cousin from Trinidad   42
Edward Baugh   The Pulpit Eulogists of Frank Worrell   43
    View from the George Headley Stand, Sabina   44
James Berry   Fast Bowler   45
Roger Bonair-Agard   Gully   47
    To Mimic Magic   48
Kamau Brathwaite   Rites   52
Jean Binta Breeze   Song for Lara   58
    on cricket, sex and housework   60
Lloyd W. Brown   Cricket Grounds, Plymouth   61
Stewart Brown   Test Match Sabina Park   63
    Counter Commentary at Kensington Oval   64
Faustin Charles   Viv   66
    Cricket's in My Blood   66
Merle Collins   Quality Time   68
David Dabydeen   For Rohan Babulal Kanhai   70
Fred D'Aguiar   Extract from *Guyanese Days*   71
Kwame Dawes   Alado Seanadra   72
Ann Marie Dewar   Cricket (A-We Jim)   74
Ian Dieffenthaller   Weather Report   76
J.D. Douglas   I'm a West Indian in Britain   77
Howard Fergus   Lara Reach   78
    Short of a Century   79
    Conquest   80
Delores Gauntlett   Cricket Boundaries   82
Cecil Gray   Sonny Ramadhin   83
    Practice   84
    Still Driving   85

A.L. Hendriks	Their Mouths But Not Their Hearts	86
Linton Kwesi Johnson	Reggae fi Dada	87
Paul Keens-Douglas	Tanti at the Oval	90
Roi Kwabena	all part of a day's play	96
E. A. Markham	On Another Field, an Ally: a West Indian Batsman Talks Us Towards the Century	97
Ian McDonald	Test Match	99
	Massa Day Done	99
Kei Miller	Drink and Die	101
Egbert Moore (Lord Beginner)	Victory Calypso, Lord's 1950	103
Grace Nichols	Test Match High Mass	105
Sasenarine Persaud	Call Him the Babu	106
Rajandaye Ramkissoon-Chen	On Lara's 375	108
Eric Roach	To Learie	110
Krishna A. Samaroo	A Cricketing Gesture	111
G. K. Sammy	Cricket in the Road	112
Bruce St. John	Cricket	114
William Walcott	Bondmen	117
Milton Vishnu Williams	Batting is My Occupation	119
Benjamin Zephaniah	How's Dat	120

FICTION

Michael Anthony	Cricket in the Road	123
Deryck M. Bernard	Bourda	126
Cyril Dabydeen	Faster They Come	131
Neville Dawes	Extract from *Interim*	137
Rayhat Deonandan	King Rice	138
Garfield Ellis	Extract from *Such As I Have*	141
J.B. Emtage	Extracts from *Brown Sugar*	152
Bernard Heydorn	Cricket, Lovely Cricket	156
Carl Jackson	The Professional	161
Anthony Kellman	Extract from *The Houses of Alphonso*	170
Ismith Khan	The Red Ball	171
George Lamming	Extract from *The Emigrants*	178
	Extract from *In the Castle of My Skin*	179
Earl Lovelace	Extract from *Salt*	180
	Extract from "Victory and the Blight"	183
	Franklyn Batting, extract from *Is Just a Movie*	186
Glenville Lovell	Extract from *Song of Night*	189

Ian McDonald	Extract from *The Hummingbird Tree*	191
Earl McKenzie	Cricket Season	195
Mark McWatt	A Boy's First Test Match	199
Edgar Mittelholzer	Extract from A Morning at the Office	208
Rooplall Monar	Cookman	209
Moses Nagamootoo	Extract from *Hendree's Cure*	214
V. S. Naipaul	Extract from "Hat"	216
Eileen Ormsby Cooper	Cricket in the Blood	218
Ivor Osbourne	Extract from *Prodigal*	223
Sam Selvon	The Cricket Match	225
Anthony C. Winkler	Extract from *The Lunatic*	229
Sylvia Wynter	Bat and Ball	237

DRAMA

| Errol John | Extract from *Moon on a Rainbow Shawl* | 245 |

ESSAYS, MEMORIES AND EXCUSES

Colin Babb	Cricket, Lovely Cricket: London SW16 to Guyana and Back	251
Edward Baugh	Speech in Honour of Allan Rae	256
Hilary McD. Beckles	History, the King, the Crown Prince and I	261
Frank Birbalsingh	Return to Bourda	267
Learie Constantine	Village Cricket	271
Kwame Dawes	A Birthday Gift	276
John Figueroa	West Indies and Test Cricket: A Special Contribution?	281
Beryl Gilroy	Village Cricket	289
Stanley Greaves	The Joys of Conjecture	291
C.L.R. James	The Window, from *Beyond a Boundary*	294
Paul Keens-Douglas	Me an' Cricket	304
Earl Lovelace	Like When Somebody Dead	308
Ian McDonald	Cricket's Most Memorable Over	311
Alfred Mendes	Extract from *The Autobiography of Alfred H. Mendes*	313
Edgar Mittelholzer	Extract from *A Swarthy Boy*	315
V. S. Naipaul	Test	316
Philip Nanton	Night Cricket at Carlton Club, Barbados	325
Christopher Nicole	Introduction to *West Indian Cricket*	326

Vincent Roth   Extract from *A Life in Guyana*   328
Chris Searle   Lara's Innings   330
Derek Walcott   Extract from "Leaving School"   341
P. F. Warner   Cricket in the West Indies   342

Notes on Contributors   347
Sources and Acknowledgements   362
Index   367

What More Can One Ask of Cricket?

To bridge continents with glorious uncertainty.
To leave a legacy of unpredictability.

John Agard

IAN MCDONALD

FOREWORD

This is the text of the Frank Worrell Memorial Lecture at the Centre of Caribbean Studies, London Metropolitan University, June 2005.

CRICKET: A HUNGER IN THE WEST INDIAN SOUL

I cannot very well explain to you what a great honour it is to have been invited to give the inaugural lecture in what is bound to become a famous series in honour of a very great man, a very great West Indian and one of the greatest and most influential cricketers in the long and glorious history of the greatest game ever invented.

A game invented, I should say, not by man but by God, as an old man explained to me a long, long time ago as I was watching a village game in St. Augustine, Trinidad, from under a samaan tree when I was a boy – and ever since then I have known the old man was right: a sublime game, a sacred game, a game of transcendental beauty and value in that beloved homeland of ours, the West Indies.

You will not need to be told that West Indies cricket has fallen into difficulties. Up to a few days ago I was in deep mourning after the painful and less than honourable losses to South Africa and to Pakistan in the One-Day Internationals. Now, I feel a lot better after we beat Pakistan conclusively in the first Test – except that I saw the empty, accusing stands at Kensington and knew that a canker is burrowing in the heart of the rose.

Problems of weak and sometimes blundering administration, team indiscipline and disunity, strife between players and management, bitter sponsorship battles, an erratic shuffling of the captaincy – and moneymaking creeping insidiously into the game as the primary concern on all sides – all have brought about a general malaise which has undermined the team's confidence, purpose and performance and diminished our pride in the team although not, I believe, our abiding loyalty.

This lecture will not be about all that. That is temporary. We need to remember that every age is not golden and some are even made of lead. But now more than ever we should recall the deeper sources of inspiration which inform the history of West Indies cricket. In our eras of greatness, when West Indies took the field, ghostly presences walked with the players representing commitment to a higher cause, loyalty to the proudest of traditions and attachment to a long line of heroes – and the twelfth man in the team always answered to the name of courage. Such inspiring presences seem almost to have vanished these days. But, you will see, they will emerge again soon enough from the shadows.

I am awed by the responsibility given me this evening. The only credentials I have for delivering this lecture are my love of cricket and my love of the West Indies. As a tennis player I became good enough, and was extremely proud, to captain the West Indies in the Davis Cup but when asked by an interviewer what my desire would be I could do nothing else but say that if given the choice by some benign deity between winning Wimbledon and winning a Test match for the West Indies by scoring a century at Lords I would choose the century at Lords. It is a game that has entered my dreams and has lifelong captured my imagination.

As for the West Indies, I have close connections by ancestry, birth or adoption with St. Kitts, Nevis, Antigua and Barbuda, Trinidad & Tobago and Guyana but it is by deep conviction and commitment that I am West Indian. I love the West Indies. I wish we were a full-fledged nation. I hope that day will come.

Perhaps I do have one other credential to give a lecture on cricket. It is that a great-uncle of mine, Major A.E. "Bertie" Harragin, once hit the immortal W.G. Grace for six sixes in an innings. It was in the first match of the West Indies tour of England in 1906, a game against W.G. Grace's Eleven, when my uncle Bertie, to our family's eternal credit, had the temerity to hit the Grand Old Man of cricket for six towering sixes in a flashing innings of 50. I like to think of that wild colonial boy smiting the revered W.G. out of the ground no less than six times on a summer's afternoon as a distant foretaste of the independence which lay in our future as a people.

Certainly my qualifications as a player to give this lecture are nil. The most I can say is that when I was a boy I was quite a good leg-break bowler who, it turned out, could only bowl googlies which unhappy fact soon enough became known to every batsman who ever faced me. My other claim to non-distinction was that I was one of those West Indian schoolboys, of which I have a feeling there may have been many, dismissed as a batsman in a way which the laws of cricket do not define. In that particular innings, coming in at number 10, I had been playing and missing for about four overs, first awkwardly swishing on the off-side, then even more awkwardly not making any connection on the leg-side. A ball came which I left alone, quite expertly I thought, but when I looked up to my horror I saw the finger of the umpire, who was also our games master, a strict disciplinarian and lover of the game, decisively uplifted. I protested, of course, and requested an explanation. "Don't argue, McDonald," he said. "Be on your way. You're out for ugly batting." It was an early and striking indication for me that the game has an aesthetic dimension which is all-important.

Can one tell the moment when one falls in love? That moment when first love crystallises and never is forgotten? I remember the crystalline instant when I first fell in love with cricket and would thereafter be eternally enraptured. I was a schoolboy at Queen's Royal College in Port-of-Spain in the late 1940s and when inter-colonial matches were played we were given half-days off and we would walk down to the Oval to see Trinidad play. There came a day when I was watching Trinidad play Barbados and Frank Worrell was batting. As time passed a realization built up in me that I was receiving a gift beyond price, a blessing that would not fade. And then Wilfred Ferguson, the wonderful and popular Fergie, sent down a lovely leg-break and Frank Worrell, all grace and perfect balance, with a dancer's marvellous, adroit step, late cut the ball most delicately to the boundary in a pure and gleaming flash of genius. I still have the image in my mind. It was the moment when my love and reverence for cricket crystallized forever.

It may or may not be a coincidence that just about that time I had discovered a love for poetry which would never leave me. And from that time have associated Frank Worrell's peerless late cut with Gerard Manley Hopkins' eternally beautiful poem "The Windhover" which about then had also transfixed me. Worrell and Hopkins – they both helped to shape my young soul.

Let me read the first few lines of that poem and imagine yourself at the Queens Park Oval on a golden afternoon:

> I caught this morning morning's minion, king-
> dom of daylight's dauphin, dapple-dawn-drawn Fal-
> con, in his riding
> Of the rolling level, underneath him steady air, and
> striding
> High there, how he rung upon the rein of a wimpling wing
> In his ecstasy! Then off, off forth on swing,
> As a skate's heel sweeps smooth on a bow-bend:
> the hurl and gliding
> Rebuffed the big wind. My heart in hiding
> Stirred for a bird, – the achieve of, the mastery of the thing![1]

Those lovely words that sum up anything greatly and naturally done.

Does that not remind you of batting at its glorious, Worrellian, God-given best – "the achieve of, the mastery of the thing!"

From the start, therefore, Frank Worrell stood for the beauty and poetry of cricket. As the years passed I grew to learn how much more he meant to West Indian cricket and cricket as a world game.

To put it simply, there was a hunger in the West Indian soul which Worrell above all came to express through his mastery of all that cricket involves and through his leadership. Through his intelligence, his unerring sense of values, his example, his calm not to say serene authority, he inspired West Indians of every stripe and colour in all walks of life and lifted up the whole game to a new level of excitement, popularity and world-importance, illuminating it anew when it had been fading almost into decadence.

It was perhaps inevitable as indigenous intellectual authority gained the upper hand conclusively everywhere in the West Indies, and political independence loomed, that the white mercantile-planter class would be dislodged from automatic domination and leadership in the game. What was not inevitable was that a man of exactly the perfect temperament, intellect, character and charismatic leadership qualities should have emerged to break the mould and make the transition seamless and inspirational. He was the perfect leader of men and he believed in the West Indies with his whole heart. Here is C.L.R. James describing with what absolute sureness of touch Worrell brought out the best in the West Indies team he captained:

> The West Indies team in Australia, on the field and off, was playing above what it knew of itself. If anything went wrong it knew that it would be instantly told, in unhesitating and precise language, how to repair it, and that the captain's certainty and confidence extended to his belief that what he wanted would be done. He did not instill into but drew out of his players. What they discovered in themselves must have been a revelation to few more than to the players themselves. When the time came to say goodbye some of the toughest players could only shake the captain's hand and look away, not trusting themselves to speak.[2]

Talk about the right man in the right place at the right time! And so he stepped with supreme assurance onto the world stage.

Worrell became captain of the West Indies at a time when cricket was losing its way. Caution was the order of the day – batsmen playing for safety, bowlers bowling defensively, captains seeking to avoid defeat at all costs. It is clear that Worrell decided to restore to Test cricket in 1960 the spirit and the fervour of the game he loved. We know what happened. Richie Benaud, the Australian captain, met him halfway, the greatest Test series ever played transformed expectations, and the West Indies, even in losing, inaugurated a cricketing renaissance. When the West Indies visited England in 1963 the Lord Mayor of London summed it up, "A gale of change has blown through the hallowed halls of cricket." Who can doubt that Frank Worrell is indelibly one of the greatest, most transforming figures in the history of cricket?

How might one convey what Frank Worrell stood for and what he wanted our cricketers to absorb into their very beings and thereby set an example to all West Indians? How might one convey what it takes to be builders of a team and builders of a nation?

There is a word which has a meaning for West Indians beyond the ordinary dictionary definition. The word is respect. Nuff respect is an expression which recognizes achievement at the very highest level, recognizes pride, excellence, superior performance and gallant behaviour which is uniquely admirable. It is a concept which, I fear, in all its West Indian ramifications and special meaning has been losing its relevance in West Indian cricket and West Indian teams in recent times. If West Indian cricket is to return to its moorings nuff respect must be shown again with the fervour which Frank Worrell and our other founding fathers of the concept taught with such absolute conviction – respect for the history and traditions of cricket, its deeds and heroes; respect for the laws of cricket, never to be denied or circumvented; respect for the umpires and officials who are given to be guardians of the laws; respect and loyalty and love as in battle for team mates; respect also for opponents for they are after all joint legatees of the great game and its traditions; respect and love of country, in the knowledge that nowhere else will defiance or surrender register so profoundly in the people's psyche; in the end respect for oneself as player and participant, keepers of the shrine, a responsibility not to be taken lightly or forgotten.

When one enters a temple, a church, a mosque one has to behave in a certain way, one has to show nuff respect. When you enter cricket for the West Indies it is like that. Not just a hunger for runs or wickets or money or fame but a hunger in the soul for something greater than personal benefit or achievement. It should be recognizable without definition. For a long time it was.

Our West Indian leaders have been struggling hard to shape our Caribbean region into a single, valid economic and, eventually perhaps, political space. For long they have recognized cricket as a vital means to achieving the holy grail of unity, come-together effort, common identity and solidarity. At their Inter-Sessional Meeting in the year 2000 it was plainly stated, "Heads of Government reiterated that cricket occupies a special place in the economic and social life of the people of the Region and that every effort must be made by all stakeholders to encourage the continued development of the game." A recording secretary's unembellished prose, it is true, but surely in no other part of the world is a game of such supreme value that concern about its future is reflected in the regular deliberations of Heads of Government.

Of course, the Heads of Government should not have limited the value of cricket to the economic and social life of the people of the Region. They will certainly have known better than that. The value and importance of cricket in the West Indies extends deep into the cultural and psychological domain of the people.

We must always begin with C.L.R. James's famous comment: "What do they know of cricket who only cricket know? West Indians crowding to Tests bring with them their whole past history and the future hopes of our peoples."[3]

It means a great deal to be a cultural leader in the world – to be prominent in the arts, in literature, in music, in theatre, in architecture, in film, in style and fashion, in scholarship. And cricket as much as any game represents an international cultural experience of abiding significance. To play an important role in cricket gives us stature in the world. There is pride and self-confidence when we compete strongly among the best anywhere. And we feel diminished when we do not.

Who can doubt that cricket is central to what keeps us together as West Indians? C.L.R. James instructed us in this in *Beyond a Boundary*, the greatest book ever written about cricket. He pointed out, by example, that English people have a conception of themselves breathed from birth. King Alfred and the burnt cakes, Richard the Lion Heart, the Crusaders, Shakespeare, Mighty Nelson, the Iron Duke and Waterloo, the Charge of the Light Brigade, the few who did so much for so many – these and such as these, C.L.R. points out, constitute a national tradition.

For West Indians our icons to a remarkable extent are cricketing icons: imperious Challenor, "Furioso" George John rolling up his sleeves as if to hurl an iron spear, the leaping Constantine, Headley in all his glorious, defiant genius, "Those two friends of mine, Ramadhin and Valentine," the silken elegance of Stollmeyer and the obdurate defiance of Allan Rae, the indescribable magic of Rohan Kanhai, Sobers the greatest cricketer who ever lived, Hall with crucifix blazing in the sun and Griffith inseparable from the other end, the great Gibbs who could spin a ball on marble ground and make it bounce on feathers, the three immortal W's, Worrell in Australia and the Tied Test and little Joe Solomon caught forever in that famous picture throwing down the last Australian wicket, Roy Fredericks hooking Lillee and Thomson again and again to the boundary at Perth, Holding of the whispering death, Greenidge of the thunder bat, Clive Lloyd and his magnificent pride of fast bowlers, Viv Richards the Master Blaster, Ambrose and Walsh saving our pride again and again, the ever reliable and faithful Chanderpaul, Brian Lara whose princely deeds will never fade despite all controversy. These and a hundred others, these are our Knights of the Round Table. And in their exploits we weave a good part of the nation's historical fabric, our own Bayeux Tapestry beyond any price.

Our nation is not fully formed. It needs its heroes and brave traditions and its sagas. I cannot believe that this tradition, this legacy, passed on from hero to hero, is at an end. Yet there are those of the younger school of commentators and scholars who clearly think so. This is what Hilary Beckles, Principal of the University of the West Indies, Cave Hill campus, and distinguished new-generation scholar of the game, has forthrightly written:

> Today's cricket hero now wishes to be identified as a professional craftsman with only a secondary responsibility to the wider sociopolitical agenda carried out by his predecessors. He does not wish to carry the burden of responsibility for nationalist pride, regional integration and the viability of the nationstate. He sees himself as an apolitical, transnational, global professional aiming to maximize financial earnings within an attractive market, and is principally motivated and guided by these considerations.[4]

Hilary Beckles continues:

The logical implication of this self-perception is that the cricket hero wishes to distance his performance and psychological state from the considerations of the 1950s and 1960s, from the political project of nation building. [...] These post-nationalist players want to function as "pure" entrepreneurs within the market economy of sport, and with a minimum emotional or ideological bond to the psychological needs of nationstates.[5]

The thought that this may be true shakes me to the core of my belief in what cricket stands for in the West Indies. In the writings of W.B. Yeats there is a wonderfully eloquent phrase: he speaks of "a community bound together by imaginative possessions". Yeats used this phrase in the context of discussing the importance of a National Theatre for his beloved Ireland. Yeats also wrote of theatre as an institution for transforming those isolated from one another into the unity of one audience. And he wrote that it was impossible for a nation to exist if they were "no national institutions to reverence, no national success to admire without a model of it in the mind of the people".[7]

When I think of cricket and the hope of West Indian nationhood the words Yeats spoke so eloquently strike with me a chord that sings. Economically, we are much divided and sometimes seem tempted to go our separate ways. Politically, we remain suspicious of each other and therefore cannot so far summon the will to come together in the many ways we must know are necessary for practical nationhood. But cricket, there I have always hoped we are different and better and more confident and more together. Truly cricket is supremely an imaginative possession which binds our Caribbean community together. If it is no longer to be so we have lost something of infinite value.

When we look around the world it indeed seems that life is only about economics, about getting and spending in the marketplace, about who comes off best and who gets the most. But of course it is not so. The historian, R.H. Tawney, author of *Religion and the Rise of Capitalism*, had a longer and better view of man's ultimate concerns when he wrote the following:

> The most obvious facts are the most easily forgotten. Both the existing economic order and too many of the projects advanced for reconstructing it break down through their neglect of the truism that, since even quite ordinary men have souls, no increase in national wealth will compensate them for arrangements which insult their self-respect and impair their freedom. A reasonable estimate of economic organisation must allow for the fact that... it must satisfy criteria which are not purely economic.[8]

One reason I know that he is right is my lifelong experience with West Indian cricket. There is a hunger in the souls of West Indians for this great game which needs to be satisfied and is part of our yearning for a more fulfilled life. When that hunger is less satisfied and that yearning less fulfilled it is an unhappy and restless time – as it is now. Our administrators and players must always remember that. They must never imagine that they are merely corporate managers, or in the case of our beloved cricketers, merely players who win or lose another game and make what they possibly can out of doing so. They are custodians who inherit and pass on what Derek Walcott named "the bread that lasts".

From the very start – the wonder of Frank Worrell's late cut, the inspiration of Manley Hopkins' gleaming lines in "The Windhover" – I have associated lovely cricket with beautiful poetry. Over the years, more often than I can count, tears have come to my eyes when I have seen displayed such surely God-given signals of man's instinct to create perfect works of art. And I think of Derek Walcott's great lines in his poem written for Joseph Brodsky, "Forest of Europe":

> what's poetry, if it is worth its salt,
> but a phrase man can pass from hand to mouth.
>
> From hand to mouth, across the centuries,
> the bread that lasts when systems have decayed.[8]

Poetry, of course. And, in the West Indies, cricket also. The bread that lasts. I have felt that all my life. If the spirit that evokes that feeling has faded in the younger generations and cannot be revived it will be a terrible loss for West Indian cricket. It will also, I believe, depress and undermine the hopes I am sure we all have for ever-closer unity and identity and, eventually, nationhood.

Vice-Chancellor, ladies and gentlemen, I thank you again. I will never forget this great honour. It is a highlight of my life.

June 2, 2005

Endnotes

1. "The Windhover", *Poems of Gerard Manley Hopkins, now first published* (London: Humphrey Milford, 1918), p. 29.
2. C.L.R James, *Beyond a Boundary* (London: Hutchinson, 1963), p. 250.
3. James, ibid., Preface.
4. Hilary McD. Beckles, The Development of West Indies Cricket: Vol 2: The Age of Globalisation, (Mona: UWI Press, 1998), p. 19.
5. Ibid., pp. 19-20.
6. W.B. Yeats, "The Galway Plains", *Collected Works Volume IV, Early Essays* (London: MacMillan) pp.156-159.
7. W.B. Yeats, *Memoirs* (London: MacMillan), p. 183
8. R.H. Tawney, Religion and the Rise of Capitalism (Middlesex: Penguin Books, 1926, 1938) p. 218.
9. Derek Walcott, "The Forest of Europe", *The Star-Apple Kingdom* (London: Cape, 1980) p. 40.

STEWART BROWN

INTRODUCTION

> Cricket has always been more than a game in Trinidad. In a society which demanded no skills and offered no rewards to merit, cricket was the only activity which permitted a man to grow to his full stature and to be measured against international standards… The cricketer was our only hero-figure. (V.S. Naipaul) [1]

Ian McDonald's beautifully written Frank Worrell Memorial lecture, which we have adapted and used here as the foreword to this anthology, establishes the foundational significance of cricket to a sense of West Indian culture and identity. This anthology of writings about cricket by West Indian writers (although that regional definition has been stretched a little here and there) sets out to demonstrate the truth of Ian McDonald's's observations. Notwithstanding the recent decline in the West Indian cricket team's performances and fortunes, nor the scandal and embarrassments of the Stanford affair, nor even the apparent decline in the West Indian public's affection for the sport as measured by attendances at big games and numbers playing the game at school and club level, still you do not have to scratch very deep beneath the surface to discover how profoundly the language, values and ethos of cricket remain as fundamental elements of West Indian life.

The variety of voices collected in this anthology speak to that important place cricket holds; writers from all corners of the "cricket playing Caribbean"[2] and its diasporas are collected here, including many of the region's major writers. There is not much that unites writers as personally distinctive as V.S. Naipaul and Kamau Brathwaite, but the affection, insight and empathy that characterises both Brathwaite's poem "Rites"[3] and Naipaul's essay "Test"[4] is remarkable. That shared engagement is evident in the attention paid to the language of the ordinary West Indian characters, spectators at test matches home and away, who become the *dramatis personae* of these two pieces (as indeed they do in many other poems and stories in the collection, whether set at a test match or a showdown between rival village teams). Listening to the West Indian crowd – the banter, the arguments, the braggadocio and the disappointment – becomes a prime occasion for writers to catch the vivid vocabularies, the music and the distinctive grammar of spoken West Indian creoles. It is those voices, those inflections, which tell the stories in this collection, for, almost without exception, the writers are fans-in-the-crowd first before they are writers. They understand the dreams and frustrations, share the emotional commitment to the players and really know what the West Indian cricket team and its star players have meant to generations of such fans. It is that insight that distinguishes this anthology from other books on or about West Indian cricket.

That crossover, from fan to writer, is one of several ways in which West Indian cricket and West Indian literature intertwine. In some ways the writers become another kind of West Indian team, representing the region, knowing that more than personal talent is being weighed and measured when their books are read and reviewed. Whether they wish it or not, the writers, like the players, become "representatives" and have to accept that particular burden, which may inspire them to greater things or may even act as some kind of brake on their creativity – hence the few writers who resist any kind of geographical, ethnic or gender tag and insist that they are "just writers".

However, as the spread and range of the contributions to this anthology suggest, and if only because it *was* such a ubiquitous presence in the background to any twentieth-century West Indian childhood, cricket as a subject does carry a particular cultural charge for very many of the region's writers. As the few excuses in the "Essays, Memories and Excuses" section of the book suggests, several writers who haven't engaged much with the game have nevertheless felt obliged to justify this omission! The schoolboy Derek Walcott, for example, declares his determination to make his contribution (to his House and, by implication, the region) in the Alpha Book for outstanding scholarship and creativity rather than on the cricket field (see the extract from his essay "Leaving School"[5]). It is interesting, though, that in his brief, self-excusing paragraph Walcott confesses to having engaged in play-acting to convince his peers and schoolmasters that, as a reluctant wicketkeeper, he was more seriously hurt by a batsman's wild flailings than was in fact the case – the budding dramatist performing for effect even as he leaves the field of play!

There are other ways that writing and cricket cross over. I have mentioned the voices and language of the crowds that commentate, one way and another, on the games, big and small, that are the focus of much of this literature. The vocabulary of those commentaries is oftentimes distinctive and unlikely to be found in *Wisden* or even the *Daily Gleaner*'s accounts of the same action. The fundamental creativity that so enriches West Indian speech is evident too in this arena, whether simply as reportage or in the imagined and embroidered dialogue of the stories the writers tell. So, for example, in his chapter "Cricket and Obeah" in his quasi-fictional *Hendree's Cure*, Moses Nagamootoo tells of the unplayable "snake-break" delivered by the local hero Johnny Pilloo. These grubbing leg breaks invariably bowled unwary batsmen behind their ankles and were greeted by the home crowd with cries of "Bite he, Johnny; bite he".[6] Other writers have proffered alternative definitions for some of the traditional language of cricket; so, for example, John Agard suggests that, in the context of Caribbean history, LBW might stand for "Limbo Beyond Water",[7] while in his essay, "The Joys of Conjecture",[8] Stanley Greaves imagines a quirkily surreal and counterfactual history of the game.

In a more serious vein there is a striking similarity between the way Alfred Mendes, one of the Anglophone Caribbean's early cultural nationalists, describes the manner in which West Indians claimed and changed the imperial game to make it something distinctively their own, and the way Kamau Brathwaite has written about the process by which the imposed language of slavery and the plantation was undermined, usurped and remade to become the creole languages of the islands, *the* medium of West Indian identity and self-expression.[9] In Mendes' words , the West Indian

> at once proceeded to impose *his* personality upon the game, *his* subtle version of its spirit, and this was vividly illustrated when teams from England played Test Matches against black West Indians.[10]

Part of the rationale for this anthology was to examine the ways in which regional writers' evocations of cricket in the West Indies differed from the versions available in the writings of British commentators. Just as many postcolonial writers felt a need to "write back to the centre" in terms of challenging the stories that had been told about their societies in mainstream imperial literature, so the representation of West Indian cricket in British (and possibly Australian) journalism and literature often reflects the prevailing values of the times in which it was written. So while, for most British writers, all West Indian cricketers – of whatever ethnic background – are to some extent exotic, black and brown West Indian cricketers are characteristically caricatured in ways that seem to carry overtones of racial disdain, even in contemporary times. Even when well intentioned, such commentators have tended to fall back on unconscious stereotypes: reference to "natural athletes", "spontaneity" and "calypso cricket" all reinforce a certain notion of the West Indian person which has its roots deep in slavery and arguments against emancipation. Learie Constantine was the first black West Indian cricketer really to make a mark in English cricket and he was often described in such terms by British commentators, even when they were ostensibly singing his praises. As C.L.R. James remarked in *Beyond a Boundary*,

> Constantine's leg glance from outside the off-stump to long leg was a classical stroke. It was not due to his marvellous West Indian eyes and marvellous West Indian wrists. It was due, if you must have it, to his marvellous West Indian brains.[11]

Constantine was himself a distinguished writer about cricket as well as an outstanding player of the game. His account of his time in the Lancashire League is revealing in all sorts of ways about the values of the society he came from and that in which he settled: his autobiography *Cricket in the Sun*[12] is a fascinating mix of social history, travelogue, philosophy, anthropology and cricketing memoir. It is perhaps the first demonstration of the truth of C.L.R. James' most famous observation, "What do they know of cricket who only cricket know?" As the poems, stories and essays collected here make plain, cricket is implicated in so many aspects of Caribbean life, from – at the public level – issues of history, politics and national identity, to – in more personal terms – matters of dignity, ambition and dream.

Indeed cricket is so entwined in a West Indian morality and system of values that many writers have understood that the language and lore of cricket is a fertile source of metaphor that will resonate beyond the usual literary domain. The image of life as a kind of innings and especially death as the final dismissal is employed in several of the pieces collected here. Interestingly both Linton Kwesi Johnson and Merle Collins, two poets who otherwise have shown little interest in cricket, employ the metaphor in poems lamenting the passing of their respective fathers. It may be a generational thing as cricket was obviously an important factor in the lives of the two men and it might also be tied to migration, as both poets moved from their islands – Jamaica and Grenada respectively – to settle in Britain (and subsequently, in Merle Collins' case, in the USA) where cricket was less central to their own lives but was part of the remembered landscape of their childhoods. In Johnson's "Reggae fi Dada" the cricket image comes in only at the very end of the poem,

> yet still yu reach fifty six
> before yu lose yu leg wicket[13]

whereas Merle Collins's poem "Quality Time" is structured around the idea of life as an innings, or more particularly that her father's response to his final illness was like his response to hostile bowling in a cricket match,

> They say, *"Go easy"*
> but his batting is steady
>
> and he's smiling. [13]

Other writers use the language and ritual of cricket as a way of talking about such big subjects as religion, history, politics and even sex. Jean Binta Breeze's teasing, sensual poem, "Cricket, sex and housework", manages to find surprisingly lubricious possibilities in the word googly![14]

Merle Collins and Jean Binta Breeze are not unusual as West Indian women writing about cricket. Just as a typical West Indian cricket crowd will include many women as informed and enthusiastic spectators and commentators, so the crowd of writers whose work is collected here includes a good share of female authors. Perhaps the most prolific, in terms of her writings about cricket, is the Grenadian/British poet Joan Anim Addo, who writes not only as an observer but in several poems presents girls and women as players, often enough resented and discriminated against by their male counterparts. Joan Anim Addo is very much a poet of the twenty-first century, but cricket has been an interest of women writers for a long time. We are glad to be able to include two previously uncollected stories, by Sylvia Wynter and Eileen Ormsby Cooper, first heard on the *Caribbean Voices* programme of the 1950s.

22

The crossover between literature and cricket is explored in other ways too. Several writers make comparisons between batting and poetry, indeed that seems the highest praise that can be given. In Bernard Heydorn's "Cricket Lovely Cricket" a batsman is described as showing "such zest and panache, it was poetry in cricket".[15] In a more fundamental way, in Earl McKenzie's story "Cricket Season", batting is presented as the language by which an otherwise inarticulate boy is able to speak, at least to express himself and release his true personality:

> Vincent did poorly at school. But, put a bat in his hand and he was transformed. He became expressive, confident and masterful. He said things with his bat that he could not put into words.[17]

That exceptional fluency, understood in terms of style, is another literary measure that applies to the appreciation of cricket and cricketers. Almost without exception a West Indian crowd applauds a stylish – even if unreliable – batsman over a workaday run accumulator. It is perhaps revealing that there are praise songs aplenty within this selection of literary responses for Brian Lara and Carl Hooper and even Chris Gayle, but no celebration of the gritty, reliable but rarely exuberant Shivnarine Chanderpaul,[18] whose runs have arguably saved the West Indies from humiliation, if not from defeat, over almost two decades. As Anthony Winkler explains in the extract from his novel *The Lunatic*, although the powerful Busha is admired by the crowd for the sheer number of runs he amasses with his heaving muscular six hitting, he "gets no appreciation whatsoever from connoisseurs", his batting is too "rude and clumsy", too "vulgar". "Him think him butchering cow," one spectator remarks, "Him swinging blind, dat's all," responds another.[19] In *Beyond a Boundary* the great C.L.R. James, trying to understand the essence of style, tells the story of his childhood encounter with Matthew Bondman, a man who in life was scorned and vilified by the community for his lack of civility and manners:

> Matthew had one saving grace – Matthew could bat. More than that, Matthew, so crude and vulgar in every aspect of his life, with a bat in his hand was all grace and style. When he practised on an afternoon with the local club people stayed on to watch and walked away when he was finished. He had one particular stroke that he played by going down low on one knee. It may have been a slash through the covers or a sweep to leg. But, whatever it was, whenever Matthew sank down and made it, a long, low "Ah!" came from many a spectator, and my own little soul thrilled with recognition and delight.[20]

But perhaps the most telling account of the importance of that sense of style, of class, is in Earl Lovelace's description of his character Franklyn's disdainful way of *not* playing a shot, of simply leaving the ball alone, in his novel *Is Just a Movie*:

> ...then the ball would come and he would leave it alone, just that, watch the ball and withhold his bat from it. And although it didn't show in the score book,

that was a stroke, that was a statement, that was an acknowledgement of the bowler and an announcement to the world that we here. We have eyes. *We ready*, just to hint to them that they can't play the arse...[21]

So the importance of style is more than just a matter of aesthetics; it reflects notions of dignity and self-respect that root back to the days of slavery and indenture. The use of "we" in Lovelace's account of Franklyn's batting suggests another way in which cricket in the West Indies has always been more than a simple game of bat and ball. As the novelist and sociologist Orlando Patterson suggested as long ago as the late 1960s in his foundational essay on "The Ritual of Cricket",[22] the game has a symbolic and cultural significance in the Caribbean where – particularly at international level – the cricket field becomes an arena for the acting out of deeply felt animosities and the redressing of old wounds. Cricket was first and always the imperial game; its manners and traditions, its language and values were part of the English occupation of Caribbean cultural space. In their usurpation, remaking and subsequent domination of the colonial game West Indians were doing more than simply winning cricket matches. As Lovelace's narrator remarks, when Franklyn is in his full pomp each stylish stroke challenges not only the particular opposing team but also that West Indian plantation history of oppression. Each shot asks the defiant questions, "How you going to stop we? How you go keep us down?" The narrator goes on:

> When Franklyn was batting was we the ones batting, and in the mirror that he had become we would see ourselves in contest with the world. He was holding the bat but the strokes was our strokes and the bowler bowling the ball was England or Australia or Pakistan: the world. Yes, the world.[23]

Many aspects and nuances of that sense of cricket as a historical psycho-drama are explored throughout this collection. Kwame Dawes' essay, "A Birthday Gift", jokingly plays with the idea of how psychically enmeshed West Indians may feel in the very existence of a "West Indies" team. The issues of race and class, morality, history and economics that are inextricably bound up in West Indian cricket are dealt with very directly in Patterson's essay: the gradations of colour around the stands, depending on comfort and shelter from the sun; the past issues of race and captaincy; the historically proletarianised role of the fast bowler; the imperial tensions of playing the English. These are dealt with more obliquely in these literary pieces, but they are there, as are the way race, class and history bear on the particular values that characterise West Indian ways of playing the game, at whatever level it is played.

The ways in which West Indian cricketing stars have been invested with heroic status which extends far beyond that fame given to sportsmen in other parts of the world is a reflection of the extent to which these figures are being applauded for more than mere athletic prowess. John Agard presents the on-field contest in Shakespearian terms in his witty poem "Prospero Caliban Cricket":

Caliban remembering
how Prospero used to call him knave and serf.
Now Caliban striding the cricket turf
like he breathing a nation,
and de ball swinging it own way
like it hear bout self-determination[24]

As a schoolboy in 1981, Roger Bonair-Agard sees that conflict enacted in the famous confrontation between Michael Holding and England's opening batsman Geoff Boycott in the Barbados test match. Boycott, in his way the quintessential English professional – stoic, patriotic, white, the opposite of stylish but grimly determined that "they shall not pass" – faces Holding, the hostile, athletic, black Jamaican fast bowler, later nicknamed "whispering death". Holding softens him up with five fiercely aggressive fast balls and then blows Geoff Boycott away with the final ball of that opening over. It was a memorable spectacle for anyone watching, but for an adolescent West Indian boy it was a life changing moment:

We could not have known
even as we started
from our cafeteria or pavilion
or wherever we gathered the next day
how much men and changed we were[25]

There are many praise-songs in this collection to great West Indian cricketing heroes who are almost always presented as representing some aspect of cultural assertion beyond their mere achievements on the field of play. It is interesting that in both the previous examples it is the fast bowler who takes on that role of avenging warrior, and there are several other pieces devoted to fast bowlers, starting indeed with Learie Constantine, mentioned by the character Charlie in Errol John's play *Moon on a Rainbow Shawl* as being among the early West Indian tourists who, by their success in England, "help put the Indies on the map". A couple of generations later it was the great Barbadian fast bowler Wes Hall who is at the centre of another event which seemed to mark a sea-change in the way West Indian cricket was regarded – especially in Australia. Hall's final over in the famous tied Test in Brisbane in 1960 is nominated by Ian McDonald as "Cricket's Most Memorable Over" and in his essay included here he vividly describes the drama and tension of the occasion. So Constantine, Hall and Holding, three wonderful athletes and world-class performers, but it is not only the achievement of the great fast bowlers that seems to have inspired the writers, it is also the very idea of being able to bowl fast enough to scare and intimidate that catches their characters' imaginations, no matter the real-life situations that confront them. So, for example, in Cyril Dabydeen's wry short story "Faster They Come", set in Canada, the central character Ron, a displaced Guyanese migrant, dreams of becoming a great fast bowler as a way of asserting his presence and dignity in a land indifferent to cricket and, by implication, indifferent to people like him. Similarly, in Ismith Khan's story "The Red Ball", the ability of the small skinny "country boy" Bolan to – with a flick of his wrist – bowl the ball so fast that it defeats his new found city friends on the Queens Park Savannah in Port of Spain, becomes the passport to his acceptance and accommodation in his new environment.

So the dignified stylish batsman and the warrior fast bowler are figures of fact and imagination that resonate at some deep and profound level in a West Indian psyche, figures that speak to dream and ambition as much as reality. But it is arguably the slow bowler, cunning and cool (to adapt Dennis Scott's famous image) who best represents that bitter strand of West Indian experience that is explored in the stories of Anansi, the trickster spider who survives and prospers, against all the odds, by his wit and guile. Anansi out-thinks his antagonists, spinning his webs of confusion. There aren't many pieces honouring West Indian spin bowlers in the collection, but Cecil Gray's praise-song to "Sonny Ramadhin" remembers the heroic achievements of his fellow Trinidadian who was immortalised, along with his Jamaican partner Alf Valentine, as "those two little pals of mine" in Lord Beginner's famous calypso – from which, incidentally, we have taken the title of this anthology. It was Ramadhin and Valentine who spun West Indies to their first series victory against England in England in 1950 and then went on to bemuse the Australian batsmen "down under". The Englishmen, Gray reports, in a wonderfully apt image, given the East Indian and plantation background that produced Ramadhin, "… fell before you like a crop of canes". And just as the achievements of the fast bowlers and the great batsmen asserted a West Indian presence and persona that defied demeaning stereotypes, so Gray asserts about Ramadhin:

> What you sent down for over after over
> Was not a ball with stitches in red leather.
> It was an orb investing us with power. [26]

The presence of Ramadhin in the West Indian side calls attention to the racial diversity of the team over time. Having Indian Caribbean players like Ramadhin in a team representing the West Indies has been read and understood in various ways – read for example as evidence of the way cricket provides an overarching shared cultural experience that unites the various communities that together make the West Indies such a cosmopolitan place. On the other hand, the presence of such players has sometimes been understood rather as a way of focusing on the particular histories and struggles of those ethnic groups within West Indian society, so that individual players become symbols of possibility and achievement for communities who feel themselves marginalised or overlooked. In terms of the pieces in this anthology, the player who seems to have best expressed "Indian Caribbean" ambition and attitude was the great Guyanese batsman Rohan Kanhai. David Dabydeen's poem "For Rohan Babulal Kanhai" draws that political background and the interracial

26

tensions of Guyanese history very vividly and speaks to the Indian community's appreciation of Kanhai's sporting achievements as representing a kind of communal assertion:

> Is round night radio we huddle to catch news
> Of Kanhai batting lonely in some far country
> Call Warwick-Shire, and every ball blast
> Is cuff he cuffing back for we,
> Driving sorrow to the boundary.[27]

In the context of the history of West Indian cricket the moment when Frank Worrell became the first non-white captain of the West Indies, chosen on the basis of talent and merit rather than because of his race or colour, is a real marker of change in the society as a whole. In some ways the politics of that event, and Worrell's subsequent career in public life, have overshadowed memories of his daring footwork and distinctive style as a batsman. Edward Baugh's characteristically witty poem "The Pulpit-eulogists of Frank Worrell" laments that turn of events, asserting that:

> Any clown can play the gentleman.
> But who could time a ball so sweetly
> Or flick a wrist so strong so featly?

And concludes:

> But I lay you odds (all death's a game)
> That God to whom they commend his name,
> *That* God remembers cut and glance,
> Designed, who knows, the deadly dance.[28]

The profound and intimate ways in which such cricketing heroes *represent* the ambitions, frustrations and dreams of their communities – extending, like Worrell, far beyond the boundary – helps to explain the active engagement of West Indian spectators, across the region and overseas, in the games they are attending. This is as true of local, village or street games as it is of test matches or inter-island games.

There are many occasions of crowd intervention in the stories and poems collected here, and many other pieces where the story *is* the crowd, the game itself going on in the background. Perhaps the most vividly realised character in the crowd is Tanti Merle in Paul Keens-Douglas's hilarious poem "Tanti at de Oval", who, when the game gets tense – seven runs needed, with nine balls to bowl and one wicket to fall – can hardly contain herself:

> Seven balls six runs to go… Tanti on top de seat.
> Six balls five runs to go… Tanti fall off de seat.
> Five balls five runs to go… Tanti wavin' de parasol.
> Four balls four runs to go… police cautionin' Tanti.
> Three balls three runs to go… Tanti climbin' over de fence.[29]

Superficially Tanti Merle is a wonderfully observed comic character but, like several other West Indian writers included here, Paul Keens-Douglas engages with the picong wit and humour of a West Indian cricket crowd as a way into an exploration of serious concerns. At the beginning of this introduction I mentioned the pieces by Kamau Brathwaite and V.S. Naipaul, set respectively at test matches played at Kensington Oval in Barbados and at Lords in London. Brathwaite's much anthologised poem "Rites" is perhaps the best-known literary account of a West Indian cricket match; it enfolds within its few pages of dialogue between a local tailor and his friends many of the issues so far discussed in this Introduction. To say that it is set in Kensington Oval is not quite accurate; the discussion takes place in the tailor's shop and opens out from an account of a local game played by the friends and contemporaries of the men gathered in the shop to a recollection of a recent match between Barbados and the MCC touring team that was played at Kensington Oval. So it's not exactly accurate to call it a test match either, but in those days – the game must have been part of the 1953/54 tour – the England test side would be selected from the MCC touring party, so it is effectively an international game. The conversation of this group of ordinary men – although in fact it is only the tailor who actually gets to "commentate" – reveals a strong sense of the historical and symbolic resonance of any game between England and the West Indies, the sense of identification with the players on the field –

> as if was *they* wheelin' de willow
> as if was *them* had the power

– and the investment of both hope and fear in the outcome of the game. It is a wonderfully rich poem but particularly remarkable for me is the way Brathwaite encapsulates in one tiny vignette all the pent-up *meaning* of the game for those same ordinary men. The sight of Clyde Walcott, the great Barbadian batsman, disdainfully driving away the best that Johnny Wardle, one of England's finest bowlers, can deliver, triggers a transformation in the behaviour of one apparently passive and demure spectator who jumps up and, pointing at Wardle, screams to Clyde Walcott

> B... L... O... O... D, B... I... G B...O...Y
> bring me he B...L...O...O...D

And the tailor comments:

> Who would'a think that for twenty
>
> five years he was standin' up there
> in them Post Office cages, lickin' gloy
> pun de Gover'ment stamps.

But as well as that release and celebration, Brathwaite's poem also, in a slightly varied refrain, acknowledges the deeply ingrained self-doubt of a colonial people who perhaps fear that when the chips are really down, they are not quite up to the responsibility of independence

> when things goin' good, you cahn touch
> we; but leh murder start
> an ol man, you cahn fine a man to hole up de side...[30]

Celebration and self-doubt are emotions explored in V.S. Naipaul's essay too. A keen cricketer himself in his student days at Oxford, Naipaul's observation is characteristically sharp – in both senses of the term. As ever he is alert to class distinctions within the diverse West Indian crowd he is moving among during the Lords' Test of the 1963 West Indies tour to England. When Basil Butcher reaches his century in the second innings, rescuing the game after a passage of play when it looked as if the West Indies batting would collapse again, the event is marked – among those Naipaul calls "the plebeian West Indians" – by ostentatious jubilation; one man:

> jumps on some eminence behind the sightscreen and dances, holding aloft a pint of bitter. Mackintoshes are thrown up in the air; arms are raised and held in massive V-signs. Two men do an impromptu jive.[31]

Among the more restrained and self-consciously respectable middle-class West Indians gathered in The Tavern (one of whom asserts that cricket is "the only thing in which I remain West Indian... Only thing"), relief seems to be the prevailing emotion: "This is historic. This is the first time a West Indian team has fought back. The first time."[33]

Despite the distinctions in class, language and attitude that Naipaul emphasises in his account of the West Indian crowd at Lords, he does write with real insight into – and understanding of – the game's *beyond a boundary* significance for all the West Indian spectators there, regardless of their social status. His essay introduces another theme that is explored by several writers in the anthology: the experience of migration and the role that cricket played in both helping to establish an identity in the new place and maintaining a sense of connection with the Caribbean. Sam Selvon, in a typically nuanced comic story, "The Cricket Match", included here, plays with the possibilities of self-invention and reflected glory that the achievements of the West Indies test side allowed recent migrants to Britain, struggling to establish an identity for themselves in their new circumstances. The characters in Selvon's story play along with the assumption on the part of their British factory-mates that all West Indians must have an interest in cricket, and that by extension they are almost certainly able – "natural" – players of the game themselves. This stereotype is quickly established in the 1950s and is perceived by some later Black British writers to be part of a process of reduction which they react against, but Selvon's characters respond in more creative and self-aggrandising ways, encouraging the stereotype and indeed turning it to their advantage.

Well in truth and in fact, the people in this country believe that everybody who come from the West Indies at least like the game even if they can't play it. But you could take it from me that it have some tests that don't like the game at all, and among them was Algernon. But he see a chance to give the Nordics tone and he get all the gen on the matches and players, and come like an authority in the factory on cricket. In fact, the more they ask him the more convinced Algernon get that perhaps he have the talent of Walcott in him only waiting for a chance to come out. [32]

Beyond Selvon's wonderful way with words and ability to create memorable characters in just a few gestures, the comedy in the story is generated by the ways Algernon and "the boys" manoeuvre between the reality of their complete lack of cricketing skills, their own mythmaking – claiming a cricketing pedigree at home and contacts with the test players on tour – and the determination of their English workmates to believe the stereotype rather than the evidence of their own direct experience of the way Algernon and his team actually perform. In *Against the Grain: a 1950s memoir*, E.A. Markham records a similar experience in which, as a relatively recent immigrant in London, he was consistently picked to represent his school team because of the assumption on the part of those making the selection that, being West Indian, he must have latent talent as a cricketer. This went on for some time – he recalls – even though his performances were consistently mediocre. He describes this attitude on the part of his white British teachers as a kind of "benign racism". [33] Markham recalls that at the time he was happy to go along with it once he realised that, while dressed in his cricketing whites, he attracted the admiration of certain girls he was keen to impress. For a later generation of children of West Indian descent, however, those assumptions and the racial stereotypes they embody were more corrosive. In its blunt enunciation of the stereotypes J.D. Douglas's poem "I'm a West Indian in Britain" suggests the frustration of a generation for whom cricket is viewed – in Colin Babb's vivid words – as "a 'West Indian Grandad's game', dull and associated with rum-sipping, calypso, dominoes and the past."[34] For this generation the tabloid simplifications are demeaning and offensive, serving only to fix them in roles they neither recognise nor accept:

> I bash me can, and beat some pan
> now you know I'm a cricket fan
> policeman steer, me no care
> I'm a West Indian in Britain [35]

Similarly Benjamin Zephaniah's poem "How's Dat" suggests the ways that stereotypes based on prevailing assumptions about black boys' "natural talent" for sport rather than more academic pursuits infiltrated the British education system so that less was offered to or expected of them in terms of their intellectual development.

Teacher tell me
I am good at cricket,
I tell teacher
I am not,
Teacher tell me
We luv cricket,
I tell teacher
Not me,
I want Trigonometry
Fe help me people,
Teacher tell me
I am a born Cricketer [36]

We are back to C.L.R. James and Constantine's "marvellous West Indian brain".

However, back in the Caribbean itself, despite, as I noted earlier, some falling away of attention and participation, especially in the shadow of the West Indies team's lack of success in recent years, cricket retains its place as the quintessential West Indian game, and continues to resonate in the imagination of the region's writers as both a characteristic feature of the life of their societies and as metaphor for deeper issues and concerns. The extent of this fat anthology gives a good impression of the range of West Indian writers who have, over time and in various forms, been inspired to write about cricket, either as the main focus of a poem, essay or short story or as an incident in a longer piece of fiction or drama.[37] To have two recipients of the Nobel Prize for literature and several winners of other prestigious international literary awards represented among the contributors to an anthology of this kind is rather remarkable, and in itself says something about the place of cricket in the life and imagination of the region.

However, this collection, extensive as it is, is only a selection of the material we might have included. There is at least one major writer whose work we had hoped to include but in the end, were unable to agree permission fees. And we have included only one calypso lyric, Beginner's "Victory Calypso", which has become so much associated with the *story* of West Indian cricket that it seemed to belong here. The original plan for the book was to include both a selection of calypso lyrics relating to cricket and a selection of critical essays written about the literature of West Indian cricket. In the end it became apparent that such a book would be impossibly vast and unwieldy, so we have focused in on the literary materials – poems, stories, extracts from novels and from one play text, and literary essays. We excluded the more journalistic material and intend to publish a separate, companion volume of critical/academic essays on the literature of West Indian cricket in the near future. We decided that, with the one exception, simply as *texts*, we could not do justice to the qualities of the lyrics of the many calypso, reggae, soca and other popular songs relating to West Indian cricket. There have been several compilations of recordings of selections from that material, in one form or another, and archived radio programmes that are able to both sample the songs and discuss them in the various contexts that bear on their reception and understanding.[38] One of those contexts *is* certainly that of West Indian literature and we intend no slight on either the form or the writers/performers of such songs by our decision not to include them here, but every anthology must set its boundaries.

Most of the material in the anthology was written in the second half of the twentieth century but we have included some earlier pieces, including P. F. Warner's account of an early tour of the West Indies by an English team – led by Lord Hawke – in 1897. Although he was born in Trinidad, "Plum" Warner may not have been considered – or considered himself – "a West Indian" but he certainly knew the region well and his report is an early acknowledgment of the potential of the West Indies to become a real force in international cricket. Vincent Roth's colourful account of a much more "local" game at Arakaka in what was then British Guiana, around the same time that Lord Hawke's team was touring, gives us sense of how deeply rooted the game was by then and, in the recollection of the Chinese players representing Ho-a-Shoo's Cricket Club, how widespread was its appeal across the diverse communities of the region. Moving forward in time we particularly wanted to include something by Learie Constantine – as a writer – and the extract from his autobiography we have chosen shows off his literary style as a complement to the several accounts by others of his style as a cricketer. Not least in the work of C.L.R. James, who, although he looks back to the turn of the twentieth century in the extract we have included from *Beyond a Boundary*, ushers in the modern era in both West Indian cricket and West Indian literature. James takes cricket and cricketers seriously, he takes writing about them seriously, and in so doing he makes them a suitable subject for the generations of writers who followed him. This anthology demonstrates the ways in which they have risen to that challenge.

Endnotes

1. V.S. Naipaul, *The Middle Passage* (London: Andre Deutsch, 1962, quotes from Picador edition, 2001) pp. 35-36.
2. The phrase first coined by Gordon Rohlehr in his introduction to the anthology *Voiceprint : An Anthology of Oral and Related Poetry from the Caribbean,* eds. Brown, Morris & Rohlehr (London: Longmans, 1990).
3. "Rites", *Islands* (London: OUP, 1969), pp. 40-46.
4. "Test", first published in *Summer Days: Writers on Cricket* (London: Eyre Methuen, 1981).
5. "Leaving School", *The London Magazine*, 1965.
6. *Hendree's Cure* (Leeds: Peepal Tree Press, 2000), pp. 92-93.
7. "Professor David Dabydeen at the Crease", unpublished.
8. Unpublished.
9. Kamau Brathwaite, *The History of the Voice*, (London: New Beacon Books, 1979).
10. *The Autobiography of Alfred H. Mendes* (Mona: UWI Press, 2002), pp. 34-35.
11. *Beyond a Boundary* (London: Hutchinson, 1963), p. 134.
12. *Cricket in the Sun* (London: Stanley Paul, 1946) pp. 32-36.
13. *Tings and Times* (Newcastle: Bloodaxe Books, 1991), pp. 34-36.
14. *Lady in a Boat* (Leeds: Peepal Tree Press, 2003), pp. 13-14.
15. *The Arrival of Brighteye* (Newcastle: Bloodaxe, 2000), p. 50.
16. *Walk Good Guyana Boy* (Ontario: Learning Improvement Centre, 1994), pp. 179-186.
17. *A Boy Named Ossie: A Jamaican Childhood* (London: Heinemann, 1991), pp. 19-24.
18. Chanderpaul does get a mention in passing in Rajandaye Ramkissoon-Chen's poem "On Lara's 375" which celebrates Brian Lara's breaking of the world record for a single Test innings, but only because he happened to be batting at the other end when Lara broke the record! He does, I'm glad to note, get appropriate – if prosaic rather than lyrical – appreciation in Frank Birbalsingh's essay, "Return to Bourda", included here. Readers should recall his astonishing assault on the hapless Steve Harmison for 26 in one over in the one-day match against England in April 2009.
19. *The Lunatic* (Kingston: LMH Publishing, 1987, 1999), p. 174.
20. *Beyond a Boundary*, p. 14.
21. *Is Just a Movie* (London: Faber, 2011), p. 88.
22. "The Ritual of Cricket", *New Society*, 1969, no. 352.
23. *Is Just a Movie*, p. 86.
24. *New Writing 2* (Minerva, 1993).
25. "To Mimic Magic", *Gully* (Leeds: Peepal Tree Press, 2010), pp. 55-58.
26. *The Woolgatherer* (Leeds: Peepal Tree Press, 1994), p. 105.
27. *Coolie Odyssey* (London: Hansib, 1988).
28. *It Was the Singing* (Toronto, Sandberry Press, 2000).
29. *Selected Works of Paul Keens-Douglas* (Trinidad: Kiskadee, 1992).
30. "Rites", op. cit, p. 46.

31. "Test".

32. *Ways of Sunlight* (London: MacGibbon & Kee, 1957) p. 161.

33. E.A. Markham, *Against the Grain: a 1950s memoir* (Leeds: Peepal Tree, 2008) p. 118.

34. See Colin Babb's essay "Cricket, Lovely Cricket: London SW16 to Guyana and Back", included in this anthology. First published in *IC3: The Penguin Book of New Black Writing in Britain* (London: Penguin, 2000).

35. *Caribbean Man's Blues* (London: Akira, 1983), p. 12.

36. *City Psalms* (Newcastle: Bloodaxe, 1992), p. 54.

37. We have included a few poems, too, where cricket is only the incidental "weft" as it were of another tale that is being told, establishing the veracity of a setting perhaps, or where the occasion or language of cricket is employed as metaphor rather than the primary subject of the poem. But these more "casual" references serve to confirm the ubiquity of cricket in the West Indian space, as it were.

38. See especially the work of Ray Funk in this regard. There is also interesting critical discussion of some of this material in the context of West Indian literature and cultural studies by such scholars as Gordon Rohlehr and Clair Westall.

POETRY

JOHN AGARD

THE DEVIL AT LORDS

There was nothing in the match.
A tame predictable draw.
A wicket without promise.
Till the Devil in inspired fit
did a lightning streak across the pitch.
A copper's helmet covering
a bifurcated prick
but unable to contain
two Beelzebub tits
swinging their googlies
with glorious certainty.
Such unorthodox phenomenon
made W. G. Grace turn in his grave.
Dicky Bird attempted flight.
Nothing in the rule book
said androgynous demons
were not the life and soul of cricket.

PROSPERO CALIBAN CRICKET

Prospero batting
Caliban bowling
and is cricket is cricket in yuh rickaticks
but from far it look like politics

Caliban running up
from beyond de boundary
because he come
from beyond de boundary
if you know yuh history

Prospero standing
bat and pad
thinking Caliban is a mere lad
from a new-world archipelago
and new to the game

But not taking chances
Prospero invoking de name
of W. G. Grace
to preserve him
from a bouncer to the face

Caliban if he want
could invoke duppy jumbie
zemi baccoo douen all kinda ting,
but instead he relying
just pon pace and swing

Caliban arcing de ball
like an unpredictable whip.

Prospero foot like it chain to de ground.
Before he could mek a move
de ball gone thru to de slip,
and de way de crowd rocking
you would think dey crossing de atlantic

Is cricket is cricket in yuh rickaticks
but from far it look like politics.
Prospero remembering
how Caliban used to call him master.
Now Caliban agitating de ball faster
and de crowd shouting POWER

Caliban remembering
how Prospero used to call him knave and serf.
Now Caliban striding de cricket turf
like he breathing a nation,
and de ball swinging it own way
like it hear bout self-determination

Is cricket is cricket in yuh rickaticks
but from far it look like politics.

Prospero wishing
Shakespeare was the umpire,
Caliban see a red ball
and he see fire
rising with glorious uncertainty.
Prospero front pad forward with diplomacy.

Is cricket is cricket in yuh rickaticks
But from far it look like politics.

Prospero invoking
de god of snow,
wishing a shower of flakes
would stop all play,
but de sky so bright with carib glow
you can't even appeal for light
much less ask for snow.

Is cricket is cricket in yuh rickaticks
but from far it look like politics.

PROFESSOR DAVID DABYDEEN AT THE CREASE

Watch him play the literary cowlash,
a stroke known as Kanhai-brash
to lovers of the game of glorious uncertainty –
backside grazing an archipelago.

Still, he's prepared to flash
the tongue of his Creole willow
oiled with the canon's orthodoxy.

So he don't expect a turf of level green.
Not when the groundsman is history
and texts are seen and unseen.

Who knows, there might be ships in the deep
and canefield odysseys in the outfield.
In that case, he can always reverse his sweep,
sometimes called the empire writing back.

He knows there'll be movement in the air,
and even if the pitch plays fair as Hogarth's blacks,
he grooming himself for unpredictable cracks,
for art and slavery make subtle bedfellows.

Leg before wicket might mean limbo beyond water,
so he treats stormy bouncers as gentle turners
and makes the scoreboard his counting-house.

JOAN ANIM-ADDO

THOUGHTS FROM A CRICKET ORPHAN

I wonder which girlchild could forgive
a mother's leaving her for cricket?
She should have known how such absence stretches
like the long, fearful hand of the jumbie
into fretful childhood dreams. I waited.

Doubtless she stood at the crease eyes alert
to the streak of red, air-borne or on pitch,
seeking the boundary. I watched sunset reds
like layered hair ribbons touched by night's stain
waiting her return. Such

devotion to hard leather on willow
is strange behaviour in a mother.
And when she was at home, dissatisfied
I listened to her voice made for stories
debating unendingly unto sleep
the intricacies of the LBW.

I picture her now, in cream flannels
made in skirted days for mums
at the old Singer, the treadled one
"so much more reliable
than these electric things." Gran's words.

I see her, plaits awry, Gran's constant cry
"She must always behave like a boy!"
Her girl. No time for dolls or housey housey games
– such shame – but give her a coconut bat
and anything would do for a ball.

Yet that cold imperative "chores first" held
then as now. Did she practise in secret
those skills denied to girls,
skills she craved? Mine remains
a grudging sympathy. I'll leave it be.

Then and to this very day
who get run out and who get duck
I never could care.
Under arm or over, fastbowl or spin
don't bother me. I always thought
this career for a mother
far from maidenly.

TAKE A PEEP AT THE CROWD

If you see a patchwork of caps with peaks
in rioting colours that play with the sun,
rasta tams in green, red and gold
crocheted or leather-worked like a dome;
if you see the odd red headkerchief
over a cap, or the day's newspaper
shading a head or two;
if you see promoters' sunshades
suggesting you drink this or that,
placed over bright cotton scarf;
if you hear claxtons or bicycle horns
persistent in their patterning of sound,
metal knocking metal, aching to be steelpan,
or the goatskin drum itself, bembe steady,
straining the nerves of visiting supporters,
you can bet is the Windies.
They might be in Bourda, Guyana,
or Oval, Barbados, but this is Queen's Park, Grenada.
Windies playing at home,
Janie sitting on concrete in the pavilion
her cropped sunhat-shaded,
tension rising like night fever
and supporters in no mood for defeat.

SHE COUSIN FROM TRINIDAD

Cousin Dolphus boy visiting from Port of Spain
shared a room with her brothers.
Whole night his singsong voice talking
Learie Constantine and André Cipriani
Trindad giving pure licks beating MCC.

The morning sun had barely glanced
at the green jalousies holding out against dawn
before calls for wickets and marking the crease
began to pepper air more tuned to cocks crowing
and he was Constantine, no matter who was Cipriani.

When they signalled her from the kitchen
made mime so mammy wouldn't know
and promised to help fetch water from the well
or even sweep the yard if she would bowl,
she cousin stood out a photograph in whites.

Like waiting for a shutter to click-freeze his image
he held aloft a shop-bought bat marked Bradman
and announced with solemnity the West Indies Team.
Then pity and laughter both she saw in his eyes
as he faced her: girl with cricket ball in her hand.

She insists she really didn't want to play
but for every cuss about small island this, that
and girls not knowing about cricket,
a stirring grew as her scamp brother winked.
First delivery went wide, second bounced high.

With the third, she declared as she caught it herself:
"Carry your bat, boy, all the way to the pavilion.
Right now, I is one girl don't care
'bout Learie Constantine and André Cipriani.
Is Trinidad getting licks. Now show me MCC".

EDWARD BAUGH

THE PULPIT-EULOGISTS OF FRANK WORRELL

They should have talked of cut and glance
described the dance
he did on such or such a day
on what green floor
on what astonished field.

Instead, they said he was a gentle man,
praised him as a model for his race,
noted with aplomb he took his place
as senator; a leader cherished
by his men, in friendship steadfast,
who, in spite of bitter recollection,
loved his country at the last.

Any clown can play the gentleman.
But who could time a ball so sweetly
or flick a wrist so strong so featly?
Yet those who saw him in his day
have left the middled things to say –
the strokes, the swing, the easy stance.

But I lay you odds (all death's a game)
that the God to whom they commend his name,
that God remembers cut and glance,
designed, who knows, the deadly dance.

VIEW FROM THE GEORGE HEADLEY STAND, SABINA

"You see, you see what I tell you,
he playing and missing, I tell you!"
"No, no, you don't read the stroke.
He know what he doing, he leaving
the ball alone. Just at the last
crucial moment, he easing the bat
inside the line and letting it pass."
"Well, all I can say is that that
is a damn dangerous way
to be leaving the ball alone."
"What you saying in truth? You mean
you meaning to tell me in this
almost-twenty-first century them white boys
making my boy look fool?" "Mister man,
all I know is it wrecking my nerves,
for just make that ball swerve
a fraction and follow the bat
and bap is a snick to slips
and, ole massa, we gone, we dead!"
"Cho, I don't care what you call it,
that is what I call a indigenous
stroke. You know what I know?
This argument can't settle, for if
him out now caught in the slips
that still wouldn't prove nutt'n
and if you ask him himself, the man
would be a fool to tell you the truth."
"Gentlemen, gentlemen, is watch
we come to watch cricket, or is
epistemology we come here to talk?
This chicken sweet, yes? Is Brenda
cook it? Say what? You mad?
You don't know long time that rum
don't agree with my stomach?
Man, just pass me the Scotch."

FAST BOWLER

Batman's nervous wait – not a bowler's worry.
Upright wickets taunt him.
Back turned. He walks on.
A journey, long, long and steep.
Eleven men toss one ball with his arm.
Yet, ball speaks *his* eloquence.
He turns. He trots. He runs. Big long limbs
fly with pounding hoofs to a leap,
releasing a bullet of a ball.
Batsman ducks. Shelters in lower air.
Okay. Okay. Next time.

Back turned. Slowly, he walks, journeying.
Each wicket stands there – an enemy soldier.
That bat on guard. A fortress door.
Ball in hand is his charge
to despatch a man.
Ball stamps the pages of a life.
He turns. He trots. He runs. Big long limbs
fly with pounding hoofs to a leap,
releasing a bullet of a ball.
Batsman pad up. Two columns of pads.
Okay. Okay. Next time!

Back turned. Slowly, he walks, journeying.
Ball in hand is a nation's voice.
Jibes of standing wickets bite him.
Ball – *be* hurricane-powered!
He turns. He trots. He runs. Big long limbs
fly with pounding hoofs to a leap,
releasing a bullet of a ball.
Batsman hits him. Hit his ball away for four.
Loose ball. Avoid that. Avoid that.

Back turned. Slowly, he walks, journeying.
Ball tests hard how two nations can rub.
Sometimes with a spear disguised, sometimes

with a sword, gaming in an open field is
a battle, but *open*. And eyes watch him while
so erect, lordly wickets mock him.

Improvised ball, go now, arrive unreadable.
A baffler with the tricks of a genius.
He turns. He trots. He runs. Big long limbs
fly with pounding hoofs to a leap,
releasing a bullet of a ball.
Batsman hits him. Hits his ball away for six.
Unbelievable. Unbelievable. Think. Think!

Back turned. Slowly, he walks, journeying.
Wickets together. An immovable barrier.
Ball unravels an opening by combat.
Ball demands a total testing.
Eyes of his team rest on him heavily.
He turns. He trots. He runs. Big long limbs
fly with pounding hoofs to a leap,
releasing a bullet of a ball.
He misses the wickets by a pinpoint.
His missile! *His* missile! Controlled!
Launch it. Launch it, again, Launch it!

Back turned. Slowly, he walks, journeying.
Fine clothes get full of a downpour:
his fit limbs are heavy with fatigue.
But his arm works his nation's arm!
So knock him for ones and knock him for twos.
Have him glided to the boundary
or fly gone past the keeper. Have him
give a wide, a no-ball, a catch dropped,
and a spell without a wicket, and remember,
always, his next ball will carry his plan.
He turns. He trots. He runs. Big long limbs
fly with pounding hoofs to a leap,
releasing a bullet of a ball,
shattering the wickets to scattered sticks.
Got him! Got him! Let him walk.
O let him walk away, dead!

Roger Bonair-Agard

GULLY

Here, the ball comes off
the bat so fast it is sometimes
a flung streak of paint.
From here, how fast I am,
how snapdragon quick
my reflexes, can dictate a whole day's play.

A cocky batsman will cut
right past me – late or square –
and then I must become a bird,
a winged reptile uncoiled to snag
the catch so fast, the commentator fooled
already looking to the boundary
for the ball.

I am trained to disappoint,
my outstretched snatch of a one-hand
catch must trap the batsman halfway
up the pitch thinking he is on his way
to more runs. In this position –
so close I could be quiet for hours –
I could also be a god, a trickster god,
a two-faced orisha, one who when prayed to
delivers in the most excruciating manners.

TO MIMIC MAGIC

*...To the umpires, he was malevolent stealth personified, so they
called him The Whispering Death.*

Wisden (on Michael Holding)

i The bowler is a shaman

Even on the black and white
we could tell the ball
was a wicked duppy

it moved furniture
spat and reared at the batsman's
throat   shot past his chest
like a comet

the bowler   a hypnotist
priest doling out a fiery eucharist
was all our fathers
a silent   stern   unsmiling man
nevertheless so smooth

we all imitated him
on the courtyard   the field   the pitch
especially next day

It was the fastest over ever

and none of the batsman's body
armour had prepared him for the placid
mat of a pitch suddenly turncoat
with grass and movement

We took turns practising
the interminable run-up
the willow of a body gathering
speed and purpose like a train
head ever so slightly turning
side to side
the soft landing of the feet

ball cupped like a co-conspirator
in a bent wrist
each stride a human gazelle's

Dexter was the closest facsimile
we were thirteen   but he was already
six foot and slightly bearded
he alone had the body to mimic
the phantom ferocity   the ninja-like
ability to approach in quiet and leave
a swathe of blood

but we all took turns anyway
giggling after each boy's gambit
and mocking excitedly the jack-in-the-box
twists the batsman needed
to avoid serious injury

Even then we knew we had witnessed
an improbable history
a black man billowing
like a sail in the distance
so fearsome that the batsman kept
his head down until the ship docked
a fierce unfurling of colours in the sun
and an explosion of gunfire
never heard before

We all saw it
We all knew it
but we never called it
by name

ii As for the batsman...

No slouch
his *Fundamentals of Batting for Young Cricketers*
was the best selling primer on the subject

Technically gifted
from foot-width to shoulder-placement
he spoke of the high backlift
against immeasurable pace
the low crouch to read
a devil of a googly emerging
like a rabbit from the hat
of a spinner's hand

He was an opener
dealt with the fastest bowlers
on the livest pitches
his history and authority secured
his defences unassailable

but nothing prepared him that day
for the shiny new ball hissing
like a hot raindrop from the pitch

Twice in six balls his body
arched parentheses into the air
to avoid the missile
while the Bajans   already drunk
on Mount Gay rum   gasped audibly
at the spectacle

At home we inched our chairs
closer to the TV screen
as if we could shed all the fences
all the limits we didn't know
we had   by bathing
in the ball's fiery flight

My mother avoided me
as one would a man
in rapt prayer   the altar moving
with each spiteful delivery
and useless attempt at parry

iii Denouement

By the time Geoff Boycott's off stump
was dislodged on the over's last ball
and cartwheeled twenty yards back
he was linked forever
with Michael Holding in cricket lore
in that way that history happens
in the past   present   future   all at once
the way that real history
is poetry in the possible tense
the way all that happens is the rain
and none of us one man's house

We could not have known
even as we started
from the shadow of the West Building or pavilion
or wherever we gathered the next day
how much men and changed we were
– school uniforms be damned –
accelerating up to the wicket
in fascinated mimicry
beginning to unfurl
our shirttails
blazing

RITES

Many a time I have seen him savin'
the side (the tailor was saying
as he sat and sewed in his shop).

You remember that tourney wid Brandon?
What-he-name-now
that big-able water policeman –

de one in charge o' de Harbour Patrol...
You mean Hop
a-long Cass? Is because a cow

give he mother a kick before he did born
that he foot come out so.
Yes, I know

but is not what I talkin' about. Ol'
Hoppy was bowlin' that day
as if he was hurricane father.

Lambert went in, play-
in' he know all about it as us'al
an' *swoosh!* there he go fan-

nin' outside the off-stump an'
is *click!*
he snick

de ball straight into de slips.
"Well boys it look like we lossin'
this match", says the skipper,

writin' nought in the exercise book
he was keepin' the score in; "you think
we could chance it an' sen' Gullstone in

before Charlie or Spooks?"
So Gullstone went in.
You could see he face whitenin'

under he tan an' you know
that that saga-boy frighten: bat
tappin', feet walkin' 'bout like they talkin'

wid ants; had was to stop meself axin'
meself if he ever play cricket on Brown's beach before.
An' I tole him,

I tole him over an' over
agen: *watch de ball, man,* watch
de ball like it hook to you eye

when you first goes in an' you doan know de pitch.
Uh doan mean to *poke*
but you jes got to *watch what you doin'*;

this isn't no time for playin'
the fool nor makin' no sport; this is cricket!
But Gullstone too deaf:

mudder doan clean out de wax in 'e ear!
Firs' ball from Cass an' he fishin';
secon' ball an' he missin', swishin'

he bat like he wishin'
to catch butterfly; though the all Gullstone ever could catch
pun dis beach was a cole!

But is always the trouble wid we:
too fraid an' too frighten.
Is all very well when it rosy an' sweet,

but leh murder start an' *bruggalungdung!*
you cahn fine a man to hole up de side.

Look wha happen las' week at de O-
-val!

At de Oval?
Wha' happen las' week at de Oval?

You mean to say that you come
in here wid dat lime-skin cone

that you callin' a hat
pun you head, an' them slip slop shoe strap

on to you foot like a touris';
you sprawl you ass

all over my chair widdout askin' me please leave nor licence,

wastin' muh time when you know very well that uh cahn fine
enough to finish these zoot suits

'fore Christmas; an' on top
o' all this, you could wine up de nerve to stop

me cool cool cool in de middle
o' all me needle

an' t'read; make me prick me hand in me haste;
an' tell me broad an' bole to me face

THAT YOU DOAN REALLY KNOW WHA' HAPPEN
at Kensington Oval?

We was *only* playin' de MCC, man;
M - C - C
who come all de way out from Inglan.

We was battin', you see;
score wasn't too bad; one
hurren an' ninety-

seven fuh three.
The openers out, Tae Worrell out,
Everton Weekes jus' glide two fuh fifty

an' jack, is de GIANT to come!
Feller name Wardle
was bowlin'; tossin' it up

sweet sweet slow-medium syrup.
Firs' ball...
"N...o...o..."

back down de wicket to Wardle.
Secon' ball…
"N…o…o…"

back down de wicket to Wardle.
Third ball comin' up
an' we know wha' goin' happen to syrup:

Clyde back pun he back
foot an' *prax!*
is through extra cover an' four red runs all de way.

"You see dat shot?" the people was shoutin';
"Jesus Chris; man, wunna see dat shot?"
All over de groun' fellers shakin' hands wid each other

as if was *they* wheelin' de willow
as if was *them* had the power;
one man run out pun de field wid a red fowl cock

goin' quawk quawk quawk in 'e han';
would'a give it to Clyde right then an' right there
if a police hadn't stop 'e!

An' in front o' where I was sittin',
one ball-headed sceptic snatch hat off he head
as if he did crazy

an pointin he finger at Wardle,
he jump up an' down
like a sun-shatter daisy an' bawl

out: "B…L…O…O…D, B…I…G B…O…Y
bring me he B…L…O…O…D"
Who would'a think that for twenty-

five years he was standin' up there
in them Post Office cages, lickin' gloy
pun de Gover'ment stamps.

If uh wasn't there to see fuh meself,
I would'a never believe it,
I would'a never believe it.

But I say it once an' I say it agen:
when things goin' good, you cahn touch
we; but leh murder start an' you cahn fine a man to hole up de side.

Like when Laker come on.
Goin' remember what happenin' then
for the rest o' me life.

This Laker a quiet tall heavy-face fellow
who before he start to do anything ser'ous
is hitch up he pants round he belly.

He bowlin' off-breaks.
Int makin' no fuss
jus' toss up de firs'

one an' *bap!*
Clyde play forward firm
an' de ball hit he pad

an' fly up over de wicket.
Boy, *dis* is cricket!
Laker shift weight

an' toss up de secon';
it pitchin' off-stump an' coat' back sharp
wid de men in de leg trap shinin' like shark.

Clyde stretchin' right out like a man in de dark
an' he kill it.
"N...O...O...O...O", from de schoolboys, "hit it, hit it".

Boy, dis is *cricket*.
Then Laker come down wid he third
one. He wrap up de ball in de palm

o' he han' like a package
AN' MAKE CLYDE WALCOTT LOOK FOOLISH.
Mister man, could'a hear

all de flies that was buzzin' out there
round de bread carts; could'a hear
if de empire fart.

An' then blue murder start
"Kill one o' dem, Clyde", some wise-
wun was shoutin', "knock he skull off;

doan *let* them tangle you up in no leg trap;
use de feet dat God give you!"
Ev'ry blabber mout' talkin',

ev'ry man jack givin' advice;
but we so frighten now at what happenin' there
we could piss we pants if we doan have a care.

"*Swing de bat, man*", one feller was shoutin';
an' Clyde swing de bat but de bat miss
de ball an' de ball hit he pad

an' he pad went *biff*
like you beatin' bed
an' de empire han' stick

in de air
like Francis who dead
an' de bess o' we batsmen out.

The crowd so surprise you int hearin' a shout.
Ev'ry mout' loss.
But I say it once an' I say it agen:

when things goin' good, you cahn touch
we; but leh murder start
an' ol man, you cahn fine a man to hole up de side...

JEAN BINTA BREEZE

SONG FOR LARA

is a young generation
comin dung sweet
nat in awe of *Wisden*
nat studyin defeat

a fresh clean page
from an islan of dreams
a bat in han an
burstin at de seams

de wicket holds no shadows
of what cannot be reached
Jus
practisin, dread,
gettin better all de time
de limelight doan mean nutten
wid a bat in mi han
liftin up mi head
an thinkin bout de glory
is a sure way to be out
before de en a de story

if de bowler fine a reason
ah will answer wid a rhyme
any kine a riddim
in mi own time

                    Pan man, hole tight.
Lara een
im tekkin up im guard
fus one straight back
dung de pitch
Dis is between we an de Lord!

We bus out a heaven gate today
wid a certain majesty
buil a hero to open space
from all dat crampin' we

lightnin flash troo de covers
breakin de boundary
den we sekkle back pon de riddim wid a
Noooo... defensively

Dance it, Lara, dance it
de march deh pon we foot
steady timin
watchful eye
wait for de tenor pan
to fly
lash it
cause it overpitch
bruk a man han
if im try ketch it
is a four, is a six, is a sure ticket
anyting ah have, Lawd,
ah gamble it

dem slow dung de riddim now, mi son,
so steady timin, bassman, come!
deh sayin we don't like it slow
deh call we calypso cricketers
say we cyaan hole dung tempo
so we sen for David Rudder now
is a ballad in kaiso
so slow... so slow
a ballad in kaiso

> "*Come mek we rally...y...y*
> *rally rung de West Indies*"

an wen we wear dem dung again
we gawn forward extempo

is a pair a eye dat see de ball
before de bowler   tink it

a pair a leg dat dance wid ease
anywhere he   lan it

a pair a han dat have more joint
dan jus elbow   an wris

is a fella dat will fine de gap
instead a mindin it
instead a mindin it

an all de time
he smilin sweet
gentle, humble
dress well neat
bat like a ratchet
in he han
slicin troo
de hard red heat

        an he playin hiself
            he playin hiself
but he doan play all hiself yet

        he playin hiself
            he playin hiself
but he doan play all hiself

yet

ON CRICKET, SEX AND HOUSEWORK

I have never liked ironing

but there's something steamy here
that softens the crease
and although I played it straight
I fell
to your googly

I came out slightly crinkly

perhaps it's the strange things
your fingers do
around my seams

LLOYD BROWN

CRICKET GROUNDS, PLYMOUTH

Movement is the seamless flow of practised repetition,
the seductive timelessness of proper form;
motion becomes a seeming immobility,
a rectangular frame of fluid rhythms
anchored to the hard-packed earth
by the imperial measures of the sovereign wicket,
and hinting at the genteel splendours of some ancient
tapestry in a noble matte finish of soft green
laced with a delicate embroidery of flannel weave,
stark-white threading over black braids
that have been stitched into place.
Play is energy becalmed, then stirred
into slow motion by an effortless elegance,
with hypnotic aplomb,
grace under the pressure of constraints sanctioned
by the quintessential gentleman's agreement;
momentary explosions are extraordinary
acts of civil obedience under stress and heat,
and these creased lines of pitched battle
are a formal declaration of lawful rule
and orderly submission.
The rocketing ball is a red-brown flash above the turf
in this Memorial Day salute to the war dead
of an empire itself presumed dead;
and that brief flash illumines
the well travelled road from an uncivil past
to a familiar destiny already grown old,
stocked, like some venerable trophy room,
with the burnished anachronisms of a far-flung order
on which time never did set:
enduring proprieties, like a tropical teatime break,
that are yesterday and tomorrow,
the inviolate rituals of a prophetic remembrance
in which memories are selected positions,
stock-still, screening the boundaries of legitimate
being on the world's assigned periphery.
This field is set, Janus-like, in time,

where the well-trained future scampers for meagre runs
between the wooden bars of its allotted space,
under the distant gaze of privileged boxes in the west
opposite the cemetery that sidelines the eastern boundary
with the mocking silence of an inexorable finality;
and looming over all,
Mt. Chance's fog-capped peak
flaunts a windblown cape of clouds,
sea-island cotton-white
trimmed with black lava rock,
in air still thick with sulphur
from the exploding furies which froze, long ago,
into an inert immensity of energy –
caged and motionless –
except for the hot springs bubbling underfoot,
beneath the calm precision of play,
from ancient bedrock furnaces, to die
on black-sand beaches below the southern boundary,
while a disciplined chorus of hands
applauds the end of a well-played innings.

Montserrat
May 1, 1989

TEST MATCH SABINA PARK

Proudly wearing the rosette of my skin
I strut into Sabina
England boycotting excitement bravely,
something badly amiss.

Cricket. Not the game they play at Lords,
the crowd – whoever saw a crowd
at a cricket match? – are caged
vociferous partisans, quick to take offence.

England sixty-eight for none at lunch.
"What sort o battin dat man?
dem kaaan play cricket again,
praps dem should-a-borrow Yagga Rowe!"

And on it goes, the wicket slow
as the batting and the crowd restless.
"Eh white bwoy, how you brudders dem
does sen we sleep so? Me a pay monies
fe watch dis foolishness? Cho!"

So I try to explain in my Hampshire drawl
about conditions in Kent,
about sticky wickets and muggy days
and the monsoon season in Manchester
but fail to convince even myself.

Eventually the crowd's loud 'busin
drives me out, skulking behind
that tarnished rosette – somewhat frayed
now – and unable, quite,
to conceal a blushing nationality.

COUNTER COMMENTARY AT KENSINGTON OVAL

Against the plummy platitudes
of Chris Martin-Jenkins
on the ball-by-ball, this broad
barefooted cane cutter,
taking his ease and Cockspur
in the Mitchie Hew…
getting drunker as the day proceeds
offers us all – can't be
restrained from – his loud
counter commentary

*CMJ: And Greenwich is being tied down just at the moment by some tight bowling
from England*

He kaahn handle it?
Why he don' jus handle it?

Good batsman, you g'now,
he ol' but he a good batsman still.

CMJ: And that's a fine piece of fielding by Smith at extra cover…

Proper fieldin', man!
Him put him fut, man,
'e hit the ball like Glory!

CMJ: And one feels that Richards is just setting himself for the battle to come…

Watchin' that man Richards is a money worth itself, man
Richards is a A class batsman, man…

*CMJ: Devon Malcolm was brave, or perhaps foolhardy, enough to say that he thought
he had the measure of Richards, we shall see…*

Yorker boy, leh go a yorker boy,
that's what you need for he

Crowd e up man, crowd e up,
put all de men around he, behind he,
inside he… Crowd e up!

He flashin at de win'!

Outside de off stump, Glory!

CMJ: What can one say, that's Richard's third six off Malcolm in two overs.... The somewhat embarrassing affliction that has been discomforting the great man in recent months* doesn't seem to be troubling him a this moment... or perhaps it is!

Bwoy him arse pain im, him arse pain im HOT!*

Malcolm, know you place when you meet the greatest, boy,
know you place

CMJ: And Malcolm, perhaps in desperation, is showing the ball to the umpire

Ball burs'? Nuttin wrong wid de ball.
The man is joke!

CMJ: One senses that the crowd have mixed feelings towards Small and Malcolm who both have family connections in the West Indies of course...

How the Englishman like black man for so!?
Dey tief Malcolm an' Small man, dey tief dem.
Englishman they like to USE yu till yu dry –
Give back Small de ball man!
He kaan bowl again a'ready? He not a black man?!

CMJ: And he's out, Richards is out trying just one hook too many...

The boy gone!
Yu see Richards get out wid that same hook he hookin'?
Too damn foolishness!

CMJ: What can one say about Richards' dismissal, Trevor, there was no need for him to play that shot at this stage of the innings but I suppose those who live by the sword will often die by it...

I come here fe watch good cricket man
Is not so me come a see.

(* Around the time of this match Viv Richards had been reported as suffering from haemorrhoids.)

65

Faustin Charles

Viv
for cricketer, Vivian Richards

Like the sun rising and setting
Like the thunderous roar of a bull rhino
Like the sleek, quick grace of a gazelle,
The player springs into the eye
And lights the world with fires
Of a million dreams, a million aspirations.
The batsman-hero climbs the skies,
Strikes the earth-ball for six
And the landscape rolls with the ecstasy
of the magic play.

Through the covers, the warrior thrusts a majestic cut
Lighting the day with runs
As bodies reel and tumble,
Hands clap, eyes water
And hearts move inside out.

The volcano erupts
and blows the whole game apart!

CRICKET'S IN MY BLOOD

Blood Fire!
Strokes in the middle of the imagination,
Fine slip-catch, stretching cat-like,
Offside, on-side feelers perched
Mid-on making style in the gully;
Bat on heat, clash, ball bouncing century.
The play is a poem.

The play is a poem
As the sun rides the boundary;
Hooked by the torrents of slashes

From the sweeping willow;
The batsman fashions play
And the game swells the blood.
The mounting runs skyward, flood-board
To the scoreboard, stroke-play, turning, pulling
The rhythm of the day.
Dancing in the cunning cut and drive, spins,
Opens up the movements of the hours,
Shattering the field
Shattering the mind
In and out of time, slips to divinity,
Swings and shines golden
For the love of the game;
Rising to conquer, propelled by a gift
And a hunger.
The ball swerves, lifts, and strikes
Widens with pain and anguish
Breaking heights beyond the sun,
And the light circles all,
Screaming in the extremity
Of lives laid out bare in the height of sacrifice.

Through the searching trees, eyeballs racing
Challenor melting boundaries spurring Warner spread-eagled
Through Constantine gliding magic cutting loose,
Seeding heroes thundering Martindale budding Ollivierre;
The fierce sun reels,
Scatters a ray of fielders
Stunned by the batsman's plunder;
The curving sling-shot of Ramadhin and Valentine
Mesmerises, and into the trap
The striker plunges.
Cricket's in my blood,
As the play tightens my soul into steel;
Blasted by the fanfare, the winds swell,
Headley wheeling the conqueror's wand
On the ticking time-bomb horizon.

Every night Worrell's ghost walks
Through the village
Delivering inspiration.

MERLE COLLINS

QUALITY TIME
for my father

They say what he has is malignant
but they promise more good years.
Now, they say, it's quality time,

so he's smiling. Words like
quality and malignant,
you could probe and unwrap them

but he's batting, protecting his wicket.
The game's going on, and he's
out in the field again

with cocoa and cashew, guava and gospo,
mango and mortelle, nutmeg and nettle,
soursop and Seville orange; he's

spending some quality time.
They say,
We got it all, but it's malignant,

and he wonders.
They say, *Go easy,*
but his batting is steady

and he's smiling.
But soon, he's brooding,
could feel strength going down, could see

suckers pushing out,
draining the cocoa tree dry,
could feel how the vines curling

and stifling. Could see how
bush growing high and it
choking the crop.

He notice how
most mornings sun blaze
boastful over mountain,

shine bright for a time, then just
sink down dying over the sea.
They say,

We tell you, it's quality time,
and he leans on his bat and he wonders.
The crowd is watching and waiting,

his batting is weaker, light getting bad,
he can't face the bowling,
sun heading down to the sea.

Bowler runs in, crowd leaning forward,
ball hit timber, wicket done scatter and
suddenly so, sun get swallowed by sea.

DAVID DABYDEEN

FOR ROHAN BABULAL KANHAI

1.

Kanhai
Cutlass whack six,
Leather-ball red
Like Whiteman restless eye.
One ton cane-runs
Cropped, all day in hot sun the man cut
And drop on he back
To hook two and lash four:
Hear the coolies crying out for more!
England glad bad when clouds
Puff and scowl and blue
Like end-of-over-bowlerman
And day done in rainburst:
God is White Overseer for true!

2.

And when darkness break and Blackman buss we head
Wismar-side and bleed up we women
And Burnham blow down we house and pen
Like fireball and hurricane
And riverboat pack with crying and dead
Like Old Days come back of lash and chain,
Is round night radio we huddle to catch news
Of Kanhai batting lonely in some far country
Call Warwick-Shire, and every ball blast
Is cuff he cuffing back for we,
Driving sorrow to the boundary,
Every block-stroke is paling in a fence
He putting down to guard we,
And when century come up, is like dawn!

* *Wismar:* Scene of massacre of Indians in Guyana by Africans, in the 1960s.
  Burnham, later President of the country, was a promoter of racial strife.

FRED D'AGUIAR

FROM GUYANA DAYS

The run home: terylene unbuttoned
Shirt-tail flying in a cooler breeze
And the paling fence I had to slip sideways
Through after working one loose stave up
To double the gap, headfirst then the rest
Follows easily, left straight as a sentry.

For I am about the yard in search of parts:
A truck from two cans halved by twisting,
Made wheels, with a stick long as my leg
Nailed to a string-steered axle that broke
Out of control when we raced invisible circuits
Raising dust till the cricket and cicada cried dusk.

Or tractor from an empty spool, each tooth
Of its threaded wheels cut one by one in its edges.
It climbed everywhere powered by a wound rubber band
On a lever pulled between a pierced piece of candle.
Or a game of hopscotch: squares drawn on ground
Pitch-clean, a dry mango seed for kicking,

Thrown and retrieved by hopping on one foot
Throughout. There'd be cheers and boos,
The index finger whipped against middle finger
And thumb, and the long, astonished whistle
At the accurate jab, the return hop heavy,
Burning; over the start-line was earth scaled.

Dusk's half-light thickening into pitch-night,
Batting till the boundary closed to the crease
Almost, flanked by house and road, having to stroke
The wooden ball under the verandah for four, fielding
On my stomach there; six if the palings cleared;
Always lashing out for runs, fast; or making a catch.

A half-calabash used to scoop water
Fetched in a bucket for a wash, the last of it
Poured by anyone nearby, the breeze goose-pimpling.
A buttonless shirt, knotted; a baggy trouser pinned;
The day's one cooked meal downed, grouped round
The gas lamp I so loved to pump, bright.

KWAME DAWES

ALADO SEANADRA

Something like forty runs to pile up in fifteen overs
with the sun round like power over the compound.
I prayed like hell out there on the boundary

far from the scorers talking Test cricket as if this game
was another day in the sun. I prayed like hell.
I had made something like twenty – out to a stupid short ball

which should have been dispatched to mid-wicket with ease.
But too greedy, I got a top edge,
and was caught looking naked as a fool in the blazing

midmorning. Now, like a mockery, the bowling was soup
but the boys still struggling to put one single before a next.
So I prayed like hell out there on the boundary, trying to will

a flaming red four my way. Still, I should have known,
after all, God's dilemma: We playing a Catholic team
that always prayed before each game. And where their chapel

was a shrine, ours, well sometimes goats get away
inside there; and once we did a play right there using the altar
as a stage. So I tried making deals with the Almighty,

taking out a next mortgage on my soul; asking him to
strengthen the loins of Washy who looking alone in the wilderness
out there in the blaze, bedlamized by the googly

turning on the rough patch outside off-stump.
Washy went playing at air, and the wickets kept falling
until it was Alado, flamboyant with his windmill stretch action,

his fancy afro and smile, strutting out to the wicket
still dizzy with the success of his bowling that morning.
And Alado take his guard loud, loud to the umpire:

"Middle and leg, please." Lean back till his spine crack.
Alado, slow like sugar, put on the tips, prolonging the agony.
Now, Alado surveyin' the field, from boundary to

boundary as if somebody was about to move a stone,
and the boys start to wonder if this was some
secret weapon, some special plan to win the match

in a trickifying way. I fantasised a miracle
in that moment, but I blame the sun for that.
And then the boy take his stance. Classic poise, bat tapping,

looking like a test class stroke-player, toes shuffling,
waiting for the pace bowler sprinting stallion along the worn
dry grass. Up to the wicket, he bowls, good length ball,

dead on mid and off. Alado shift the front foot forward,
sheer poise and style, head down according to the Boycott book,
elbow up, and unleash a full cover drive,

bat like flying fish catching the sun. And even when we heard
the clunk of the stumps, and see the bails take off,
we all still searching the extra cover boundary

to see the ball slap the boards. Alado Test stay posed off
like that for Lord knows how long. Big smile in his eyes
staring at the ball he must have hit in his dreams.

The umpire signal end of play with the gathering of the bails
and the pulling of the stumps. My soul was saved that day,
the year we never made the finals.

ANN MARIE DEWAR

CRICKET (A-WE JIM)

What a carry-on a Sturge Park!
How de crowd a stomp an roar!
Fo combine play Guyana,
An a-we Jim tap de score!

Lek water fram a bus pipe,
Lek bullet fram a gun,
Lek how lang-foot Sue mek baby,
A so Jim put on run!

You shoulda hear how Montserrat neaga
Shout an clap out dey a Park!
You shoulda see how neaga proud off
When Jim reach de hundred mark!

When Jim a bat, ee no mek joke –
Cricket ball a fly all over
To slip, mid-on, boundry, square leg,
Fine leg and extra cover!

Miss Mary shout an carry on,
Mas James tun up ZJB,
An every Stratian heart rejoice
When Jim reach hundred twenty three!

What a ting fo poor Guyana!
Dem try dem bes keep dung de score,
But no matter wha dem do,
A-we Jim a mek run by de four!

Miss Mary great-granmudda
Stay home, cause she couldn see,
But hear she mek some loadn noise
When Jim reach one-fifty!

She tell Miss Mary dat she sure
Goat water do de trick;
An how dis Montserrat food
Does mek man muscle start get thick!

If Jim didn pick pan Combine
Is how Combine woulda cope?
When Guyana man confront dem
Is pan Jim dem heng dem hope!

Mas James tell ee daughta husban
Fo mark ee wuds: ee say
Dat West Indies woulda beat Australia
If Jim mi dey!

So me joyful, and me head up high!
Me heart cyan full no more,
Fo Combine play Guyana
An a-we Jim tap de score!

Ian Dieffenthaller

WEATHER REPORT
for Chris Gayle

Is a strange wind blowing man
Insouciance and scattered inconsistency

A driving hurricane – mashing up the boundary rope
Mashin up Australian car behind de Oval stand

Rainfall of a cricket ball, a music
Better than the 1-2-3 ah Strauss
Dey say it soundin like a reggae show
But no, de storm was writin kaiso

Then in de eye
De bails dem flyin regular
I never see a storm wid so much I
Mus be an optical allusion

Dat gale
Big man wid twenty-twenty vision
Really test we patience oui

A strange wind blowing Windies outa Englan

Yet dat small red sun, rising from
De storm at Kennington, June 6,
Two thousand nine, was fine
They say an ill wind blow no good

J.D. DOUGLAS

I'M A WEST INDIAN IN BRITAIN

*All of us knew our West Indian cricketers, when they made
their first century, if they drank whisky instead of rum.*
C.L.R. James

I support a cricket team
whose players I shout when on de field
I bring me booze, forget de wife
I just wanna get tight
I'm a West Indian in Britain

I arrive at de cricket ground
and stop a cricket tout
"Got a spare ticket?"
I'll pay yu price and shut me mouth

As de match begin
whole lotta grins
shirt sleeves and shades, surround de field
come on Lloydy, bounce them Andy
I'm a west Indian in Britain

I bash me can, and beat some pan
now you know I'm a cricket fan
policeman steer, me no care
I'm a West Indian in England

Match finish, time to celebrate
I wish I'd brought a bloody crate
never mind I'll find some liquor
I can't stand that white man bitter
I'm a West Indian in Britain

I think of home and carnival
long time since I saw bacchanal
I think of Worrell, Sobers and Griffiths
Lance Gibbs, Wes Hall and Rohan Kanhai
now even you can't deny
I'm a West Indian in Britain.

HOWARD FERGUS

LARA REACH

Lara jus reach
jus reach to de crease
and he reach century aready

Me here all de while
jus a blot jus a blot
jus a blot up mi piage with singles and dots

Lara settle and shuffle
he eye like a hawk
he leggo de bat firs ball, four, aff de mark

Me fire and miss
me miss like a piston dat sick,
a heart outa rhyddim; ball jus miss me right stick

Me put arn me helmet
me still a get hit
a get hit from de bounce of de bullet

Dey say me a run short
a run short of breath
me bound to get caught, caught out of me depth

De high-handed umpire
stick me up wid wan finger
wan wutless finger out me short of me number

Lara jus reach
jus reach to de crease
and he reach lord aready

SHORT OF A CENTURY

for George Allen, island player, died 1990

After hitting out at Hugo's
lightning pace your innings ended
with a short-pitched ball
ten before the century closed

You gave us oohs and aahs of ecstasy
and pain when you missed five score
by inches. The umpire's lean finger
checked the reign of runs

And gave you out. Your sun stood still
and shouted cheat at destiny
for breach of morning promise
a well-run field of gold

All-round player you stringed
your Wisden willow for guitar
and scored harmonies to thrill pavilions
at Bourda, Kensington and Cuba

Boos for the umpire over, I hear voices
glory day now de morning come
crowds are standing all over the pavilion
sing and shout now de morning come

My pen a primitive bat turned
upside down enters the chorus
to score a silent interlude
of hope and sorrow till morning come.

CONQUEST
1986

Bow to Richards, you northern stars;
panmen, beat his team a roll of honour.

Hitting for the skies,
you brought to earth our dreams,
although your temper on the turf
echoed the pitch of childhood.
Children of the empire,
we did not dream to zero England.

We played in gullies, mountain climes,
brandishing cedars imaging the willow,
trained coconut fronds for guerrilla combat
or pitched battles
on placid English fields.
Children of the empire,
we did not dream to capture lords.

Marching in an epic line of marshals –
Worrell, Sobers, Kanhai, Lloyd –
you infected us with victory,
levelling Montgomery's England.
We shall be generous in glory,
wielding words Great Britain taught us,
send horns of mercy, VSO,
to bring the mother country into line
lest *lesser breeds without the law*
of cricket hit her past the boundary
to decline. Orphan lambs of empire,
we did not think to tame the lion.

Beat the pan for Richards,
stream in praise, you northern stars.
Drunk on dank tobacco leaves,
Warner poisoned us with cane;
your deadly strokes are balm
for the sugar in our brain.
Washing marbled Albion,
you bathed us black with pride.
Children of the empire,
we did not mean to trouble England.

Children of empire,
defend your wicket-gate
from wicked men who batten
on an orange black free state;
we observe the truce
but not declare the innings closed,
we play to win the war.

Bow to Richards, you northern stars
beat a paean, panmen, for his company.

Delores Gauntlett

CRICKET BOUNDARIES

The victory of losing
is sometimes lost
and the answers
wag anxiously
in search for change

which when summoned
will be enclosed
by doors of skin
long before
the anaesthetist needles
its subconscious
between seams of stones

and the process of evolution
will spin
to the test

SONNY RAMADHIN

They said you kept a wily secret
up your rolled-down sleeve, the Englishmen
who fell before you like a crop of canes.

Three steps and a subtle turn of wrist
wrought apertures spread-eagling their stumps.
They looked behind bewildered, open-mouthed.

Here in these islands we screamed joyous shouts
as every wicket fell. We'd taught our masters
how to play the game. The name of Ramadhin

made pride flush our veins. Then we sent you
with your guile to beat Australia. Our little marvel
off to twist the mighty giants by their tails.

At four o'clock one morning, Christmas Day,
you had Doug Ring out. We'd won. The umpire
said no. Oceans away here, like you, we wept.

What you sent down for over after over
was not a ball with stitches in red leather.
It was an orb investing us with power.

So in our hearts we placed your statue up.
How strange that time has caked its bronze with rust,
and children playing now trample your dust!

PRACTICE
for Peter

There's a spot in that yard which was worn.
It's all grassy now though.
It had served as the crease of a wicket
once when a father inveigled his son
to come bravely out to learn cricket,
to hold a straight bat, to drive through
the covers, pat the ball past the slips.

The boundary, of course, was the hedge
with magenta hibiscus flowers.
The glass louvres shone in the house
solvent in soft saffron sun
so hooks and sixes were out.

It was a makeshift scramble at dreams.
In late afternoon light two teams
took the field, one the father never played on,
and one that he wanted his son
to fit into at school. In that yard then
the past was entreating the future
to make good on a promise time seemed
to have made then deserted the picture.

There, taking his stance at the patch,
a reluctant boy, tense and nervous,
gave all that he could to the task
as if knowing his was the innings
counted on for winning a match,
that he had to defy any risk
to dip into time's fictions and snatch
for his father a refracted glow of success.

STILL DRIVING

Shuffling legs, shaking like dried razor
grass in the wind, sidled jerkily on
before me. The lean of the head
made an image tremble to life from
the bottom of a schoolyard's memories.

I saw the shuffle across the crease
Babsie Fraser used to be famous for,
at least to us. He would bring the pads
out to the yard to have us bowl at
his stumps. Every hit got you six cents.

On the playground he scored all around
the wicket and piled up the runs, but
only against us. On Saturdays
when he played on Queen's Park Savannah
he showed good style but was bowled early.

His glory belonged to us. We saw clearly
the oxides of failure left no rust on
his dignity, his humour held defeat
at bay. A little smile of mischief always
played round his lips, notching up centuries.

Here he was, still driving the ball death
kept sending up, straight down the line back
to that bowler, shuffling on. I stepped
quicker to face his open-eyed stance,
to ask if he remembered. He did.

A.L. HENDRIKS

THEIR MOUTHS BUT NOT THEIR HEARTS

The Englishmen who live beside me
Remind me of the indentured teachers
Who used to be shipped out to us,
Perspiring, pink, athletic men
With English names, Weatherby,
Gladstone, Barnes, Hawthornden;

Their mouths turned against Kipling
With his "lesser breeds without the Law",
And Milton whose God revealed everything
"First to His Englishmen"; but not their hearts,
For, as we all eventually saw,
We had to learn their games, their history, their arts.

They almost speak our language – went to same type schools;
They are kind, keep tidy lawns, small well-swept drives,
Sleek healthy dogs, and tailored, fresh-cheeked wives
Whose eyes lie still, like silent, unfished pools.
They treat me civilly, are indeed polite,
Always choose quickly to discuss
Sunshine, bananas, rum, calypsos
And inevitably cricket,
("Once saw your cousin keeping wicket,")
But wonder if their women dream at night
About the things they've heard about us.

French, German, Dutch, Italian,
They regard as people they always used to beat
In sport, and war, and colonisation,
And to whom they now repeat
The lesson in peace, democracy,
And how to lose a struggle gracefully.

They say they do not like the diplomacy and tact
Which made them Europeans,
Received Uganda's Asians,
And sift the rest like us through their Immigration Act!

LINTON KWESI JOHNSON

REGGAE FI DADA

galang dada
galang gwaan yaw sah
yu nevah ad noh life fi live
jus di wan life fi give
yu did yu time pan ert
yu nevah get yu jus dizert
galang goh smile inna di sun
galang goh satta inna di palace af peace

o di waatah
it soh deep
di waatah
it soh daak
an it full a hawbah shaak

di lan is like a rack
slowly shattahrin to san
sinkin in a sea af calimity
where fear breed shadows
dat lurks in di daak
where people fraid fi waak
fraid fi tink fraid fi taak
where di present is haunted by di paas

a deh soh mi bawn
get fi know bout staam
learn fi cling to di dawn
an wen mi hear mi daddy sick
mi quickly pack mi grip an tek a trip

mi nevah have noh time
wen mi reach
fi si noh sunny beach
wen mi reach
jus people a live in shack
people livin back-to-back
mongst cackroach an rat

mongst dirt an dizeez
subjek to terrorist attack
political intrigue
kanstant grief
an noh sign af relief

o di grass
turn brown
soh many trees
cut doun
an di lan is ovahgrown

fram country to toun
is jus tissel an tawn
inna di woun a di poor
is a miracle how dem endure

di pain nite an day
di stench af decay
di glarin sights
di guarded affluence
di arrogant vices
cole eyes af kantemp
di mackin symbals af independence

a deh soh mi bawn
get fi know bout staam
learn fi cling to di dawn
an wen di news reach mi
seh mi wan daddy ded
mi ketch a plane quick

an wen mi reach mi sunny isle
it woz di same ole style
di money well dry
di bullits dem a fly
plenty innocent a die
many rivahs run dry
ganja planes flyin high
di poor man him a try
yu tink a likkle try him try
holdin awn bye an bye

wen a dallah cyaan buy
a likkle dinnah fi a fly

galang dada
galang gwaan yaw sah
yu nevah ad noh life fi live
jus di wan life fi give
yu did yu time pan ert
yu nevvah get yu jus dizert
galang goh smile inna di sun
galang goh satta inna di palace af peace

mi know yu coudn tek it dada
di anguish an di pain
di suffahrin di prablems di strain
di strugglin in vain
fi mek two ens meet
soh dat dem pickney coulda get
a likkle someting fi eat
fi put cloaz pan dem back
fi put shoes pan dem feet
wen a dallah cyaan buy
a likkle dinnah fi a fly

mi know yu try dada
yu fite a good fite
but di dice dem did loaded
an di card pack fix
yet still yu reach fifty-six
before yu lose yu leg wicket
"a noh yu bawn grung here"
soh wi bury yu a Stranger's Burying Groun
near to mhum an cousin Daris
nat far fram di quarry
doun a August Town

TANTI AT DE OVAL

Yes, ah come back.
Ah bring back Tanti Merle too.
Look, woman, don't ask me no foolish question – yu hear?
Where yu see ah sit down here, is trouble yu lookin' for.
Yes, ah know Trinidad lose.
Yes, ah know Combined Islands beat we,
Yu should ask Tanti Merle 'bout dat, she should know.
Why I vex? Who tell yu ah vex? Yu find ah look vex?
Yu didn't study dat
When yu make me take Tanti Merle to de Oval?
Ah know we been through all dis already,
But never me again, never, never, never
Ah not takin' no relative with me to de Oval, not me,
Next time is me one alone an God goin' in de Oval.
Ah mean to say, yu had de whole year
To send Tanti Merle to de Oval,
But why today, eh? Today of all days,
Trinidad versus de Islands, ah big match like dat,
An' you want me to take Tanti Merle to see cricket match.
Ah know is she birthday,
Ah know she from St. Vincent,
Ah know she always talking 'bout de Islands,
But Tanti Merle livin' in Curepe fifteen years
An' she never put foot in de Oval,
So why today, eh? why today? tell me dat.
Yu have transistor,
Yu have radio,
Yu have television,
Right here in dis god-bless house,
Tanti Merle could ah well come an' enjoy de match,
Instead of dat, yu take de woman an' sen' she
Quite in Port of Spain to see cricket
An' nearly kill me dead, dead, dead
Dis April month of de Lord, 1975
An' Tanti Merle is sixty-five years old.
Woman, yu don't know what confusion yu put me in, eh?
Woman, yu don't know how yu nearly lose a husband , eh?

Yu see dat woman yu callin' Tanti Merle?
Well, let me tell yu 'bout she…
First of all, we leave late.
Ah tell Tanti Merle to get ready for ten o'clock,
Match startin' eleven,
We had ah good hour to reach de Oval,
But Tanti Merle wouldn't leave de house,
She only tittivaying, packin' basket with ah set ah food,
Sayin' how nobody eh go' starve she in Port of Spain.
An' yu know who end up carryin' de basket … me!
Ah man like me who does go in de Oval
With me money in me side pocket,
Ah petit-quart in me back pocket,
An' me two hand swingin' free.
But see me now, looking like some kind ah market vendor,
People only askin' me' what yu sellin'?
An' of course Tanti Merle had to take she parasol too.
Ah tell she de stands have roof, but not she,
She eh takin' me on at all,
Talkin' ah whole lot ah stupidness 'bout sunstroke,
An' on top of dat is ah pink parasol she bring.
Imagine me in de Oval with ah pink parasol.
People must ah tought it was Carnival.
Any way, ah take de basket.
De nex' set ah horrors was de taxi.
You self know how taxi hard to get in Curepe,
Every time I stop one, Tanti say she not goin' in,
Either de driver look too funny,
Or de passengers look too low-class,
Or de car look like it go fall down.
So ah tell she "choose yu own taxi".
She say she want ah red taxi.
Now tell me why your Tanti Merle must drive
In ah red taxi?
Yu see dat woman is like she wukkin' Obeah yu know
Is like yu tanti is ah real bad Obeah woman.
Tank God ah taxi come dat lookin' kind ah red,
Because she decide to take it.
An' yu know how she do dat?
De woman just step off de pavement
Right in front de taxi, an' say "hold dat"
Well yu could imagine brakes,

Ah never hear ah taxi-man cuss so yet.
But Tanti Merle eh take he on,
She just freeze him with one bad eye
Haul open de back door,
An' take over de whole backseat
As if she is de Queen of Sheba.
An' me self with dis big basket, smellin' like ah snackette.
Nex' ting de taxi-man switch on music, reggae.
Tanti Merle tell him take it off,
She say she want to hear cricket.
Well, dat was de only good ting she say,
From de time we leave Curepe
To de time we reach in de Oval.
De taxi-man put on de cricket,
An' from dere on Tanti Merle take-over.
Nobody mus' talk, Islands batting,
Tings in de Oval goin' good an' Tanti Merle grinnin',
Hear she, "Dats me boys an' dem, dey go bus' allyu tail."
De taxi-man made de mistake an' ask she
Where she come from.
Well is who tell he say dat,
We get de whole history of St. Vincent,
How it came Hiroona an' one set ah ting.
All dis time I vex, match start an' ah missin' play,
An' on top of dat Tanti Merle carryin' on 'bout St. Vincent.
Ah eh know how de taxi-man eh turn over de taxi
De way he begin to drive fast,
Ah never seen ah man drive so fast yet,
Fus he want to get Tanti Merle out de taxi hurry.
He take we straight to de Oval, non-stop.
Den Tanti Merle start to talk 'bout fifteen cents.
Well ah sure dat taxi-man must be tink she mad,
Is me wha' had to put peace again,
Ah just hand he five dollars
An' tell him tank you.
Yu tink wha' ah just tell yu bad?
Wait till yu hear wha' happen in de Oval.
Dat Oval was something else, is den story start.
Tanti Merle try to go through de people gate
With she parasol open,
Because she say she 'fraid she catch "sun stroke".
Well you self know how de gateman an' dem in de Oval stop,

Some ah dem does jus' watch yu hand with de money,
Dey doesn't even watch yu face
Fus dey couldn't care less, 'bout yu,
Is just de hand de money an' de ticket,
De hand de money an' de ticket,
Well dey had to watch Tanti Merle,
She nearly jook out dey eye with she parasol.
All dis time I apologisin',
An' yu know what one ah dem turn 'round an' tell me?
Why ah eh leave me wife home if she 'fraid sun.
He eh say aunt, he eh say granny, he eh say cousin,
He say wife. Yu know how ah feel? Yu laughin'!
Is because ah make de sign of de cross
When we reach inside de stand an' get we seat.
An' guess who is de first man ah see?
Boysie an ah whole side feting up with one set ah rum,
An' me with Tanti Merle.
An' when dey see me, yu could imagine de scene.
"How de madam?"
"Ae, ae boy, where yu get dat one"
"Make sure she have ah will."
"How yu selfish so, yu can't introduce de boys?"
"Where yu get dat nice woman, boy?"
"Dat is de one yu always tellin' us 'bout?"
An' dey start to carry on.
Is tank God de cricket so hot
Dey eh have time to take me on for long.
Islands battin' an' Trinidad bowlin',
Islands have runs to make,
Trinidad have wickets to take,
Time runnin' out an' is excitement in de Oval,
If Islands win dey get de shield
Tension in de place like steel.
I settle down to watch de game,
An' is den Tanti Merle start up.
She tell ah fella in front she to take off he hat,
She say it barrin' she.
Well he start to cuss she, an she start to cuss he
An' I trying to put peace but ah frighten,
Because is ah real "Bad-John" Tanti interfere with.
Tank God jus' den Richards get out stupid,
Cause dey say he not in he crease

An' de ball fall out de bowler hand an' hit de wicket
An' so he stump out stupid, stupid so.
Well Tanti Merle forget de Bad-John an' start with de umpire,
She say how he blind like ah bat,
She say is how he have lumbago,
She say is how is teaf he teafin' for Trinidad,
She say how he lucky she eh out dey
Because is wha' she would do an' wha' she wouldn't do to he,
An' she start to carry on.
But she quiet down when Allen start to blade ball
An' de score start to move
An' every run dat make de crowd makin' noise,
Tanti like dat.
Next ting braps! Shillingford gone,
Braps! Eddy gone, braps! Coriette gone,
Imtiaz an' Jumadeen spinnin' ball like joke,
An' wicket fallin' like smoke.
An' every wicket dat fall de crowd makin' noise,
Tanti eh like dat, she get vex,
She say how de crowd too hypocrite,
One minute dey cheerin' de Islands,
De next minute dey cheerin' Trinidad,
Den she turn round an say how Imtiaz stonin'.
Well ah fella tell she how spinner can't stone
An' ask she where she come out.
Well who tell he say dat?
We get de whole history of St Vincent again,
Only dis time she stan' up on de people seat to explaciate.
Ah had to beg she quick, quick, come down Tanti
Open de basket, let we eat.
Dat was de fus time ah glad we bring dat basket.
She open up de ting, an' was like Christmus, if yu see food.
Den Tanti start to share out, was like ah picnic, everybody get,
She even give de "Bad-John" piece.
Nex' ting ah know Allen out at ninety-six tryin' to vup
An' everybody forget food, tension high in de Oval.
Finlay an' Roberts battin', thirteen runs needed.
Den Tanti decide she want to change she seat,
She say de pole barrin' she.
So I behind, Tanti down front.
Roberts attempt ah six an' he out, the crowd roar,
Den Tanti start to shake she fist at Gomes for makin' de catch.
She say de way Gomes jump is like he eat Dominica Mountain chicken.

Ah man tell she move, an' was go' drop ah lash on she,
But jus den Willet out an' town in ah mess.
Islands need seven runs, with nine balls to bowl
An' one wicket to fall.
Dis time I forget 'bout Tanti Merle
Excitement in de Oval like yu never see in yu life,
Gore come in to bat an' is den de action start.
Nine balls seven runs to go…noise in de place.
Eight balls six runs to go…Tanti start wavin' de basket.
Seven balls six runs to go…Tanti on top de seat.
Six balls five runs to go…Tanti fall off de seat.
Five balls five runs to go…Tanti wavin' de parasol.
Four balls four runs to go…police cautionin' Tanti.
Three balls three runs to go… ah can't even see Tanti.
Two balls three runs to go… Tanti climbin' over de fence.
One ball three runs to go…Tanti on de people field.
Gore hit de ball, an' he an' Finlay pelt down de wicket for two run,
An' is den de bacchanal start, score tie at 283
An' everybody say Islands win.
Nex' ting ah see
Is Tanti parasol high up in de air,
An' she in de middle of one set ah people,
An' dey on de people pitch singin', an' dancin', an' carryin' on,
Ah whole heap of small-island people, and Tanti in de middle,
An' Tanti parasol only goin' up an' down, up an' down, up an' down.
Nex' ting loudspeaker say match eh tie, it draw
So Islands eh win de shield is Guyana.
Well who tell dem say dat, Tanti nearly cause ah riot.
She start to carry on.
She say dey teaf,
She say dey eh like de Islands,
She say change de rules,
She say tie and draw, same ting,
She say she forming delegation to see de Doctor,
She say she declare war,
An' she have one big, big crowd round she,
An' she on top one ah dem ting dey does roll de pitch with.
Dat same Tanti Merle dat look as if butter can't melt in she mout.
It take me 'bout two hours to get she out de Oval,
She lose de basket an' de parasol mash up,
But she eh study dat, is noise de whole way home.
An' yu know what dat woman have de heart to ask me when we reach de gap?
When nex' we goin' back in de Oval?

ALL PART OF A DAY'S PLAY

Three runs to go. This
conch shell
blows to cool the tension.

Five of our boys
out for duck. Even a half-crack spectator
fire the team. By this time almost
everybody feel we gave away
the match. So say what you want,
west indians could survive anything. We

just love cricket. Leg before wicket.
An anxious wicketkeeper sucks his teeth.
Time too good to waste. Rain
could even upset play.

A naked tourist
scampers near the pitch.

E.A. MARKHAM

ON ANOTHER FIELD, AN ALLY: A WEST INDIAN BATSMAN TALKS US TOWARDS THE CENTURY
for Malcolm Marshall and Michael Holding, resting…

Into the nineties, into the nineties
Ten to go, ten runs, don't panic…
Think Bradman… never got out when into the nineties

Nerves of steel, drive them through legs
Beginning to buckle *think* the three W's *think* Clive Lloyd
Think Richards and all those ruling heads

On the coin of cricket. And relax. Now where am I?
Lost in the arms of voluptuous Anna. *Fin*
de siècle, recalling the days of immortal Kanhai

Hooking to the boundary from a prone position.
Cravats & decadence. Good ball. *Christ!*
Man in white coat weighing the decision

To point the finger, legalized gun
With power to run the "Man of the Match"
Out of town. Not guilty. Not guilty, my old son

If I say it myself. A lapse
In concentration quickly repaired by nailing
The Will against any further collapse

This side of the century. Here behind the barricades
Stretching from "Clifton" and Gordon "Le Corbusier" Greenidge
Through "homelier" architects of our days

Of glory – the team's Frank Lloyd Wrights –
Up against pollution, thinning ozone, treeless forests
In the tropics etc., each run lifts you to the heights

Of vertigo. And for you down there, Miss X, Mrs Patel
At the corner-shop, this wicket guarantees
Orgasms, guarantees that this last exile suits you well.

And damn it, I'm out. *Out?* There's no morality to this game.
Protesting genocide and burying your head
In sweet Anna's thighs, it's all the same.

The butcher of dreams, man in white coat
Offers no reprieve, his butchershop in Hounslow in need
Of more meat. Yet again I've missed the boat

Of the century. Breath in the wall.
Bowled through the gate. Marooned from the grand
Ocean liners: SS Sobers & Headley; not by formidable Wes Hall

Line of destroyers; no *chinaman* or finger-lickin' spin
To obscurity – just a *gift* with your name on it
Lacking spite, Physics or Philosophy, innocuous as sin.

Like I say, there's no morality in this game.
Protesting genocide or burying your head
In sweet Anna's thighs, it's all the same.

IAN McDONALD

TEST MATCH

When cricket is playing
This place has a special mood.
Naturally, in the town there's little else.
For miles and miles and miles around
Attention centres on the Test Match ground:
Stands besieged from early morning;
Transistored cyclists weave one-handed,
Risking crashes every wicket down.
Heroic men are just down there
And the greatest heroes are our own.
Latest score is all that counts,
There is a feel of fairground in the air.

It catches on in Mercy Ward,
The excitement rises in the days before,
The desperate centring on self departs.
The subject concentrated on is changed,
The endless question unexpressed:
How much time have I got left?
Now other questions supervene:
The boys in trouble or the boys on top?
Their minds, diverted and released,
Fly out to where the cricket plays.
For a little while at least
Those broken on the wheel of life
Feel at their throats a different knife.

MASSA DAY DONE

Viv in a mood today, you only have to watch,
see the jaw grinding, he stabbing the pitch, backlift big.
Look how he stare down the wicket, spear in he eye,
he going to start sudden, violent, a thunder shock.
Man, this could be an innings! This could make life good.

You see how he coming in, how he shoulder relax,
how he spin the bat, how he look up at the sun,
how he seem to breathe deep, how he swing the bat, swing,
how he look around like a lord, how he chest expan'.
You ever see the man wear helmet? Tell me?
They say he too proud an' foolish.
Nah! He know he worth, boy;
the bowler should wear helmet, not he.
Remember long this day, holy to be here.
See him stalk the high altar o' the mornin' air.

You ever see such mastery in this world?
You ever see a man who dominate so?
This man don't know forbearance,
he don't know surrender or forgive,
he lash the ball like something anger him
Look how the man torment today!
He holding the bat, it could be an axe.
Look how he grinding he jaw again, boy.
how he head hold cock an' high
and he smile, he gleam, like jaguar.
Don't bring no flighty finery here; it gone!
Bring the mightiest man, Viv husk he.
He always so, he stay best fo' the best.

I tell you, he smile like he hungry;
you ever see this man caress?
That mood hold he, it bite he!
He pound the ball, look at that, aha!
Like he vex, he slash, he pull, he hook,
he blast a way through the cover, man,
he hoist the ball like cannon ball
gone far and wild, scattering the enemy,
and foe turn tremble, danger all about.
It's butchery today, bat spill blood,
and he cut like he cutting hog on a block;
nobody could stop he in that mood.

Almighty love be there! Almighty love, boy.
We know from the start, he one o' we.
Something hurt he bad, you could see,
as if heself alone could end we slavery!

DRINK & DIE

1 shot sambuca
1 shot tequila
4 dashes of Tabasco sauce
Layer in order in a glass

Paul, I coming
but I coming late.
Irene won't leave
me alone until
I read the front page
of the Gleaner and drink
the damn banana porridge.
Then only after she kiss
my forehead, and ask –
Papa you will behave
youself today? and I say
yes, does she go
on her business.

So Paul, I coming
but I coming slow.
These days the rum bar
seem further away
than time before when
we was young men returning
from a black day at the tire factory.
And recently, I been losing
my way and is long
after morning done
I finally find myself through
the doors.

Paul, I coming,
please wait on me
and I will tell you
about West Indies cricket,
how Carlooper is our
salvation, and as always
you won't agree with me.
And today, if someone ask
who the hell I talking with –
if I don't know is six years
you been dead now, Paul,
I will hit the brute down –
for not knowing how spirit
and spirit is always talking.

And Paul, these days I feel
my bones being pulled
into the earth
and my skin lifting
to show the duppy-self
underneath. So I know
I coming, Paul, real soon.

Egbert Moore (Lord Beginner)

Victory Calypso, Lord's 1950

Cricket, lovely cricket,
At Lord's where I saw it;
Cricket, lovely cricket,
At Lord's where I saw it;
Yardley tried his best
But Goddard won the test.
They gave the crowd plenty fun;
Second Test and West Indies won.

CHORUS:
With those two little pals of mine
Ramadhin and Valentine.

The King was there well attired,
So they started with Rae and Stollmeyer;
Stolly was hitting balls around the boundary,
But Wardle stopped him at twenty.
Rae had confidence,
So he put up a strong defence;
He saw the King was waiting to see,
So he gave him a century.

CHORUS:
With those two little pals of mine
Ramadhin and Valentine.

West Indies first innings total
was three-twenty-six
Just as usual
When Bedser bowled Christiani
The whole thing collapsed quite easily,
England then went on,
And made one-hundred-fifty-one;
West Indies then had two-twenty lead,
And Goddard said, "That's nice indeed."

CHORUS:
With those two little pals of mine
Ramadhin and Valentine.

Yardley wasn't broken hearted
When the second innings started;
Jenkins was like a target
Getting the first five into his basket.
But Gomez broke him down,
While Walcott licked them around:
He was not out for one-hundred and sixty-eight,
Leaving Yardley to contemplate.

CHORUS:
The bowling was superfine
Ramadhin and Valentine.

West Indies was feeling homely,
Their audience had them happy.
When Washbrook's century had ended,
West Indies' voices all blended.
Hats went in the air.
They jumped and shouted without fear;
So at Lord's was the scenery
Bound to go down in history.

CHORUS:
After all was said and done,
Second Test and West Indies won!

GRACE NICHOLS

TEST MATCH HIGH MASS
(at Bourda Green, Georgetown, Guyana)

If Jesus was pressed into playing
a game, I'm sure it would be cricket
and he – the wicketkeeper
bearing open-palmed witness
behind the trinity of stumps.

Watching his white-clad disciples
work the green fields –
tracking the errant red soul
of a ball – arcing gloriously
across the turf of uncertainty.

Watching his flocks, especially
those in trees (reminding him
of Zachias in his sycamore).
Now see them they flapping wings
at every six and four.

Meanwhile the sun
casting benediction down
but the two umpires
like judgement-day-vicars
casting fate with a lift of finger –

Dis is high mass. Dis is Bourda.
We the heaving congregation,
with a Job-like patience,
wonder what miracles will spin
to feed a hungry multitude?

SASENARINE PERSAUD

CALL HIM THE BABU

Kanhai in Calcutta and the swarm
of crowds, waves of Indian Ocean
roaring in the stands. Once *Aja*
stood on docks nearby, boarding
for Indies Cristobal, the Baptist
Navigator, christened this land.

But mother, you let us go, did not
look back. And I am returned bitter
and thrilled – Whack! to the boundary,
whack! to the Indian boards. Two tons
this score.

It seemed he didn't care but stroke
played all around, inventing the
backsideboundary hook from the Indus
batsman's flicker. The alwayswrong
critics dubbing him another calypso
cricketer and finally silver fox.
Another black lie: ferocity and catness
the Bengal tiger's where *Aja* boarded
and *Ajie* waved to *Bharat* to ocean to
Guiana of El Dorado, D'Aguiar's XM whiterum
bitter and sweet – land of many waters.

We called for *The Babu*: whoelse?
with Jagan CIA-ed and raced from
office, with rainbows of rigged
elections, Korean mass games; our
voice stifled, our 50 + 1 %
minoritied for years…

We made him *Hanuman* and sat on his shoulders
when he flew to wicket, cutlassblade in hand.
Each ball a soldier struck, or a chicken-
in-the-rough traffic cop stopping Indian
taxidrivers for lunch, breakfast, dinner

cut to the root: bladed every comrade of
The Party not least The Comrade Leader
who would ban him from cricketplaying in his
land, who would send the military to
canefields when the Indian cutters striked.

That day in Bourda sunshine: his score
a ton like the graceful Bajan Sir; bats
flashing and glinting like sun on
"twenty-twos" cleaving burntcane,
like the nickel-coated golf clubs sparkling

           in this late summer sun
a thousand miles north we still call
The Babu for the great white lie, *The*
Babu for the unreturning, *The Babu*
for the cold...

ON LARA'S 375

They bowl fists of cheer
their arms in line and length
through the air.
They chip, they *wine*
calypso reggae meringue combined.
The conch horns blow
to spoon on bottle, the merry tambour.

He removes his cap to the applause
a record red with the flash of runs
lifts the bat historically high, each arm
above his head and wide.
He walks the victory sign.

He bubbles like the unstoppered
cola he advertises, hugs his little
partner on the pitch
with the weight of his emotion,
with arms that unite
beneath an uncertain sun.

Humbly like a hero
he bows to the wicket
that held the bales
in a three-staved parapet.
He kisses the earth
that drove his knocks
beyond the boundary of the furthest count.

His team are all soldiers
pitched in the field of cricket.
They tip bats on each side
in a high vaulted avenue
for his triumphal walk-through,
each extended handshake in linkage.

They stole his gear, but not
his run to stardom.
The clouds parted their rain
heavy shades of drape
on a blue window of sky
upon our islands strung
on a nylon sea.

He colours hope on the nation's flag
sliding down with fading values
almost to half-mast,
and for the young restless
on the winds of the times.

St. 3 L. 2   Shivnarine Chanderpaul
St. 6 L. 1   It was claimed that Lara's cricketing gear was stolen,
*   but was subsequently returned.*

ERIC ROACH

TO LEARIE

Of famous father a most famous son
Wherever cricket has been greatly played
Wherever men discourse of wonders done
By wisden wizards – of fine feats displayed
In the great empire game, – there in renown
Is known the name of Learie Constantine
Who won and wears now cricket's triple crown.

Here in our native sun, in the cold clime
Of Northern England are his praises loud.
Here have we seen him hit a hundred, take
A grandest catch, and give the thundering crowd
A smile as though he'd done it for our sake,
And we have seen him run and leap and swing
The ball with havoc down the taut matting.

KRISHNA A. SAMAROO

A CRICKETING GESTURE

This is not cricket. A finger spun
a leather ball down a wicket
worn to the bone, cracked
like a skull unearthed by
a spade clearing space for
another soul in this cemetery
of dreams we call hope.
The umpire stood unmoved,
and the ball at the stroke
played, elbow squaring with shoulder,
bit into the flesh and flashed
to first slip; a quick grip
ended a career that spanned
passages beyond the boundaries
of this field; the slow gait,
the dropped head, the gritted teeth
tell the tale only too well;
the pattering palms in irony
flood with the horror of memory.

G.K. SAMMY

CRICKET IN THE ROAD

The Bowler:

"Howzat, Umpire? Send him out,
that was plain caught behind!
How you could say the ball miss bat?
You stupid or you blind?"

"This man done score a set of runs.
He plan to bat whole day?
If I could bowl one fast straight ball
I'll knock his stumps away."

"Is Malcolm Marshall bowling here –
my bouncers could break bones!
You shut your mouth! Don't say my pace
is more like Larry Gomes."

The Wicket-Keeper:

"Oh God, he voop and hit again.
Look how far that ball fly.
Is like when Vivi hitting out:
ball bowl – bat swing – goodbye!"

"Aye, look, you see Old-Lady yard?
Don't hit in there at all,
because that stroke is six-and-out
and we will lose the ball."

"Old-Lady dog eat seventeen
wind-ball this year alone.
So every time I get the chance
I pelt him with a stone."

"Look, all-you try and out this man
I tired wicket keeping.
Howzat!! Not out? Look, Umpire,
you either drunk or thiefing."

The Bowler:

"You see how fast I bowl that ball?
You see how much it swing?
Not Greenidge, Haynes nor Carlyle Best
could put bat to that thing!"

"You 'keeping or you liming, man?
Look, they just take a bye!
I know your name is not Dujon,
but try nah man, just try."

The Wicket-Keeper:

"This batsman just like Larry Gomes –
he steady as a rock,
but if he bat till darkness fall
I wouldn't get my knock."

"Look, Captain, change the bowling round.
We want a Tony Gray,
a Holding, Walsh or Patterson –
we want to bat today."

"This batsman feel he's Richardson.
He wouldn't out at all.
That's it. Game done. I going home.
Give me my bat and ball."

CRICKET

Boysie uh has was to tel yuh
How yuh touch muh soul de edduh day
When yuh talk 'bout cricket an' de Lord;
Yuh know yuh right 'bout backbite an' backslide
Um at de church, boy, more than at Kensington.

Doan min' how tick de crowd is,
Duh will size roun' an' gi' yuh a lil scotch
An' if yuh hip kin pullup a flask at lunchtime,
Yuh eatin' like a gues' at Cana feas'.

Le' muh tell yuh somet'ing Boysie boy,
De Lord got somet'ing to do wid cricket
De wicket does remin' me o' de Trinity
God in de centre of de three,
Holy Ghost pun de lef' and Jesus
Pun de right an' de bails like a crown
Joinin' dem an' mekkin' dem Three in One.
De pitch like an altar north and south
Wid de sun transfigurin' de scene
An' de umpires like two high priests
Wid de groundsmen as de sextons, Yes, Yes.

When two batsmen stick pun a side
Jookin' like a dog an' peltin' willow like a
Hog an' yuh see de captain change up de
Fiel', da is toilin' all night
An' ketchin' nutten; den all of a sudden
De man in de slips ketch a fish!
De Lord revelation da captain.
Yuh remember da match 'gains' St. John
W'en de winna wuz t' get a demijohn?

Big Joe David did de captain
An' So-So Johnny open de bowlin'
When David call de team roun' de South stumps
An' mek evah man kneel down

Den sprinkle de Stades between de wickets
An' pass de flas' from mout' to
Mout' an' hol' de empty bottle
Till de sun dry out de dregs, you ain' remember?
Lord, Lord, de St. John people laugh
Dem cry, dem hol' duh belly an'
Roll pun de groun', some pee an' all!

 Johnny run down like a bull-cow did
 Behin' 'e an' he le' go de fus' ball
 Like a jet! "Father", "Son", an'
 "Holy Ghost". De "Trinity"
 Lick from behin' dem star!
 Da Sunday mornin', Pastor Worrell
 Eye pop out when 'e see de five dollar
 Pun de plate. He sing de t'anksgivin' hymn
 Like a angel, an' he preach 'bout David
 An' Goliath…

Why yuh fink dem W's did so good?
Turn de stumps upside down an' yuh see?
W–man! De whole "Trinity"!
Doan bring down de wrath o' de Almighty!

Three shots I remember to me grave
A square cut from de Son for a four
Uh see de shot, uh hear de crack, but Boysie!
To tell God's trut' uh en see de ball
Yet; a gal from de boundary pelt it
Back…

De "Holy Ghost" stretch down de wicket
An' 'e jook an' 'e poke like t'ings tight,
All of a sudden 'e step back
An' 'e stretch up in de air an' 'e smack!
A fielder pun de boundary pounce
Like a cat! Down han' 'pon de ball
An' de ball twis' out 'e han' an' de man
Eatin' grass an' de ball hit de board
An' bounce back!…

De "Father" did a master 'pon de bat
Nuh lot o' crack no lot o' smack but de grace when 'e place,
Divine like de dawn foreday mornin',
Three men pun de off stan'in' close,
An' 'e drive t'rough de covers smooth an' sweet
Duh get so close dat dem butt up an' fall down
An' de ball tek it time t'rough dem han'
T'rough dem foot kiss de board an' stan' still.

Cricket is de game o' de Lord
Cricket is de game o' de Master
Play de game right, Boysie boy
An' you stan' a good chance hereafter.

WILLIAM WALCOTT

BONDMEN

Fourteen West Indians on the field.
Who has heard the crickets?
Who has seen the bats?
Who has cleared the bawl?

Fourteen West Indians on the field.
Who has kept the pace?
Who has lined the drive?
Who has filled the bowls?

Fourteen West Indians on the field.
Who has torn the covers?
Who has saved the pitch?
Who has squared the boundaries?

Fourteen West Indians on the field.
Who has razed the stakes?
Who has missed the blot?
Who has borne the loss?

Fourteen West Indians on the field.
Who has shaped the sentries?
Who has seized the runs?
Who has kept the stations?

Fourteen West Indians on the field.
Who has milled the ground?
Who has soiled the plot?
Who has stalled the boss?

Fourteen West Indians on the field.
Whose charges will we fear?
Whose banner should we wear?
Whose conscience must we bear?

Fourteen West Indians on the field.
Whose converts must we hold?
Whose letters will we fold?
Whose bounties must we mould?

Fourteen West Indians on the field.
Whose captain will we name?
Whose battle should we blame?
Whose victory must we claim?

MILTON VISHNU WILLIAMS

BATTING IS MY OCCUPATION

Batting is my occupation;
both by inclination and gift.
I am interested in correct strokes
to suit the occasion – a great match.
The match is cohabiting. The strokes
must be keen, sharp and cleanly struck,
as if Peter May, Cowdrey or Sobers or I
could never be out.

And in truth my blade flashes
from all angles.
It would take a genius of high character
to distinguish and plot them,
for my ingenuity is stamped everywhere.

O womb bowlers, stir up the sleeping tribes
stuck in you. Wicketkeepers are idling contentedly.

BENJAMIN ZEPHANIAH

HOW'S DAT

No Sir
I don't play Cricket,
One time I try
Fearing a duck
I watch de ball fly towards me,
I recall every spin
An unforgettable air speed,
It bounced before me
Jus missing a two day old ant,
Up it cum
A red flash
Lick me finger so hard
I thought me finger would die.

Teacher tell me
I am good at cricket,
I tell teacher
I am not,
Teacher tell me
We luv cricket,
I tell teacher
Not me,
I want Trigonometry
Fe help me people,
Teacher tell me
I am a born Cricketer,
But I never......(well only once),
I don't play cricket.

FICTION

MICHAEL ANTHONY

CRICKET IN THE ROAD

In the rainy season we got few chances to play cricket in the road. For whenever we were at the game, the rains came down, chasing us into the yard again. That was the way it was in Mayaro in the rainy season. The skies were always overcast, and over the sea the rainclouds hung low and grey and scowling, and the winds blew in and whipped angrily through the palms. And when the winds were strongest and raging, the low-hanging clouds would become dense and black, and the sea would roar, and the torrents of rain would come sweeping with all their, tumult upon us.

We had just run in from the rain. Amy and Vern from next door were in good spirits, and laughing for oddly enough they seemed to enjoy the downpour as much playing cricket in the road. Amy was in our yard, giggling and pretending to drink the falling rain, with her face all wet and her clothes drenched, and Vern, who was sheltering under the eaves, excitedly jumped out to join her. "Rain, rain, go to Spain," they shouted. And presently their mother, who must have heard the noise and knew, appeared from next door, and Vern and Amy vanished through the hedge.

I stood there, depressed about the rain, and then I put Vern's bat and ball underneath the house, and went indoors. "Stupes!" I said to myself. I had been batting when the rains came down. It was only when *I* was batting that the rains came down! I wiped my feet so I wouldn't soil the sheets, and went up on the bed. I was sitting, sad, and wishing that the rain would really go away – go to Spain, as Vern said – when my heart seemed to jump out of me. A deafening peal of thunder struck across the sky. Quickly I closed the window. The rain hammered awfully on the roof-top and I kept tense for the thunder which I knew would break again and for the unearthly flashes of lightning.

Secretly I was afraid of the violent weather. I was afraid of the rain, and of the thunder and the lightning that came with them, and of the sea beating against the headlands, and of the storm-winds, and of everything being so deathlike when the rains were gone. I started again at another flash of lightning and before I had recovered from this, yet another terrifying peal of thunder hit the air. I screamed. I heard my mother running into the room. Thunder struck again and I dashed under the bed.

"Selo! Selo! First bat!" Vern shouted from the road. The rains had ceased and the sun had come out, but I was not quite recovered yet. I brought myself reluctantly to look out from the front door, and there was Vern, grinning and impatient and beckoning to me.

"First bat," he said. And as if noting my indifference he looked towards Amy who was just coming out to play. "Who second bat?" he said.

"Me!" I said.

"Me!" shouted Amy almost at the same time.

"Amy second bat," Vern said.

"No, I said 'Me' first," I protested.

Vern grew impatient while Amy and I argued. Then an idea seemed to strike him. He took out a penny from his pocket. "Toss for it," he said. "What you want?"

"Heads," I called.

"Tail," cried Amy, "Tail bound to come!"

The coin went up in the air, fell down and overturned, showing tail.

"I'm *not* playing," I cried, stung. And as that did not seem to disturb enough, I ran towards where I had put Vern's bat and ball and disappeared with them behind our house. Then I flung them with all my strength into the bushes.

When I came back to the front of the house, Vern was standing there dumb-founded. "Selo, where's the bat and ball?" he said.

I was fuming. "I don't know about *any* bat and ball!"

"Tell on him," Amy cried. "He throw them away."

Vern's mouth twisted into a forced smile. "What's an old bat and ball," he said.

But as he walked out of the yard I saw tears glinting from the corners of his eyes.

For the rest of that rainy season we never played cricket in the road again. Some-times the rains ceased and the sun came out brightly, and I heard the voices of Amy and Vern on the other side of the fence. At such times I would go out into the road and whistle to myself, hoping they would hear me and come out, but they never did, and I knew they were still very angry and would never forgive me.

And so the rainy season went on. And it was as fearful as ever with the thun-der and lightning and waves roaring in the bay, and the strong winds. But the people who talked of all this said that was the way Mayaro was, and they laughed about it. And sometimes when through the rain and even thunder I heard Vern's voice on the other side of the fence, shouting "Rain, rain, go to Spain," it puz-zled me how it could be so. For often I had made up my mind I would be brave, but when the thunder cracked I always dashed under the bed.

It was the beginning of the new year when I saw Vern and Amy again. The rainy season was, happily, long past, and the day was hot and bright and as I walked towards home I saw that I was walking towards Vern and Amy just about to start cricket in the road. My heart thumped violently. They looked strange and new as if they had gone away, far, and did not want to come back any more. They did not notice me until I came up quite near, and then I saw Amy start, her face all lit up.

"Vern…" she cried, "Vern look – look Selo!"

Embarrassed, I looked at the ground and at the trees, and at the orange sky, and I was so happy I did not know what to say. Vern stared at me, a strange grin on face. He was ripping the cellophane paper off a brand new bat.

"Selo, here – *you* first bat," he said gleefully.

And I cried as though it were raining and I was afraid.

BOURDA

It was only last Saturday that we agreed to come to the test match on Easter Monday. "We" meant three of us; Baps, Bingie and I. We worked it out that since play started at eleven, and the gates were often closed by nine o'clock, we would have to start queuing by six-thirty in the morning. This created serious problems since that meant leaving home by five-thirty. The preparation of the food we would need for our day's nourishment would need to start on Easter Sunday night.

Negotiations for the food added complications to each of our domestic lives. Baps was married but was not on very good terms with his wife since he had returned home from his last job. He had got himself involved with a plump young girl while in the bush and word of his indiscretions had seeped all the way back to the coast. His wife had raised bloody hell over the story and suspected, quite rightly as it happened, that the young woman had made substantial inroads into the money Baps had earned on the project. He has had to make numerous promises and compromises to restore normal relations.

Bingie is not married, he is "living home" with a country girl he met last year. One Saturday night, he slapped her around because she had cursed him and refused to cook for us when we had assembled at his house drunk. After the first few slaps, she had run to the kitchen for the chopper, threatening to cut off his right hand. Bingie had to back off and apologise. We had to restrain Betty from getting us all into trouble with the police.

I am a bachelor and I still live at Ma's house. She and I are at war over remarks she made from the kitchen when Dolly was last by our yard. Dolly is not pretty, I know, but she is a good girl, easy to please and quite content with the sporadic attention I am able to give. There was no reason, however, for Ma to call her a "foffie-eyed wretch". Sometimes I believe if even Shakira herself were to visit, Ma would find something mean to say about her.

In our crowd, you cannot arrive at Bourda without a basket full of food and drink. That is how you convince your friends and admirers that you have your womenfolk under control. To sustain this masquerade, we made demeaning compromises. Poor Baps may never be able to see his fat girl again. Bingie had to promise many gifts and jewellery. I suspect, though, that the women all recognised that their own reputations were on the line if any of us were to arrive at the ground with a less than perfect lunch kit. So five-thirty Easter Monday morning found us at the Pike Street bus stop waiting for the first Kitty/Regent, each with a basket and numerous other bags and appendages. I had my mother's best ice-flask and several bottles of Coke, in addition to chow mein, fowl curry, rice, patties, pine tarts, half a sponge cake, two plates, two spoons and four plastic cups. Bingie and Baps brought the rum, two large bottles each, in addition to food. I was not allowed to keep rum in the house since my mother had joined the revival group last year.

Getting on the bus was another story. The old Motor Transport buses had narrow turnstiles that made entry with two or three bags per person a hazardous business. Since most of the other passengers were also on their way to cricket there was much good-natured badinage, and eventually we helped each other, passing bags, baskets and even one or two small boys over the turnstiles to get things going. We reached the North Road gates at six o'clock to find Bourda already alive. There were hundreds of diehards already in line, and fellows from the country who had come down by train from Berbice for the weekend and were camping out in the open on the grassy stretch on the North Road. The out-of-town guys had used up all their cooked rations by this time and were buying food at cut-throat prices from the city food vendors, always on the ready to cash in on a good thing.

Some of the country boys were in a sorry state. Many had come by train since Friday night to see the great local hero Rohan Kanhai make a big score. Kanhai had made a majestic 89 on the first day and, though he had not got to his century, it was clear to all concerned that at his second go on Saturday he would pulverise the Australian bowlers and make his first century in a home test. Many of the boys had come laden with food, money, drink and high expectations of a good time. Kanhai was the first master batsman of Indian descent in the West Indies team, so he generated special reverence from people of his own background, especially those from the sugar estate villages from which stars like Kanhai had been recruited. Unfortunately, before a roaring crowd on Saturday, an Australian fast bowler named Hawke found the ball of his life, completely defeated the local hero and bowled him out. The crowd went as quiet as if it was church.

Many of the fans were in a dilemma; their hero was out and would not have a chance to redeem himself. Why bother to stay? Some had spent most of their money and not a few were without the ready to afford the train trip back home. Many had bet huge sums with speculating Georgetown fans on Kanhai's hundred, and had had to pay up when he was defeated. They hung about squatting on the grass, their new shirts and picnic clothes now bedraggled, and their unshaved, unwashed faces highlighting their pitiful stories.

We joined the queue for the Northwest stand since it was covered and since a large number of our drinking buddies and fellow cricket arguers were going to be there. Those who got there first tried to preserve some room for those further back in the line. This was possible because "Mammy Eye" was counted as one of our gang and had long since been deemed a "rogue and a vagabond" by the city magistrates for persistent assault, battery, and "resisting a peace officer in the carrying out of his duties". Anyone trying to get a seat in our corner was frightened off by his growl, and by the advice of people knowledgeable about crime and vagabondage in Kitty and environs. We joined the queue about half a mile down the road and as we inched forward the morning sun rose in our faces, reminding us how long we had been awake.

Queues are jolly at Bourda. Preliminary arguments begin about the blindness of the selectors, the arrogance of the cricket board of control, players selected who should not have been and forgotten players who should have been. Controversy was also generated because a local writer had suggested that Nurse, the Barbadian, had not earned his place and that Cornelius, the local boy, should have played in his stead. Since Nurse was my favourite player at the time I could not let this go unanswered, but since I am short, thin and bespectacled, and without the necessary loud voice that helps in these quarrels, I was shouted down. My lack of patriotism was denounced by several large and voluble diehards, and Baps and Bingie had to save me from myself despite their disgust at my open heresy.

The talk then drifted to the local officials who had made fools of themselves by refusing to allow our leading umpire into the stands because the local umpires were on strike. Unfortunately for them, when the Prime Minister arrived at the game on the first day, he had joined the umpire in the bleachers, where they sat on a soft drink case together, and the resulting publicity put the board in a bad light. They had no defenders in the North Road queue.

By the time we got to the bridge over the canal the queue started to disintegrate, since latecomers from the Scheme walked straight to the head of the line and tried to muscle their way in. Early birds such as ourselves from Campbelville, Lodge and Kitty were not going to allow these hooligans to do us out of our hard-won seniority, and eventually the pushing match threatened to become ugly. The lone policeman on duty could do nothing about it and looked away until a few guys fell off the end of the bridge into the canal. This sobered everyone down a bit, though some unfortunates lost their lunches and spent the day looking bad and smelling worse.

We got into the ground about eight-thirty and wove our way through the; crowded wooden stand to the gang in "our" corner. Even though it was over two hours to start of play the stand was almost full and the gates were closed about half an hour after we got in. The trouble with getting up so early to watch cricket is that by the time you get to a seat, you are already hungry and thirsty so you have to open the food, start eating, open the rum and start the drinking. This is also advised if your lady made mistakes about the time it would take before your food went off. One fellow opened his chow mein at lunchtime only to find it had expired some time before.

You cannot eat alone at cricket. You have to pass your bowl, flask, cake-tin and anything else around your friends. Your friends would have brought friends and would pass your fried rice or roti to them. Of course, a friend of friends will pass you some of their food. Flask and bowl covers were pressed into service when plates ran out. The drinking was even more serious. Each large bottle is ceremoniously produced, the seal is broken and a few drops are sprinkled or thrown over the shoulder to appease the spirits. The drinking commences. Muddy, a loudmouthed accountant in the civil service, had walked with a bottle of scotch that he had brought to impress the gang. Unfortunately, he passed his bottle around before taking a drink himself, and by the time it returned to him there was only a tiny drop to be squeezed out. Muddy began to recoup his losses by making major inroads into any bottle passed to him. By ten o'clock, Muddy was drunk and fast asleep. I do not believe he saw a single ball played even though he remains an authority on the events of that day.

You have a lot of time to waste before the game starts. You could watch the players warm up in front of the pavilion. You could try to guess the names of the visiting team, quite a feat since they all looked alike. You could stare at the signs encouraging you to drink Russian Bear Rum and rub with Canadian Healing Oil. You could stare at the trees rising over the tops of the stands and admire the birdmen perched high on the Regent Street side. You could eat again or vary your diet by getting boiled channa from Channaman or boiled corn from Beaks. Channaman was expert at throwing his parcels to his patrons no matter how high up. By game time we were so bored we applauded everything. The groundsman putting in the stumps, the umpires walking out, the drunk who managed to get on the field and give the police a good run around. You could look up in the pavilion and wonder at the big shots watching cricket in dark suits and ties.

By the time the day really got started, we were bored enough to get into pointless arguments and ridiculous bets. What a day it was. I made a bet about Nurse with a large red-skinned guy from Buxton. Nurse promptly got out first ball. Then Sobers came in and started to hit the Australian bowlers all over Bourda. Bets about the great man began to fly and Bingie bet a guy from Courantyne that "Sobers will fifty". As Sobers approached the half century mark, Bingie, now under the cloud of rum, scotch and overeating, became abusive and insulting to an equally drunk Berbician. On the brink of his fifty, Sobers got out and Bingie refused to pay up. The gang turned on him and in the ensuing scuffle, my glasses and my mother's favourite ice-flask were broken. Bingie did not learn. When the Australians began their second innings, he started an argument with everybody because Sobers was opening the bowling from the top end instead of Hall. He claimed that the skipper was a selfish "pro" and a brainless captain. This enraged the whole collection of drunks, including complete strangers who attached themselves to our well-fed and watered company. When Simpson the Australian captain and opening batsman clouted Sobers for a four, Bingie made large bets waving the entire contents of his pocket in reckless abandon. Sobers promptly bowled Simpson two balls later, knocking the stumps out of the ground in spectacular fashion. Bingie could not pay all his creditors and almost had to give up his shirt to a big fellow from Mackenzie who was late in the queue to collect his winnings.

As the day grew hotter and the hard greenheart stand began to hurt our backsides, and the cramped postures in which we were crouched began to take effect, cricket watching became hard work. Everyone had to stand and stretch in between overs and during water breaks to keep off cramp and stiffness. The standing break took longer and longer until the crowd waited till the bowler was running in for the first ball to sit down. Also the sun now beat straight into our faces, unlike the faces of the big shots in the pavilion and the rich people in Flagstaff stand. And we were drunk and tired and sleepy. The cricket was fascinating that day but most of us were tired out by liquor, loud arguments and the heat of the sun, and so missed all the subtleties of a masterly display by the spin bowler Gibbs. As he wove confusion amongst the Australian batsmen, we were too beaten up to appreciate the subtle arts of the Guianese master. Australia was routed.

But so are we. We are walking home elated but tired and sore. We have to walk since there is no chance that there will be any room on the bus. Baps has spent the money he promised his wife and Bingie has no hope of getting his madam her bangles for some time. And me, I have to explain to Ma about her special ice-flask.

CYRIL DABYDEEN

FASTER THEY COME

> Whoa di big man inna cricket.
> – Jamaican saying

Ron fancies himself a fast bowler. He comes at it full speed, then lets the ball out of his hand with all the force he can muster. He's imagined doing it a hundred times before. And he *is* a celebrated cricketer, isn't he? The ball leaves him in a rhythmic, swinging motion, then rockets down to the batsman. The spectators applaud, the sound resounding in his ears.

"Yeah, yeah!" voices cry from black and brown faces.

The batsman, still poised at the other end, shuffles forward to play the skidding, rocketing ball. Suddenly he misses. The ball races through bat and pad, the bails fly, the stumps spread-eagle.

Bowled!

Ron replays the ball's movement in his mind as the crowd cheers. The next batsmen are from Australia, England, India, Sri Lanka, Pakistan. All have familiar names – Neil Harvey, Bobby Simpson, Peter May, Geoff Boycott, Khan, Gavaskar, Tendulkar. Each batsman is at the top of his class. The crowd at the SkyDome in Toronto cheers Ron on.

"What's the matter with you, Ron?" his wife, Doris, asks, awakening him from his dream.

"Eh?"

"You hear me. Why you play-actin' like that for, an' smilin' so?"

"Smiling?" Ron wants to return to his reminiscing. Once more he takes the long run up and imagines he is faster than the legendary West Indians – Hall and Griffith, Roberts and Holding. Or the other greats from England and Australia – Lindwall, Trueman, Statham, Davidson, Thompson, Lee. In his mind he sees Learie Constantine, George Headley, Sobers, Richards, Kanhai, Lloyd. *Who else?* Was that Brian Lara eyeing him? Canada and the Caribbean together. The Atlantic's waves beating. Trade with rum and codfish. Oh, the Maroons long, long ago. Did anyone forget history? Sea chests of silver and gold in sunken ships.

Look good, Doris. See me in action now. You could be cheering me on, you know!

But Doris sneers and scoffs at his play-acting. Then he hears another voice. A stranger's. *Who is he?*

"Man, you can't be living in Canada in ice and snow and thinking you're still back there. Who do you think you really are?"

131

"I am the best. Besides, Canada's now different."

"Really?"

"Who the blasted hell are you, anyway?"

"An immigrant, just like you, Ron."

"What kind of immigrant?"

"Just an immigrant, that's all."

"Ever been a fast bowler, stranger?"

"It's cricket you're talking about again?"

"You heard me!" Ron snaps.

Cricket, sea dogs, buccaneering – the images appear again, and Ron is back at it. He still thinks of the one who calls himself an immigrant and watches him from somewhere in the crowded stadium. Ron's fans are everywhere in Canada. No longer just at the SkyDome but at the Woodbine Racetrack where cricket can also be played in wide-open spaces. These are the same fans who are also patrons of hockey, baseball, basketball, and horse racing, no?

Doris still sneers, scoffs.

A fast bowler is like a thoroughbred racehorse, flying up the green, hooves pounding. Ron sprints up again, then hurls the ball at full speed. *Yeah!*

Let them snicker – Doris and the one who calls himself an immigrant!

Ron dreams of Canadians by the thousands playing cricket everywhere, in every town and city, the new and not-so-new Canadians. All watch him as he takes the long run up once more.

Now the batsman might be from somewhere like Nova Scotia, Quebec, Ontario, Manitoba, Alberta, or British Columbia and will play him with confidence, not unlike a Donald Bradman or W G. Grace. *Who?* You heard me, didn't you? Don't deny who they are! The batsman is so confident. He comes down the pitch, ready to hit the ball through the covers for four!

Suddenly Ron is just a slow-paced, ordinary bowler being taken advantage of. No more horse's hooves galloping, pistons pounding, wings flying. He is just himself, alone, forlorn. Is the immigrant still watching him and commiserating?

Doris laughs again. The ball soars in the air as the batsman hits out again with a mighty whack. Ron's eyes burn as he sees the ball go straight into the sun. And the immigrant in the stadium is pointing at him. Who is he, anyway? Where did he come from?

"Stop it, man!"

"You again?" Ron screams.

"I can't bear to watch you being so humiliated by the batsman."

"Humiliated?"

"The ball being hit so easily, I mean. What kind of fast bowler are you, anyway?"

"I am, uh, the best!"

"Ah, still thinking you're back there?"

"I am *here*,"

"In Canada, eh? You know you can't keep fooling yourself or Doris any longer."

"I'm not trying to fool anyone!"

"Ron, see, you're in Canada now, a place that's cold in winter and ice is everywhere on the hard ground. It's a place where cricket's not yet appreciated. It's just hockey and baseball."

"Cricket could become a national sport soon." Ron still thinks he is the best, though he can't quite muster the long run up anymore. He grips the ball in his hand.

Were the thousands of spectators in the stadium awaiting his next move? He knows he mustn't disappoint them. They watch him on national TV, too, on prime time no less. Yet he has difficulty now lifting his arms and legs in the familiar rhythmic motion, even with the easy follow-on down the wicket. He can't bowl the ball to strike terror in the batsman anymore.

"Ron, you're hardly payin' much attention to me," Doris says. "What kind of marriage are we havin', anyway?"

"Leave me alone, woman."

"It's time you stop your foolish play-actin', I say!"

But Ron wants to be the best and keep his pride and self-esteem intact. Then who would ever doubt him? He imagines Doris on the cricket ground like a cheerleader, applauding him the loudest. *Is she really?*

"Look, immigrant, whoever you are!" Ron cries. "Look at her, eh?"

Doris is with her friends from the office. They all watch him as he starts the long run up. Yes, he feels a new energy inside, in every muscle and nerve of his body. They are all rooting for him.

"Look good at my husband, everyone!" Doris yells.

"Is it him striding up to the wicket like that?" asks another, a blond named Carey. "Gosh, he's so sexy."

"Look at him throwin' his arms an' legs in the air like that – look good!" Doris urges.

Ron glances up to wave to Doris in the stadium and loses his concentration a little. In the sea of faces before him he recognizes Doris and her friends, and Carey and her boyfriend, Jake – a hirsute Englishman, she calls him.

Instinctively Ron waves to them. He feels his old form returning. Now he will bowl faster than ever.

Doris cheers him on. "Everyone see him good, my husband, eh?"

Carey, with Jake next to her, also cheers. "Yes, it's him."

But in another moment Doris says to him, "Oh, the fun we used to have, Ron."

"Yes, Doris, I remember when we were first married and came to Canada to start a new life. We wanted to try out all the new Canadian things, didn't we?"

"We used to like watchin' hockey, too, no?"

"Indeed, that bodychecking along the boards is really Canadian."

Doris smiles. "Good skatin', too. That Wayne Gretzky, ha."

"Not Mario Lemieux?"

Doris laughs. "Paul Coffey an' the others."

"Stop it, Doris," Ron suddenly says.

"Stop it? Christ, what's gotten into you?"

Did she forget that Ron is still in the middle of the cricket ground? Everyone expects him to bowl again, faster than ever. The one who calls himself an immigrant is watching, isn't he? But he and Doris seem to want only to be themselves in their new country.

Something else seethes in Ron now. He doesn't know exactly what it is. Perhaps Canada is making him rethink things he doesn't want to re-examine. He feels a strange paralysis. His legs are almost numb. Let the one who calls himself immigrant look at him, too, whoever he is, wherever he comes from.

Doris has such a sweet smile. Ron remembers embracing her when they first arrived in Canada more than a decade ago. It was like a dream come true. They pledged always to be happy together. But not long after he sensed her withdraw from him. She didn't seem to recognize him anymore as her husband.

The cricket ball is in his hand, his sleeves are rolled up, his mouth is set, and he is ready to bowl fast once more.

But the immigrant accosts him again. "Who are you really, Ron?"

"What do you mean?"

"What kind of sportsman do you want to be?"

"I can blasted well play cricket if I want to, can't I?"

"Not play hockey then?"

"That, too. I will learn to play hockey – later."

"And baseball?"

"Baseball, too, later."

"Christ, but you've been a cricket fast bowler only."

"*Been?*"

"Can you still bowl like the best of them? Or is it only your ongoing fantasy, Ron?"

"Who the hell are you, anyway?"

"I told you, one just like you – an immigrant."

"From where?"

"Once you're here, does that matter?"

Ron isn't sure what to say next.

"Now about your cricket fantasy, Ron."

"It's real, I tell you. It's what I am!"

"Not who you were?"

"I am still a… a… fast bowler," Ron says. "And soon the sport of cricket will be played in every part of Canada. I've seen some good batsmen here, too."

"Have you really? On TV, you mean?"

Ron squirms. "Ask my wife, Doris. She'll tell you. Ask her for God's sake. Ask her friends, too, especially that one called Carey."

Suddenly Ron isn't sure what he is saying.

The immigrant smirks. "That English boyfriend of hers, he, too, used to be a cricketer? You think they like the long run up, how you leap in the air striking fear in the batsman's heart? Is that what you're thinking?" He laughs.

Ron frowns. "Christ, that's what Doris has been saying to me."

"So Doris really is in the stadium watching you?"

Ron isn't sure of anything anymore. Gosh, what is happening to him? He rubs his eyes hard.

What is real?

He grips the ball firmly in his hand. Maybe Doris is no longer applauding him. Maybe she and her friends are only humouring him and this was all planned. Carey and her boyfriend, the hirsute Englishman, are probably in on it.

Ron moves forward for the long run up. He's coming full speed. Thousands watch and cheer him on. People from all walks of life, all races and ethnic backgrounds. Many come from places the world over, too. White, brown, black – all complexions and colours.

A new spirit surges in his veins and he starts to laugh. Then he hurls the ball in that rhythmic bowling action he's perfected so well. The batsman at the other end is laughing, too, for the sheer joy of cricket.

Wild applause erupts as if coming from all parts of the world where cricket is played – Australia, New Zealand, England, India, Pakistan, the entire Caribbean, Sri Lanka, South Africa, Kenya, and Zimbabwe. He figures the batsman will be unable to cope with the ball's flight down the wicket, and no matter how good he is he won't be able to hit the ball.

Yet strangely the batsman does just that. He hits the ball with a mighty whack, and it floats high in the air toward the boundary in a veritable home run! Ron is astonished and begins to clap. Then he looks at the batsman to see who he is. It's Carey's boyfriend, Jake.

No, wait. It is the one who calls himself an immigrant. And he's laughing, the bat still in his hand.

Laughter overtakes Ron. It doesn't matter that he's been hit for six. The entire stadium is standing and cheering. *Cheering who?*

Doris runs forward onto the middle of the pitch. She shouts to him that he is the husband she loves no matter what the others think of him. She admires his spirit and zeal for the game.

"Doris, is it really you?"

"Who else d'you think? Christ, you've changed, Ron!"

"Changed? Have I?"

"Ron, it's not the same anymore, is it?"

Immediately he wants to tell her what his real thoughts are, everything that now pumps through his veins. And the immigrant comes toward them, too, bat in hand. He watches Ron and Doris embrace in the middle of the stadium.

The crowd applauds wildly. The ball still soars as Ron looks up into the sun. He doesn't care for anything else now.

Nothing else is real on such a splendid day. It's like being back on a tropical Caribbean island, if you can believe it. It is no other place but Canada now. It is nowhere else in the world. Not India, Pakistan, Australia, South Africa, England, or the United States. Ron feels this new energy will be in his veins for a long time to come.

Who will tell him otherwise?

The immigrant waves to him. Carey and the hirsute Englishman, Jake, do the same.

Oh, the sweet, sweet sound of applause.

EXTRACT FROM INTERIM

I remember that Nattie Barrett, the butcher, was there, seven feet of him, strong and lanky, plodding with his seven-league boots. He was a young man, still under thirty, and had learned the butcher's art before he was fifteen. He had three of his nephews as apprentices. Nattie talked endlessly, without ever stopping for breath or listening to anybody else. His talk and laughter were intermingled with the cutting and weighing of the meat and the announcing of prices – even the cow-horn laughed and talked with his voice. He had elaborate excuses for not attending church (my mother was very concerned about this), long, amusing stories of travelling all over the district on Sundays looking for a good cow or goat to buy. He was the only person in the village who owned a bicycle and we often asked him to tell us again the story of how he was nearly killed in the Bay when a policeman gave him a wrong signal. For this story, the sharp knife was his bicycle, one corner of his tray was the junction of roads, the goat's head was the approaching car and the goat's liver, the policeman. He sometimes left two or three stories half-finished and then on other days, he would continue them where he left off (without establishing context) so that time and place were confused and all you could do was laugh.

When he left the yard, his presence echoed for a long time. He stood out, too, as a cricketer, one of the village's fast bowlers – long loping run-up, high dropping trajectory, an expert at "bailers" and at bruising fingers. Like everybody else, he had a little piece of ground which he farmed. His only worry was that his wife could not produce a child.

With him was his close friend, Alex Barrett, the shoemaker. Together they made a unique pair of fast bowlers, a study in antithesis. Alex was short and thick, a silent man with dreamy half-closed eyes, who hardly ever spoke. He made excellent boots and shoes with leather which he cured himself from Nattie's slaughtered cows. He re-cased old cricket balls and then soaked them in annatto so that they were red and shiny and new. As a fast bowler, he took two or three steps to the crease and then released scarlet lightning, round-arm, low-trajectory, thunderbolts hugging the ground, bruising toes and cracking the bases of stumps. He was an erratic bowler (Nattie was very steady) but he was capable, on his day, of dismissing any of the teams our village played for less than ten runs. He was our mightiest hitter and he lost many a ball at Mary Bottom ball-ground. In between his lofty generous sixes he would drink a wine-glass of rum. Unlike Nattie, he had many children, at least twelve, scattered all over the village – we recognised them by their sleepy dreaming eyes. He was a regular churchgoer but had long been excluded from the communion-table.

KING RICE

Okay, this is what we Creole-speakers call a longtime story, something that happened a good many years ago. It's about a man named Bungy, or at least that's what people call him. Back Home, nobody really knows anybody's real name, and if they do, they never admit to it in polite company. So, as far as anyone need know, this man's name was Bungy.

I should know a little something about Bungy, since he is, after all, almost family. My mother's brother married a woman whose cousin's granddaddy was, you know, Bungy. So he is almost family.

Now, Bungy was one funny man. That's the way my daddy describes him. To men of my daddy's generation, anybody willing to make a fool of himself is a funny man ranked high with the likes of Milton Berle and Jack Benny. It occurs to me now that maybe Bungy was a little sick in the head, like North American big-city people who holler at phantoms and direct imaginary traffic.

In Guyana, though, no one's mad if he can feed himself. It's a good rule to control the number of loons in the bin.

Maybe Bungy wasn't so much mad as he was daunting, the way bank robbers and Evil Knievel are. A psychiatrist friend told me once that that kind of people are called "psychopaths", a term usually associated with criminals, though most of them never get around to actually committing a crime. So maybe Bungy was a psychopath, but one fully able to feed himself.

Now, the entire village was mad for cricket. The Windsor Forest team, despite being made up of underfed farmers and farmers' sons, had been making dramatic gains on the national circuit. Every man and every man's son came out to cheer them on, for they represented, not only the proud dung-ridden west-coast village of Windsor Forest, but all villagers who owned and worked their own land.

Bungy, of course, was madder for cricket than most.

Bungy went to every single game, regardless of the distance he had to travel. That was also the magic of the day; cricket gods unfailingly allowed for good weather during game days, so that the most psychopathic of fans could cycle through the mud-gutted unpaved roads to cheer on their feckless heroes. Bungy would push that old bicycle to its rusted physical limits, packing a lunch and a cricket bat (which, of course, required him to steer dangerously with one hand for the entire journey) so that nothing, not hunger nor an obstructing head, could deny him the pleasure of witnessing firsthand a Windsor Forest victory.

Bungy was so fanatical, in fact, that he had been known to be provoked to physical violence if his team were slandered in even the mildest of ways. And this was many decades before British football hooliganism, let me tell you. This was something *we* gave to the English.

My mother's brother, who would later marry Bungy's grandson's cousin, told me that Bungy at one time threw him from Bungy's house because he had *implied* that maybe, perchance, by the will of God, it was conceivable the Windsor Forest team might fail to win the Demerara Cup that year. Not even deference to the will of God had been sufficient to quell the ire of our man Bungy.

So the *grande finale* approached: the final match between the rice farmers of Windsor Forest and the sugar plantation workers of neighbouring Eyeflood. It was a poetic ending to a versified season indeed, as this match-up would pit the imperialist-sponsored sugar team against our intrepid heroes from the autonomous mudlands.

And the venue would be the enemy's home fortress, the Eyeflood Cricket Grounds, built and maintained splendidly with imperialist sugar money; a far cry from the dung-scattered sandtrap against the seawall back in Windsor Forest. Back Home, the practices had to be cut short twice a day because the rising water level made it a submarine game. Not many people have played cricket well *under* the Caribbean.

No, the odds were definitely against the rice farmers this time. But there was confidence all around, because the rallying power of Bungy's madness was renowned and highly revered by supporters and antagonists alike. The team itself was wary of playing if any rumour reached them that, for whatever reason, Bungy would not be in the stands inciting lunacy.

Perhaps I've not stressed sufficiently the uniqueness of Bungy's dementia, the humour of his approach. Back when Mr Carruthers, the brand-new Governor General of Her Majesty's Guyanese Territories, had first risen to power, he decided to celebrate his recent appointment by personally visiting every last miserable village under the Queen's protection. The villagers had dressed in their Sunday best and politely lined up to shake the undoubtedly distinguished hand of Lord Carruthers.

Bungy had not disappointed. He, too, had dusted off his suit, lain unused since he had had to appear in court many years ago on an unsubstantiated public indecency charge. Instead of a tie, though, he had worn about his neck, for the plain view of Lord Carruthers, a noose fashioned from the finest Indian jute.

"Why are you wearing a noose about your neck?" Carruthers had foolishly inquired.

"Because I, Sir," Bungy had replied, full of airs, "am a slave."

On another occasion, Bungy found himself in the capital city, Georgetown, with no money to get home again. Luckily, he was aware that my mother's brother's future wife's cousin was visiting in the nearby town of Lenora, equipped with a very useful automobile.

So Bungy, penniless, boarded the bus bound for Lenora and waited for his stop. When it was time to pay, he ambushed the ticket collector, crying, "Is this *Ninora?* I have to be in *Ninora* to be in court!"

"You fool," the collector had said, "you're in *Lenora!*"

"Oh no!" Bungy had exclaimed. "You'd better let me out!" The driver complied, and so Bungy had managed to get himself a free ride to his grandson's auto.

With such precedents, it wasn't surprising that the gathered onlookers expected much from our hero. Not just that he would serve to entertain them during the duller moments of an otherwise gripping cricket match, but that, in the event of athletic tragedy, Bungy would be able to lift his team's spirits from the clean-swept Eyeflood field and onwards unto victory.

And so, on the grand day in question, the Windsor Forest contingent had been nervously silent until the appearance of the fabled Bungy, who had arrived uncharacteristically late. He had walked there, leaving his bicycle at home, and was curiously without his lucky cricket bat. This was enough to set some players and spectators aback, to be sure, but they were quelled by the sight of Bungy's little brown bag. At least he had brought his lunch, they saw, so some holy customs were to be maintained.

The game went off to a terrible start. The Eyeflood team, their brilliant white cotton uniforms blinding in the tropical sun, terrorized the awestricken lads from Windsor Forest. Our champion bowler, Big Castro, actually missed the wicket on two occasions. And the rice fields' favourite son, James Caan Number Two, bungled at least three easy catches. The sun was in his eye, onlookers said, no doubt reflected off those overstarched Eyeflood shirts.

The boys were bumbling and fumbling, their muscles tight with fright. As one miserable beast, their pleading eyes looked up to the stands, meeting those of solemn-faced Bungy. His forehead was creased in vexation, his lips pursed in sobriety.

Then, without warning, he stood and raised his paper bag before him. The crowd went silent, and even the players paused anxiously in their match. From somewhere off in the adjacent meadow, a cow was heard to bray, a curiously melodic note against the rhythmic background of Caribbean waves.

Bungy reached into his bag and pulled out a handful of the finest Guyanese rice he could have purchased, grown, no doubt, in the muddy fields of Windsor Forest. He scattered them over his audience, bellowing: "King rice!" Then, in a more guttural tone, he gestured to the bewildered Eyeflood team and cursed: "Slave sugar."

A resounding cheer erupted from the stands, drowning the feeble protestations of the very proper Eyeflood backers. Big Castro screwed up his courage and bowled straight from then on, and James Caan Number Two made the most thrilling catch anyone had ever seen.

The Demerara Cup still went to Eyeflood that year. But nobody ever forgot the brilliant madness of Bungy, my mother's brother's wife's cousin's granddaddy.

FROM SUCH AS I HAVE

1

They met again on a cold summer morning just as the sun began to push the mist from the face of the Puddin' Pan and the dew dripped like icy teardrops from the leaves. It was a few days after the fateful duck at the christening of the new pitch. Headly was on the final leg of his usual morning jog around the Puddin' Pan. His jogging partner and best friend, Dezzy, had just disappeared down the hill towards his house to prepare for work in the sugar factory of Caymanas. Headly remained behind to continue his exercises with one eye peeled for the first boy he could coerce into throwing a few balls at him.

Headly did not work. For him cricket was work. He put more of his time, dreams and energy into cricket than most men put into two jobs. His mother took care of him. What she did not have, his father sent from England, and for whatever else he wanted, the people of Slygoville were there. A while back, he had got a job in the textile factory at Twickenham Park. The captain of the cricket team there had got the job for him so he could be the opening batsman for the factory team. After a year of working there, he got into a fight with his foreman and left the job, even though they promised to place him in another department. He hated being bossed around by unintelligent people. His dreams did not lie in some menial job in some factory. He wanted to be drafted into the Jamaican team. He had already mastered club level and his name was being suggested to open for St Catherine in the inter-parish competition. Everything he did was for that. He was good. It was his batting that had brought the Slygoville team to the semifinal of the St Catherine League for the first time. It would help them win the match against Caymanas the next weekend, and it would help them beat the St Catherine champions from Old Harbour in the final at the Puddin' Pan.

So Headly spent his days practising his cricket. Dezzy would start with him early in the morning and jog around the Puddin' Pan for an hour or so, till Dezzy had to leave for work. Sometimes, if they were planning some event or were caught in some long argument, he would follow Dezzy halfway to work. But most of the times Dezzy would leave for work and Headly would remain to continue his training and practise his cricket, using the boys from the hill to throw balls at him until their time too was up and they had to be on their way to school.

That morning, he finished his exercises and began to examine the pitch. He stood at its northern end and relived the fateful delivery that Dwily had made. Then he checked the surface of the clay to see if there was indeed a hard spot or grass root where the ball had pitched and shot so viciously to destroy his stump. But the wicket was clean, the clay smooth and flat and even.

Suddenly he heard the sound of cows. A boy of no more than eight was chasing a herd of twenty or so across the Puddin' Pan. They were heading straight for him and the brand-new pitch.

"Go the other way! Go the other way! You don' know you mustn't run them 'cross the field?" Headly shouted angrily at the boy, who had the cows at a gallop.

The boy was almost invisible behind the herd of cows. He was evidenced only by his stern shriek: "Cow... cow. Move cow...," and the yelps of two mongrels.

The cows were suddenly upon Headly and he had time only to jump out of their way as they thundered across the pitch. As the cows passed, Headly grabbed the shirtless boy from behind by the waist of his pants and lifted him clear of the ground. The boy yelped in surprise, his feet still going through the motions of his stride.

"What you doing?" demanded Headly. "You don' see the pitch? You don' see you a mash up the pitch?" Headly shook the boy firmly, dropped him and slapped him in the head just before he scampered off.

A look of sheer pain crossed Headly's face as he saw the multitude of hoof marks that spoiled the surface of the clay. He stood for a moment then walked away, angry and disgusted. All the boy had to do was walk his cows to the side and avoid the field, but he had to chase them across the pitch and spoil it. They had spent so much time preparing that pitch and now the smooth clay was violated with a hundred hoof prints. He walked toward the guinep tree to pick up his bat, cussing loudly to himself how the stupid boy had mashed up the pitch with his stupid cows and mangy dogs.

It was then that he noticed her standing off to the side of the road, near where the boy had thundered down the hill with the cows. From where he was, she appeared as just a dark form against the breaking day. At first he thought she was another boy, but as he drew closer to his bat, he began to see her better. He stopped beside his gear, and for a minute they stood looking at each other across the field.

She had watched the whole episode and had stood there as he came across the field, mad and cussing as if someone had just slapped his mother. She thought how little he had changed. He was still tall, red and arrogant, his ass cocked off into the air, his shoulders broad and swaying, pivoted on a narrow waist and a stomach that looked as hard and flat as the Puddin' Pan itself. And Maizy said he had changed, that he was very nice and not a show-off as people thought. But Maizy must have been thinking from the wrong place. He was the same show-off she remembered. He had lifted the boy and dropped him with the same disdain he had shown when he had kicked her dog years ago.

Their eyes met – his aloof with rhetorical enquiry, hers sad, with a hint of scorn.

"Little idiot," he murmured angrily.

"Thought you were going to kill him," she told him, fingering the bag in her hand. She was on her way to the shop in the town square.

"That I should do. You know how much work it going take to roll the pitch and get out the cow foot them? I should bruck him neck."

She was not even amazed at his response. "Why? He was just taking his cows to bush."

"Well make him walk round the field." He pointed behind him to the bushy periphery of the Puddin' Pan. "Make him walk there so."

"In the bush?"

"Yeah! No cow him have? No bush him going? Plus that is bush?" he hissed his teeth. "Which part you see bush? Where him come from have more bush than that."

She winced at that. Her face tightened like wet cow skin under the sun. She lived a stone's throw from the boy. For some reason Slygoville people regarded everyone who lived north of the Puddin' Pan as living in some sort of dense rurality, as if Slygoville was not itself one big bush, twenty miles in from the Spanish Town highway and halfway up the back of a hill.

"You own the place?" she asked him. "Is it your place? People used to have cows all over the hill before all of onoo christen it and block it off like onoo own it."

He hesitated in whatever he was about to say and took a good look at her. She stood with haughty defiance. Her hair was cut short, close to her head, shorter even than his. She carried a handbag made from crocus bag and lined with plastic. She stood with feet slightly apart, bottom cocked off, chest forward, like a game-fowl spoiling for a fight. Her eyes blazed and glistened in the early light. He remembered her instantly – the way she stood: "Like them market woman ready to trace," his mother used to say. *Junjo Head* – he remembered her now – *African Perch*.

Pam – her name was Pam. He had not seen her in years. He had heard that she had passed her exams and had gone down to Linstead or some place like that to live with some relative and to go to high school. He had hardly even missed her from the village. She had not been important any more, for when she left, he must have been close to seventeen, and it was no longer cute to chase her up the hill to the shack she shared with her obeah mother. So she had dropped from his list of diversions as old skin drops from a snake, and he had forgotten she existed. But now, as he saw her standing there, he remembered how she was always dirty, unkempt and aggressive. He remembered her always tracing, flinging stones like any boy, taking on anyone of any size. She had even beaten Dezzy once, had collared him and rolled with him down the hill. He had taken months to live that down.

Headly had never spoken directly to her before; she had never spoken to him. They were from the two extremes of their society. He was the son of the leading dressmaker, with family abroad. He was the boy every man wished was his son, every boy wanted to be, and every woman wanted to be with. She was at the bottom of the ladder – a nobody, whose mother was an obeah-warner woman who sold coal and washed people's clothes in the village sometimes. She was a loner, always dirty, a mongrel. Her hair always stood on end. No one played with her. So Headly had had no reason to speak to her except to chant "Junjo Head" or "African Perch" at her as he chased her up the hill with the boys after school, or lay in wait for her as she came from the shop. He had never spoken to her directly and she had never dared open her mouth to him.

But now there was something about her that was different. It was not just her skin, which was now neither crusty nor coarse, nor her figure, which had matured and ripened to a compact and sexy shape; nor was it the sense of danger that seemed to lurk inside her. No, there was something more about her, about the way she spoke, the way she met his stare, as if all the feistiness and fight of her younger years had aged into that knowing half-smile which seemed to say that she knew something no one else did, that she had looked deeper inside him and had seen some fallibility that he did not recognize, that she alone had discovered and was amused by.

"Is I own the pitch?" he echoed. "Is your son? You take up for him like is your son. You own him?"

She ignored that. "You see, you Slygoville *men*. You see onoo. All onoo do is show off. You only have strength for little boys." She began to walk off.

He hated that she might have been alluding to his duck of the Saturday before. "Is we Slygoville *men* who give Slygoville playing field and put Slygoville pon the map," he sneered at her.

"Cricket can eat?" she said sarcastically, half to herself.

"What you say?" he said, giving her his hold-on-little-bit tone.

"All the same, this is a pointless conversation. I won' bother talk. The same stupid people come out to worship onoo every Sunday, as if they don't have a thing to do – as if the Puddin' Pan is church."

His chest heaved with anger as she swished away, leaving him standing there.

"But is who this gal talking to? But wait… but wait… hold on…"

But she was halfway down the road by then. He kicked the grass and cussed at her disappearing back. His face was set against the morning. The sudden glow beyond the hills that signalled the day's awakening was like the sudden hot glow in his stomach that told him, in some mysterious way, that she had come to change things.

The following Saturday they won the semifinal match. They went to Caymanas and caused weeping down there.

When Headly went in to bat, they shouted: "Send back the boy Headly, quick." But by the end of the day, he was "Mr Headly".

He stopped traffic with his stroke play. Men on their way to the golf course stopped to watch him. Gana ganas loaded with sugar cane paused on the street as their drivers and sidemen stopped for a peek at the batting genius from Slygoville hitting the ball to every corner of the field.

After the match Caymanas put on a dance so big it was as if they had won and not Slygoville. They brought in King Stitch from Kingston as DJ, and the whole Slygoville team stayed to see the famous dance-hall artist in action. It was two o'clock Sunday morning before Maizy was able to drag Headly and Dezzy out of the crowded school auditorium, where the music thumped like thunder on a six-hour roll. Most of the team had gone with the last bus, but they were stranded in Caymanas and would have to walk all the way back over the hill from Caymanas to Slygoville. Dezzy dug the captain of the Caymanas team out of some corner where he was locked in some kind of rub-a-dub, and persuaded him to take them halfway.

So, three o'clock caught them at the foot of the Slygoville hill, staggering along the road, like ants who had diverted through a jar of cured molasses. There were about eight or so of them, including Maizy, Pam and another woman from the club. The women were not as drunk as the men, but tired from partying. They walked silently ahead, almost huddled against the cold that slid down the Slygoville hill and burned their faces. Headly and the boys were a space or two behind, singing and shouting in loud raucous voices, each hand filled with a bottle of Guinness. They rocked and rolled and sang like men around a nine-night fire. Every now and then the women would turn to look at them, make sure they were still on course and shake their heads in wonder.

"What is mi name?" Headly shouted.

"Mr Headly," the voices chorused around him.

"I say, what's mi name?"

"I say, Mr Headly." The voices approached song.

"What I bring come bat?"

"Mrs Esmie door."

"What I bring?"

"You mother door."

"Who can pass that?" Headly bowed and danced and cupped his hands to his ear.

"We mother door," the chorus sang.

"Me say who can pass?"

"We mother door."

"No, not a man can pass?"

"Mi mother door."

"Caymanas can' pass?"

"Mi mother door."

"Kingston can' pass?"

"Mi mother door."

"May Pen can' pass?"

"Mi mother door."

"Next week, when Old Harbour come?"

"Them better bring bulldozer – we going lock we mother door." They erupted into laughter and danced across the street.

Dezzy waited until they lulled a bit, then cupped his ears and wailed, "And Central Village?"

"Bulldozer Dwily broke the house to rass boy," yelled Hozzy, falling to the ground. This time even the women laughed. Headly laughed loudly, this match had wiped away the bitterness of the duck he had made against Central Village.

He was slightly ahead up the road so he waited for the group to catch up as the chuckling died. He hugged Dezzy and they walked together behind the women. The rest of the group made up the rear. The legendary cold of Slygoville drifted down the hill like icy mist. It did not bother them. They were used to it – in any case they were filled to the brim with warm Guinness, and the cold served to sober them a little.

Headly drained the last of the Guinness and dropped the bottle in the grass by the road. He nodded in the direction of the women ahead of him. "The obeah thing don' look too bad at all."

Dezzy smiled in the half-darkness. "Me you a tell?"

"Me tell you," Headly sighed. "Look like she could take a nice ride, boy."

"A nice back shot, yea." The words passed Dezzy's lips as if caressed slowly from his breath by his tongue.

Headly nodded, like a connoisseur. "Yeah, yeah man, you see how her bottom just cock off and round, yeah, a nice back shot. Just press her over like, you know."

"Boy, me a tell you. She don' look too bad at all." Dezzy licked his lips. His voice was almost sad.

"So what happen? You a go move it later?" Headly asked.

"Move?" Dezzy groaned as if the pressure of the cold was forcing the word back against his tongue. "Move? No, sah." He shivered and stumbled on.

"Then no you me see dancin' with her whole night? Maizy no set you up?"

"Well me dance with her," said Dezzy. "But every time a dub start, she sit down."

"How you mean?" Headly exclaimed. "You never rub it?"

"Rub! Neither rub nor dub."

Jest crept into Headly's voice: "Man have to celebrate later. Man just win match."

"I hear you, sir. Have fi find the little thing roun' the corner near you later, boy."

Headly ribbed him: "You a lose you touch, mi frien'. You have a thing like that in front of you and talkin' 'bout the little dry-foot schoolgirl."

"At least that sure," Dezzy shrugged.

Headly hissed his teeth and nodded towards Pam. "So what can hard 'bout that?"

"Say she don' wan' no Slygoville man."

"A wife you a look?"

"Well it look like you have fi a look wife fi get that."

Headly laughed loudly and slapped his thigh. "A wife you a look. Oh, now me know, a wife you a look."

"Me never say that, you know," Dezzy defended himself. "Me never say that."

"What you tell her say?" the master enquired of the student.

"Tell you the truth, you know, I don't even remember what I say. Prob'ly ask something 'bout independence party or so. Because we talkin' good, good, you know. We dance a song and the dub start play, so me ask her why she have to sit down. So she say she not in any rub-a-dub business. Something like that, I don' remember everything. Then me ask her something else, or drop a lyrics or something, and I think I ask if she have boyfriend or something like that."

"So what that have to do with it?"

"Me just ask her. And she said no. So me say what happen, something wrong with me? So she say no, nothing not wrong with me, she jus' don' want no Slygoville man. Say we just friends an' me mus' leave it at that."

"Lie you a tell!" Headly mused. "She say that? She should glad Slygoville man a wan' talk to her. So what she want – a car man, a big man from Beverly Hills?"

"Well, you will have to ask her that yourself."

Headly laughed madly. "You see me. You see me is one friend me want, you understand? Me not looking wife, is one frien' me want and is the nusnie."

Dezzy was silent.

"You know what is your problem?" Headly continued. "You makin' test match out of the little ketchie shubbie. You lookin' wife, man, a pick-up team, a organize big test match. Is just little ketchie shubbie, a pick-up game with sponge ball, nutten no inna it."

Dezzy gave a small chuckle. They were cresting the hill into Slygoville and the fog that lingered seemed to cover the hills around them. They could hardly see the houses along the sloping hillsides as they neared the town proper. But they were made aware of them as the various members of the group dropped away. Soon there were just four. Headly and Dezzy moved forward to join Pam and Maizy for the rest of the way.

The road to Dezzy's home veered away to the southwest of the town on the side of a valley called Little Valley. As they entered the town, he said goodnight and turned away.

Pam lived the farthest of all. She had to walk through the village and up the hill, past the Puddin' Pan and on nearly half a mile in the bush. Maizy elbowed Headly in his side and asked if he could walk Pam to her house. But Headly had other things on his mind. He dropped his hand from Maizy's shoulders to rub her bottom and mumbled suggestively in her ear. She allowed him a generous rub, and as they got to the town centre she blurted out to Pam that he had promised to walk her home.

"Is all right," Pam said, sensing the mood. "I'm not afraid."

"It too late. You alone can' walk so far alone," Maizy told her as she elbowed Headly's side. They approached Maizy's gate, and the women said their goodbyes.

Headly quickly realized that his joy that morning would be directly linked to his helping his woman's friend. He asked Pam to wait a while as he squeezed a promise from Maizy.

"Yes, I will wait. Jus' knock at the window," she told him.

"You sure?" Headly asked.

"Yes. You think it going run 'way?"

In the light fog her brown skin looked almost pale and her half-Indian hair was slightly damp with dew. She trembled with sincerity and desire. He recognized that she wanted him then, just as he wanted her. But he did not trust leaving her to a warm bed for an hour.

"You sure?" he asked.

"Headly, make haste and go on. The quicker you go, the quicker you come back."

"All right. Make sure, you know," he whispered hoarsely.

He waited while she closed the gate behind her and ran to her door, which opened from inside. Then he turned to join Pam.

They walked in silence up the hill – the smug silence of people who were in control of their spaces. But there was a tension between them, like current in a high-voltage electric wire; a sense of anticipation – not that of circling contenders before a cockfight, nor of a calm before a storm – but a waiting like that of two mongrels watching each other across a barbed wire fence; an anticipation, not of the mongrels, but of the fence itself; an expectation that they will tangle there at the fence, at the dividing line – that they will hurt themselves there, scar themselves and bleed.

As he walked beside her, he was aware of how she leaned forward to meet the hill. He walked straight and erect – others might bend, not he. But she had a special way of leaning forward. She walked with a deliberate determination as if each step was a statement against the incline, and every inch covered was movement against some wager.

He had walked beside her before. They were children then and they were coming home from school. He remembered her walking that slow, purposeful stride, biting her lips and fighting back tears as she walked ahead of the jeering bunch of boys he led. She had been in a fight at school. Her uniform was dirty and torn. Her hair, which always seemed to be plaited in ugly lumps, was dirty and two of the plaited lumps were loose, her only exercise book was clutched in her hand, and her bare feet slammed into the dust of the hill with the determined steps of a tired mule. Her feet were white and dirty with marl, and her skin was black and coarse.

They had walked beside her all the way from school, he, Dezzy and a few other friends. They called her Junjo Head and teased her about her clothing – her having one uniform, her never wearing shoes to school, her always smelling of smoke and coal. And all the time she just bit her lips, held back the tears, hugged her exercise book tightly, bent to the hill, and marched deliberately on.

Then Dezzy had said something about her mother being an obeah woman. She had spun and sprung so fast that Headly could not remember seeing her move. In a flash she and Dezzy were locked together rolling back down the hill in the loose dirt. It seemed to Headly that she was throwing all the punches and making all the scratches while poor Dezzy was just holding on. It was Old Naya, the coal man, who lived in the hill near her, who finally broke through the ring of children to drag her from the battered Dezzy. Days after, her exercise book was still snagged in a cold bush vine along the road. But they never teased her again, at least not that close. After that they kept out of her way and watched her from afar, old Junjo Head, always dirty and barefoot, with her one exercise book, trudging up and down the hill.

Headly smiled to himself as he sensed her beside him. Who would have known it?

Junjo Head look like somebody now.

"How you so quiet?" she said, breaking the silence.

"Man don' have to talk all the time."

"You, you always talking, always have something to say."

He smiled to himself. *She have talk, too, big talk now.*

She had rarely spoken to people then. She had lived alone on the hill with her mother, a slim, black woman who only left the hill to warn, with her head wrapped in red cloth, or to wash for people in the village who did not have the time. She walked around with a stern, angry look on her face and stared at people as if she was ready to fight or trace at the drop of a word. They said her father was some man who drove gana ganas for Caymanas, but no one was ever sure. Slygoville people hardly spoke to her – just a few like Maizy did, whose parents her mother washed for regularly, or those who bought coal from her at her house. But they were few, as her mother sold most of her coal to a big fat man who drove an old Bedford truck up the hill to her house once a week.

People said she would never come to anything good, that Pam, that natty-head girl. No one played with her except for Naya's sons, who were around her age, and everybody knew what kind of playing that was – always going and coming all sorts of hours, in and out of the bush that surrounded the Puddin' Pan.

Now Junjo Head looked like somebody. Her natty head was now cut short, halfway between bald and a good Napoleon, and her angry eyes seemed magnetic and bright, the angry pout to her mouth now seemed sensual and in the half-light her skin was cool and smooth.

She could take a brush, he thought. *Don' look too bad at all. Maybe I should take a brush off Junjo Head to rass.*

They came to the Puddin' Pan and then swerved left and upwards towards her house. Here the semi-paved road ended, and the way was just a track made in the grass by feet and trucks and dray carts. There was dirt and gravel where wheels had erased the grass and growth with time, and left broom weed and stumpy grass in the centre. She took the right track. He took the left, and they were separated by a strip of grass and broom weed.

"Puddin' Pan," Headly mused as they passed the field. "Ol' Puddin' Pan."

"Field a day, bed a night," she mimicked his tone.

"Wait! What you mean by that?" he said surprised. "Where you get that from?"

"So my mother call it."

"Why she call it that?"

"How you mean?" she said casually. "That's where Slygoville men play cricket during day and screw off the people them gal pickney them a night time."

Must a talk from experience, he said to himself, bristling. He would have said it aloud had he not begun to modify his intentions toward her. "How you and your mother so sure 'bout that?"

"I know. I see onoo over there all the time. You think is few nights I over there and see onoo."

"Mind yourself, you know." He tried to keep his voice light and controlled. "Mind yourself. What you doing over there late night to see people?"

"Eemm, I see onoo though."

"Mind this *onoo* thing you know. You ever see me over there yet?"

"Eemm, no you them name the guango tree after?"

Headly laughed and shook his head. "Guango tree? You no easy, you know. You not easy at all."

"You mean onoo Slygoville men no easy."

They were halfway to her house now and the dew was falling like thin, wet powder on their heads. It soaked into Headly, and he began to feel a little irritated.

"What you have 'gainst Slygoville men?" he asked. "What Slygoville men do you so? Everything is 'onoo Slygoville men'. What Slygoville men do you?"

"Nothing," she said, shrugging her shoulders as much as she could while hugging herself against the cold.

"No, but we mus' do you something, why you hate we so."

"I didn't say I hated anyone, you know."

He sensed she was on the defensive and dug for every bit of sarcasm he could find. "Bwai, I wouldn't like to hear you talk 'bout somebody you hate," he said, "if you talk so 'bout people who you love."

"Who I say I love now?"

Headly left that alone. Some balls were like that. You just didn't play them – a little wide, a little high, close enough to the bat, but so perilous that all one could do was to cover the stumps and leave them alone. So he covered his stumps, lifted his bat and did not play a stroke. He let the morning and the dew and the cold settle between them so that not another word passed until they got to the little plateau where the hill veered away to the right and the path cut its way to the little wooden gate and bamboo fence of the yard where she lived. Even then he did not speak; he just bowed to her.

As she cracked the wooden gate, a window opened slightly and her mother's voice came through strong and clear: "Pam, is you that?"

"Yes, Mmm."

She turned around and secured the gate. "Thanks, Headly. I know you didn't have to come."

He wasn't sure if it was gratitude or an attempt to defuse an awkward situation.

"No problem," he replied.

The voice from the house was insistent: "Pam is who that you talking to? Is who and you that out there?"

"Is nobody, Mmm." She shrugged knowingly at Headly – he too understood a mother's concern.

"Make haste come out of the dew." The voice was now at the door, which creaked inwards. "Is who the young man?"

"Is Headly from down the road."

"Esmie' Headly?"

"Yes, Mmm."

Her mother grunted something.

Pam turned again towards Headly and avoided his eyes. "Thanks."

"What she say?" Headly enquired. "What she just say?"

"Nothing."

"Why she sound so?"

"She don' like you."

EXTRACTS FROM BROWN SUGAR

The voice of Dr. Pierce drifted up again.

"What's this I hear, Branker? You all walked off the field when you were playing Sunbury Plantation?"

"It was de ball, suh. We did wish a new ball, an' dey would not use another."

"What was wrong with the ball?" Branker shuffled uneasily.

"Some of us see dem put *obiah* 'pon dat ball. Our boys could not bat against a strong *obiah*."

"*Obiah*, Branker! Your boys put *obiah* on themselves by believing such nonsense. You cannot bewitch a cricket ball. Bring it and show me."

"Dillon," he called, "please come down here a minute."

"Help! What is the M.C.C. ruling on *obiah*?" He put on a tattered bathrobe, and stumped off downstairs muttering: "Books in the running brooks, sermons in stones, and spooks in cricket balls."

Dr. Pierce sat in a canvas chair beneath the huge bearded fig that gave shade to the yard. At one side was a row of servants' rooms, and Branker soon emerged carrying the ball which was possessed by a devil – and one well versed in the tactics of cricket. It was almost new, and stamped with the name of a reputable firm. Dillon examined it and frowned. Branker watched him with the profound respect, almost reverence, due to one who had played the game at international level.

"There has been some monkey business here," he said, "but it is not *obiah*. Look, the seam has been opened slightly with a knife. Also it feels a shade light; I think it has been cooked in a slow oven. And it has been polished like a mirror. Bowled into the wind this ball would swing about."

"Well, well, *well*! Dat jes' what he do. Our boys could scarcely get a bat to he." Branker gazed at the ball with affectionate understanding. He was learning something, and knowledge was power. No use against Sunbury, of course; they were already well-versed in these mysteries. But the next match, with Lemon Arbour, might be enlivened by an *obiah* ball of his brewing.

"This must be Sunbury's ball," said Dillon. "How come you got it?"

"We hide it from dem, Mas' Dillon." Branker smiled uncertainly.

"Well, you leave it with me. This sort of thing is illegal."

"Cricket," said Dr. Pierce, "means fair play – in one sense. It is a formal game in which the players dress properly and behave well." He checked himself there, unwilling to embark on a sermon.

*

By noon the city was almost deserted. Banks and stores were closed, the courts adjourned, and the House of Assembly risen in haste. The *mawby* sellers, unconcernedly balancing on their heads the five-gallon cylinders of their strange beverage, joined the stream of chattering citizens hurrying on foot or wheels along the coast road to Fontabella. Schools and colleges took half-holidays and contributed bus-loads of children to the traffic. While in the country, planters left their canes to nature, doctors were difficult, and parsons prayed for deliverance from sudden deaths – and burials. At Fontabella, the scene of the battle, the roar of the crowd was continuous and could be heard far out over the Caribbean. Besides the packed official stands, private enterprise reared platforms on crazy stilts to overlook the walls; and these, at moments of high tension, sometimes crashed down in ruin beneath the stamping feet of patrons. Beside the main gates were two banners with letters a foot high: REPRIEVE CUDGER and HANG JENKIN; and a gallows between dangled a limp figure with a coconut for a head.

Coming upon the scene unbriefed, a tourist might well have thought he had stumbled upon a revolution, the overthrow and impending liquidation of a hated tyrant. But he would be mistaken. Mere affairs of State could never have aroused such passions, which were in fact centred upon a game of cricket. It was Big Cricket, of course, the final Trial to decide the team to tour India and Australia.

Cudger, whose reprieve the posters demanded, was the best slow bowler in the Caribbean – a junk-pitcher of class, Americans would say. His fingers, long and of exceptional strength, could spin a ball so that it hummed in the air. Unfortunately he had used them, three months ago, to choke his wife Rhoda in novel fashion. Returning after absence on a tour, Cudger had found several letters in the house addressed to Rhoda, which was surprising as Rhoda herself could not read. Cudger, however, could read, and did. Neighbours had noticed the unusual circumstance of frequent mail for Rhoda, and the mystery was now solved, for the letters were from the postman himself. They were frank letters, and Rhoda would not have kept them had she known their contents. In which case she would not have had them thrust down her throat by the long fingers of a talented spin bowler.

Jenkin of Guiana was called in to fill the vacancy resulting from Cudger's absence in jail, awaiting execution. But on his first appearance the previous day, besides bowling poorly, he had dropped two easy catches. Hence the growing feeling, expressed in the posters, that Jenkin should be hanged in place of the more valuable Cudger. The posters perhaps expressed the view of a few extremists, for there was a large body of more sober-minded citizens who were not prepared to go so far as to hang Jenkin for dropping catches, but considered only that Cudger should be released just for the Tests in Australia, and then return home to be hanged. Shrewd economists in the group pointed out that the Cricket Board of Control would be put to pointless expense paying Cudger's return fare, just for his execution on arrival. But the difficulty, others pointed out, might be avoided if the Australians would agree to hang Cudger (for a small fee) as soon as the Test Series was decided. Then there were others who took the even more liberal view that Cudger should be allowed to continue indefinitely in Test cricket as long as his form justified it. When in the course of time this failed him, he could then return and pay the penalty of his misdemeanour. The debate continued.

The noise from the crowd inside was non-stop, every ball bowled receiving its share of commentary, knowledgeable and caustic. Controlled defence, following a scoring stroke, was particularly relished; "NOoo, tell he, NOoo," would be shouted in unison as the batsman, refusing to be drawn, played a furious delivery quietly back down the pitch. Angry cries of "Don' *hide* de ball!" greeted the bowler who, to avoid punishment, bowled wide of the wicket. And the ball itself, being chased by a fielder towards the boundary, would be urged on by cries of "Run, ball, RUN." Betting was continuous, often on such frivolities as whether or not the next man in would wear a cap; and areas of shouting and clamour developed as these wagers became due for settlement.

Flannel, the barefoot groundsman of Dillon's club, conducted his betting in the grand manner. He circled the ground, bottle of rum in hand, haranguing each section of the crowd, leaving a trail of bets. He freely staked any of his possessions, from trifles like his wife and hut, to a serious status symbol like his cart and donkey. When the Island XI was losing (which was rare) he sat on the ground and wept. On one such occasion he tried to drown himself in the harbour; but this proved impossible as he could swim like a fish.

Dillon had arrived early, and left the car in a reserved park. A horde of barefoot boys circled dizzily around this manoeuvre, screaming his name. They did not want his autograph, they wanted to be left in charge of the car. Dillon selected one he knew, and awarded him the contract. The car was now safe from sand in the petrol or flat tyres, although its small guardian would leave it unattended; protection from the parking gang had been properly arranged.

An hour later, he was in more real danger than most bullfighters.

Two boundaries past cover, and Jarman had stamped his foot in anger. He waved the four slips over to crouch on the leg side, and prepared to bowl bodyline to maim. Experts judged him the fastest bowler in the world, with a speed of well over ninety miles per hour. At twenty yards' range this gave two-fifths of a second to judge length and direction, to make skilled play with an over-two-pound bat, and to avoid the red flash of a projectile whose effect would vary from bad bruise to fatal. Earlier in the game he had smashed a stump in bowling a famous run-getter for nought. He had rushed down the pitch and held aloft the broken pieces to the frenzied delight of the crowd.

Now, his next delivery bounced head high, and was taken by the keeper fifteen yards back. Dillon walked down the pitch and waved to the pavilion, and a player ran out with his pith helmet. He adjusted this head protection with care, while the crowd buzzed like swarming bees. The next ball reared so high that he needn't even duck; but the one after swung in, rose sharply from a length, and crashed into him like the kick of a mule. He stood still, conquering *angina pectoris*, while Jarman leapt with the bellowing crowd. As the pain dulled, red anger flooded in. The last ball of the over he square cut at a height of five feet, and they ran three while third man just cut it off on the boundary. This brought Dillon to the bowler's end.

"You aim at scalping me?" he asked.

"I bowling the ball, Mist' Dillon. You mus' play it," was the aggressive reply.

Dillon now faced Jaipal, of mixed Indo-Chinese blood, who traded silks and ivories in the town, and dealt in polished googlies at the Oval. Jarman at forward short leg was covered beyond by deep mid-wicket, but there was a gap in the field at square. Pain and anger in his chest, but bland of face, Dillon staked his maturing innings on a show of indiscretion. To the first two deliveries, of impeccable length, he moved yards out of his crease and played them back straight. Jaipal was surprised at this unprofitable rashness, but he remained as inscrutable as his Chinese ancestors. His action was unchanged, but the next was a little quicker, and pitched a shade shorter. This was just what Dillon had banked on, and sound tactics would have been to turn it through the gap at square. Instead he moved right back to make it shorter still, spun on his right heel, and slammed it with all he had into Jarman at four-yard range. Jarman collapsed, hugging his stomach and spitting obscenities. Dillon walked over and helped him up, saying: "I played the ball, Jarman. Why didn't you catch it?"

Shaken, and still massaging himself, Jarman retired to field on the boundary during convalescence. Here the fickle crowd barracked him by chanting: "Go back to Africa" as it was known that he had at one time attended Rasta meetings.

Strangely enough the incident converted Jarman to a reluctant support of Dillon, whose cricket he had previously tried to belittle. In his cups, which were deep, he would now say: "Ah! He does know the game. It is blow for blow, and an eye for an eye wid he."

CRICKET LOVELY CRICKET

Bat and ball cricket is a delightful game, played at all levels from the street corner to the Test arena, it is the national game of the West Indian people. On his return to British Guiana, cricket provided Stephen with a diversion from his private studies in preparation for the General Certificate of Education Examinations. He was invited to join a cricket team, sponsored by a store on Water Street, the commercial centre of Georgetown. His team, the Crusaders, played Sunday cricket at a ground on Thomas Lands, by the Seawall. The team was inherently weak but recruited a few "professionals" to join the ranks, cricketers who played for teams at a higher level.

The Crusaders were an illustrious band of jokers. The captain of the team was a small, brown-skinned man called Kelly, who always had a slight smile on his face as if he was enjoying a private joke. Kelly was a captain who often let his team members do whatever they wanted. He was the constant butt of jokes, but he didn't seem to mind. One of the fast bowlers was a man called North, noted not for his speed of delivery, but the rate at which he consumed the Russian Bear rum, before, during, and after matches! The other fast bowler was a tall, black man called Slam, who got his name from the fact that he slammed the ball down on the pitch, when he bowled, barely missing his own toes! His run-up to the wicket was usually faster than his delivery. There was a red-skinned man called Fanner, a born joker, who was a "passenger", who kept his place on the team by telling jokes and having the players and spectators in stitches, laughing. There were some older Portuguese men on the team, who had retired from work but not from drinking rum. Stephen joined this distinguished company of cricketers for some of the best days and laughs of his life.

Sunday cricket never started on time. One or more team members was always late or absent altogether. Each absent player, if and when he showed up, always had a "good" excuse. He was partying the night before and his "'ead 'urt, bad, bad." He had a fight with his missus and she was about to throw him out, which was probably true. He forgot the time, lost his watch, or his bicycle had a flat tyre. One excuse, which no one believed, was that he had gone to Church.

The players arrived in different stages of dress or undress, and different levels of sobriety. Their mental states improved little during the game, as they often picked up their drinking where they had left off, from the Saturday night before. They arrived at the cricket ground with white shirttails flying out of cream flannel pants, which had seen better days, cricket boots hanging from bicycle handle bars or loosely off feet. Each arrival was greeted with howls of derisive laughter, comment and counter-comment, "Maan yuh look beat up!" "Like duh wife lock yuh out las' night!" "Yuh sleep in duh dog 'ouse?"

Eventually the game would get started and Kelly, the captain, would send in the "professionals" to open the batting. These would paste the ball all around the ground, having great fun at the bowlers' expense. After a couple of hours, with almost two hundred runs on the board for the loss of two wickets, the innings would be declared closed. This brought forth a lot of good natured comment from players, like Farmer, who never got a chance to bat at the wicket, but were batting the rum in the pavilion. They always complained that they wouldn't return to play for the Crusaders, but showed up the following Sunday, anyhow. There was nowhere else they'd rather be.

During the innings, Farmer gave a running commentary on the play. He demonstrated how each ball should have been hit by the batsman, and what he would do instead, if he was batting. On one occasion, Kelly did promote Farmer in the batting order, to see if he could put his money where his mouth was. Stephen watched as Farmer walked out to the wicket and called for his guard, "Centah empire!" With all eyes glued to him, he made a couple of awkward shuffles down the wicket to the first two balls, failing to make contact, the balls hitting his pads. For the third ball, he decided to change his strategy and stayed back in his wicket. "'Owzat!" roared the bowler and surrounding fielders, as Farmer was hit plumb in front of his wicket. He jerked away quickly, to camouflage his position, looking like he was stung by a bee. Up went the umpire's finger, supporting the appeal, and back came Farmer to the pavilion, complaining bitterly, "Maan look at dat! Look 'ow duh empire t'ief out meh ricket!" No one believed him.

While there was cricket action on the field, outside on the red, dirt road, dramas would often be unfolding. On one occasion, a getaway jackass cart came careening by, tearing down the road, minus the driver, completely out of control. Soon after, the driver came running by, shouting and cussing as the donkey brayed up the road, Hee-haw, hee-haw…! The animal was then caught and given some good licks with a tamarind stick by the driver.

On another occasion, the game was interrupted by the potato ball man, who did a brisk business every Sunday, selling his roti and potato balls to players and spectators. On that occasion, he had difficulty negotiating his carrier bike down the steep, bumpy path leading from the road to the bridge, which entered the ground. His front wheel got caught between some loose, rotting boards on the bridge and down he went, bike and all, into the muddy trench! When the players and spectators saw this, they laughed riotously. The unfortunate vendor, covered in slime, mud and tadpoles, tried to retrieve his bicycle, while his roti and potato balls floated away down the trench, heading for Camp Street.

In the hot afternoon sun, players often took shelter under trees around the boundaries. Their only other respite was the crush-ice man who dished out shaving cones from a big block of ice, covered with a sugar bag, resting on his push cart. He shaved the ice with a black, steel shaver, packed it down in a cup, and poured dripping red syrup on top. For an extra penny, the thirsty customer got a double cup or double syrup.

The result of a game was never an issue; the fun was in the playing and the endless good-natured banter, on and off the field, which kept up all day long. The breeze blew off the Seawall on glorious sunny Sunday afternoons, the skies always fair, except for the occasional shower. This was culture beyond class, and the players and spectators loved it. Fun in the sun; eating, drinking and joking under a West Indian sky, were the soul and spice of Sunday cricket. One people, one love, one life to live, and Sunday cricket provided contentment for the rest of the week, for players and spectators alike.

Test cricket, the pinnacle of the game, was played at the Bourda cricket ground of the high falutin' Georgetown Cricket Club. Test match days in British Guiana were memorable occasions. Businesses shut down, schools were closed, and a carnival atmosphere enveloped the country. The trains were packed and the streets were crowded for many country people had come to town. There was great drama in the air, as all work stopped to focus on cricket. All roads led to Bourda, everyone excited and decked out in colourful clothes, carrying picnic baskets and blasting portable transistor radios.

At the Bourda cricket ground, the playing field looked like a billiard table, smooth and green, shining in the sun, ready and waiting for the encounter. The batting pitch, marble-like, had the best Guiana mud rolled into it, the cricket announcer on Radio Demerara calling it a batsman's paradise that should last for days. The West Indies were playing England and Stephen knew there was going to be fireworks!

Long before the half past eleven start of the game, people were lined up to enter the grounds, the lines snaking around Regent Street and North Road. Policemen, some of them on horses, called horseguards, were there to make sure the crowds were orderly. The spectators usually cooperated except once when England was beating the West Indies in 1954 and some unruly people threw bottles onto the field, bringing a halt to the game. This forced Ozzie to say, "Yuh see why duh white maan don' like to play in cockroach places like dese!" He always supported the visitors, especially if they were the Englishmen. Soon the two teams would be pitted against each other, like gladiators of old, and no quarter asked or given!

Outside the ground, behind the ten foot high fence, before the first ball was bowled, the tall, thick flamboyant trees would be packed with people. These people were usually of the lower classes, men and boys who could not afford to buy a ticket to gain entry. High up in the trees, sitting on branches, they secured for themselves what Ozzie called "bird tickets". Ozzie sometimes showed up at a game, riding and parking his bicycle under a tree, outside the ground by Regent Street. He would try to peep over the fence to see the game for free.

Once, as he sat on his bike, peacefully watching the game, minding his own business, a branch snapped high above his head, and down crashed a "birdman", branch and all, barely missing him! This caused a commotion as bystanders helped the unfortunate man by throwing ice water on him. Undaunted, the "bird-man" was up in the tree again, as soon as he could catch his senses, determined not to miss his cricket.

The game continued and Ozzie was taking it all in, when he heard a voice in the tree above him say, "Alyuh-dis move. Leh meh see if ah can spit on dat red maan bal' 'ead dong deh." The "birdman" then started to clear his throat to hawk. Ozzie had heard the comment, and the clearing of the throat, and realized that he was the target. He quietly walked his bike away from under the tree, trying to find a safer place to watch the game, but enraged at the un-provoked insult. That evening he told the family, angrily, "Ah gun kick a 'bird-man' before ah die!"

While Ozzie was outside, Stephen sat in a pavilion, crunched up between a fat woman, and a man drinking rum like it was going out of style. The West Indies were batting and the English fast bowlers were slinging the ball down so fast, Stephen could hardly see it. The sun poured down from a heavenly blue sky. Occasional wisps of high-flying, cottonwool clouds drifted by. At tea time, a shower of rain burst, cooling the grounds, spectators and players. Snow cone, crush-ice, ice cream and soft drinks, were all in great demand. Roti and potato balls, channa and nuts, were being devoured by hungry patrons. Stephen felt his shirt sticking to his back, soaking wet in sweat from the excitement, heat, hu-midity and crush of people.

In the high falutin' Georgetown stand, the players and elite of British Guiana were seated. The ladies, decked out in white cotton dresses and fancy broad hats, sipped wine or orange juice. The men, some in suits with collar and tie, others in open-necked sports shirts, drank whisky and beer. Across from the main pavilion, the spectators in the open air grounds, the cheapest seats, sat crowded together on hard benches, with no shade from the penetrating sun, except a few umbrellas sticking up.

Out on the field, the West Indies were batting beautifully, forcing Ozzie to say, "Englan' gettin' a leaddah 'unting today. Like dey buck sick." Sonny Rooplall, the East Indian batsman from the Corentyne was in full flight. Stephen remembered seeing him bat at the Mental Hospital ground in New Amsterdam. It looked like half the Corentyne had come down to see him play. In an outrageous assault on the English bowling, he was hitting the ball like a buccaneer. He fenced and lashed, inventing new ways to hit a cricket ball, fall-ing all over the wicket, especially in his hook shot. Puncturing the English ego, Rooplall was proud, free and fearless, putting on a display of stylish cricket. The local people loved it, many of them having travelled far, just to see this. The English supporters suffered in silence, and Ozzie went home with a sour face, saying, "'Ow come a coolie baay from duh Corentyne can savage duh Englishmen so? Dems duh people who invented duh game!"

Rooplall passed his century in fine style, to great applause, and continued to score freely. Stephen thought the batsman had such guts, such glory, such zest and panache, it was poetry in cricket. Eventually, close to his second century, he drove a ball hard, past the bowler and charged down the wicket to be unluckily run out. The stands rose in unison as Rooplall departed to the sound of thunderous applause, a deserving ovation for a brilliant West Indian.

On the English side, a fiery fast bowler seemed to be getting the crowd's attention. This man who came from the coal mines of Yorkshire was quite a character. He bowled fiercely, giving nothing away, his mop of black hair blowing in the wind. He took the ball from his captain, a staid Englishman, and as he was about to bowl, rubbed it suggestively in his groin area. This made the spectators laugh and comment, the ladies saying, "Look weh 'e puttin' dat ball." He then grinned at the crowd, turned around and began his angling run up to the crease, to deliver a lightning thunderbolt. It was his favourite yorker, and it took away the batsman's middle stump, sending it cartwheeling backwards toward the sightscreen at the Regent Street end. As the crowd sat in shocked silence, the bowler turned around, bowed, and took his sweater from the umpire.

He then went down to field by the long leg boundary, where he entertained the crowd by putting his hands underneath his sweater, pretending that he had big boobs! He talked to pretty girls and signed autographs, all to the crowd's delight. Stephen had heard that this bowler was as irreverent off the field as he was on it, pinching the Governor's wife's backside at a cocktail party, after he had had a healthy drink of Guiana's fireass rum. This Englishman added colour to West Indian cricket and the local people loved it, although his captain and the English selectors were not amused.

For West Indians, cricket was more than a sport or a game; it was the national pastime. It gave the natives an opportunity to confront their colonial masters on a level playing field. It represented a microcosm of West Indian society: one people, one destiny. It was colourful and comic, dramatic and entertaining. People came to the game for a holiday, a respite from their daily lives. It was an opportunity to view a spectacle in a carnival, theatre-like atmosphere. Whether play was interrupted by the arrival of the Governor, a shower of rain, or a local character dressed up in a canary-yellow suit, waving the Union Jack, it mattered not. This was "cricket, lovely cricket" which the calypsonians sang about.

Men, women and children had come out to watch their heroes, admire their talents, and gloat in their achievements. Every boy dreamt that he could be out there, playing calypso cricket for the West Indies, in all its glory and splendour, under the blue Caribbean skies. When it was all over, when the explosions of the thundering drives along the boundary boards had faded into silence, when the dying sun had set, slipping into the West over the top of the stands, then the only things remaining were sweet memories, burned forever in the pavilion timbers and the faraway places of the heart.

THE PROFESSIONAL

He lay face down on the bed with the woman above him kneading the muscles in his back and shoulders and the scent of embrocation and body heat swirled pleasantly round the room. He rolled on to his side. The woman let herself fall next to him.

"I still have to rub that knee," she said.

"Later."

"You won't be able to bat tomorrow if you don't get the knee rubbed."

"You comin' to see the game?" he asked, his mind far away.

"No. I'm taking Thomas to the doctor."

"I forgot. How is he?"

"The fever is going away, but the doctor says bring him back tomorrow."

Thomas was the youngest of their three children, and the only boy. The two girls were robust enough, but with Thomas it was different; rather like his mother.

"Do you need any money?"

"No I can manage."

She was asleep when he left her. He threw on a dressing gown and went out. He looked in on the children on his way to the kitchen. Thomas was running a fever. Asleep, his resemblance to his mother was even stronger. He rested his hand against the boy's cheek and kept it there.

He opened the refrigerator and took out a bottle of beer. I must start going easy on the beer, he thought. Too much weight. And with the knee starting to go, he really needed to keep the weight down.

He pulled a chair over to the window and sat looking at the night sky. Sitting there in the darkness alone, drinking beer, he knew suddenly and with absolute certainty that the best years were already behind him and that he was now a good player when once he had been a great one. The last season had been a disaster. The press had not made it any easier.

He went to the refrigerator and got another beer. The familiar sensation of cold beer on a warm night sparked a train of memories. Like winning that first Test match in Australia, and sitting in St. Auric's hotel room drinking beer out of overgrown bottles until the sun came up. There had been a lot more drinking after that, most of it to defeats. After fifteen years in Test cricket a man learned to smile at both victory and defeat, he thought, but it was never that way. Losing always hurt.

The conversation he had with the secretary of the English county where he was a professional came back to him.

"We're not firing you," Ned Whitlaw had said. "But I think you'll agree you didn't have a very good season. The committee feels the team needs a younger man. Perhaps if you'd managed to keep your place on the West Indies team, the vote would have gone the other way. In fact, I'm almost certain it would."

The West Indian Cricket Board had that same week announced the names of the professionals who would form the core of the team to play against England in the West Indies. His name was not on the list.

"Everybody hits a bad patch now and then," Whitlaw said. "Yours came at the wrong time that's all. Go down there and show the world the great Johnny Kane isn't finished."

Kane paid his way from England. The first thing he did when he got to Barbados was to tell the press that he was available and would play if selected. They invited him to practice but he knew they wanted him to fail.

At the far end of the village, a dog howled at the moon and others took up the chorus. He drank some more beer. Another thing he didn't have was time. He had perhaps another year in Test cricket, and with luck another five as a professional, and after that final Test, a farewell dinner and a speech. If he was lucky. He had known players who had not been given that much. Perhaps somebody might give him a job in a department store. He winced at the thought of himself behind a counter trying to sell socks and underwear. Or he might end up as a sports officer – except that the country already had more sports officers than it knew what to do with. It was not that he had not earned good money over the years, but looking back now he could see there had been too many card-games, too many parties and too many women. It was all Giles St. Auric's fault. A superb athlete, undoubtedly the finest batsman and all-round cricketer in the world, he had as captain of the West Indies team done a lot to set the tone.

He opened another bottle of beer. The game had started badly for him. He was too tense. He tried everything he knew to help him relax but nothing worked. Then he dropped the opening batsman in the first over. The fielders sniggered and the batsman said, "Thanks old man." He came to bowl when the score was fifty-four. Two runs came off his first over. He settled down in the slips feeling a little more relaxed.

The other bowler started his run-up. The first ball, a outswinger took the edge of the bat, bounced off the wicketkeeper's glove and struck Kane in the chest. Boos came from the pavilion.

Some of the fielders laughed. The booing was still there when he began his second over. The first ball went by outside the off-stump.

The next one came back off the seam and struck the batsman on the pad.

"How's that?" Kane shouted.

The umpire shook his head. Kane shouted again. The umpire ignored him. He bowled a long-hop next ball and the batsman hit it over mid-wicket for six.

He forced himself to be calm. He bowled an outswinger next ball. The batsman drew away to cut it past point but edged it to gully instead. Gully dropped it. Kane counted to ten slowly. He tried a yorker next ball. The batsman caught it lowdown on the bat and it sizzled past Kane to the boundary. He delivered the last ball from two feet behind the bowling-crease. The batsman came on to the front foot, too early. The ball hit high on the bat and lobbed gently to Kane. He was too quick. The ball struck the tips of his fingers and dropped at his feet. One of the fielders fell down laughing. St. Auric walked over to him.

"Man, you're trying too hard," he said. "Relax. When you tense up like that it ain't no good."

St Auric took him off and put himself on. The fifth ball of the over struck the edge. This time Kane took the catch. The pavilion applauded sarcastically. One of the players came over and said, "You only caught that because St. Auric is the captain and you don't want him to send you off." Kane could not be certain the man was joking.

They are anxious to see me fail, Kane thought. Being dropped from the Test team would reduce him to their level. It always pleased the mediocre to see a new face among them.

"See how easy it is?" St. Auric said.

By close of play that evening the other team had scored three hundred and fifty-seven runs. St. Auric took five wickets for seventy runs, and Kane, brought back against the tail finished with two for ninety-three. A schoolboy whom Kane had never seen before, had scored one hundred and thirty and Cliff Ashton the West Indies opening batsman had made another century. Big Leo Slade the fast bowler had come in at number ten and struck two enormous sixes before being bowled.

Rosa's voice cut across his thoughts. He hadn't heard her come into the room.

"Shouldn't you be sleeping?" she asked. "It is nearly four o'clock."

"I'll be all right."

"Let me get you some milk," she offered. She had seen the empty bottles at his feet.

She left and came back with the milk. Kane leaned over and kissed her breasts through the nightgown.

"I looked in at the children," she said. "Thomas seems to be feeling better."

Kane sighed wearily. He had hoped that the boy would one day be an even greater cricketer than himself. He knew now that was unlikely. And Thomas was his only son. He shook his head.

"You go back to sleep," he told Rosa. "You had a rough day."

He closed his eyes, and behind the lowered lids he played the kind of innings he wished to play that day. He thought about Slade. Slade liked to hit batsmen. He had already put two players in hospital that season.

"It'll be a little difficult at first with the dew and all," St. Auric said. "But it ought to ease out after the first hour or so. You'll have to watch Slade. But I know you can handle him."

They were in the dressing-room. The umpires were walking onto the field. Johnny Kane was down to go in at number three. St. Auric was following at number four.

"Lord in heaven," a voice said. "You seen that?"

A ball from Leo Slade had just passed through the batsman's hair. Kane drew a hand across his brow. His hand shook. He smiled to hide his fear and the worry in his eyes. Slade was in one of his moods. He wasn't really afraid, Kane told himself. He still played fast bowling well, but an injury now would put him out of the game for good.

He found himself thinking about the number of batsmen he had seen injured on that very ground. There had been the Indian Test Captain, and a few years later, a West Indian batsman. Both men had been put in hospital with fractured skulls. There had been others too, but none as serious as that unfortunate pair. There was some talk of getting padded vests and helmets. Baseball had had them for years. Perhaps one day cricket might too.

"You're in Kane," St. Auric said.

He looked up. A fielder was retrieving the bails from fine leg and the batsman was walking back to the pavilion.

Kane adjusted his gloves. He picked up his bat and walked down the steps into the sunlight. He walked slowly giving his eyes time to adjust to the light. He muttered an automatic "hard luck" as he passed the batsman. The man seemed dazed.

Kane began gathering his concentration in at the edges. His mind registered every detail on the field of play; like the way the wind blew the umpire's coat as he bent forward to adjust the stumps, the boot-marks near the edge of the crease, and the clean well-manicured look of the outfield, the flight of sparrows against the blue sky.

Slade had taken that wicket with the last ball of the over. At the other end, Mort Hayes faced the other opening bowler. He pushed the first ball behind square-leg and they ran two. The next he hit away to the left of cover-point, an easy run.

Kane called, "Yes." Hayes sent him back

Hayes played out the rest of the over. A good player, Kane thought, but not quite up to Test standard. He too is afraid of Slade.

Kane took guard. Leg stump. He looked around the field then crouched over his bat and waited for Slade. Easy now, he told himself.

Hands tight around the bat. Weight forward on the balls of the feet. Head and eyes straight down the pitch. Knees bent. Upper body completely relaxed. Head still.

Slade came up to the wicket with long hungry strides. Kane's bat swung up, his eyes on the ball as it left Slade's hand, his right foot coming across to cover the line of flight.

Zip! The ball whizzed past outside the off-stump. It had been very quick. The wicketkeeper tossed the ball back to Slade and he went back to his mark rubbing the ball on his flannels. He turned. The run-up was smooth, fast, and controlled. Kane knew this would be a good ball. He saw the yorker just in time. The ball skidded off the bottom of his bat and streaked through the leg-slips.

"Yes," Kane shouted.

Hayes hesitated, then came through for the run. Kane knew he had been lucky. Hayes glanced quickly around the field. He gripped his bat tightly and seemed to freeze as Slade thundered up to the wicket. The ball went through his tentative prod and tore out his offstump. He cast an angry glance at Kane as he left for the pavilion. Giles St. Auric came down the pavilion steps and the crowd stood up and applauded until he reached the wicket and took guard.

He drove Slade's first ball past mid-on for two. He had, it seemed, all the time in the world in which to play the shot. He played the next ball quietly back to Slade, then flicked the last ball of the over through the leg-trap for a single.

He took eight runs off the next over. His innings had begun with that calm assurance which Kane had come to know so well. St. Auric was on his way to another century.

Now Kane faced Slade again. Slade's hand flashed over. Uh-h-h! The ball zipped past Kane's head buzzing like an angry wasp. Kane's mouth felt suddenly dry. That ball could have killed him, he thought. He hardly saw it. Sweat poured down inside his shirt. He gripped the bat tighter.

Slade turned at his bowling-mark gathering speed like a medium-range jet. The arms went up. The great shoulders rolled. What was it this time, Kane wondered. Not another bouncer. No, a yorker perhaps. Yes, a yorker. That would be good tactics.

The ball was quicker than any of the others before it. And it was a bouncer. Kane, halfway into a defensive prod, felt an explosion under his heart. Through a faint red haze, he saw the sightscreen tilt, then the coconut trees, then the horizon. They wavered for a moment then crashed back to the horizontal.

His vision cleared slowly and painfully. He was surprised he was still standing. He forced his mind to focus. People were around him. His bat had fallen from his hands and he was swearing in a steady monotone.

Upstairs in the VIP enclosure of the players' pavilion, one of the selectors turned to the President of the Board of Control.

"He ought never to have come back," he said. "Getting too old for the game."

"Always quit when you are ahead I say," the President said. "Five years ago, he'd have hit that for six." He shook his head sadly and drank some more whiskey and soda. "Two years ago even."

St. Auric put an arm around Kane's shoulders.

"You're feeling all right?" he asked. "Need a doctor or anything?"

Kane pushed him away. He bent and picked up his bat. There was a red hot iron ball in the centre of his chest, and it got in the way of his breathing. He was certain something was broken.

The umpire said: "Bat or go in. You're keeping back the game."

The crowd was applauding. Kane felt a terrible loneliness. He staggered back to the crease. The fielders drifted to their positions. His vision was normal now, but his knees felt weak, and he wanted to go to the washroom desperately. Slade was waiting impatiently at the end of his bowling mark. He sped up to the wicket and bowled Kane a fast yorker. He managed to keep it out of his wicket by a combination of batting instinct, experience, and luck.

"Yes!" St. Auric shouted, already halfway up the wicket.

Kane scrambled gratefully for the other end. The crowd jeered. He breathed a silent thank you to St. Auric for taking him away from Slade.

Giles St. Auric leaned on his bat and smiled serenely at Leo Slade. Slade read the challenge in that smile and his head lifted and he rubbed the ball into the sweat on his brow and stood looking at St. Auric a long time. He thundered in and unleashed a perfectly straight murderously fast bouncer at St. Auric.

St. Auric swung his bat in a lazy arc. There was a crack and the ball seemed to hang motionless against the blue sky above the pavilion before disappearing beyond the stands. St. Auric smiled innocently at Slade. Slade swore under his breath, hitched up his trousers and walked away. The ball came back. Slade waited at his bowling mark rubbing it gently in his flannels to keep the shine. The stands waited. The next ball was a better one. It pitched closer to the batsman, on off and centre, and leaped from the pitch like an enraged panther straight at St. Auric's head. St. Auric leaned on his back foot and hit it into the back seat of the pavilion at mid-wicket. The crowd stood and chanted his name. He played the last ball of the over past cover for a single. Still keeping me away from the bowling, Kane thought.

His breathing was less painful now. Another ten minutes and he'd be fine. St. Auric took fours off the second and third balls of the next over, then a single. Kane managed to play out the remaining two balls.

"How you feeling man?" St. Auric asked him.

"I can handle Slade," Kane said.

St. Auric smiled. "Of course. But don't hurry. He's still dangerous. You just stay there and watch."

St. Auric drove Slade straight for four, then pulled a fractionally short ball through the onside for another four. Slade was taking a hammering and he did not like it. Kane faced the next over and pushed the last ball past gully for an easy single.

He was facing Slade again. He felt uncomfortable and afraid. He sensed the ring of fielders tighten around him. He pushed forward at the first ball and it struck the edge of his bat and streaked low through the slips for four. The second ball found the middle of the bat. He felt better. Slade is getting easier, he thought. He felt some of the old confidence coming back. Slade ran in again. The ball was short and very fast and on his body. It left the pitch at over ninety miles an hour and in the fraction of a second he stood there trying to reach it, he knew that if it hit him it would kill him. He threw himself backwards desperately. His feet became tangled, and as he went down, he felt the rush of wind as the ball passed in front of his face close enough for him to smell the scent of the leather. He sat on the ground and hoped that when he tried to get up his feet would support him. He got up slowly. The field, the stands, everywhere was still. Kane looked away into the distance. Slade walked up to him.

"Ever think of taking up boxing?" he asked gravely. "With footwork like yours you could make a fortune."

Kane looked through him at the distant hills. He did not say anything. His mouth was dry. His tongue felt like sandpaper against the roof of his mouth. They may see me get hit or even killed, but they will never see me run or flinch. The words seemed to come from a long way off, but he knew he had spoken them.

Slade tramped back to his mark. The great shoulders drooped.

Kane nodded. Even a giant like Leo Slade had to tire at some time, and that last, searing bumper had drained the last of his reserves.

The next ball was a half-volley; fast, but a half-volley. Kane hit it past Slade for four. Slade took his sweater at the end of the over.

Giles St. Auric reached his half-century with a four past extra-cover and kept the crowd on its feet for the next fifteen minutes as he pulled, drove, and cut his way into the eighties. He was batting now with awesome command, driving the fielders back towards the fence by the sheer power of his hitting and still the ball got through; all the time smiling his gentle and faintly melancholy smile like a commanding general observing a gallant but battered enemy gather for another hopeless rush against a position they knew they would not take.

Kane thought: If St. Auric makes a hundred today, nobody will remember that I played in the game.

St. Auric hit past cover's left hand to reach ninety-six and stepped down the wicket to the next ball and crashed it through the ring on the offside and stood poised on the balls of his feet watching the ball race away, enjoying the moment, revelling in the powers of a great batsman at the top of his form. But the fielder had had his pride dented too often that day. The ball seemed already past him when he threw himself at it sprawling full length. The ball met his outstretched hand and stuck. There was no danger to either batsman as long as they did not attempt a run. St. Auric was still silently applauding the fielder when through the corner of his eye he saw Kane dash past.

Kane had not called, neither had he. The fielder threw the ball to the far end. St. Auric stranded halfway down the pitch turned towards the pavilion.

"Sorry," Kane muttered as St. Auric passed.

Giles St. Auric's smile was still gentle. "You son-of-a-bitch," he said.

The crowd booed. Kane leaned on his bat and waited for the uproar to subside. He felt better now that St. Auric was back in the pavilion. It is not enough to do well, he thought. I have to do better than everybody else. Soon, he was playing with a fluency that reminded him of the old days. He heard applause and he glanced up. He was surprised to see he was fifty. He immediately forgot about it and started to bat again as if he had just come in. He was on ninety-three when Slade took the second new ball. Kane flicked the first two balls through the onside to reach his hundred. Batsmen came and went. Kane hardly saw them. All he could think about was not getting out. At close of play, he was one hundred and ninety not out. The spectators stood up and applauded as he walked towards the pavilion.

St. Auric was not in the dressing-room. Kane wanted to find him, to say thanks and to apologise. He sat down and took off his pads and felt weariness wrap itself around him like a cocoon.

The knee hurt. The stiffness was spreading through his entire body. The spot where Leo Slade hit him hurt. He undressed and stepped under the shower.

He found St. Auric leaning against the bar frowning into his beer. Kane went over to him.

"I'm sorry, Giles," he said.

Giles St. Auric looked at him, then he said. "Have something to drink." He nodded towards the barman. "Another beer here for my friend."

"I ran you out on purpose," Kane said.

"I know."

"If you'd made a hundred out there today nobody would've remembered me."

St. Auric shrugged. "Have another beer."

"No thanks. I'm out on my feet already."

He had proved he was still a good player, but he had needed St. Auric's help to do it. And he had run out St. Auric to keep the spotlight on himself. Thinking about it now, he had no regrets. Professional cricket was hard and when a man was fighting for his life he was capable of anything. He hoped St. Auric had no hard feelings.

"You began to look like the old Johnny Kane out there today," St. Auric said.

He sounded casual enough. Kane could not tell if St. Auric was angry or not.

"Sure you won't have another?" St. Auric said.

Kane shook his head. "Got to get home," he said. "Rosa's expecting me."

St. Auric rested his glass on top of the counter and regarded Kane thoughtfully. Kane waited.

"Slade was bowling to instructions out there today," St. Auric said. "He had orders to shake you up a little. Keep you from staking a claim."

"Instructions from whom?" His throat was dry. He held out his hand for another beer. "No matter," he added. "No matter."

He sipped the beer. His knees felt weak. They really did not want him in the team. And Slade had been ready to put him in hospital. Son-of-a-bitch! St. Auric was smiling. Kane held his breath. He felt alone, cut off, surrounded. The young man before him was still smiling. He only had to say the word and Kane was finished. My God, they had pointed Slade at him and pulled the trigger. He waited. If St. Auric had given the instructions he would not now be telling Kane.

"How's the knee? I saw you limping."

"Fine. The knee is fine."

I'm putting you in the team for the first Test," St. Auric said. "That's the most I can do. The rest is up to you."

"Thanks." Kane's voice was hoarse.

"Work on that knee," St. Auric said. "My specialist batsman is no good to me if he doesn't pass the fitness test."

They shook hands. Kane went down the steps and into the warm night thinking about the man, St. Auric. Outside the gate he paused and took out his hankerchief and wiped away the speck of dust the wind had blown into his eye.

Extract from THE HOUSES OF ALPHONSO

From where I sat, I could see a group of boys playing cricket not far down the road. For stumps, they used a rectangular piece of wood which they'd no doubt propped from behind with a stick. The bowler and fielder on the leg side had their backs to me, but I could see the faces of the batsman and the mid-off fielder. The latter stood on the vacant lot. The lads appeared to be between ten and fifteen years old. I heard their shouts, laughter, and occasional disagreeing tones. The bowler, left-handed and imitating the slow hunched crawl of Sir Gary Sobers, delivered and struck the stumps. The batsman shouted, "Man, no, man! I didn' ready, man! I ain' out!" The others quickly gathered around him, and one of them attempted to wrench the bat from his hands. The batsman was adamant. He also looked like the oldest in the group. Soon, the others succumbed to his terrible mood and, frowning with defeat, resumed the game. The next ball was a full toss which the batsman struck high and hard. The furless tennis ball struck one of the royal palms, rolled along the grass and stopped a few feet from the step on which I sat. Smiling, I moved towards the ball. The young bowler came running up to the hedge.

"You guys having a good game?" I asked. The boy nodded. "But don't hit the ball too hard, you know. You don't want your parents to have to pay for broken windows." I held the ball as I spoke.

The boy, hands held out in anticipation of my throw, said, "You see how we out him just now and he say he wasn't out?"

THE RED BALL

"Aye... Thinny Boney! You want to play?"

One of the boys called out to him, and although he had heard and knew they were calling him, he kept pulling out the red petals of the hibiscus flower, tore off their bottom ends and blew into the fine pores of the needle holes at the base until the petals swelled out into a thin balloon of pink skin which he pierced with the straight pin which kept his shirt front closed.

"Match-stick foot! You playin' deaf. You want to play or you don't want to play?"

In his childish way, the boy had understood that if he answered to any of the names they coined for him, he would have to live with it forever. For two weeks now, since they moved to Port of Spain, he had been coming to Woodford Square in the evenings. At first he sat in the fountain with his long thin legs dangling in the water, the spray falling on his face, and when no one was going past he waded across the waist-high water to the green and mossy man-sized busts where there was a giant of a man standing lordly among four half-fish half-women creatures, a tall trident in his massive arm pointing to the shell of blue sky. He had touched the strong green veins running down the calves of the man's legs with fear, half expecting the severe lips to smile, or even curl in anger at him, but the lips stood still in their severity. He then held his cheek close to the small breast of one of the smiling women seated back to back at the feet of the standing man, and she seemed to smile. That was the first time he felt as though he were back in Tunapuna, before they moved.

"Aye you! What you name? You have a name or you ain't have a name?"

He looked at the boys through slitted eyes, still seated on the foot-high cement runner that ran around Woodford Square with tall iron rails pierced deep into the runner. On previous evenings, when the city workers were still wending their ways home through the short-cut square, he had stayed away from its centre and its fountain, catching the flowers of the yellow and purple poui as they spun sailing earthwards. He waited like a small animal scenting the wind with his nostrils until some small gust unhinged a flower and he went racing below the path it was slowly tracing as it came spinning and dancing slowly down to earth. During the past week he came and sat on the runner where the boys played cricket until the fireflies came out into the square and the boys went home with their bats and wickets and balls, then he got up and caught some fireflies and put them in a small white phial to put under his pillow so that he could watch them glow when his parents blew out the kerosene lamp.

"Aye – no name – that is your name?"

"I name Bolan," he said sullenly as he eyed the six or seven boys who had stopped their game and stood about from their batting or bowling or fielding positions waiting on him.

"Well… you want to play or you don't want to play? Cat bite you tongue or what?"

His parents had left their ajoupa hut in Tunapuna and loaned out the two cows to his uncle so that his father could work as a cutlassman at the air bases the Americans were building at Chaguaramas, and the boy went to the "Market School" in the back of the Eastern Market with its thousands of voices of buyers, vendors and live animals screaming through the windows of the school so that he could not hear what the teacher was saying sometimes. That cost six lashes in the palm for what the teacher called "daydreaming". And when he finally understood what was meant by "daydreaming" he could not help but feel that the teacher had pierced deep into him and discovered a secret he kept from everyone else. Because his mind *did*, indeed, run away to the smells and sounds of Tunapuna that the crowing of a fowl in the Eastern Market stimulated. And he came to the square in the evenings because it had in some way seemed like the only place in the city of Port of Spain where people were not chasing him down. It was quiet in Woodford Square, a strange brooding quiet, not of loneliness or nothingness, but of someone having been there long, long ago who had left an insignificant footstep on the landscape. For that was Woodford Square, and the Trinity Church beyond, and the Red House and the Public Library, footsteps left behind by unknown people called British and Spaniards who had gone back to their homes to bury their bones a long, long time ago, leaving Woodford Square behind for him, a Tunapuna boy from the sugarcane fields, to come to spend the evenings in.

He still sat on the runner, his long-boned hands hung down between his knees, admitting to himself that the cricket set the boys had was good, three wickets made from sawn-off broomsticks, which they had nailed into the ground, two bats, one made from a coconut branch, the other a real store bat that smelled of linseed oil, and a cork ball that still had red paint on its surface. He rose, took up the ball, and began hefting it, tossing it up in the air, then catching it to feel its weight, while the other boys looked on in silence.

In Tunapuna he had played with used tennis balls which rich people sold for six cents apiece after they had lost their bounce and elasticity. Only on Sunday matches had he seen a real cork ball and the touch of this one, its rough texture between his fingers, its very colour, gave him a feeling of power. He knew that he could bowl them all down for a duck with this ball.

The boys first looked at each other questioningly, then they began moving to their playing positions as they watched the thin boy count off fifteen paces. He turned and his feet slapped at the turf moving him along like a feather; his

172

long thin body arched like a bow, the ball swung high in the air, his wrist turned in, and he delivered the shooting red ball that turned pink as it raced to the batsman. The batsman swiped blindly and missed, his head swung back quickly to see how the ball could have gone past him so fast. "Aye, aye, aye," the wicketkeeper cried out, as the ball smacked into his hands making them red hot. The fielders who were scattered far off moved in closer to see if they could catch the secret in his bowling, but each time he sent the ball shooting through the air, they missed some small flick of his wrist that made him bowl them all down before they could see the ball.

"You want to come back and play tomorrow?" they asked as they stood about the corner of Frederick and Prince Street, eating black pudding and souse from a vendor who had a charcoal brazier going on the street corner.

The boy jerked his shoulders up and down in an indefinite gesture as he watched the other boys buy an inch, two inches, three inches of the black blood sausages, sizzling in a large tray on the pale red embers.

"How much *you* want?" the vendor asked, as he stood staring at the heap of hot pink ash in the mouth of the brazier, his thumb hooked in his pants' waist. And again he jerked his shoulders up and down in the same indefinite gesture, and when he thought that the vendor was about to offer him a piece of black pudding for nothing, he moved to the back of the clique of boys and disappeared before the fat old woman turned around to look for him again.

It was turning that salmon and orange light of the evening when the sun's rays and the shadows of the trees in Woodford Square were playing tug o' war, both stretched out thin in the evening as they pulled upon each other until that singular moment when no one was looking, and night fell upon the ground like a ball of silk cotton descending through the air with its infinite fall until it touched the grass and settled there as if to remain for ever. He turned into their long tunnelled gateway on Frederick Street and walked to the far end of the deep backyard, for theirs was the last barrack-room close to a high wall that separated the yard from the next street.

As he entered the room he smelt cooking, the smoke of the kerosene lamps, fresh cut grass from his father's clothes, and the faint odour of cigarettes and rum that his father's body exuded.

"Boy, where you does go whole evening instead of stop home here and help your moomah?" his father asked. The boy saw him only late in the evenings now, and each evening he brought home a nip of Black Cat rum. At first the boy thought that they were rich as they said they would become when they left Tunapuna, where a nip of rum meant that it was a holiday or a celebration and there was laughter all around.

"Nowhere," he answered, as he hid his phial of fireflies under the straw mat on which he slept.

"No-way, no-way… You beginning to play big shot! You could talk better than you moomah and poopah. Boy! You don't know how lucky you is to be goin' to school. When I was your age…" His father left the sentence incomplete as he put the nip to his mouth and gargled the rum as though he were rinsing out his mouth, then swallowed it.

"Leave the child alone! If that is the way they teach him to talk in school, that is the right way," his mother put in his defence.

"Yes… but No-way is a place? Show me where No-way is, show me!… you or he, where No-way is, where this boy does go and idle away he time. You know where he does go?" his father shouted, and then it was one of those moments when he felt as if he had held his mother in front of him as a sort of shield to save himself from a rain of blows.

His father then fell into one of those silences. He looked like an old man. He let his hair grow on his head and face unless they were going to Tunapuna. Then he would get a shave and a trim, and tell everyone that he was making three dollars a day at the American Base.

His mother meantime moved about in the series of quick motions that came as she was close to finishing up her cooking for the evening. She seemed to get a sudden burst of energy towards the climax that would make the whole evening's preparation of dinner come to an end with a soft breath of finality.

"The man for the room rent come and he say that next week the price goin' up by two shillings," she said, as if she were speaking to herself. They lived in one of a long line of barracks that you entered after passing through one of those deep dark gateways on Frederick Street. Inside the yard was a stone "bleach" made up of large boulders whitened by the drying of soap as clothes were spread out in the sun to bleach on the hot stones. There was a yellow brass pipe in the centre of the yard tied to a wooden spike driven in the ground.

"It look as if everything goin' up since *we* come to live in town. Is always the same damn thing. Soon as you have a shilling save… two shillings expense come up. As soon as we did have a li'l money save we have to go and get a…"

"A child?" his mother asked.

The boy's eyelids jerked up and his eyes met his mother's and he saw her look back quickly into the brazier.

The same feeling flooded across his heart as it had in those days he sat on the runner in the Square, waiting for something he could not describe. As he left the Square that evening he had felt suddenly released from it, now it was upon him again, clinging to his eyebrows and eyelashes like those invisible cobwebs that hang from the trees in the Square in the early darkness of the evening.

"Boy, why you don't go and sleep instead of listening to big-people talk," his father said, and the boy started to get up from the low stool on which he sat.

"He ain't eat yet," the boy's mother said. "At least let him eat. What you want the boy to do? Go out in the road so he can't hear what you saying? It only have one room and the child have ears just like anybody else. Now come and eat too before you drink any more."

The boy felt more and more that there were things which he had not noticed about his father before. The way he let a long silence linger between the moment he was spoken to, and his reply. And during a lapse like this, he would press his jaw together and make a terrible grimace, then swallow hard before he spoke again.

"Before I drink anymo'! Huh! It ain't *have* no mo' to drink," his father said as he turned the small green bottle upside down, from which two or three drops of amber liquid fell on his protruding tongue.

They had finished eating their dinner in silence when his father said, "Boy, go and full this cup with water." The boy unwound his thin long legs from his squatting position and hurried out to the pipe in the yard. He returned and handed it to his father.

"All right, boy... go ahead and sleep now."

As he started over to the mat in the corner of the room where he slept, his mother said, "*Boy* this... *boy* that! What come over you at all? The child have a name, and it look as if you even forget that too."

His father let his body slowly fall backwards and when he was flat on the floor, he stretched his limbs with a sigh of relief and tiredness. His eyeballs were dancing in a frenzy under his closed eyelids. Then he spoke after a short silence.

"I too tired to argue with you... you hear, woman. I goin' to sleep, so I could go and do the white people work tomorrow, please God."

She turned the lamp down low and went out into the yard to wash the iron pots and enamel plates, and when she returned the boy could hear her talking out loud to herself as she often did these days, yet talking unmistakably to his father, as though she were trying to cloud over what she was saying in a kind of slant by not speaking to him directly.

"Is true," she mumbled, "that we ain't save much, that you believe you work hard for nothing, but don't forget how much we had to borrow to move to Port of Spain. One day when we pay back everybody we will be able to save something..."

From the darkness he heard his father, whom he thought was sound asleep, ask her, "And how much we have save in the can?"

She took out the Capstan tin in which she kept the money, and counted out all the coins which they had saved above all their expenses since they had come to the city.

"It have eight shillings save up in the can," she said, in a tone of voice which the boy felt was a disappointed one, as if she too felt that there should be more in the cigarette tin. His father let out only a small noise, and as though he had dreamt the little incident, he went back to sleep again.

The following evening the boy went to Woodford Square again. He was a little late, for he had gone down to the foot of Frederick Street on an errand, and when he entered the square, he saw the boys sitting on the grass, the wickets nailed in the ground in readiness, the bats leaning against a berry tree, and the ball at their sides. Someone caught sight of him and shouted to the others, "Look Bolan!" and the boys all stood up now. He began running towards them, filled with an excitement such as he had never felt before.

"We was waitin' for you, man... what make you come so late today?" The boy was pleased beyond words that they had not started the game without him. He squeezed out a shiny red cork ball, brand new, from his pocket with a wide smile on his face such as they had never seen before. They all ran to their places and they played cricket until it was dark in the square. The boy was to be their star bowler from now. At the vendor's stall afterwards, he paid for all the black puddin' they could eat.

"Gimmie a two-inch piece," someone would call out, and the boy foraged in his pocket, fingering the surface of the red ball each time he reached for a coin to pay the vendor. Along the emptiness of Frederick Street they heard someone calling. The boys looked in turns to see if it might be any of their parents, then fell back to their black pudding.

Suddenly the boy recognised his father in the cutaway trousers that came three-quarters of the way down his legs. "I have to go," he said hastily, and he ran up Frederick Street. As they turned into the gateway, his father took hold of his ear and tugged him close. "I goin' to give you a cut-ass that you go remember so long as you live," he said, as he led the boy to the back of the yard where an old carpenter had left hundreds of switches of sawn-off wood. The boy danced up and down as the lashes rained now on his feet, now on his back. His father shouted at him, "It ain't have no thief in my family... We never rob nobody a black cent." The boy's mother hovered about, trying to catch the switch from his hand, and each time she caught it, he took another from the large pile that lay about on the ground.

"All right," his mother said. "Nobody ain't say that your family rob anybody... why you don't leave the boy alone?" For each moment of defence from his mother, the boy got more stinging lashes on his legs.

"And where this boy learn to thief from... where? Where he learnin' these *bad bad* habits from... not from me!" his father said.

"Don't call the child a thief... he is not a thief, he just take the money to buy something."

"He is a thief... thief," his father insisted, and the switch whistled with each word.

"When I get through with him he never thief in he whole life again, he go remember what it mean to be a thief." The boy's legs were marked with thin red welts from the lashes and he stopped jumping up and down from the switches now. His father, too, seemed tired, and now his mother took hold of the switch in his hand.

"You ain't have no feelin's... you done gone and kill the half of this boy that is you half, now leave the half that make out of my body, if you still have any feelin's for that."

She took the boy to the standpipe and mixed some salt in a cup of water and made him drink it down, then she took out the ball from his pocket and the few pennies of change he had left. She had gone to the square several days looking for the boy and seen him on the runner watching the other boys play, and she had gone away. When she saw the ball, she knew that they had finally asked him to play.

"You still remember how to bowl?" she asked him, and the boy nodded, his eyes fastened to the ground. After they blew out the kerosene lamp the boy rolled from one side of the mat to the other, trying to find a position in which his body would not be painful. He heard his mother talking to his father in whispers, and he was afraid another beating would follow. He stopped his ears so that he would not hear their conversation, and long afterwards, when he had fallen asleep with his arms around his head, he dreamt that the great green man standing in the cauldron of water in Woodford Square had moved his lips and spoken to him saying, "I didn't know, boy... is for you we doin' all this... only you. We love you like nothin' else in the whole whole world... must always remember that."

And when they were all awake in the morning and he wondered if he had dreamt the words that still sang in his ears, he remembered that he had smelt his father's body as he came and lay close to him in the night.

George Lamming

Extract from THE EMIGRANTS

All dese people in de West Indies, brown skin, black skin, all kind ah skin, dose wid learnin' an dose wid no learnin', them all want to do something. All them want to prove to somebody dat them doin' something or that them can do something. Poor man prove him can get rich. Rich man prove him can get as rich in a next country. Him with no education prove education is what him want. Him with education prove de education him got is equal in quality wid education other country give. An' politician prove dat what Colonial Office doin' them can do better. West Indies people, whatever islan' you bring them from, them want to prove something. An' dose who dance calypso an' shango them want to prove something too. When them call it art form that them study an' want to do correct, them tryin' to prove somethin' too. In cricket same thing. When them win England or Australia, them win to prove something. Them all want to prove something. Me serve in de R.A.F. three years, an' the only thing that West Indians in de R.A.F. dint want to prove, de only thing him feel no need to prove is his capability wid a bottle or a blonde. Him never worry to prove 'cause such operation was natural. Him just perform widdout giving a rassclot 'bout provin' anything. An' de reason is simple as A.B.C. Him feel no need to prove 'cause him know what him can do. Him know his potentiality, an' when his performance take place them who witness can reach what conclusion them like. 'Cause him know his potentiality. Him sure o' himself. Him feel no need to prove nothin'. Him sure. In everythin' else him feelin'. Him searchin'. Him trying to prove that him know w'at is w'at. Him quarrel if him no get respect 'cause him afraid that him not really provin'. Him take criticism bad 'cause him feel him not provin'. Doctor, nurse, lawyer, engineer, commercial man, women and men, them all that study an' call themself West Indies people as though them was a complete new generation or race the Almighty Gawd create yesterday, them all want to prove somethin', an' them sensitive, them 'fraid, 'cause them ain't want the foreign man to feel that them ain't provin'. An' if you ask what it is them want to prove the answer sound a stupid answer. Them want to prove that them is themself. That is w'at them want to prove.

He knew Trinidad through the annual cricket tournaments which were played in the two islands. One year Barbados invited Trinidad to compete in the game, and the following year Trinidad would invite Barbados to play at Trinidad. There was a tradition of tournaments that had helped more than books, newspaper reports or history lessons at school to remind the people in Barbados that there were people with similar habits and customs living in Trinidad. The tournament sometimes included British Guiana and now and again Jamaica. But Jamaica was the least known. They were farther away, and for various reasons their cricket teams came less frequently. Yet Jamaica cricket had captured the Barbadians' imagination. Every boy who felt his worth as a batsman called himself George Headley. In most cases the only knowledge most people might have had of Jamaica was the fact that George Headley was born there. The shoemaker looked up at the partition directly behind him. Pasted in two rows on the boards were the press photographs of cricketers he had clipped from the daily paper. Some wore caps and blazers and the sweaters with the colours that could only be used by those who had represented the territories combined against England or Australia. The players were of mixed colours. Slightly above the top row was a picture of one George Challenor who might have been a white planter in Barbados. Beside him was George Headley against whose name was printed in pencil the words, THE BLACK BRADMAN. The shoemaker looked at them and recalled the stories he often told of each. Learie Constantine, Derek Sealey whom he called the wonder boy of West Indian cricket, Clifford Roach, Mannie Martindale, and Bertie Clarke who was going to be the best spin bowler the world had ever seen. The baggage man who went by the name of Flannigan had made the prophecy, and Flannigan was never wrong. The shoe maker made another stitch in the boot and looked out at the people pushing around the cart. He was thinking about the strike and the riots in Trinidad and the cricketers, and in a way he couldn't explain to himself they all seemed to belong to the same line of events.

Extract from SALT

"Alford [...], go to the schoolmaster and ask him to send two sticks of chalk for me. You know what to say?" she encouraged. "Say, 'Miss say to send two sticks of chalk for me.'"

"Miss say send two sticks of chalk for me," he had repeated.

"Please," she added.

"Please," he said.

And that was how he grew up at school, running errands for his teachers, cleaning the blackboard, collecting homework assignments and maintaining silence in the teacher's absence. On some days he occupied the teacher's chair, surveying the class with strict humourless zeal, his eyes alert to discover the slightest breach of order so he could dutifully report it, so that by the time he entered Standard Two his classmates had already given him the nickname Sir.

It was his air of Sirness, his stiff, grave, wooden intensity, as much as his greater size, that in the beginning set him apart from his fellows and kept him an outsider for most of his school days.

He was older and bigger than almost every boy in his early classes. In their games his solemnity and awkwardness made him appear a bruising giant among them. Seeing how the tiny tots were bowled over by his charge, teachers and bigger boys cried shame on him. After a while, his very classmates, seeing him approach the playing-field, not even considering that they were in many cases more adept at games than he was, would withdraw to the sidelines complaining that, as they put it, "We not playing any game with that man."

Just a little ashamed and believing that they had made a mistake that they would want to rectify, he would walk away slowly, wanting to remain longer within earshot of them so they wouldn't have to shout to call him back. The call never came.

Among boys closer his own age, Alford didn't do any better. Their play was a rough, boisterous affair open to anyone with the ability to rush and push and bluff and bully, each man for himself. And Alford tried, but, inhibited by his reserve and lack of confidence in his talents, he handicapped himself from the beginning. He began to develop into someone tentative, ungainly and suspicious, never quite able to trust the competence of his natural instincts to get the hang of things, needed something less fallible, more guaranteeing of success than the blind imitative venturing of most of his fellows.

On the few occasions when he did get a kick of the ball or managed to get to bat, he addressed his opportunity with a solemnity that suggested that his very life was at stake and there to judge him was a tribunal of not only the players around him but all those who had mastered the game and, more than they, the very implements he was seeking to manipulate. Seeking the perfection that such an audience demanded, to the delight of the other boys, he failed. It must have been, he reasoned later, his ambition to be better than his gifts dictated that vexed them. They readily accommodated fellows who accepted their own limitations, who did not take themselves at all seriously, were content simply to get an opportunity to take a swing at the ball and hope to the gods that they connect. They cheered such fellows with as much gusto as they did the heroes, for what by luck and by chance and by enterprise they eventually were able to achieve. Alford's efforts irritated them. And they began to punish him. Even in scratch games the captains were reluctant to pick him and, rather than choose him, they would play with a man short or call to some indifferent boy passing and invite him over while Alford stood by dying for the opportunity to play.

He began to arrive at the playing-field earlier than anybody else. He began to provide the wickets and the ball or bat for the game, to sweep the pitch in preparation for cricket or put up poles for goal posts for football. He would go into the forest and cut lengths of wood, take them home and shape them into wickets. Occasionally, he produced a tennis ball which he taped over and polished until it bounced and looked nearly like a real cricket ball.

But even such contributions were not enough to guarantee his selection.

One day he arrived on the ground with his own wickets, a bat he had himself fashioned out of the root of a bois canot tree, one of his taped and polished tennis balls. He was setting up the wickets when the other boys arrived. One took up the bat, another the ball. He went behind the wicket and they began a game. Then more fellows came and it was decided to play a match. The two captains selected themselves and began to pick two teams, Alford looking on anxiously, counting the fellows to be sure that there would be an even number so that there would be no excuse for him not to be picked. There were eighteen boys, enough for each side to play with nine. Each captain had chosen eight, and left to be picked was Alford and a thin Indian boy who had proven before that he could neither bat nor bowl nor field and who didn't really care either. The boy was selected. Alford was already beginning to move to join the other team. Perhaps the eagerness in his eyes, in his gait, struck that team's captain. He held up a hand. He didn't want him.

"You take him," he said to the other captain.

But the captain of the first team did not want to have any such advantage. They argued back and forth for several minutes and then the thin disinterested boy decided that his time was being wasted and left. That left seventeen players. Each team already had eight. Alford was out. He thought of taking his wickets and his bat and his ball and leaving, but he felt that to be too easy. He wanted them to think, to feel guilty. He wanted somebody to remind them that it was his ball and bat and wickets.

181

"Keep the implements for me," he said to Victory, one of the three fellows who had begun the game. Then he turned to leave.

"Wait!" Victory said. Alford stood and waited for Victory's intercession. "Why we don't let Alford umpire?"

Alford couldn't move. He couldn't look at anybody.

"You want to umpire?" one of the fellows enquired, impatient to get on with the game.

Alford was surprised that his voice carried any sound; he heard himself answering, "Yes. I will umpire."

From that day and for the duration of his time at Cunaripo Government School, Alford became the umpire at cricket matches and, as an extension, the referee at football games. Later, it would be forgotten by everyone but himself that he had any other ambition.

It was here, in this role, that for the first time in his life he had a taste of the exercise of power. There were those who, thinking him still the diffident apologetic Alford, wanted to challenge his decisions; and for a time he tried his best to please. He wanted to be fair, to give correct decisions. And in the beginning, what errors he made stemmed from this concern, but then he discovered that he was the power, that his was the final authority. He established his control by his recitation of the rules which nobody else had read and by an inflexibility of will. All timidity left him. He penalized for the most minor infringements, delivering his judgments not as an upholder of the law but as an angel of vengeance victoriously punishing sin. Sometimes he would wait long seconds deliberating after an appeal had been made, while the player over whose fate he was about to adjudicate did his best not to look up lest he see the sword of Alford's index finger pointing him back to the pavilion.

He worked himself into the drama of the game, signalling boundaries with the elegance of a dancer, redrawing the bowling crease, calling no-balls, turning down appeals, making a theatre of his adjudication until he became as much of an attraction as the star batsman or bowler at school. He so impressed that captains of adult clubs asked him to stand in their games; and the schoolmaster, delighted to have in his school a young man with such a sense of force, invited him at sixteen to become a Pupil Teacher...

"And you know how I get this clipper? A pardner send it from the States for me. The latest. You know who send it? Rupert, the fast bowler from Wanderers. He gone up there in the States and see this clipper and he say, 'Victory will like this' and he send it for me."

"How long he away now?" Pascal asked.

"Four, five years. Last time I hear about him he was living in New Jersey. I always wonder why he send me the clipper."

"Maybe he didn't like how you used to trim him," Brown said.

After the laughter, the barbershop was filled with the sound of the clicking scissors, with Brown and the fellar named Ross intent on their game.

"Those was the days when Wanderers was Wanderers," Brown said. "This barbershop was the centre. On a Saturday morning you couldn't get in. All the young teachers and civil servants lined up to talk cricket and boxing and waiting to trim. Those days real draughts used to play, with Castillo and Cecil and Mr Arthur leaving Libertville to clash with Paul. Now Paul, too, gone away."

"The worst thing this government do is to allow people to go away," Victory said. And he swung the barbering chair around to get to tackle the other side of Pascal's head.

[…]

"So, Victory, what is going to happen to your side now?" Pascal asked, idly. With Victory working on the front of his head, he was looking at the photographs on the wall.

"Which side?" Victory answered.

"You know who I mean, Wanderers. Your side."

"Wanderers is not a side. Wanderers is a club. A club is not a side. A side is when you pick up eleven fellars to play a match and next week you have to look to pick up eleven fellars again. A club is solid. It is something to belong to."

"What going to happen to your club when all your players gone away?"

"All? All the players?"

"Well, the stars. Prince, your fast bowler going to Canada. Murray going. Ali gone to the States."

"Who else going?" Victory asked. He didn't like this talk.

"Is your club. You should know."

"What you want us to do? They going to study. They have to think about their future. They have to get their education. Just now, just from the fellars who leave and go away from Cunaripo and they come back with their BAs and MAs and Ph dees they could run the government."

"I wish I was one of them going," Brown said. He was relaxed now. Ross had miscalculated.

Victory was ready now to clean the edges of Pascal's head with the razor. Quickly, he lathered the shaving brush and brushed it across the edge of hair he was going to remove, then, tilting the chair, bending at the knees, he swept the razor in brisk, deft strokes at the base of Pascal's head and behind his ears, nobody saying anything, Pascal sitting very still. Then Victory attacked the head once more with the scissors; then, with a powder pull, he puffed some white powder over the places where he had wielded the razor. He took up a comb and handed it to Pascal. He was going to do the final shaping of the hair now.

"Comb out your hair," he said to Pascal. "Wait. Is so you does comb your hair?" he asked, seeing Pascal combing from back to front.

"I combing it *out*. I usually comb it backwards."

"Well, comb it backwards, just as you does comb it when you dollsing up." Watching Pascal comb his hair, Victory continued talking. "You build a club to last, to stand up. They say nothing can't last in Cunaripo. They say we can't build nothing. And you build a club and next thing you know, bam! fellars you building it with gone away."

"What you want them to do?" Pascal asked.

"You think I going to stay here just to play cricket?" Brown said.

"*Just?*" Victory asked. "*Just* to play cricket? How you mean just to play cricket? What you think put us on the map, make us known in Pakistan, England, Australia? You all don't know what to care about?"

"You have to be able to afford to care," Brown said. "How you expect a fellar like me scrambling for a living, to care about cricket?"

"And how you will care about anything? Somebody will pay you to care? They will give you money and then you will care, eh, Brown? Money will make you care?" Victory had stopped work on Pascal's head.

"I would go away to better my position," Brown said. "Not because I don't care."

"Betterment? By the time you come back you stop playing cricket, you seeing 'bout wife and children, you get fat. It was like if you was never here. Sometimes I look through the scorebook and see the names of players who used to play: Bridges, Kedar, Housen, Francis, Lee, Bisson, Griffith. Was like they was never here. Maybe the government should give a subsidy to care, eh, Brown, eh?"

"Is not the going away," the fellar named Ross said.

Victory turned upon him, "Is not the going away? Wait! You come in this barbershop a stranger and making more noise than anybody and now you telling me 'is not the going away'?"

"Is not the going away," Ross said, holding his ground in the now silent barbershop, "What it is? Is what they do while they here… I see Housen. I see him play in Arima and I see him play in 'Grande. I remember him like today, and is how long ago I see him play? He bring an excitement, a magic, a life. You see him on the field and you see life. You see yourself. Is like that, I miss a man like Housen. I glad he was here."

The silence deepened in the barbershop.

"Is true, Victory," Pascal said. "I play against him once. He playing for Dades Trace, I playing for Colts, and when he finish bat... I mean, when we at last get him out, the whole field was clapping, not because we out him, because of the innings he play. Is true. The man coulda bat."

Victory spun the chair around and crouched and looked at Pascal's head, then he spun the chair again and looked at the head as a surveyor looking for an angle. Then he rose up.

"So you does play cricket?" Victory asked, turning now to the fellar named Ross, his scissors clicking once again. "What you do? Bat? Bowl?"

"Open bat and bowl medium pace. Inswing mostly, but now and again I does get one to move away."

"Ross, you say your name is? From Arima. It had a fellar used to work with the electricity company. Gerome Ross. Tall, kinda good looking, always with his hair cut neat and his moustache trimmed?"

"Gerome? That is my first cousin."

"When he was up here, he was my good pardner. Neat, clothes always sharp, dressed to kill when he playing cricket, but he couldn't play fast bowling. Bounce one at him and he start to dodge away. Rupert used to have him hopping. What about him?"

"He get kinda fat," Ross said.

Victory looked down at his own middle, "Just now I have to start some jogging. Or maybe start to referee some football. Pascal; you don't remember Gerome? Coulda kick a football *hard*. Goalies used to cry when they see him coming."

Brown had been studying the draughts board and now, as if he had the whole game worked out, he pushed a knob and said to Ross, "Your play."

Victory finished touching up Pascal's head, went around behind him and unpinned the cloth, taking it off carefully so that the hair wouldn't fall on Pascal's clothes. He brushed the tufts of cut hair off the cloth into a heap on the floor, then went to the door and holding the cloth with two hands dusted it out, flap, flap, flap, then he began to fold it. When he turned it was to see Pascal standing in front the mirror looking at his head admiringly.

"You still think I shoulda clean it?" Victory asked, still folding the cloth.

Pascal turned his head this way and that. Then a smile broke onto his face, "How much I have for you?"

"The price aint gone up," Victory said.

As Pascal put his hand in his pocket, Brown let out a big exclamation and slapped a knob down on the draughts board, same time springing to his feet just as the legs of the bench gave away, upsetting the whole game, but not before Ross, with a quickness that amazed Victory, had leapt from the falling bench. Victory thinking, yes, he's an opening bat in truth.

Franklyn Batting

In Cascadu, when Franklyn went in to bat, around the ground the talking would stop, people would look for a good place to sit and from the savannah the word would go out, little fellars taking off running in different directions to make the announcement, "Franklyn batting! Franklyn batting!"

Through the whole village it would go, *Franklyn batting*, and before she go out her door, Miss Dolly would pull out the firewood from the fireside and add some water to the pot she cooking so it would bubble slow while the wood glowed to ashes, Rabbit and Jerry would get up off the bench in front the rum shop, people buying in the grocery would hurry up with their message and even down Eight-mile it would reach, Kenny slowing down his taxi to shout out as he passing to the people bathing by the spring, "Hey, all-you, Franklyn batting! You hear what I saying: Franklyn. Franklyn batting. *Franklyn batting*," and would drive maybe another five minutes, making the announcement, before he turn around and pick up those who ready and carry them back up to the cricket ground. Old cricketers like Housen and Montiqueu and Hercules would leave from in front Cyril house where they stand up talking and Bank and Pico and Copper and George, from different starting points, not even knowing exactly where they going, seeing people moving, would feel the tug of a grand event and begin to follow and only after they on their way they would ask, "Where we going?" and the answer would come, "Franklyn batting. Franklyn, yes, batting."

In the club, fellars playing knock rummy would take up their money and pack up the cards and head for the Savannah and even Melda, clerking in Mendoza shop, would ask Ross to hold on for her with the selling so she could go and see Franklyn bat. Just for one over. Just one, holding up her finger, "One, Ross. One." And Ross would hold up his finger too and his eyes would open and his moustaches would tremble, "OK. One, you hear. One."

And in the gallery of the house behind the savannah, Manick father, off today from driving the steamroller, sitting down in his hammock, would make sure he have a big cup of water and peanuts in a bowl beside him on the floor so he wouldn't have to move while Franklyn batting. In the savannah, people there already on the mound of the hill that was the pavilion would dress-round to make room for old man Castillo and his two pardners and feel the pathos as these men contemplate then laboriously engage the Herculean task of sitting down, their bones creaking as they hold out their hands, feeling for the ground and with a sigh in salute to the pain in their knees, in their bones, would ease themselves down, *Ahhh!* on the grass. The girls who had been modelling their lithe limbs and their Sunday fashion would settle down in front the Community Centre near where my aunt Magenta was selling coconut drops and sour sop ice-cream and nobody would say nothing, just watch Franklyn with the bat in his hands walk out to the ground with his slouching walk, bending and unbending his shoulders like the two ends of an accordion, lifting his knees high, one first then the other like the limbering up exercise of a high-jumper. Then he hold himself down and walk off again, nonchalant, this time, like a prince who never see a day of trouble, his head in the air like he walking on a rope stretched across the sky, so confident his balance that he not even looking down to see where he putting his foot. After he mark with chalk the spot on the matting where he would take his stand, Franklyn would settle over his bat, casting to one side with a shrug the cape invoked on his shoulders and look now at the bowler run up to release the ball.

People look at cricket for the runs, but with Franklyn it was the runs, yes, it was runs, but his batting wasn't only runs, it was the spring in his step, it was the dance of his body, the confident readiness of muscles to move forward or sideways or back: to tiptoe or pivot or kneel or duck; and then the ball would come and he would leave it alone, just that, watch the ball and withhold his bat from it. And although it didn't show in the score book, that was a stroke, that was a statement, that was an acknowledgement of the bowler and an announcement to the world that we here. We have eyes. *We ready*, just to hint to them that they can't play the arse, that they have to put it on a length, we not going powerful-stupid chasing after wide balls. *Put it on the stumps. Put it on the stumps. Until I ready for you.*

Franklyn had three leave-alones. He would leave alone in acknowledgement of a good ball, not even having to shake his head, not even doing nothing like that, just a ordinary leave-alone, and he would leave alone as a warning to say don't put it there again. Sometimes with a smile, to mask his perplexity and to acknowledge that the pitch of the ball or its flight or its pace deceive him a little, a wee bit, he would leave alone, measuring the distance from the ball so as to know exactly what to do when the bowler put the next ball in the same spot. He had a lot of no's, that is, when he actually play the ball for no runs, "Noo!" He had a lot of no's. As if he knows that it have time in the world. And all that is batting and he ain't even start to score yet. I not even talking yet about Franklyn going down on one knee and sweeping to square leg or climbing back on his back foot and slapping it back past the bowler, not a man move.

I ain't talking yet of Franklyn up on tiptoes, his eyes fixed big on the ball he been watching its whole journey from the bowler's hand, and even after it pass his waist and look like it about to go past his wicket, he had already pivoted like he doing a bullfight dance and just when the keeper feel he have the ball in his fists, his bat come down sweet and long, long and sweet, slap, between the keeper and slips, *How you going to stop we? How you go keep we down?* And all round the wicket, each in its own time, each off the chosen and appropriate ball would be the music of bat on ball, punctuated by the chorus of our applause – not really applause – we didn't really applaud Franklyn. When Franklyn batting we was the ones batting, and in the mirror that he had become we would see ourselves in contest with the world. He was holding the bat but the strokes was our strokes and the bowler bowling the ball was England or Australia or Pakistan: the world. Yes, the world. And when he finish batting, when he get out, a curtain of silence would fall like when the sun that you know going to rise tomorrow goes down.

Nobody would move yet, we would wait and watch him come back under the mango tree like a dancer who just finish dance a set and is walking the girl who partnered him back to her seat, and put down his bat and sit down and take off his pads and then you would hear the voice of a mother – Miss Ruby – calling her boychild Glen to come now and do what she tell him to do so long before but which he must do now. And if you look across at the gallery of Manick house you would see the father putting on his slippers and taking up his cutlass with a sense of urgency, as if Franklyn's batting had imposed on him and his family and indeed the whole community the need *to do* something, to exert on the world an equivalent force and style. On the mound, with the same Herculean straining, the old men would push themselves up with their hands to their feet, making sure of their balance on the slippery deck of age. People would start talking again and Pico would reassemble the Four for the knock rummy and Melda would run past everybody, her slippers flapping, screaming, "Ross going to kill me," but in her heart knowing that Ross will understand how she lose track of time, and a girl and a boy would walk slow close-close together and shy, their swinging hands touching, holding just briefly and letting go so as not to make a spectacle of their feelings.

Rain could fall now. And gradually argument would start up again in the rum shop, the Four would reassemble in the club, music in the snackette next door would begin to play and the old men, walking slow, would lift up their hands in a hello, walking a little straighter today, and that night men and women would make love as if they have the world of time, paying attention to details, to the no's and the yeses as of a Franklyn's innings, and others, in company, over a nip in the snackette or with their elbows on the wappie table in the gambling club would take their time with one another, *Nooo!* And people would restore in themselves the patience, the un-hurry, to let a slight pass, to leave a bad situation alone, to not be inveigled by shit, to resist having to agree to stupidness, to say no, thank you. No, and lift a glass to their lips and down a drink in salute of each other, with the same smooth un-hurry of Franklyn dispatching a ball to the boundary.

EXTRACT FROM SONG OF NIGHT

A man crawled out of a nearby shop and braced himself against the kicking wind. Lemuel. In his youth Lemuel had been a strapping cricketer who played for the island, and many said he was good enough to play for the West Indies. Now his body was crooked. Still, there was a residue of virility left to defy Nature.

He was coming toward her. She turned, not knowing whether to flee or stay. She didn't feel like talking.

He stopped in front of her, putting his crookedness under her nose, daring her to ignore him. He was nothing much to look at. Yet something about him seemed to hypnotize her. His eyes were proud and compelling as if they were the only things he had of worth now.

He did not speak. She eyed him in silence.

"What you want?" Her voice as angry as it was puzzled.

"You better watch you'self, girl." His deep voice came out of a cave.

"Who you telling to watch themself?"

"I used to know your father real good. We used to play cricket and nick dice together. I know what people 'bout here think 'bout him. They would like to destroy you for being his daughter. Don't let them."

"Nobody can't do me nothing."

"I used to feel like that, too. I know that feeling good. Young and strong, that's what I was. Indestructible. It don't last forever, yuh hear me. God could take it from you like *that*. Remember that. And watch out for your sister too."

"Why you care what happen to we?"

"Faith ain't measured in nuggets of gold, but in the things you do. You father was the onliest body in this village who truly believe I coulda make the West Indies team. Everybody else try to bring me down, to belittle me. Them cheer for me when I was playing local cricket, but the minute my name get mention for big cricket, the minute I get call to trials, them turn on me, like them couldn't stand to see me get through. Them say I would never be good enough, that I was too worthless. That I drink too much rum, that I had too much women, that I too lazy. Not your father. He believe in me. Used to tell me all the time I was the best fast bowler he ever see. That I was better than Wes Hall. I wasn't very careful with money in those days, and when I didn't have money to get a good pair of shoes for the trials, Steel give me the money. And he come and watch every match I play.

"And when the radio announce that I make the Barbados team and everybody start saying how them know I was gonna make the team, Steel and me, we just stand up and listen to them and laugh.

"I play twelve matches for Barbados, and who knows, if what happen to me didn't happen, I mighta make the West Indies. But I got good memories 'bout cricket days and I would never forget your father. And I promise myself when I hear that he was... you know... going to be... you know, I promise myself I would look out for his children as much as I could."

Then he was gone. Crab-walked across the street so fast, it surprised her. A car zipped past. When she looked again, he had disappeared into the tiny space between two houses.

IAN MCDONALD

EXTRACT FROM THE HUMMINGBIRD TREE

The village lay about a mile away from our house. It was not very big, about twenty-five families, hardly more than an impermanent settlement really; the huts were quite new, for the first villagers had only come there about three years back. These had broken off from a much larger village and come to this place where the Government had let them have enough land to graze cows, keep donkeys and goats and fowls, grow rice and ground provisions. The first-comers had been joined by others. They all complained that there was no op-portunity in the big village they had come from. "A man don' like to change whe' he live jus' fo' so but dat place choke up wid people." The young people couldn't find new land or new jobs. "Up dere so you never see such idleness in you' life. Saga boy an' small t'ief mounting up like a rage. Why you think I bring me fam'ly right down here so?" Kaiser said that his family had been one of the first to come; his grandfather, Old Boss of the village, had negotiated with the Government for the small piece of land. Not very many others had been as lucky.

The main occupation of the villagers was working in the canefields, which covered rich swathes of land in the neighbourhood. In season they cut the cane and carried it to the small factory in the district. Some of the men worked in the factory; though they did the crudest work there, carting the heavy jute bags of brown sugar, cleaning dirty vats, they proudly called themselves "engineers", and had a certain prestige in the village. The magic and power of industry and the world of machines touched them. All the young men would have liked to work in the factory.

In the season there was enough work for the village. But in the slack time of the year, when the growing cane needed little attention and the factory was shut down, time hung heavy on the hands of the men there. Petty thieving increased nightly in this off season and there was sure to be a rapid rise in the number of cases of drunkenness coming up before the local magistrate. In all these cases he [my father] meted out the customary admonition: "Why don't you get out of the rumshops and find some work to do, man?" Some did find work. They took odd jobs at rich houses like ours, or at the Government Farm, or at Mr Trotter's dairy. One or two went far afield to find work picking fruit on citrus estates or in part-time jobs on the Port of Spain wharves. Some stayed at home and just spent more time in tending their plots of corn and rice and sweet potato, yams and beans, and in looking after the few cows and donkeys and goats and poultry which they kept. Then perhaps their wives and daugh-ters could sell more vegetables, eggs and milk in the rich houses. But whatever they did, it was still a bad time in the village. Tempers went bad and wives were beaten. There were fights.

Ramlal must have rubbed his thin hands, because his rumshop was always full. However, more often than not even he had to give credit, for pockets were empty at that time of the year. Underemployment made everyone in the village restive.

The most innocent way of relieving this strain of having nothing to do came in epic village cricket matches which sometimes lasted right through the day from early morning until nightfall. They were played on the rough village pasture where in the dry season a dirt pitch, more or less than the regulation length, was hacked out of the grass and smoothed out as carefully as possible. The village didn't have a coconut matting to put over the pitch so at least the menaces with which its uneven surface bristled were visible to the eye. The outfield layout was littered with clots of dung.

I watched one of these big cricket matches once with Kaiser. He was in the village team. They were playing a side from the old village. It was a game hilariously, intensely, and fiercely contested. The day's casualties were high, several bruised heads and broken shins and three fractured noses, but the game seemed to let loose a surge of good humour in the villagers. There was one fight, between a visiting batsman and one of the home umpires, but this was soon over, with the umpire, chosen for his toughness, an easy winner, and the game continued smoothly after it.

Each team consisted of fifteen or sixteen men. I noticed that on Kaiser's side anyway the best batsmen opened the innings and then later, when the opponents could be supposed to have half-forgotten what they looked like, in again at number thirteen or fourteen they strode, wearing different caps. There were complaints, but never successful complaints, about this practice: it was the caps rather than the men who batted.

I gathered these caps were all-important in the game. The team which appeared with the most memorable caps was well on its way to triumph. The village team was pretty well unbeatable, for in its ranks, a Bradman of headwear, it boasted a green Trinidad XI cap. Its authenticity was questioned many times but never disproved. One day at the Oval a great star, as he walked in through a corridor of people applauding a brilliant century, threw his cap nonchalantly to those worshippers, and it had landed straight in the hands of a little boy from the village. He came home with it and sold it to the cricket team for five shillings. Now it starred in every game. In this particular match it made four appearances in the batting order and each of its scores was a highlight of the innings. Kaiser was one of those honoured with the green cap. He let me touch it and examine the treasured emblem on it, the Trinidad crest, the black-masted ships of Columbus in a blue harbour and in the background the trinity of green mountain peaks. Beneath had been sewn the Latin motto of the island: Miscerique Probat Populos Et Foedera Jungi.

"Oh, God, I hope I score big," Kaiser said fervently as he put it on to go in to bat.

After a nervous start he hit seventeen fiery runs. He hooked one ball into the casuarina tree which grew in the bush in front of Old Boss's hut; the game was held up twenty minutes while both teams searched the undergrowth; the ball was finally recovered from a patch of razor grass into which Kaiser, protesting, was made to go and whence he emerged ball in hand but woebegone, slashed by the delicate, sharp, green blades. The next ball he lifted for another six and hit his mother's cow in the field adjoining; it began to moo disconsolately. In the midst of the cheers for such a fine hit, his mother rushed out into the playing field shouting angrily.

"You crazy or what, boy! Look what the hell you do now! You want to kill we cow or what, eh! Come out from dey an' see what I going gi' you here today!"

She advanced towards the pitch; Kaiser retreated from his wicket. The bowler took off his cap and fanned his face. The other fieldsmen flopped down on the grass and took a rest. The two umpires conferred quickly and then told Kaiser's mother she must go. She refused.

"Le' me get me han' on that wotless chile an' I going beat he like I beat a donkey. You hear me cow, you hear it!" The cow was still mooing as if it had all the woes of the world on its back.

Confusion reigned. The umpires conferred again, but could reach no decision. The rest of the village team came streaming out on to the field. A babble of voices and a waving of arms began. In the middle of it all Kaiser's determined mother stood firm, cursing.

"All you big men like baby or what? What you playing this dam' foolish thing for? Why you don' go an' work, eh! You only was'ing you' time wid this chupid little ball an' piece of ol' wood. You' brain mus' be sof'ning fo' true. You think you going stop me bus'ing his little arse fo' him. Look what he do me cow, eh! You hear it?" The cow was still mooing, distraughtly now.

At last they called Kaiser's father. He was in Ramlal's rumshop where he had gone for a rum. He was slightly drunk. He commanded his wife to go off the field when he heard the story.

"Woman, ge' off this fiel' here today," he said ponderously, "or I going well beat you. You hear me. Gawd, if you had Bra'man fo' you' son you would vex if he hit you' cow or what! The dam' cow not dead. Go, move, cle' the field, play, play!" he ended, flushed with triumph.

His wife went off crying. Play was resumed. The bowler swung his arms, glared at Kaiser, pounded down and delivered his stock ball, a fast full pitch. Kaiser swung hugely, missed, and was clean-bowled. The fieldsmen clapped the bowler. Kaiser walked away from his wicket, head bowed. As he came to the boundary edge his father caught hold of him and began to beat his ears mercilessly.

"Who you think you is, eh, firing shot at we cow like you mad. You don' know cow cos' money or what!"

Kaiser slipped through his arms and ran for his life, the green cap awry on his head; as he ran he straightened it proudly.

The team scored 123 runs of which Kaiser's 17 was top score. This total included eight byes scored when two short-pitched balls had rocketed prodigiously over the heads of both batsman and wicketkeeper and sprung with one leap over the boundary. There was then a chatter of awe amongst the spectators.

The score of 123 was too formidable for the opposing team. The village's star fast bowler, Burnley Hing, a Chinese-Indian who shared a hut with two brothers, who mended motor cars when he wasn't drunk, and who consumed more rum than anyone else in the village, really mowed down the visiting team. He took eight fair wickets and dismissed two other men with broken noses. His fierce slinging delivery was suspect and he was volubly accused of throwing the ball.

"Gawd Almighty!" the visiting captain, a dour, grey-haired old man wearing a flashy, floppy Panama hat circled with a red ribbon, said in an explosion of righteous despair. "Gawd Almighty! What kin' of game this is! Gawd, man, me di'n' come here to pelt mango, oui! I never see a man pelt so. Eh, what you saying, umpire?"

The umpires shook their heads sadly. The only consolation that the captain had was in scoring ten runs out of their small total of 44, and that ten was top score. Burnley Hing, in whose face lurked a thousand smiles of triumph, was hugely cheered. As he wiped his sweating face with a large silk handkerchief, he expressed himself:

"Where dat rum now, boy? I could drink a barrel o' rum here tonight!"

These matches, especially in the slack season when thirsts were so high, were profitable occasions for Ramlal, the richest man in the village. After the game both teams invaded his rumshop. It was now that the glum visitors recovered their spirits.

Kaiser and I slipped in too and had a sweet drink each that evening before I had to go. Kaiser took a Ju-C, I took a 7-Up; I paid for them both.

CRICKET SEASON

Uncle Basil, the soldier, gave Ossie money as a gift the day before he returned to England. Ossie met him on the parochial road. He came up the slope wearing his felt hat, white shirt and brown tweed trousers, and he stopped to talk with Ossie. He had bright, intelligent eyes which looked at Ossie kindly, but Ossie also noticed a touch of sadness in them; he returned home to a hero's welcome after each promotion, but they said he cried each time he had to leave. Ossie loved his stories and photographs of the places he had visited. He remembered Ossie and stopped and talked with him each time they met.

"Ossie, you are walking like a big-shot," said Uncle Basil, grinning. "Seems you own the place, man."

Ossie laughed.

"What games do you play?" asked Uncle Basil. Each time they met they talked about a different topic. The last time they had talked about school.

"I like cricket," said Ossie.

"Are you a batsman or a bowler?"

"A bowler. A spin bowler."

"A spin bowler, eh. Maybe you will be another Alfred Valentine. We have had lots of talented cricketers in these parts, but so far no one has made it to the national team. But maybe you will."

Uncle Basil reached into his pocket, took out a coin and gave it to Ossie.

"Thank you, Uncle Basil," said Ossie. He was thrilled. Nobody had ever given him so much money before.

"I am leaving tomorrow," said Uncle Basil. "Don't know when I'll be back. You may be a big boy by then." He began walking up the road.

"'Bye, Uncle Basil."

"And when you bowl remember this – keep your eyes on the stumps."

When Ossie got home he saw his father chopping wood in the yard in front of the kitchen. He told him about the money that Uncle Basil had given him. His father stopped chopping the wood and looked at him.

"You should save it," said his father. "I will show you how. Just a minute."

His father went into the house and returned with his saw. "Follow me," he said, as he led the way into the kitchen. He chose a bamboo joint on one of the kitchen posts – choosing one which was in Ossie's reach – and, using his saw, he cut a slit near the top of the joint.

"This is your savings box," he said. "Put in the money."

Ossie slipped the coin into the opening and heard it drop to the bottom of the joint.

"When you have enough saved you cut the bottom of the joint and take out your money. That was how I used to save my money when I was a boy. Now save your money and get rich."

His father returned to the yard to continue chopping wood.

Ossie decided to save up to buy a cricket book. He found ways of increasing his earnings, and his savings grew in the bamboo joint. He collected cocoa beans that fell from the pods eaten by rats, dried them in the sun, and sold them to Miss Enid the shopkeeper. When he saw fit soursops on trees he picked them and asked the higglers to sell them in Kingston. He made yo-yos and gigs and sold them to boys at school. He weeded his aunts' gardens and got paid for his labour.

Then the cricket season came. The West Indies team was playing against England at Sabina Park, and the excitement spread even to the remote villages in the hills. Men gathered at the shops to listen to the commentary on the radio. Each day at the school the headmaster left his desk to play with the boys in the schoolyard; he was a big man who hit powerful fours and sixes, and small boys spent hours searching for the balls that landed in the bushes. A match was planned between a team from Ossie's village and one from another village some miles away. It would be played in the churchyard on a Sunday afternoon.

Small boys did not get to play with the headmaster; neither were they selected for the matches between villages. But they enjoyed the game nevertheless. They made bats from coconut fronds and, using stones as stumps, played the game in the road. The big boys who played well were their heroes; and they argued about their favourites among the test cricketers whom they heard described on the radio.

Ossie began making a cricket ball. First he carved a spheroid from a bamboo root. Then he wrapped it tightly in a piece of cloth: After this he knitted a thick covering over it; the covering was made from string and he used a nail to do the knitting. The knitted patterns made the ball very attractive. The covering of string would give the ball its bounce.

The day of the cricket match arrived.

In the morning, Ossie and his parents went to church. Ossie's father did not go to the church often; on Sundays he liked to sleep late and then relax at home dressed in pants and vest; but his wife sometimes persuaded him to go. On this occasion she said that the church would be welcoming a new minister, and a large turnout would make a good impression. So he put on his navy-blue suit and accompanied them to church.

When they returned home they changed into their Sunday-evening clothes. Ossie sat in the sitting-room and skimmed through a religious picture-book while he waited for dinner to be served. His mother passed through the sitting-room on her way to the kitchen. A few moments later he heard her cry out in the kitchen. "Tief! Tief!" she cried. Ossie rushed to the kitchen.

"The dinner is gone!" his mother exclaimed. "The pot with the curried chicken and the pot with the rice. Both gone!"

Ossie turned to look inside the bamboo joint which contained his money. The thief had chopped an opening at the bottom of the joint. Ossie stuck a finger in and found it empty.

"My money is gone!" he wailed. "All the money I saved!"

His father came into the kitchen and they told him what had happened.

"They watched us," he said. "They knew I wasn't here. And it is somebody who has been here before, somebody who had the time to notice Ossie's savings box."

Ossie thought of the faceless persons who had caused this distress. They were people who struck when you were not there to defend yourself. Perhaps they were people he knew, who had other faces – ones of evil that he had never seen.

"Perhaps they are hungrier than we are," said his mother charitably.

"The food is bad enough," said his father, "but to steal from a child!"

"Uncle Basil would be very sorry to hear they stole the money he gave me," said Ossie.

"But he would want you to continue saving," said his mother.

They had sardines, bread and tomatoes for their dinner.

After eating, Ossie got his ball and set off for the churchyard to watch the match. If the match ended early he would probably be able to play with his friends. He was hoping that the big boys would not capture the pitch after the game.

The team from Ossie's village won the match after a close and exciting contest. The hero of the team was Vincent, a slim sixteen-year-old with straight hair. Vincent was the son of a prosperous truck operator. It was well-known that Vincent did poorly at school. But put a bat in his hand and he was transformed: he became expressive, confident and masterful. He said things with his bat that he could not put into words. Today he gave one of his best performances and led his team to victory.

After the match, men and boys followed Vincent and other members of the team to the stonewall. Ossie was so thrilled by Vincent's performance that he forgot about playing and followed Vincent and his admirers. They sat on the wall and discussed the match. In the heat of the discussion, some of Vincent's admirers, on remembering one or other feature of his performance, went up to him and shook his hand. Ossie sat on the base of the wall and listened while fiddling with his cricket ball.

Vincent was so elated with his performance he wanted to continue playing. He took the stumps from Reggie, the manager of the team, and set them up in the road. Then he took a ten-dollar bill from his wallet and held it up in the air.

"Any man who bowl me get this money," he said.

"Give me the money to hold," said Reggie, a fat young man in a colourful shirt and blue pants.

Vincent gave Reggie the money.

Boys rushed forward to take their turns bowling to Vincent. But he was too good for them. He played virtually every stroke in the book. He talked to the bowlers while he batted, and he hit each ball with scorn and contempt.

"Nobody can bowl him," said Reggie. "He is seeing that ball as big as a breadfruit."

But the bowlers persisted. It would soon be dark. They wanted to get him before bad light stopped play.

Ossie went out to bowl. There was loud laughter from some of the men and boys. But a few of them cheered him on. Vincent grinned when he saw Ossie.

"Don't laugh!" shouted Phonso. "Ossie is a good bowler."

Ossie faced Vincent. He remembered Uncle Basil's words: "Keep your eyes on the stumps." He studied Vincent for a few moments thinking about some of his characteristic movements. Then he ran up and, aiming at the stumps, bowled. Vincent shouted "No!" as he played the ball back to Ossie. Ossie bowled again, getting the ball to spin more this time and it beat Vincent and hit the middle stump.

"Clean bowled!" the shout went up from the wall.

"Lucky ball!" cried one of the big boys.

"Lucky ball nothing," said Reggie. "He was bowled fair and square."

"He said any 'man' who could bowl him," said another boy, "he didn't say any 'boy'?"

Reggie laughed. "Come take your money, Ossie," he said. Grinning happily, Ossie took the money and pocketed it.

"Good ball, Ossie!" shouted Vincent as he went by.

The session was now over and the men and boys left for their homes.

Ossie's parents were having supper when he rushed into the house; he joined them and shared the news of his good fortune.

His father laughed. "You made a fast comeback. You are earning money from cricket and you are not a test player yet."

"Isn't that more than you lost today?" asked his mother.

"Yes."

"Imagine that, eh?"

"Are you still going to save it?" asked his father.

"Yes. I may never know who stole my money. Let them take it. But I am not putting this in a bamboo joint."

"Bamboo joints are not as safe as when I was a boy," said his father.

"I heard Teacher talking about a Post Office Bank," said Ossie. "I am going to find out more about it."

"It is now you are going to want to buy that cricket book," said his mother.

Ossie grinned. "I am going to study bowling. It has been good to me."

MARK McWATT

A BOY'S FIRST TEST MATCH

On a Friday morning in the middle of March, 1958, I awoke with an inexplicable feeling of excitement – until I remembered why – it was a holiday from school and I was going fishing with two of my classmates. They were going to pass for me at seven-thirty and we would ride our bikes to the Fort Groyne in Kingston and try to catch pakoo off the rocks there. My hooks and lines were ready (for pakoo you don't need rods). As I remembered all this I leapt out of bed and hurriedly bathed and gobbled down breakfast; I put on my "play" clothes, grabbed my bags of fishing tackle, shouted "Gran, I gone!", and was halfway down the stairs when I was stopped by a loud shout:

"Young man, you stop right there!" and I turned to see my grandmother frowning fiercely at the top of the stairs.

At that time I was ten years old and lived with my grandparents on the top floor of the big house in Kitty. An uncle also lived there with us, my father's youngest brother, who had finished school a few years ago and was working with a shipping firm in Georgetown. My own parents and younger brothers lived in the North-West, where my father was district commissioner. I'd been sent to live in town the year before, to attend a "proper" school and prepare for the scholarship exam that would determine which high school I would attend. It was at first a strange and lonely life, as I missed my family and especially the hills and forests and rivers of the North-West. But I made several friends at my Georgetown school, and we found lots to do in our spare time, in the huge yard around the big house, and all over the city and the nearby sea-walls and east-coast road – so much so that my grandmother began to complain to anyone who would listen that I was becoming too "wild", never at home and rushing through chores and homework in order to go "gallivanting with that bunch of ruffians he calls his friends".

And this was the lady who now stood at the top of the stairs, a shocked and offended look on her face:

"Just where do you think you're going, Mister?"

"Gran, Desi and Cleevie coming for me just now, we going fishing on the Fort Groyne and – "

"And what about school, may I ask? It's Friday, you know, not Saturday."

"Oh, Gran, I must have forgot to tell you, we got a holiday today; you don't think I would skip school just so – "

"I don't know what to think these days, with you getting on so wild with these friends of yours – and how come I haven't heard about this holiday? Look, your uncle is already dressed for work…" And there was my Uncle Gordon, a huge smile on his face, adjusting his tie as he stood behind her and savoured my discomfort.

"Oh Gran, is a holiday for true – you can ask anybody. Is a holiday for cricket: West Indies playing Pakistan at Bourda, and the schools in Georgetown got a holiday today," I said triumphantly, half-turning to resume my flight down the stairs.

"You hold it right there," Gran said, and then she turned to my uncle: "Gordon, you know anything about a holiday for cricket?"

"Well," he said, "it's the second day of the test against Pakistan and the schools do often get a holiday on the Friday of a test."

"Huh!" my grandmother said, clearly disappointed.

"So can I go now?" I asked quickly, trying to seize the moment of her uncertainty – but I did so with a sinking feeling, knowing that it's not going to be that easy… she was dead set on thwarting me this time.

"Not so fast, my boy, you come up here and talk to me properly. I'm not sure I like your attitude… nor the idea of you going fishing all morning with those friends of yours; besides, the school didn't give you a holiday for that."

"What?" By now I'm back up in the living room standing beside her.

"Tell me again what the holiday is for."

"I told you Gran, is for the cricket."

"So how come you're going fishing?"

"Oh Gran, those who interested in cricket can go, especially the older boys and the teachers, but all of us don't *have* to go – it's still a holiday though, and me and my friends made all these plans to go fishing."

"Well, you can forget about that: you're not going fishing. The holiday is for cricket, you try and find yourself at the cricket. They give you the holiday so that you can go and learn more about the game – "

"But Gran, I already know about cricket, I like to play it with my friends. Up to yesterday I was playing cricket with my friends in the schoolyard before the bell ring; but I don't like to sit down all day and watch it, that's not my idea of fun…"

"And who says that everything in life has to be fun, young man?"

"Oh Gran – "

"Don't give me that look and that tone of voice; that's rude! You're going to cricket. To besides, think of your family name; do you know that Clifford, your father's cousin, used to keep wicket for the West Indies?"

"Yes, I know all that, Gran, but you have to pay nuff money to get in to watch the game, and I don't even know what gate – "

At this point Uncle Gordon put his mouth in the story: "Mother, why don't you call W— ? He's bound to be going, he's a member of the board, after all. Ask him about the holiday for schools and where in the grounds the schoolboys should go."

My grandmother welcomed this suggestion and immediately picked up the phone. I knew my fate was sealed, so I put away the bag with the hooks and lines and sat looking miserable, waiting, like a convicted prisoner, to hear the details of my sentence.

"Well, that's settled," Gran said, putting down the phone, "Mr W— says he will be happy to pass for you at half-past nine and take you to the ground… Now go and change out of those rags and put on something decent. Did you bathe?… Properly?… Washed behind your ears?"

And that was it. As I was in my room, sulking and slowly changing my clothes, I heard her shooing away poor Cleevie and Desi and telling them they should be going to cricket, instead of courting death by drowning in the muddy Demerara. A smile came over my face when I pictured their expressions as they quickly backed away and bolted down the stairs. By the time I slid into the front seat of the Morris Oxford, next to Mr W—, whom I vaguely remember as one of my grandparents' acquaintances whom I'd seen from time to time in the house, I was not just resigned to a day at cricket, but was even somewhat looking forward to it: I'd been given a whole dollar to buy something to eat and drink, and then my grandfather, who spent all his time in bed since he'd suffered a stroke over a year ago, took pity on me and talked to me about the excitement of cricket and made the idea of sitting in the stands and watching the game seem almost interesting. On top of that, he made me go to the bookshelf and take down the big leather case with his binoculars.

"Take these with you, boy," he said, his hand on my upper arm; "remember when I showed you how to use them?"

"I remember," I said, brightening, "that time we were looking through the binoculars at the house at the corner, and we saw Miss Herbert making black pudding in her kitchen with all her bubbies showing, and you said – "

"Yes, yes," he said firmly, but in a lowered voice, looking quickly around the room, "but that's not what the binoculars are for – they are really for cricket: you take them with you and watch carefully the bowler's action as he delivers the ball and the batsman as he plays his shot, you will learn a lot about the game."

My grandmother didn't want me to take the binoculars because she said I was too careless and would either get them broken or else leave them somewhere and lose them, but I was most indignant, and my grandad said: "Oh, let him take them, nuh, all they do lately is sit on the shelf and gather dust."

So there I was, sitting in the front seat next to Mr W— with the leather strap of the binoculars case around my neck, a blue cap on my head and four 25-cent coins in my pocket: this might turn out even better than fishing for pakoo with Desi and Cleevie.

As we got close to Bourda Mr W— said: "So you want to go into the school-boy stand?"

"I don't mind," I said, "is it a good place to see the game?"

"Well actually," he replied, "you'd be better off in the North Stand, in terms of watching and learning the game, because there you will be behind the bowler's arm and – "

"OK," I said, not wanting him to get into too many details that I might not understand, "the North Stand sounds good." And after he'd parked the car in a spot reserved for him, he reached into the back seat and retrieved a bright red cushion: "Here, you'll need this in the North Stand; it's just the hard wood of the stand itself you'll be sitting on."

As we walked around to the entrance to the North Stand we passed the schoolboys' stand and I was not sorry that I wasn't going to be there: all the "schoolboys" looked rough and much older than me. Mr W— walked me past the man at the gate of the North Stand, telling him something I did not hear. The stand was like a flight of broad wooden stairs going up from the front to the back and he pointed out a spot about halfway up, in front of a group of mostly men, just two or three women, and no children. He said that would be a good place to sit, right behind the bowler's arm. I put down the red cushion and sat on it; the people around nodded at Mr W— as he retraced his steps to the gate. I suddenly felt privileged to have been taken there by Mr W— and smiled at the nearby spectators and waved at the retreating form of my escort and benefactor.

It was still some time before the day's play would begin, so I looked around and soon discovered a nest of food vendors near the gate. Before the first ball was bowled I'd devoured a bag of hot, peppery boiled channa, two paper cones of fried channa, two frozen custard blocks and a large potato ball with sour sauce. When the Pakistan fielders came out, followed by the West Indian batsmen, it was like an unwelcome distraction from my feast of snacks. I would look at a few balls, make a show of looking through the binoculars, then pop up and go and buy a peppermint stick or some other snack or sweetmeat. I had begun to notice that every time I got up in my seat an elderly, balding man behind me would suck his teeth and grumble. When he'd had enough of my jumping up and blocking his view of the pitch, he shouted:

"Hey you! Yes you, little boy... why can't you sit still and watch the game? You got ants in your pants?"

And the man to his right said: "You father is a glass-maker? You think you transparent or what? At least wait till the over done before you jump up in front of people and block their view!"

I mumbled "Sorry" and sunk back onto my red cushion to watch the last two balls of the over. When Garfield Sobers hit the last ball of that over for the first four of the day, the stand applauded noisily and I took the opportunity to run down to the vendors and buy four sweets, so I wouldn't have to get up again too soon. When I returned to my seat the first man who had shouted at me said: "You, little boy, come here."

"What?" I said as I walked up the two steps and stood in front of him.

"Sit down here," he said, moving over a little so there was a space next to him. I stepped over a large basket filled with a flask and other stuff and sat down next to him where he had indicated.

"What is your name?" he asked.

"Why you want to know?" I said with an edge of defiance in my voice.

"Everybody see when Mr W——, big member of the Cricket Board and a fine gentleman, bring you in here and put you to sit down and we thought you was a youngster interested in the game, but all you doing is jumping up every few minutes to buy sweetie and channa and food that ain't good for you... What's your name?"

"Mark."

"Mark what?"

"Mark McWatt."

"McWatt? – any relation to the wicket keeper?"

"I think he's my father's cousin..."

"Well," he said, "with a name like that and a relative who used to play cricket for the West Indies, I'm disappointed that you're not more interested in the game."

"And more considerate of your fellow spectators," added the other man on my right.

I began to feel ashamed. "Sorry. But I didn't really want to come," I said apologetically, "Is my grandmother who said I have to come and learn more about the game."

"She's quite right," the old man said. "You're at the age when you should be showing interest in important things, like school work and cricket. Is no accident that the schools get a holiday for cricket, you know; you could learn a lot about many things by watching cricket."

I look at him sheepishly. "And what is *your* name?" I ask. But before he could reply the man on my right says:

"Uncle. Everybody does call him Uncle, so you can call him Uncle too."

"Uncle what?" I asked.

"Don't bother with that," the old man himself said, "I'm Mr Armstrong, but just call me Uncle – like he says." And he nodded at the man on my right.

I looked from one to the other: "OK Uncle," I said, "but why I must sit down up here?"

"So you can learn something about the game, like your grandmother says, and so that we can keep an eye on you."

So I ran down and retrieved my red cushion and placed it between the two men. At this point the water-cart left the field and play resumed, so we all sat and watched.

"You know who batting, boy?" Uncle asked.

"The West Indies."

"Of course the West Indies! I mean which batsmen?"

"Garfield Sobers."

"Very good... And who's at the other end?"

"Ahmm... I can't remember – oh yes, Clyde Walcott, because Conrad Hunte get out."

"Hmm, I'm surprised that you were following the game enough to know as much as that." He looked at me and frowned. "Are you bright at school?" he asked.

I shrugged. "So they say, but they put on my report that I could do better if I wasn't so careless."

"That I can well believe," the man on my right said with a chuckle.

Over the next several overs they talked constantly to me: about what Fazal Mahmood was bowling, the strategies of the batsmen, the field-placings for the different batsmen – even the differences between umpires Kippings and Gilette. I found it very illuminating listening to them, I had no idea that so much was involved in the game of cricket, nor that there were people who knew so much about it and who took it so seriously.

When Sobers began to score fluently Uncle said to me: "Take those binoculars of yours and look at Sobers as he waits for the ball: look at his feet."

"But why Sobers?" I asked. "Walcott got more runs than him."

"Sobers' technique is better, you will learn more from looking at him."

So I looked at Sobers' feet and he hit another four. "But I can't see where he hit the ball when I'm looking at his feet through the binoculars," I complained.

"Don't bother with that, that's not important, just see how his footwork prepares him to hit the ball where he wants. Some batsmen just stand in one spot and swing the bat – "

"That's what I do when I play," I said.

"Well," Uncle said, "you'll never be a good batsman that way. Sobers' secret is in his footwork. Look again and tell me what you see."

After a couple more balls I said, "I think I see what you mean."

"Good. What?"

"Sobers got... what you call that thing again?... Parrot toe... yes, his toes turn inward, he got Parrot toe!"

And the whole group around us exploded in laughter.

"Yes, yes," Uncle said, "he has parrot toes, but that's not what I'm talking about – that's got nothing to do with his technique – "

I know," I said with a huge grin. "You mean the way he moves either forward or back after the bowler let go the ball."

"That's correct, you little joker," he said. "Sobers moves his feet so that he gets to the pitch of the ball and can therefore hit it where he wants with less risk."

And I spent the next several overs looking at Sobers' feet.

As the players went off for lunch Uncle said to me: "Boy, you ent bring nothing for lunch? What you going to eat?"

"I'm going to buy a phuri and a potato ball with nuff sour…"

"That ent no proper lunch, boy, come have some lunch with us."

And one of the women who had been sitting in the back came forward and opened the big basket; she took out a large pot wrapped in newspaper and kitchen towels, and a large spoon. When the pot was uncovered there was a familiar and most delicious smell.

"You like metagee, boy?"

"It OK," I said, my mouth watering.

"OK!, what you mean OK? This is proper BG food, boy," Uncle said, as the woman dished it into enamel plates and handed them around. "Mavis, dish out some for this lil boy, let him taste some good creole food… and pour him a glass of cold mauby."

And I got a plate with eddoes, cassava, plantain, yam, pig tail, salt fish and dumplings and nuff gravy. It was the most delicious metagee I ever ate.

"I never eat metagee like this before," I said. "It really really good – especially the dumplings and the sauce."

"Much better than phuri and potato ball, eh?" Uncle said, and a strange-looking man in a pink Panama hat sitting off to the side near the back of the stand looked at me and laughed loudly.

"Just ignore him," Uncle said, as he saw the question in my face.

The play after lunch was thoroughly enjoyable: the West Indies batsmen dominated and both Sobers and Walcott made centuries. And apart from the cricket, now seen by me through different eyes, the comments and the enthusiasm of the crowd in the stand were wonderful to hear and witness and I felt privileged to be part of it. Towards the end of the tea break, the man in the pink Panama hat shouted down to me:

"Hey, youngster, come and sit up here with me, I want to take a look through those binoculars."

"And we all know what you will be looking at through them," somebody just behind me said, " – and it won't be the cricket!" At which the whole stand erupted in derisive laughter.

"Don't bother with him, boy," Uncle said to me quietly, and the man on my right said: "If you go up there, boy, he will teach you more than cricket!"

I smiled knowingly, though I didn't have a clue at the time what they were talking about.

"Don't let Uncle keep you to himself all the time, my friend," pink Panama hat persisted; "come up here and talk to me."

At this Uncle turned around and gave him a fierce look: "You just behave yourself Rosie," Uncle said, "before I have to come up there and teach you a lesson."

And I watched as the man laughed, but seemed to shrink in his seat and turn away.

"Rosie?" I said, "but that's a girl's name…"

"Correct," said the man on my right, " – and everybody could see he's a frigging anti-man."

I still was not too sure what this was all about, but I firmly decided to keep as far from "Rosie" as possible, while at the same time enjoying the idea that I was learning all kinds of new and different – and perhaps even frightening – things while watching the West Indies play cricket at Bourda…

By the end of play I decided I'd had a wonderful day at cricket – and I repeated as much to Gran when I got home. She beamed with satisfaction and said: "You see… and if it were not for your old fogey of a grandmother, you would have missed it all and spent the day dabbling in the river mud with those useless friends of yours…"

Next morning I was "soaking" in bed around seven-thirty, thinking about the day before, when Gran called: "Mark, look, your friends are here for you again… Don't tell me you all made plans to go fishing again."

I missed a heartbeat, but leapt out of bed, scrambled into old clothes and rushed to the door, aware that my grandmother was near the kitchen door, watching me.

"Hi," I said to Cleevie and Desi.

"Boy Marko," Cleevie said, "we had nuff bites yesterday and a big one actually came up out of the water before he fall off the hook and get away… I tell you we bound to ketch one today."

"Sorry," I said, "I can't go fishing this morning."

"Don't tell me you going back to cricket again!"

"Uh-huh – Mr W— coming to pick me up at nine-thirty, and some friends are looking out for me in the North Stand. The cricket really interesting, you know, I wish you all could come, we would have a great time."

"Nah," Desi said, "it's Saturday… me and Cleevie can't spend our good weekend time watching boring cricket."

"It not boring at all, I tell you. Yesterday was great, and I learnt a lot about all sorts of things…" and I could feel my grandmother's smile warm my back as I watched my two classmates descend the stairs and hop on their bikes.

That was my first experience of test cricket, and I suppose I was fortunate: I saw both Sobers and Walcott make centuries and West Indies win the match. From that time on I've been an avid cricket follower and fan of the West Indies team – was overjoyed when Worrell became captain and we tied that historic test in Australia, ecstatic at the early World Cup victories and I luxuriated in the West Indies' years of complete dominance of the game under Lloyd and Richards and others. Like everyone of my generation I was bewildered by the team's sudden fall from grace and felt gloomier as they sank deeper into the abyss of defeat and non-performance, even as the game changed to include more one-day matches and T-20 tournaments, and as the players collect unprecedented salaries and awards... But I remain a fan and will always be a fan – in memory of that first test match I watched at Bourda as an impressionable ten-year-old, in the company of people I did not know who troubled to take an interest in me and teach me to love the game.

EXTRACT FROM A MORNING AT THE OFFICE

...Mr. Lopez' friends were of little use to him in his career as a cricketer, for in cricket – and all cricket in the British West Indies is non-professional – race and class play no part. Cricket is taken too solemnly. In the newspapers a forth-coming series of matches against the M.C.C. is given the prominence of a royal wedding or the invasion of one European country by another; it is an event discussed and speculated upon months in advance; every detail relating to it is big news. Intercolonial test matches – hardly less momentous – rank as front page news, and during the two weeks of the Tests every radio set in the islands opposed on the field blares out a running commentary of the game. Business offices and stores close half-day to permit their employees to attend the matches.

The name Raffy Lopez was known throughout the British West Indies; it was synonymous with "century"; if Raffy Lopez failed to score a century in any innings he was considered to be off colour – and he was rarely off colour.

Under these circumstances, there could be no race and class prejudice in cricket; a superb batsman was a superb batsman, a first-class spin-bowler was a first-class spin-bowler; no one stopped to ask what was his shade of com-plexion or his position in society; his performance was enough. Was he capa-ble of wiping up the Barbados bowling? Was he capable of mowing down the Barbados wickets? The hero who could answer these questions in the affirma-tive received recognition and its concomitant privileges without stint or re-serve...

COOKMAN

Ask any local cricketer from Leonora to Blairmont Estate who is this chap call Pandit, he would watch you straight in you face as if you stupid, click he tongue like turkey, inhale one draught fresh air, and sigh as if you miss something precious.

"Ha boy! Pandit! Eh-eh, he is a specialist in cooking mutton curry," he would say, smacking he tongue as if the mutton curry in front he eye... Anytime ahwe cricket team going to play against Lusignan team, by hooks or crooks, I bound to get in the team. Know why? Is Pandit self cooking the mutton curry and dalpurri for the two cricket team. He is Lusignan cricket team master cookman, you hear? Boy, is a love to eat Pandit mutton curry while them two team retire fo lunch. Eh-eh, is like you get new life in you body. You could bowl more longer than Wesley Hall in the hot hot sun.

Pandit rep gone so far that even them sport-loving whiteman and white woman from Georgetown city who does attend presentation in Lusignan Community Centre does be carried-away like a child seeing Father Christmas the moment Pandit curry drop in they mouth. If they ain't careful they could bite off they tongue. Them whiteman does sigh yeh yeh, the mutton curry gravy running down they lip, eye red and watery, the taste biting they tongue.

Eh-eh, they eating mutton curry as if is the last time they seeing it. Some filling they stomach until they can't move, lost to know how mutton curry could be prepared in such a mouthwatering manner. The garlic and geerah still on they tongue. Is like reading good poetry one whiteman say.

"Them Indian hand set to prepare mutton curry," Mr. Douglas tell them chaps one Sunday afternoon in Lusignan Centre. This time he come pissing drunk after he stuff down bowl after bowl, using he finger like fork. Then he lick them fingers as if them fingers is mutton self, sucking them chu chu...

With all due respect, them chaps had to lift-off Mr. Douglas from his chair that afternoon. All the while he belching, belching, then he let-go a fart that smell pure mutton curry. But you dare not laugh. Mr. Douglas is a big thing in Bookers. Was in the 1960s time when Bookers own most of the sugar plantations in Guyana. One bad word from he mouth and Lusignan cricket team come in shambles. A good word from he, and any member in the cricket team could get an office job. You only have to know to spell you name and add two and two...

In truth is Pandit mutton curry does take Mr. Douglas to Lusignan Community Centre whenever the cricket team invite another team to play cricket.

Them chaps say Mr. Douglas navel string left in the Centre – in the kitchen – where Pandit does cook the mutton.

"Never know a whiteman who like mutton curry like Mr. Douglas," them chaps does say. "If all whiteman been stay like Mr. Douglas ahwe Indian people coulda be far in dis country."

One Sunday evening, Lusignan cricket team was celebrating victory. They wash Enmore team for a song. Two to one. Them chaps say Enmore cricketers stuff so much mutton curry during the luncheon interval that they couldn't able to bowl when they land in the ground. The Lusignan star batsmen Hakim and Solo hitting the ball blam bladam. Is sheer four and six. Them chaps say if B.L. Crombie was present he woulda turn commentator.

And if you see sluggish fielding! Eh-eh, them Enmore players claim the ball was too quick for they grasp. They been moving as if egg stick between they leg. They say Lusignan team get them drunk on the mutton curry. They only belching and farting in the field, and they coulda empty-down mugs of ice-water. And the joke is, Enmore is a strong team.

Them Lusignan spectators really taunt them bitch. "Stuff more mutton curry. Stuff more..."

While celebrating this victory, Mr. Douglas, the curry gravy dripping down he lip blop blop, shout, "Where is the cookman?" just like how Estate manager custom to bark at you.

Meantime the Lusignan cricketers serenading in the Centre hall, drinking and smoking, laughing he he he. And cricket history flying out they head. Eh-eh, is Hall and Griffith, Sobers and Kanhai, Godfrey Evans and Wally Grout! Kensington Oval, Lords, Bourda Green... Is like the whole *Wisden* in them cricketers' head. But centre caretaker, who sent to find him, can't see Pandit there.

Caretaker heart in he hand. Can't afford to vex Mr. Douglas who look ready to fall down. Where this blasted man Pandit, the caretaker say, checking the Centre kitchen, the film store and the storeroom. Can't vex Mr. Douglas...

"Is where de hell you been?" the caretaker ask when at last he spot Pandit, standing outside the hall smoking and watching the empty ground.

"Is what you mean?" Pandit ask. "Mean to tell me the mutton curry done?"

"The big man self, Mr. Douglas, want to see you," the caretaker talk. "And is important."

Sametime Pandit feel a chillyness run thru he spine, he heart beating bap bap... Mr. Douglas! That big man! But is an order. Pandit had to go. He out the cigarette quick time and follow the caretaker, thinking how to answer the big man soon as he start to talk to him in backraman English. Them words so crisp and cutting, you would believe is Dutch. And the big man self want see me.

Soon as Pandit glimpse the big man in the Centre bar corridor he start tremble.

"This is de cookman, baas," the caretaker point at Pandit. Then he hurry to refill Mr. Douglas glass.

Mr. Douglas eye red and the words gurgling in he mouth, "Take a seat, man," he order Pandit.

Quick time Pandit find a chair, still trembling. This time the cricketers and a handful of fans still drinking and gaffing, guffawing like pigs. Some seated in chairs; others with full glass in they hand saunter about the centre, the scent of brown rum and mutton curry rolling about like rainclouds.

"Tell me the secret of your cooking. Why your mutton curry is so tasty?" Mr. Douglas ask, smacking he tongue, eyes flitting drunkenly. Mutton curry still settle on he lip.

"Me, me na know, baas," Pandit say uneasily, the words choke in he throat. He could never make head-an-tail of this backraman language, never mind he working in Lusignan Estate donkey years now...

"But how you don't know, man?" Mr. Douglas question impatiently, eyeing at Pandit.

Pandit feel Mr. Douglas eye want bore he inside. O God! This is a big man and me can't displease he. But is what me going tell he? Is how me does do the mutton piece by piece til it done cook, eh? But me have to tell Mr. Douglas something. Then in a flash Pandit recall he baap...

"Never fraid white people na matter you can't spell you name. Always get commonsense in you head. They would respect you fo that..." he baap, a darkskin Madrassi man always drum them word in Pandit ears.

[...]

The only virtue Pandit possess is he commonsense. He always keep he head cool like cucumber. But when Mr. Douglas question he, he make sure he watch Mr. Douglas lip before he answer. "Once you put correct geera and garlic and salt in curry, then you stir, then you taste, you bound to get correct taste," Pandit clear he throat and say. He want disappear.

Mr. Douglas shake he head, drain he glass of rum and declare: "I will get you a job as a chef in a hotel. Think about it and let me know."

"Yes baas," Pandit reply and vanish out of the Centre.

Hotel chef! Ever see such eye-pass? Pandit think next evening. Me going make meself one jackass when them big tourist and big-shot clap they hand and order in backraman English to bring this dish and that dish. Eh-eh! He was in his front verandah, regaling. He just bathe he skin after arriving from the canefields.

Me damn happy, Pandit remind himself. As a bull-boy in the backdam the job paying well. Is a lot of overtime specially when loaded canepunt stuck in the canals and them bull and mule had to take rest three-four times before they pull in them punts at the Sugar Factory.

Beside, Pandit get he own house, built with a loan from the Estate. He wife still working as a weeder. He four children look healthy. Is what the ass me want with hotel job. Me getting all the satisfaction cooking mutton curry for them cricketer. That is me happiness…

[…]

Come a time in the country now when local politics was swinging people head left to right like soldier marching. Some people coulda give up they life for the PPP, the PNC or the UF party. Who couldn't read and write get sense overnight. Eh-eh, is Colonialism, Capitalism, Communism… words rolling out they mouth like poetry. How England is a bitch. Take out all the country wealth. How it doesn't want to grant the country independence…

"Them English people think we still ah slave?" them people does talk in the streets sucking they teeth schuu schuu… "And Duncan Sandys tekkin all order from America. Dis kiss-me-ass eyepass!"

"Know how much CIA in this country? Why the hell they na leave ahwe in peace?" them young boys does talk. They coulda kill they self for the PPP.

True to God, politics make people come wise overnight. The atmosphere tense. It does want to explode like a cannon whenever them politician done address people in the country areas and in Bourda Green.

"Independence. Independence. Why the hell the Queen don't give the country independence?"

Then bladam, like bullet, one proclamation come from the Queen that the country would be granted its independence soon after the general election in 1964. And which political party commands a majority of the voters, the leader of the same party would be Prime Minister, and usher the country in independence.

Eh-eh, you would believe is Carnival break out in the streets. Jubilation in the air. And everybody calling each other Comrade. Was 1962 before the big race riots.

"When you too hasty to get something which you don't know about, you does land in hot-water," Pandit tell them boys one midmorning by the streetcorner. Them workers had a go-slow exercise. One driver been curse one canecutter. Soon as the canecutter talk for he right, the driver tell the overseer to suspend he from work.

"This independence thing na look too nice," Pandit say. "Jagan and Burnham should use more commonsense. Boy! When you playing with fire you bound to get burn. Is what really happen with Jagan and Burnham. They swell-headed. To run country is not plaything."

You see it had a set of younger people, among them is the local cricketers, who like the British rule, who want to keep they British passport. But soon as the country come independent you come Guyanese overnight. You getting Guyanese passport. When the set of young people hear that, them fart same time. Think is joke! Who want Guyanese passport?

212

Then the big emigration thing start. Them young people, sportsman and teachers, forsaking the country for England. Who want Guyanese passport? Even them who can't read and write like Baij, Soony and Speedy, hustling to get British passport to exit the bloody country. Was like a fever gripping the country. Is pure England, England in they head…

This time them politician want cut each other throat. Say how Jagan going to sell the country to the Russians. How Burnham taking ahwe back to Africa, D'Aguiar to America and is confusion and commotion among them country people. Worse yet when them men drink bush rum. Is only Burnham and Jagan in they mouth.

"People getting damn stoopid nowadays," Pandit does talk, sad to see that them good cricketers too going away to England. "England running this country so nice. Independence going make it worse, mark me word…"

True! He would miss cooking mutton curry and dalpurri for them cricketers. Schuu schuu schuu… Is so nice he feel while them cricketers stuffing the mutton, calling fo Pandit, Pandit, smacking they tongue. Is like he fulfilling a calling. And he love to watch the game.

Suddenly one evening during this time, the Lusignan Cricket team captain and vice-captain arrive at Pandit house. "We taking you to England, Pandit," the captain say. "You would do a hefty business with mutton curry and dalpurri among the West Indians in London…"

London! England! Pandit eye want pop out. Then he mind flash at the language. God! Is there the backraman English born. Chu chu chu! Me just going to make meself a damn fool. Is everybody talking the backraman language in London.

A chill invade Pandit inside. He watch the captain straight in he face and say: "All yuh go first, me going come later." The captain believe.

With the departure of the captain and vice-captain to London the Lusignan cricket team come in shambles. All the best players gone to England. Pandit job as cookman end. Pandit feel empty like one barrel. He couldn't catch he bearings.

Eh-eh, three months later Pandit start play the tassa-drum at wedding-houses. Watching Pandit playing you believe he merge he entire soul in the drum as if he whole body inside the goatskin, eyes closed as though in trance.

When them chaps ask why he playing the tassa-drum now, Pandit clear he throat and say: "When one door close, another door open. This country like that. Always have to find something to pass you spare time. Life is not work, eat and sleep. Is something else. Use you commonsense and living get a purpose."

EXTRACT FROM HENDREE'S CURE

Cricket and Obeah

As he grew up, Hendree had heard the pundits in the coconut-branch tent at the ball field talking knowledgeably about the game. "Glorious cricket; a game of glorious uncertainty". But "uncertainty" could not be associated with Whim. The home team had an answer for that: solid batsmen like Brother Permaul and Raddy Ragnauth, and bowler Johnny Pilloo. More importantly, Whim had an assorted array of see-far practitioners and obeahmen.

The "official" see-far practitioner was Uncle Willie Marshall, father-in-law of Radio – the cow-minder who had hung himself on the *gubby* tree. Marshall seldom went down to the ground himself, but operated from his house up the market dam, and kept his own scorecard while the game progressed. He had a fearsome reputation as he claimed mastery of the sixth and seventh Books of Moses. For many years he exercised a monopoly over the Whim turf.

He was, unofficially, the fourteenth man on the Whim team. The thirteenth would be one of the two umpires, who knew how to bury his hand in his right pants' pocket when the home side was batting, and the game was tight. The hand would remain there every time a visiting bowler appealed, "Umpayaah!" or "How's dat?" for leg-before-wicket.

Marshall would plot the game before it started, and would allocate runs for each side. If the visitors appeared in his crystal ball as formidable, Marshall would recommend "tying" the pitch. That required procedures that would give the bowling and batting strip mystical powers of its own. Like flour rising with yeast, the ground would come alive with the application of ingredients such as dried bird peppers, strands of horse's mane and dog's teeth.

On cricket day, Whim would come out in royal glory. All the local Madrasi eminences would be there – including the former superfast bowler, Frederick Peters, his cousin Victrin Peters, and some of Busscutt's many sons – Dasrath, Motilal, Bhirbal, Nandlal and Jailall – all dressed in white in solidarity with their team. They walked, though, not with bat and ball, but with baskets of liquors and cutters – the favourite being *bunjaaled* and *pepper-pot* pork. Naga would be there too, also in whites, with his friend Gunn. In Naga's case, he was reliving his own triumphs as captain of the village's second eleven. His biggest trophy was, of course, his wife Chunoo, given him in marriage by Captain Wailoo.

The women came too. Kaboolay and Seppa would be prancing and dancing around the ground, waving red and yellow *jhandi* flags, and even their own rhumals, to cheer their boys to victory. At this time, the Whim players were mostly Christian boys from the Sukhu and Ragnauth families. Kaboolay was the mother of the Ragnauth brothers – Bennett, Elick, Harry, Baker, John and young Raddy, the last being the most adored, stylish and accomplished of Whim players.

They never lost any of the big matches. That was mostly due to the ingenuity of the lanky Johnny Pilloo, who invented a style of bowling known locally as "snake break". This was a kind of leg break that would spin in behind the batsman's boots, and hit the wicket. When he bowled, the stand would roar, "Bite he, Johnny; bite he".

Consistent batting from Raddy and Harry Ragnauth, Hector Sukhu and Brother Permaul made the side invincible. When he was on song, Gopalasammy's boy, Brother Permaul, was devastating. Once he hoisted Sugarboy, who played for the West Indies Test side, for four or five sixes, hit consecutively high out of the ground. It was from this feat that Brother Permaul became celebrated for "mekking ball turn to banga-seed".

In this effect, folks said that Brother Permaul was the exact opposite of his father, Gopalasammy. Born in South India, he had an extravagant memory of his original homeland that made every small thing look real big.

"In Hindia, mey," Gopalasammy boasted, "vee gattam vell. When am ring 'veeling vladang; veeling, vladang', de whole cuntry frigging." He couldn't say "frighten", which made the story of the village bell sound obscene every time he mentioned it. In deeds as well as words, Gopalasammy was larger than life. When, for instance, young Baby (whom he lived with after his wife died) delivered twins and she was crying incessantly over that, Gopalasammy soothed her, "Oow Vevee gal: wha cry cry so? Dat time me eatam hot vepper, an' mekam twin!" Long after Gopalasammy's passing, the hot pepper remained in Permaul's blood, and had made him one of the most belligerent batsmen on the Whim field.

But if the Whim players were not daunting enough, visiting teams had to face Willie Marshall's arsenal of tricks and the public spectacle of Kaboolay's and Seppa's support for the home team. A visiting fast bowler could find his feet trapped by long horse hair – strong like twine; a batsman tapping the pitch or doing some gardening in the middle might come across a bird pepper or a dog's tooth. These were not good omens.

V.S. NAIPAUL

EXTRACT FROM "HAT", FROM MIGUEL STREET

Hat loved to make a mystery of the smallest things. His relationship to Boyee and Errol, for instance. He told strangers they were illegitimate children of his. Sometimes he said he wasn't sure whether they were his at all, and he would spin a fantastic story about some woman both he and Edward lived with at the same time. Sometimes again, he would make out that they were his sons by an early marriage, and you felt you could cry when you heard Hat tell how the boys' mother had gathered them around her death-bed and made them promise to be good.

It took me some time to find out that Boyee and Errol were really Hat's nephews. Their mother, who lived up in the bush near Sangre Grande, died soon after her husband died, and the boys came to live with Hat.

The boys showed Hat little respect. They never called him Uncle, only Hat; and for their part they didn't mind when Hat said they were illegitimate. They were, in fact, willing to support any story Hat told about their birth.

I first got to know Hat when he offered to take me to the cricket at the Oval. I soon found out that he had picked up eleven other boys from four or five streets around, and was taking them as well.

We lined up at the ticket-office and Hat counted us loudly. He said, "One and twelve half."

Many people stopped minding their business and looked up.

The man selling tickets said, "Twelve half?"

Hat looked down at his shoes and said, "Twelve half."

We created a lot of excitement when all thirteen of us, Hat at the head, filed around the ground, looking for a place to sit.

People shouted, "They is all yours, mister?"

Hat smiled, weakly, and made people believe it was so. When we sat down he made a point of counting us loudly again. He said, "I don't want your mother raising hell when I get home, saying one missing."

It was the last day of the last match between Trinidad and Jamaica. Gerry Gomez and Len Harbin were making a great stand for Trinidad, and when Gomez reached his 150 Hat went crazy and danced up and down, shouting, "White people is God, you hear!"

A woman selling soft drinks passed in front of us.

Hat said, "How you selling this thing you have in the glass and them?"

The woman said, "Six cents a glass."

Hat said, "I want the wholesale price. I want thirteen."

The woman said, "These children is all yours?"

Hat said, "What wrong with that?"

The woman sold the drinks at five cents a glass.

When Len Harbin was 89, he was out lbw, and Trinidad declared.

Hat was angry. "Lbw? Lbw? How he lbw? Is only a lot of robbery. And is a Trinidad umpire too. God, even umpires taking bribe now."

Hat taught me many things that afternoon. From the way he pronounced them, I learned about the beauty of cricketers' names, and he gave me all his own excitement at watching a cricket match.

I asked him to explain the scoreboard.

He said, "On the left-hand side they have the names of the batsman who finish batting."

I remember that because I thought it such a nice way of saying that a batsman was out: to say that he had finished batting.

All during the tea interval Hat was as excited as ever. He tried to get all sorts of people to take all sorts of crazy bets. He ran about waving a dollar-note and shouting, "A dollar to a shilling, Headley don't reach double figures." Or, "A dollar, Stollmeyer field the first ball."

The umpires were walking out when one of the boys began crying.

Hat said, "What you crying for?"

The boy cried and mumbled.

Hat said, "But what you crying for?"

A man shouted, "He want a bottle."

Hat turned to the man and said, "Two dollars, five Jamaican wickets fall this afternoon."

The man said, "Is all right by me, if is hurry you is to lose your money."

A third man held the stakes.

The boy was still crying.

Hat said, "But you see how you shaming me in front of all these people? Tell me quick what you want."

The boy only cried. Another boy came up to Hat and whispered in his ear.

Hat said, "Oh, God! How? Just when they coming out."

He made us all stand. He marched us away from the grounds and made us line up against the galvanized-iron paling of the Oval.

He said, "All right, now, pee. Pee quick, all of all-you."

The cricket that afternoon was fantastic. The Jamaican team, which included the great Headley, lost six wickets for thirty-one runs. In the fading light the Trinidad fast bowler, Tyrell Johnson, was unplayable, and his success seemed to increase his speed.

A fat old woman on our left began screaming at Tyrell Johnson, and whenever she stopped screaming she turned to us and said very quietly, "I know Tyrell since he was a boy so high. We use to pitch marble together." Then she turned away and began screaming again.

Hat collected his bet.

CRICKET IN THE BLOOD

The boys from the village met frequently to play cricket on the common in Mr. Hewitt's pimento pasture. Here the grass grew close on the hard clay soil, providing an excellent pitch, and with the warm sunshine beating upon their small black figures, the wind blowing from the sea to ease the heat, and the strong heady scent of spice in the air, the fun of the game was the supreme joy of their lives.

Dan began playing cricket here from as far back as he could remember. In the early days he was forced to be satisfied with a bat cut from the thick end of a dry coconut bough, and with it a round green orange as a ball. Sometimes when the orange split and fell short, if he made a good stroke, or the makeshift bat caused the ball to fall right into the hands of a boy on the field, Dan would emit a strange weird sound, as if his soul were being wrung by the agony of frustration and on one such occasion he actually ran and hid himself in the bushes, so that his fellow playmates would not see the tears which he could not prevent from running down his cheeks.

As time passed and Dan grew older he hewed himself a bat from a piece of wood and by saving the odd pennies which his mother gave him from time to time, to buy something to supplement his lunch, he was eventually able to buy a hard rubber ball from a Chinaman's shop in the village. After this cricket flourished for a while but gradually Dan became still more ambitious and his mind grew filled with the overmastering desire to hold a real bat in his hand, and to play with a real cricket ball. Meeting Mr. Hewitt's son one day when he was home on holidays, Dan spoke to him.

"Mister Johnny, yu don't hab no cricket bat yu isn't using? We is wanting a bat real bad, to play a match 'gainst the team from Knockton village. Please Suh, try fe help we."

Johnny Hewitt thought of the old school bat lying discarded in a cupboard in his home. Maybe his father would permit him to give it to the boys. That was how Dan came to feel his hands grasping the handle of a real bat at last. But what was the use of a bat without a ball? This time he went boldly to the big property house and tackled Mr. Hewitt himself.

"Busha," he began, his bright black eyes shining with eagerness, "I'se beggin yu a job. I can work when school let out. I want fe get the money to buy a cricket ball."

Busha Hewitt, who had always been partial towards a game of cricket himself, agreed to give Dan a few odd jobs about the yard, and eventually he himself selected the cricket ball in Kingston, when he drove to the city on some business.

Thus, at last, the team of youngsters in the village were in possession of a bat and ball and were able to take up the challenge of the lads from Knockton to a cricket match.

On the appointed day the sun shone in its splendour and Dan, as captain of the eleven, felt hopeful of victory, in spite of the fact that Knockton had won the toss and the match would be played in a pasture near to that village. As the afternoon advanced there was no doubt whatever that Dan's team was the better of the two, as Knockton had only one player of consequence, and that one was its captain, Benjy. From time to time play was interrupted by the shouting of the rivals, by free fights amongst those fielding and by the arguments with the umpire, but at length the last man had been bowled and Dan was the victor by a total of fifty-seven runs to Knockton's forty-nine.

As there still remained some time before the short tropical dusk would fall, Dan agreed to Benjy's suggestion that they should bowl at each other for a while, and took his stand before the wicket. His first ball ran along the field and was stopped short of the boundary. His second rose in the air and as he watched it Dan's heart and spirit rose triumphantly with it. In the small object flying in space before his eyes he saw, personified, the dreams and yearnings of his soul for years. No one was tall enough to stop the progress of the ball, so it passed over the boundary line and plunged into the bushes.

Speeding from his position at the wicket Dan pushed his way into the heavy growth, intent on finding his precious ball, while Benjy followed closely behind.

Suddenly Benjy flung himself forward, but not before Dan had spied the object of their search lying among some twigs. He pushed Benjy aside, in an effort to retrieve the ball, but only to find that it had completely disappeared.

"Gi it to me!" he growled at the thickset lad beside him, but Benjy only shook himself free of the bushes and ran out into the open.

"It's fe yu ball. Look fe it yuself," he retorted with vehemence.

"Gimme me ball. Ah seh gimmie me ball – yu TIEF!" Dan shouted.

Instinctively both teams began to separate and to stand together at a reasonable distance behind their respective captains.

"Yu 'ere him? Yu 'ere him?" Benjy called to the air at large. "It's him as bat the ball into the bushes, so it's him fe look fe it."

Dan was standing with his feet slightly apart, his elbows jutting out and his hands pressing against his hips. His eyes were fixed in a piercing glare at Benjy, and his breath came in short sharp pants. Then, as he suddenly made a rush forward, Benjy turned and took to his heels as if the Devil himself were after him. Dan followed in pursuit, pausing only once to stoop down and pick up a round rough stone from the ground.

Benjy's progress was eventually retarded on his reaching a barbed wire fence, which separated adjoining pastures. Dan saw him begin to climb over this obstacle, looking back in an endeavour to gauge the chances of escape. Thus, for a moment, he was almost stationary, and within range of attack.

Standing still, while his fingers gripped the surface of the stone that he was holding, Dan quickly lifted his arm to take aim, but as he did so he became aware of a strange unaccountable feeling of power which was rapidly taking charge of his body. It rose upwards from his foot, spreading until it reached his arms and thence to his fingers. Did it spring from the anguish of his mind? He could not tell, but be that as it may, he knew, without the smallest shadow of a doubt, that if he threw the stone it would speed through the air in obedience to his will; it would smash in the temple of the boy before him and in a fraction of time Benjy would be lying dead upon the ground.

It is said that one can dream at great length in a matter of minutes; that a drowning man can visualise his entire past, so that, perhaps, there are times when in the grip of extreme stress or emotion, one may be able, by some mysterious inner vision, to comprehend the true purpose of one's mind, as in a flash.

Standing there, with his fingers twitching from the sense of power which controlled them, Dan realised that it was *not* his wish to recover his ball by killing Benjy. What, after all, would one ball matter compared to the innumerable ones that he would one day hold? His arm fell limply to his side and waiting inert he watched while Benjy scaled the fence and disappeared into a gully on the other side.

For a moment he stood hesitant, as if unaware of his surroundings, conscious only of the force within him and of an urge to put it to the test, so as to fully justify his action in permitting Benjy to escape. A mango tree grew close at hand and hanging from one of its uppermost limbs was a red ripe mango. He stepped back a couple of paces, swung his arm round and set the stone free in the air. It moved with such velocity that he could not follow its progress, but he saw when the mango fell, as the slender stem which had held it on the branch was hit and severed.

Trembling in every limb Dan retraced his steps and collecting his team returned home to the village. He had lost his ball but in its place there had come to him the knowledge that under stress his aim was faultless, his speed of delivery miraculous, and that only the future could tell to what purpose he would use this power.

He knew now that cricket was in his blood and that he never again would be able to bring himself to play with an orange or rubber ball, so procuring a job in the nearest town he began to hang around the cricket pavilion, begging to be allowed to join in a game whenever the local club was playing.

At length one day his persistence was rewarded when a member of the eleven fell ill on the field. Dan, who was now a tall lanky lad in his teens, was called forward to fill the gap and strode out to take his place with the members looking on good-humouredly.

Before long he was being spoken of as the promising young player of the parish. His never-failing enthusiasm, his inborn sense of sportsmanship and his quiet disposition, won favour with everyone and resulted in an influential member of the cricket club obtaining a position for him in Kingston, so that he would have the opportunity of practising with the best players in the island.

Sometimes when Dan handled a bat, or idly tossed a ball in the air, he would remember the day of the match against Knockton and his mind would relive the experience which had come to him then. During the intervening years he had often heard of Benjy, who was now being spoken of as the outstanding bat in the country, but they had never met in a match. This event was not destined to take place until the captains of the clubs, and members of the cricket board, were engaged in deciding who should be chosen to represent Jamaica in Test matches abroad.

Dan had a favourable batting average but was particularly brilliant as a fast bowler, and fielder, but Benjy could be relied on to pile up the runs, and was now sometimes mentioned as a coming "Headley".

Dan said nothing when he heard that Benjy was being brought to Kingston so that he could practise and be tested along with the best, but he knew that his own possible selection on the team would rest on how he played during the next few weeks.

Sometimes he sat with his long slim body huddled together on a seat in the pavilion and watched Benjy, who had developed into a strong, heavily built young man, stand like a solid wall between the ball and his wicket. The air often rang with the howls of delight from spectators when his runs mounted steadily higher. People began to prophesy that either Dan or Benjy would be included in the final selection, and this was how the situation stood when Dan found himself at Sabina Park one day, as a member of a picked eleven, who were to play a match against a team which included Benjy.

The ground was in excellent condition and the sun, hiding behind an occasional cloud, gave the crowd and players a chance to keep reasonably cool. In the distance the great range of Blue Mountains rose majestically, like a fitting background for the setting of a play. His opponents had won the toss and Dan was selected to open the bowling. As he crossed the field to take up his position his fingers closed spasmodically over the round hard object which he held. A cricket ball! A dream of youth which had crystallised, and now lay safe in his grasp! He stood in his place with his eyes fixed on the ground, then he lifted his head to take aim. There, at the other end of the pitch, stood Benjy holding his bat.

Dan never quite knew what happened. He was only aware of a strange uncontrollable feeling of power mounting within him. A quiver passed over his body and he stepped back a few more paces. Then, as if something apart from himself had taken charge of his movements, he ran forward, swung his arm round and sent the ball on its way.

Almost instantaneously a roar went up from the crowd, and Benjy, with his head bent and his bat swinging at his side, was walking off the field, while the wicketkeeper began collecting the scattered stumps.

Dan continued to bowl and the spectators watched him "mow them down" as they termed it, until at length he walked back to the pavilion, still tingling in every limb of his body.

On the third day of the match Dan was fielding at mid-on when Benjy went in to bat, and it looked to him after a time as if Benjy was deliberately making an effort to keep the ball out of his path. It is not always possible to control one's direction, however, and eventually as he hit out in his strong sure style and began to run Dan saw that the ball was speeding towards him. Like one possessed he sprang forward to meet it, and with movements so quick that they could scarcely be followed he stopped the ball and sent it back with deadly aim to the wicket. The crowd, holding its breath, saw the bails fly in the air before Benjy had had the time to complete the run.

Thunderous applause rent the air and the sun, as if curious to see what was taking place, slipped from behind a cloud and flooded the field with its glory.

In the pavilion members of the cricket board were talking excitedly together.

"He's uncanny," one said.

"He's never played better," another commented.

"This removes all doubt," said a third, with the voice of authority. "Dan will go with the team – no one can dispute the selection."

IVOR OSBOURNE

EXTRACT FROM PRODIGAL

In Mocho we used to play cricket with bats we made from coconut boughs with green oranges for balls. Then we graduated to "cork and tar" balls and homemade hardwood bats. The balls used to split wide open when we hit them too hard. I remember that very well. We didn't have to be members of any club to play. We didn't have to wear white flannels and pullovers. Anyone, everyone, could play ball if they wanted to.

In England however, it was different; I had to be a member of a club, I had to have white flannels and special boots, special bats, and with all those special things I still couldn't play just anytime I wanted to; I had to wait until the club and the weather said it was alright. I couldn't afford any of those things. Obviously, I was the wrong class of fellow to join up at any of the clubs. I can just imagine the sort of uproar it would have caused in the press if I had gone to Edgbaston or Lords to join up… "'Wogs' taking up our places at the clubs!" "Dark clouds over the future of English cricket". As it was, we were (according to the press) already threatening to take away the jobs. The writing was already on the wall. "Darkies, Wogs, go home." There was no way we blacks were going to ball in England unless we built our own clubs. Only the liberals would tolerate us and then only up to the point where we granted them their greatest wish, that of touching our hair.

"Oh!" they would exclaim in surprise, "Doesn't it feel… woolly, sort of springy". And then they would recoil, bubbling with pride in their achievement.

After that, one was dead. Just another nice black man – at best.

I lost count of the number of times I went through that little routine with friends of Sally. Friends who were either discreet enough to keep their knowledge of Sally's affair with me a secret, or liberal enough to regard the whole thing as cute; a nice but hopefully brief experience for Sally. Whatever, I didn't receive any invitations to go out and play cricket, so I stayed indoors and read. In the end I lost touch with cricket completely. I didn't even think of reading the reports when MCC played the West Indies in 1960. I was so far gone by then. And it was that same year, 1960, January, I'll never forget, when they were making all that fuss about this Jamaican fellow, a soldier in the British army, whom they had accused of giving false evidence in a murder trial right there in Birmingham. We sort of fell from grace then, whatever grace we had, us blackies, with everyone thinking that this poor fellow had committed the murder.

I really did sort of go into hiding in that period of my life. I went into my solitary reading with a tremendous fortitude. I guess I wanted to find some sort of equilibrium inside myself, something that the society outside my room was never prepared to give me. I felt as if all of Birmingham, all of England was saying silently, "Go and play ball, John Brown, you have to play ball because that's all you are good for, but you won't play your ball here!" All the English fellows were always asking me something or other about cricket whenever they spoke to me. In the end I really felt that playing cricket was all that I was good for. I hated this. It was almost a pleasure to confess that I didn't know the latest score, didn't in fact know that there was a game being played anywhere. Then I would stand back and watch their faces pale with astonishment.

THE CRICKET MATCH

The time when the West Indies cricket eleven come to England to show the Englishmen the finer points of the game, Algernon was working in a tyre factory down by Chiswick way, and he lambast them English fellars for so.

"That is the way to play the game," he tell them, as the series went on and West Indies making some big score and bowling out them English fellars for duck and thing, "you thought we didn't know how to play the game, eh? That is cricket, lovely cricket."

And all day he singing a calypso that he make up about the cricket matches that play, ending up by saying that in the world of sport, is to wait until the West Indies report.

Well in truth and in fact, the people in this country believe that everybody who come from the West Indies at least like the game even if they can't play it. But you could take it from me that it have some tests that don't like the game at all, and among them was Algernon. But he see a chance to give the Nordics tone and he get all the gen on the matches and players, and come like an authority in the factory on cricket. In fact, the more they ask him the more convinced Algernon get that perhaps he have the talent of Walcott in him only waiting for a chance to come out.

They have a portable radio hide away from the foreman and they listening to the score everyday. And as the match going on you should hear Algernon: "Yes, lovely stroke": and "That should have been a six," and so on. Meanwhile, he picking up any round object that near to hand and making demonstration, showing them how Ramadhin does spin the ball.

"I bet you used to play a lot back home," the English fellars tell him.

"Who me?" Algernon say. "Man, cricket is breakfast and dinner where I come from. If you want to learn about the game you must go down there. I don't want to brag," he say, hanging his head a little, "but I used to live next door to Ramadhin, and we used to teach one another the fine points." But what you think Algernon know about cricket in truth? The most he ever play was in the street, with a bat make from a coconut branch, a dry mango seed for ball, and a pitchoil tin for wicket. And that was when he was a boy, and one day he get lash with the mango seed and since that time he never play again.

But all day long in the factory, he and another West Indian fellar name Roy getting on as if they invent the game, and the more the West Indies eleven score, the more they getting on. At last a Englisher name Charles, who was living in the suburbs, say to Algernon one morning:

"You chaps from the West Indies are really fine cricketers. I was just wondering… I play for a side where I live, and the other day I mentioned you and Roy to our captain, and he said why don't you organize an eleven and come down our way one Saturday for a match? Of course," Charles went on earnestly, "we don't expect to be good enough for you, but still, it will be fun."

"Oh," Algernon say airily, "I don't know. I uses to play in first-class matches, and most of the boys I know accustom to a real good game with strong opposition. What kind of pitch you have?"

"The pitch is good," Charles say. "Real English turf."

Algernon start to hedge. He scratch his head. He say, "I don't know. What you think about the idea, Roy?"

Roy decide to hem and leave Algernon to get them out of the mooch. He say, "I don't know, either. It sound like a good idea, though."

"See what you can do," Charles say, "and let me know this week."

Afterwards in the canteen having elevenses Roy tell Algernon: "You see what your big mouth get us into."

"*My* big mouth!" Algernon say. "Who it is say he bowl four top bats for duck one after the other in a match in Queen's Park Oval in Port of Spain? Who it is say he score two hundred and fifty not out in a match against Jamaica?"

"Well to tell you the truth, Algernon?" Roy say, now that they was down to brass tacks, "I ain't play cricket for a long time. In fact, I don't believe I could still play."

"Me too, boy," Algernon say. "I mean, up here in England you don't get a chance to practise or anything. I must be out of form."

They sit down there in the canteen cogitating on the problem.

"Anyway," Roy say, "it look as if we will have to hustle an eleven somehow. We can't back out of it now."

"I studying," Algernon say, scratching his head. "What about Eric, you think he will play?"

"You could ask him, he might. And what about Williams? And Wilky? And Heads? Those boys should know how to play."

"Yes, but look at trouble to get them! Wilky working night and he will want to sleep. Heads is a man you can't find when you want. And Williams – I ain't see him for a long time, because he owe me a pound and he don't come my way these days."

"Still," Roy say, "we will have to manage to get a side together. If we back out of this now them English fellars will say we are only talkers. You better wait for me after work this evening, and we will go around by some of the boys and see what we could do."

That was the Monday, and the Wednesday night about twelve of the boys get together in Algernon room in Kensal Rise, and Algernon boiling water in the kettle and making tea while they discuss the situation.

"Algernon always have big mouth, and at last it land him in trouble."

"Cricket! I never play in my life!"

"I uses to play a little 'pass-out' in my days, but to go and play against a English side! Boy, them fellars like this game, and they could play, too!"

"One time I hit a ball and it went over a fence and break a lady window and…"

"All right, all right, ease up on the good old days, the problem is right now. I mean, we have to rally."

"Yes, and then when we go there everybody get bowl for duck, and when them fellars batting we can't get them out. Not me."

But in the end, after a lot of blague and argument, they agree that they would go and play.

"What about some practice?" Wilky say anxiously. Wilky was the only fellar who really serious about the game.

"Practice!" Roy say. "It ain't have time for that. I wonder if I could still hold a bat?" And he get up and pick up a stick Algernon had in the corner and begin to make stance.

"Is not that way to hold a bat, stupid. Is so."

And there in Algernon room the boys begin to remember what they could of the game, and Wilky saying he ain't playing unless he is captain, and Eric saying he ain't playing unless he get pads because one time a cork ball nearly break his shinbone, and a fellar name Chips pull a cricket cap from his back pocket and trying it on in front a mirror.

So everything was arranged in a half-hearted sort of way. When the great day come, Algernon had hopes that they might postpone the match, because only eight of the boys turn up, but the English captain say it was a shame for them to return without playing, that he would make his side eight, too.

Well that Saturday on the village green was a historic day. Whether cold feet take the English side because of the licks the West Indies eleven was: sharing at Lord's I can't say, but the fact is that they had to bowl first and they only coming down with some nice hop-and-drop that the boys lashing for six and four.

When Algernon turn to bat he walk out like a veteran. He bend down and inspect the pitch closely and shake his head, as if he ain't too satisfied with the condition of it but had to put up with it. He put on gloves, stretch out his hands as if he about to shift a heavy tyre in the factory, and take up the most unorthodox stance them English fellars ever did see. Algernon leg's wide apart as if he doing the split and he have the bat already swing over his shoulder although the bowler ain't bowl yet. The umpire making sign to him that he covering the wicket but Algernon do as if he can't see. He make up his mind that he rather go for lbw. than for the stumps to fly.

No doubt an ordinary ball thrown with ease would have had him out in two-twos, but as I was saying, it look as if the unusual play of the boys have the

Englishers in a quandary, and the bowler come down with a nice hop-and-drop that a baby couldn't miss.

Algernon close his eyes and he make a swipe at the ball, and he swipe so hard that when the bat collide the ball went right out of the field and fall in the road.

Them Englishers never see a stroke like that in their lives. All heads up to the sky watching the ball going.

Algernon feel like a king: only thing, when he hit the ball the bat went after it and nearly knock down a English fellar who was fielding silly-mid-on-square-leg.

Well praise the lord, the score was then sixty-nine and one set of rain start to fall and stop the match.

Later on, entertaining the boys in the local pub, the Englishers asking all sort of questions, like why they stand so and so and why they make such and such a stroke, and the boys talking as if cricket so common in the West Indies that the babies born either with a bat or a ball, depending on if it would be a good bowler or batsman.

"That was a wonderful shot," Charles tell Algernon grudgingly. Charles still had a feeling that the boys was only talkers, but so much controversy raging that he don't know what to say.

"If my bat didn't fly out my hand," Algernon say, and wave his hand the air dramatically, as if to say he would have lost the ball in the other county.

"Of course, we still have to see your bowling," the English captain say. "Pity about the rain – usual English weather, you know."

"Bowling!" Algernon echo, feeling as if he is a Walcott and a Valentine roll into one. "Oh yes, we must come back some time and finish off the match."

"What about next Saturday?" the captain press, eager to see the boys in action again, not sure if he was dreaming about all them wild swipe and crazy strokes.

"Sure, I'll get the boys together," Algernon say.

Algernon say that, but it wasn't possible, because none of them wanted to go back after batting, frighten that they won't be able to bowl the Englishers out.

And Charles keep reminding Algernon all the time, but Algernon keep saying how the boys scatter about, some gone Birmingham to live, and others move and gone to work somewhere else, and he can't find them anywhere.

"Never mind," Algernon tell Charles, "next cricket season I will get a sharp eleven together and come down your way for another match. Now, if you want me to show you how I make that stroke…"

FROM THE LUNATIC

It was Saturday morning of the big cricket match and Busha was grimly at bat. The first ball bowled to him was a wicked inswinger that bounded towards his unprotected head at some 100 miles per hour. Busha took a desperate slice at it with the bat and missed by a mile. He spun in his tracks, certain that he would see the stumps of his wicket go flying. But the ball zoomed over the bails and plopped harmlessly into the gloves of the wicketkeeper, who immediately appealed that Busha had nicked it.

"Hoowwzzhhee?" the wicket keeper roared.

The umpire, a parson from a neutral mountain village, turned up his nose scornfully at the appeal.

Muttering under his breath about thiefing umpiring parsons, the wicketkeeper returned the ball to the fast bowler, who began leisurely pacing off his length.

The sun beat down on Busha's head like a teacher's switch. He was dressed in the garb of the cricketer: he had on his whites; his legs were ensheathed in thick pads, his testicles baking in a protective metal cup. His fingers sweated under the rubber bristles of the batting gloves. On top of everything else his throat was dry and his belly hung off him like a dead weight.

Twenty-two yards from where Busha stood nervously at the wicket waiting for the fast bowler to reach his mark, Dr. Fox, the other opening batsman, smiled encouragingly at him.

The sidelines of the playing field were thick with spectators. They spilled out over the boundary lines and dripped from the limbs of surrounding trees; they gawked from thick hillsides and peeped from car tops. Parasols bloomed thick in the air like wild flowers. Women were resplendent in their best dresses Men had squeezed calloused feet into leather shoes and now pranced on the sidelines like newly shod horses. Everyone smelled of Saturday-night baths and Sunday-morning scents.

The children had caught the excitement in the air and danced about their mothers, poking their heads through the thick crowd to ogle the cricket pitch. A babble of voices rose and crested and broke, punctuated by occasional laughter and shouts.

The fast bowler, a beefy cultivator from Walker's Wood who was usually murder on the Moneague batsmen, had reached his mark. He turned, pawed at the ground like an enraged bull, took a deep breath that blew him up to a frightful size, and began cantering towards the crease where he would deliver the ball.

Busha crouched and waited, his breath coming in sharp spurts.

"Duck" popped into his mind just as the bowler hurtled down on him, whipping a vicious bouncer towards the wicket.

Busha closed his eyes and swung the bat like an axe. The seasoned wood clouted the ball and sent it sailing over the boundary lines to carom off the asphalt road.

The umpire's arms stiffened into the air, signalling that Busha had hit a six.

The crowd bellowed deafeningly with one enormous mouth.

Padded and waiting his turn at the wicket, Mr. Shubert was sitting with the other batsmen and talking over his shoulder to $78.59, who stood behind him shielding her head from the hot sun under a gaudy parasol.

In the eyes of the world $78.59 was a good-natured, big-batty widow who had eight grown children, lived in an unelectrified mountainside settlement where she minded goats and chickens and was known to God and her neighbours as Mrs. Sepole. But because of tension Mr. Shubert could not remember the old lady's name, although he clearly recalled that her balance in his credit book was $78.59.

On all sides was Mr. Shubert hemmed in by other figures from his book. To his right was $130 dressed in a serge suit and putting on airs for a flirtatious young woman. Two rows deep behind Mr. Shubert, standing side by side, were $55.23, $98, and $210, who was in arrears and needed a good dunning. Before becoming aware of Mr. Shubert's presence, $210 had been blaring out to the whole world his vainglorious opinions about cricket. But one glimpse of the shopkeeper had caused the wretch to lower his voice and skulk away into the thicket of cloying bodies.

It was all in Mr. Shubert's book – the whole sorry story of the village – and only he knew the truth. Only he knew that that one over there with the big mouth carrying on like a fowl that just lay egg was down in the book for $86.29. Only he knew that a certain sister sweating under crinoline and umbrella on the sidelines and holding her head high like she was bound to go to heaven owed the shop $126.78 mainly for white rum purchases.

No matter where the shopkeeper looked, he could immediately pick out a face in the throng that owed him money. Even the fast bowler, now pacing off his fearful length, was down in the book. It was a comfort to Mr. Shubert to realize that no one, with the exception of Almighty God who had every name down in the Book of Life, kept more complete accounts on this horde of people.

"Mr. Shubert," a voice from behind sang pleasantly, "we expect a good knock out of you, you know, sah. You mustn't let us down today."

Mr. Shubert turned and looked into the homely brown face of a scrawny village woman whose husband operated a bus. He smiled wanly and mumbled that he would do his best.

$98.67, thought Mr. Shubert, as he settled down again in his chair. And come to think of it, the wretch had missed her payment last week.

The crowd thundered as Busha hit another towering six.

But Busha's heroics earned him no glory. For in cricket it is written that the properly stylish batsman should drive the ball low and humming over the turf where it can't be caught, should do so while striking iconic poses for the benefit of spectators and wearing a mien of effortless imperturbability like a Colonial English governess making doo-doo on the potty.

None of this is possible if one is hitting sixes. It requires such a wrenching effort of brute strength that the batsman invariably looks rude and clumsy. It is all too American and vulgar. A roar from the partisan crowd no doubt, but no appreciation whatsoever from connoisseurs.

So Busha was applauded but not valued. He appeared to some sideline critics to be wielding his bat like it was a machete and he was a garden boy chopping grass.

Busha swung viciously at a yorker and sent it flying for another six.

"All dis rass white man can do is hit six," a spectator grumbled.

"Him think him butchering cow," another remarked.

"Dem soon bowl him," scoffed a third.

"Him swinging blind, dat's all," muttered another.

Moneague wickets began falling steadily all around Busha. Dr. Fox was stumped for one run and had to shamble off the field looking like he'd been caught thiefing a chicken. Mr. Shubert came on and was immediately clean bowled for a duck. As he was walking off doing his best to look dignified, Mr. Shubert paused to remind the bowler about the balance he owed the shop. The bowler got vexed and answered with a bad word.

Mr. Shubert muttered uglily that sooner or later the bowler would want credit again at which time his goose would most certainly be cooked. The bowler sneered that it was duck that was cooked not goose, a taunt which goaded Mr. Shubert into such an abusive tirade that the umpire had to walk over and order him off the field of play.

The spectators from Walker's Wood jeered the shopkeeper with a loud quacking as he took the long humiliating walk to the sidelines.

"Better luck next time, Mr. Shubert," $98.67 muttered to the shopkeeper as he sat down and began tearing off his pads.

Mr. Shubert turned on her savagely.

"How come you miss you payment last week?" he bellowed.

The woman blushed with shame.

"Lawd, Missah Shubert, sah," she whispered, "is not me bowl you, you know, sah."

By noon the Moneague side was in collapse. Busha was grimly hanging on to his wicket with a score of forty-six. He had belted five sixes over the parked cars. One had landed in the bush of the church graveyard and the ball nearly lost. But it was found under a mass of tendrils smothering a weathered grave slab and returned to play.

Aloysius, the last batsman on the side, came to bat barefoot and clad in a crushed pair of white pants that Busha had lent him. Busha's belly was so much bigger than Aloysius's that the waist of the pants had had to be fastened with an old necktie, which drooped down the seams like a ill-fitting cummerbund.

The captain of the Walker's Wood side flew to the umpire and protested a madman being used by the other team.

"Damn out of order, man!" the captain raged. "We have madman in our village too, you know, sah! I could fill me side wid a whole lunatic asylum if I had a mind to. But dis is supposed to be a friendly game! You don't use you madman in a friendly game!'

"Play de game, man," the umpire snapped. "Nothing in de rule book 'bout madman."

The captain retreated to his fielding position, muttering threats about next year filling his team with eleven raving lunatics.

Aloysius stroked a long four through cover point on the next ball. The next delivery he lofted toward the long-on boundary where it was gingerly caught by a fielder. Just like that the side was all out for 95 runs.

There was a break for a curry goat lunch served under a poinciana tree. Everyone on the Moneague side admitted that things were looking grim. The players tried to cheer each other up, but in spite of all the heartening words mumbled through mouthfuls of chewed goat, a thick gloom had settled over them. Across the field, where the Walker's Wood side ate its lunch, there was a constant sound of lighthearted banter and laughter. Jokes were being told in boisterous voices and greeted with squeals and backslapping.

The same contrasting moods had settled over supporters of the two teams. On the Moneague sidelines a fight broke out during which a woman held down her husband and flogged him with a switch. Three special constables had to drag them both away to the police station accompanied by a frightful hissing from the unruly crowd. Children were cuffed, scolded and occasionally gave vent to an animal shrieking. Men were drinking themselves into a stupor. Women squabbled over old grievances.

But on the Walker's Wood side, there were no shrieking children, no fighting women, no drunken men. The crowd was in a jovial and happy mood. Laughter occasionally floated over the background jabber of voices. So many people scaled a lignum vitae tree, jostling for a place on an overhanging limb, that it broke with a loud snap and sent a mass of bodies tumbling headlong into the thick of the crowd. But even this accident was greeted with good-natured laughter as the fallen spectators picked themselves up off the ground, dusted off and began anew a scramble up the tree-trunk.

A drunken woman, her eyes afire with rum, her voice thick and slurred, elbowed her way to where the dispirited Moneague team sat.

"You say you name cricket players?" she shrieked at the subdued men. "Is so you name? Cricket players? Well, listen me now, if you don't win dis game, we goin' ration pum-pum on you like de Socialist used to ration butter. You hear me! No pum-pum for you if you don't win!"

A few of the bystanders sniggered at her antics. Some scowled and muttered under their breaths. But most of them just looked away and shuffled their feet with painful embarrassment.

The players sat under the tree toying with blades of grass, twirling their shoelaces, or staring idly at the lines of spectators that twined thick and colourful over the hillside, draped off the branches of the surrounding trees, and curled over the eaves of neighbouring rooftops.

After lunch the Walker's Wood side stepped to the crease and began hammering the Moneague fast bowlers. The batsmen immediately drove the new ball to the boundaries for two fours. By the time the pacemen had worn a scuff into the new ball, the score was thirty-one runs for no wickets.

A water boy came on the field and the players took a short break for bellywash and bullah cake.

"No pum-pum for de whole o' you!" the nasty drunken woman bellowed from the sidelines.

"I goin' get a constable to lock up her rass," the inspector glowered.

"Leave de damn drunk woman, man," Busha mumbled. "She just telling de truth."

"Let's just do our best and lose honourably," the parson counselled.

"'Honourably' you bumbo!" Dr. Fox snapped. "We goin' be de laughing stock of de parish."

Busha inspected the ball to see whether it was sufficiently worn to bring on the spin bowlers. Then he tossed it to his best spin bowler, who was Aloysius.

The strategy in cricket is dictated by the condition of the ball. A new ball is hard and shiny like a marble, slippery to the grip and cannot be delivered with any appreciable spin. But the fast bowlers can bowl it with tremendous speed, get it to carom wickedly off the pitch, and take wickets by scaring the daylights out of the batsmen.

After the fast bowlers have had their innings, the ball becomes scuffed and worn, its seams raised and rigid like an old man's veins. Then the spin bowlers come on. For now they can grip the ball and spin it with a flick of the wrist, making it arc through the air with tantalizing slowness and jink erratically at the stumps.

The pace of the game slows. The fielders draw perilously close to the batsman. The wicketkeeper's gloved hands hover inches over the wicket. Deceit and swindle hang heavily in the air. Sudden death lurks for the unwary batsman.

"How you do today?" Aloysius murmured to the ball as he paced off his two-step length.

"Ahh me son!" the ball replied. "Times hard 'pon me. Me back nearly broke wid all de licking dem give me."

"De bat hard, eh?" Aloysius asked sympathetically.

"Hard!" the ball became indignant. "Hard, you rass! You don't know 'hard' yet? You should be born in a world where people batter you up wid a piece of wood, den you'd know 'bout 'hard.'"

"Is true, you know," Aloysius muttered.

"Where dat white man? Him not batting now?" the ball asked anxiously.

"No, man. Him 'pon we team."

"Him nearly kill me Puppa wid all dem six. Hard knock to rass!"

The captain of the opposing team, who was at bat, strode angrily over to the umpire.

"De man is talking to de ball!" he bellowed. "Dey bring a madman to bowl to us! What kind a thing is dis? Out of order to bring madman to bowl to us!"

On the sidelines the indignation was echoed by the supporters of Walker's Wood.

For the sake of peace, the umpire strolled over to Aloysius and asked him to please refrain from talking to the ball while he was bowling since it distracted the batsmen.

Aloysius took his mark.

His face wreathed in a ferocious scowl, the captain of the opposing team assumed his batting stance, slapping the tip of his bat angrily against the crease.

The crowd quieted down expectantly.

Aloysius took two steps and let the ball go. It floated high in the air, landed three feet outside the wicket, then darted like a snake at the stumps. Fooled by the sharp break, the captain mistimed his swing and nicked the ball into the hands of the fielder crouching at first slips.

"Howzzeee he?" the team roared.

The umpire's finger stabbed the air, signalling an out.

The fury of the captain was uncontrollable. He ranted and raved at the umpire.

Moneague had emptied its lunatic asylums to come and bowl against their team, the captain bawled, and here they had been decent enough to leave their own demented citizens behind. The umpire took a dim view of the clamour and ordered the irate captain to leave the field and bring on the next batsman.

Scowling ferociously, the captain stormed off to a hail of applause from his own crowd and a chorus of boos from the Moneague supporters.

The next batsman marched bravely to the wicket. He tidied up the crease, got the umpire to give him mid-stump, sniffed suspiciously at the crouching fielders, and turned to face Aloysius with a threatening glare.

The first ball uprooted his leg stump.

The Moneague crowd exploded in a wild thundering of joy.

With the help of obeah, the devil, and lunacy (according to the captain of the other side) Aloysius took wickets like they had never been taken before. He got a hat trick by clean bowling three. He got one for leg before wicket. Two others were caught.

The solid centre of the Walker's Wood batting order, where were planted three big-belly batsmen of enormous size and a gluttonous appetite for scoring, fell meekly for fewer than twenty runs. Every falling wicket brought the captain of the Walker's Wood team raving onto the field. Bad words flew out of his mouth like bats from a cave. He stormed up and down at his own players, screaming at them for being fooled and frightened by a madman. He protested to the umpire, the heavens, the spectators. He popped oaths and blasphemies and named some private parts old women on the sidelines had not seen in years.

But nothing he did or said made any difference. It still rained wickets. And when Aloysius was not bowling Parson Mordecai was wreaking havoc with his googly ball – one that bounced trickily and lured two batsmen out of their creases to a merciless stumping.

The final two wickets fell in quick succession. One batsman was run out as he tried to scratch two runs from a ball driven weakly past the mid-on fielder. The last man at bat, the beefy cultivator who was the Walker's Wood fast bowler, hit a mighty six on his first swing, and popped up the ball to the long-on fielder on his second.

A tremendous roar erupted from the Moneague supporters, who surged onto the field, engulfing the players in an ocean of flailing limbs.

Moneague had won the game by twenty runs.

Late that night Aloysius straggled past the glare of the last street light on the edge of the village and tramped his way slowly up the empty and unlighted country road with crickets hissing in his ears and croaking lizards groaning at the darkness.

He had been overwhelmed by the crowd, carted off bodily to the nearest bar, and drenched with glass after glass of free white rum. The sound system had been turned up to its loudest volume and the vibrations of the reggae rhythms had pounded all evening through his body giving him a splitting headache. He had been hailed and slapped on his back and celebrated and told jokes like never before in his life.

The drunken woman had caught up with him and hauled him into a backyard where she dropped her panties and attempted to reward him with pum-pum on the roof of a rickety chicken coop. But even while Aloysius was groggily trying to make her understand that he could hardly stand up straight because of his great weariness, she passed out and fell on the ground, causing the penned chickens to explode in a noisy cackling.

Now, as Aloysius slowly scraped his way up the dark road, his eyes picking out the familiar shapes of trees and the low outline of the wall, he was aware that a sinister silence had descended on the darkened woods and fields. No bushes, no trees called out his name as he passed. The only sounds he heard were the shrieking of the insects, the cries of the frogs, and the hawking of the lizards.

He climbed over the wall and by starlight followed the narrow path that wound into the thick bushland where he had lived for many months alone with only the flame heart tree for company.

Inga and Service had not come to the cricket match. Inga said she did not understand cricket. Service said he had no use for watching grown men play a child's game.

Sitting on the stoop of the house, they would be waiting for him in the faint glow of the kerosene lamp.

On the night wind he could hear the sound of a file whetting a blade. It made the noise of an old man grinding his teeth during a bad dream.

BAT AND BALL

Paradise was the long, narrow strip of land which prolonged our backyard and vegetable garden into an estate. Thickly covered with "sinkle bible" cacti and divi-divi trees, this strip had long resisted my mother's pioneering attempts and remained stubbornly jungle. For Rance my elder brother, progress to Paradise was simple. He was the eldest, a manchild, and as such, born to freedom. Apart from these natural privileges he had gained, from the test of early severe illnesses, a strength of spirit which caused everyone, openly the maids, secretly my mother, to be at the same time proud and afraid of him. His escape meant no more than a lordly stepping out of the breakfast room, down the stone steps, into the backyard, down through the vegetable garden, and under a tangleful of bushes unto the rough clearing originally intended by my mother for lettuces but now serving as our cricket pitch.

My younger brother Timothy made his way to Paradise under the protective shadow of Rance, but for me escape was a different matter. First of all I was a girl and should help in the house. The fact that I hated housework and hated being a girl had nothing to do with it. My younger sister Ruby loved housework... she can sew, embroider, bake cakes..." Stella," my mother would continue, "Ruby can wrap you round her fingers when it comes to housework... and she prettier than you... you is my child but I have to let you know that you won't have much to offer by way of looks... so how you think you going to catch a husband if you don't leave off boygame, stay in the house and learn to cook?"

My mother would have thought it sour grapes if I had protested that I didn't want to catch a husband. If I had gone on to explain how every night I placed my bible under my pillow and prayed to awake and not find myself still a girl in everyone else's eyes, how I threatened to pierce the ears of a seemingly dear God, she would have been horrified at my blasphemy. Especially if she had realised the significance of the macca thorn which I carefully sharpened and kept ready inside the bible.

The only escape from household chores, then, and to Paradise was, as I soon discovered, to break one of my mother's treasures, or to spill water on her highly polished floors or some such deliberately stupid act. When her anger would flare out, she would catch hold of the nearest object, and it was quite in order for me to run. The path to Paradise streaked itself out through blurred glimpses of stone steps and the side of the house jumping up to nearly graze my head, the beaten earth of the backyard hot with sun under my feet, the sweet stinging smell of limes as I flew past, the hens squawking and fluttering under the breadfruit tree, the ducks in ordered line alongside the mud trench placidly drinking in spite of my furious flight, then zig-zag through the vegetable beds, a quick dodge around "okra" frames, my mother still flinging at me whatever came to hand, pots and pans, scrubbing brushes from off the cistern, a broomstick, her slippers, and finally the spent force of her rage in the threat: "…Alright, run go on, Miss Stella, but see if you get any lunch in here today! If you think you bad!"

And although she had given up the chase my feet would wing away elatedly past the plum-tree where, stretched out along the topmost limb, I did my infrequent studying, past the pigsty where Rance conducted his diamond digging operations (the former owners used to burn charcoal there and Rance had learnt at school that diamonds had to do with coal), cutting down through the long grass, pushing through the undergrowth, and finally onto the cleared pitch with Rance eyeing me coldly and Timothy faithfully replicating his look:

"What you come down here for? Who ask you? Why you don't stay at home and do girl-work?"

"Oh, I finish all that. I just thought I would do a little fielding no!"

I knew that the bait wouldn't be resisted. Neither one of my brothers, nor any of their friends for that matter, considered fielding to be a necessary part of the game of bat and ball. One should have a caddy to collect the ball and that was all. Real players only batted, though they may occasionally bowl since good batsmen needed good bowlers. My offer to field was always accepted, though reluctantly of course, on principle:

"Alright, but see you bring back the ball quick!" As I usually had to crawl under barbed wire and through thorn bushes, this admonition only served to get me more severely scratched and bruised than I already was. But the only thanks for my pains:

"Man, girl careless me son! And their skin red and ugly sir!"

I didn't mind all this however, because once accepted as a fielder, however grudgingly, I became one of the gang and life demanded nothing more of me than that I should obey and be loyal. And my loyalty, what I had to do, and what I had not to do, were clearly marked out by Rance. Life, which had been rather a lonely parcelling out of twenty-four hours in a day, became a sum total of hours spent scrambling after a ball. Days which had formerly slipped purposelessly through the numbers on a clock's face, now began and ended with the clear summons of bat hitting ball.

The sun fell in love with us that summer holidays and browned us gently. The sound of ball on bat re-echoed in my dreams at nights, and I took pleasure in the smarting pain from my scratches. For now every day I fielded and was still the sole fieldsman, although two boys from next door had joined the gang. It didn't even matter to me that the newcomers lolled under a guinep tree awaiting their turn to bat while I fetched busily. It didn't matter because now, every morning, Rance demanded my presence of my mother and led me out, loudly declaring that as I was so ugly he had to see to it that I was good at algebra. In return for this I was a willing slave; I mixed lemonade, ran to the shop for cakes (bullas), kept score and fielded zealously. The bible and the macca thorn lay neglected, until my mother threw away the thorn and replaced the bible on the shelf.

The two boys from next door had an elder sister called Melba. Her mother was a German woman from the German colony at Seaforth Town, and unlike her more Indian looking brothers, Melba had been born with golden curls and grey-blue eyes. Someone, for whom princesses were always blonde, had told her that she looked like one, so she had adopted a princess quality and wrapped it about herself. I hated her on sight. On this particular day her mother had gone out and she had been left in charge. When I went to summon the boys she insisted on coming along to find out what I was putting her brothers up to. I looked forward to the withering which Rance would apply to this symbol of the "girl-thing" which he hated. At first I thought that he was saving up his scorn for later because he merely nodded jerkily to her "good-morning", turned his back on her, and proceeded to give us our orders for the day. Timothy would start off with the batting, Rance with the bowling, the two boys could explain to their sister the fine points of the game, whilst they awaited their turn to bat, possibly their sister would keep score? He half-smiled to her fluted "yes", then turned to me with his fullest expression of authority. I was to sharpen up my fielding, not keep the others waiting, so that "their sister" could see the game at its best. And by the way, he continued, as a gold curl glanced off a shaft of sunlight, couldn't I do something about my hair instead of having it flying all over the place?

An apprehension of betrayal flashed by. It came back, and this time entirely to take hold of me, when just before the game began, I saw Rance spread a newspaper on a clear patch of grass, and heard him say in a loud voice: "Any-one who want to sit can sit!"

Melba sat and thanked him prettily. The fierce protuberant black eyes and the wolfish expression of the lean face which had awed me for years, melted into a shy smile. My stomach squeezed up tight.

The game began and Rance had bowled the others out before they properly knew what they were about. He then went in to bat and batted invincibly. The others bowled and bowled until the still air patterned itself with arcs of arms. The ball and the bat fused themselves together into a summer's day dance, as inevitably right and perfect and with the same feeling of ritualistic splendour as one occasionally gets at a good bullfight. For a while we were all caught up in it, for a while we understood that together we were part of the sun and the growing green things and that this game marked our recognition of the unconsciousness with which we had grown with the green things, woken up and gone to bed with the sun. Years later I learned in school a Latin phrase and thought that surely I had heard it somewhere before – *Ave atque vale*. Our moment of recognition was also, necessarily, our farewell. The silence with which our eyes marked the soaring of the ball was our tribute and our goodbye.

The shadow under a solitary mango tree began to slip out thinly into late afternoon. As our bodies became tired, our spirits drooped away from exaltation. I fielded each time more reluctantly, each time more slowly as I noticed every stroke of Rance's performed in the admiring mirror of Melba's eyes. Even his voice seemed to echo in her eyes as he yelled at me to fetch the ball quickly. Yelled at me impersonally and without animus. If I hadn't been a girl I would have sat down and cried. Instead anger shook me and I turned:

"I tired of fielding! I want to bat too!"

The wind was still yet the trees leaned to listen. The hush of the others was like that of an old and faded photograph.

Rance turned, very slowly, to Timothy who had draped himself against the mango tree and was mopping his brow:

"Did I hear that girl say something... say that... say that she want to bat?"

"Is same way so she say," Timothy answered wearily.

"And is what wrong with you, now?"

"Well Rance man, even though we can't bowl you out, is time you declare yourself out now man. All of us go in and bat and bowl out, but you batting now for two-three hours!"

"And what is wrong with that? None of you don't bowl me out yet."

"I know... but I tired. I not bowling anymore!" Timothy's tone was final.

Rance looked at the others and saw their refusal. He saw Melba's eyes and two of her plump fingers absorbedly chasing an ant.

"Alright," he said, for the first time acknowledging me as a person able to lay a claim, "alright! If is bat you must bat, bowl me out first!"

The sun cut the sweat off my face. I stood rooted by the frightening possibility of choice. If I returned to fielding the others would return to bowling and after a few overs Rance would graciously declare, we would break for lemonade (me as usual buying the sugar, picking the limes, stealing ice from the box, mixing and serving), then afterwards the others would bat, Melba would watch, and I... I would continue to field. If I did not, no more bat and ball, bat and ball being so many things, even more than those I was consciously aware of... like showering together, seeing who could hold one's breath the longest underwater (the conclusion a foregone one in our autocracy), happily unending arguments as to whose hen had been foolish enough to lay its eggs from the heights of a breadfruit tree (never Rance's), cooking together over open wood-fires, ackee and saltfish, rice and dumplings excellent appetizers to our main meal... no more money-making ventures like the time when we had given picture shows and charged a penny for admission...

240

...my mother's cotton slip, purloined by me, paid for by me with six strokes of the tamarind switch, the slip stretched over a box to serve as a screen, lighting provided by a tiny tin lamp, figures drawn by Rance, cut out by Rance, story composed and narrated by Rance, the figures glued onto sticks by Timothy and me, figures animated by Timothy and me, Timothy and me animated by Rance... money at performances collected by Rance, to be spent by Rance...

Sweat beaded itself on my forehead. If I did not return to fielding I would be excluded as my sister Ruby had been on the evening of our show's third performance, when one of our audience, idle-brained, had jeered that the rabbit shown on the screen was as big as a horse, and the whole show was therefore "foolishness" and he wanted his money back right that minute. There was some craftiness in his suggestion as it was apparent that the picture was drawing near its end. The rest of the audience became restive. Rance had halted the proceedings, fixed the dissenter with his most dominating stare, waited for the silence, and then quietly declared:

"That rabbit is a living replica of a rabbit I had. You remember it, Timothy?"

"Yes man... that grey one that had the white star on its head!" Timothy's nonchalance effectively capped Rance's assertion, but he thought it wiser to keep the ball rolling..." You remember that whale of a rabbit, don't you Stella?"

"If I remember, man! Rabbit big like that I couldn't forget! You remember how we did tired of cooking and eating it, Ruby?"

The afternoon was suddenly twilight as I remembered how confidently I had passed the thread of evidence onto Ruby. Before our credulous audience, now totally convinced by the sum of our imaginations, without reason, irrelevantly, Ruby had broken the thread with a snap:

"No, I don't remember. We never had a rabbit as big as that yet!"

Ruby's voice was mixed up with that of Rance's shouting:

"Alright Miss Hurry-come-up, bowl me out!" And now the afternoon was as it had always been, blue-bright with not a hint of cloud. The sun slivered down, seeming to pull my hand towards the ball that lay where Timothy had flung it. It was gaping in air through a squashed-in hole in its side.

Rance's yells had become a chant echoing the insistence of a drum:

"Want to bat bowl me out, to bat bowl me out, bat, bowl, bat, bowl..."

The ball fitted itself into the curve of my hand. The bat in Rance's hand poised itself, a thing of elegance and surety waiting to wing the ball away to the oblivion of a six. I didn't throw the ball over with the fanfare of flourishes which I had seen Timothy use. Instead my arm whipped under, my wrist twisting itself in some preknown rhythm, and the ball hurtled away in an inverted arc which trailed in its wake the whittled sticks of the wicket.

Timothy and the two boys, without turning their backs nor closing their eyes, managed not to see me. Melba's eyes mirrored a silly, uncertain smile.

241

Rance's were two stone marbles, heavy and without light. Timothy gathered the fallen sticks of the wicket and Rance pounded them into place…

"This is cricket we playing you understand, cricket! In cricket everybody have to field. We don't want no hangers-on running after the ball… and we don't want nobody watching neither!"

I walked slowly up to the house with the earth still warm under my bare feet and the smell of limes bittersweet.

DRAMA

FROM MOON ON A RAINBOW SHAWL

Ephraim comes in carrying a shopping bag. A second-hand sailor's pea-jacket is stuffed into it. He hurries up the steps to his room.

CHARLIE. Hey, Epf!

EPF. Hey, Charlie!... Looks like yer got him down to it, Mrs Adams.

Sophia ignores this remark and goes into Rosa's room.

The lady like she out of humour this morning.

CHARLIE. Yer know how she is sometimes. Boy, look – I show yer this.

He reaches for one of the bats.

Look at this bat, boy – and he's been using it most of the season!

Epf has put down the shopping bag and has come back into the yard to examine the bat. He wants to go about his business – but he forces himself to stay.

EPF. Whose own?

CHARLIE. Young Murray.

EPF. Royal College?

CHARLIE. That's right. Look at the face of that bat, Epf. Hardly an edge. An' he been using it most of this season. Epf! Young Murray is going to be one of the real big ones in a couple of years!

EPF. Yea.

CHARLIE. He's goin' be a useful little bowler too, yer know.

EPF. The selectors plannin' big things fer him, I hear.

CHARLIE. Yes. But they should ease him. He's kind of young, yer know. Try to break them in too early sometimes. And they get break fer good. That new one over there is his as well. Gets new bats by the dozen, that boy. His ole man holding a lot of dough.

EPF. Yes. So I hear.

CHARLIE. In my day, Epf – I use to get my bats second-hand. An' sometimes they had to last me from season to season. But my big talent was with the ball. I used to trundle down to that wicket – an' send them down red hot! They don't make them that fast these days. The boys don't keep in condition. Today they send down a couple of overs – they are on their knees. But in my time, John, Old Constantine, Francis, them fellas was fast! Fast! Up in England them so help put the Indies on the map.

EPF. I only saw you once on the green, Charlie. Yer was kind of past yer prime. But the ole brain was there! And batsmen was seein' trouble! Trouble, man!

And I say this to you now, papa – You was class!

CHARLIE [*laughing as he warms to old memories*] Ever hear about that time when I knocked ole Archie Seagram's bails back fifty yards from the wicket?

Epf laughs sympathetically.

EPF [*leaning on the bat*] Charlie... What was the plan?

CHARLIE [*startled*] Plan?

EPF. Your dream!

CHARLIE. It was something more real than a dream that went from me.

EPF. What?

CHARLIE [*smiles*] Boy – I was pushing thirty. Hard. Strong as a bull – and at the height of mey power as a bowler. None better, boy. Nowhere – None better. Ask the ole timers – they tell you. But for the West Indian tour to England that year – I didn't even get an invite to the trials.

EPF. Why, Charlie?

CHARLIE. In them days, boy – The Savannah Club crowd was running most everything. People like me either had to lump it or leave it.

EPF. It ent much different now, Charlie.

CHARLIE. Is different – A whole lot different. In them times so when we went Barbados or Jamaica to play cricket they used to treat us like hogs, boy. When we went on tours they put we in any ole kind of boarding-house. The best hotels was fer them and the half-scald members of the team – So in Twenty-seven when we was on tour in Jamaica I cause a stink, boy. I had had enough of them dirty little boarding-house rooms. I said either they treat me decent or they send me back. The stink I made got into the newspapers. They didn't send me back. But that was the last intercolony series I ever play. They broke me, boy.

EPF [*quietly*] Fer that?

CHARLIE. I should of known mey place. If I had known mey place, Epf, I'd a made the team to England the following year. And in them days, boy – the English County clubs was outbidding each other fer bowlers like me. But the Big Ones here strangled my future, boy.

EPF. Just like that.

CHARLIE. Like that.

EPF. Jesus Christ!

CHARLIE. Don't beat yerself up. All that is – long ago. And is possible perhaps that some men wasn't born to make it.

EPF [*bitterly*] This country, Charlie? Jesus Christ! To think that a man who could of play class cricket like you.

CHARLIE. Boy – There were other things. Little things. Big things. Altogether pushing yer out of the stream – and on to the bank – So that yer rot slow in the sun... You don't know yet, boy – what life is like – when things start to slide from under yer.

Sophia comes into the veranda from Rosa's room. She glances scornfully at the two men.

SOPHIA. Ephraim! Yer ent have nothin' better to do than to keep Charlie outside here talkin'?

CHARLIE. Is awright, Sophie. Is jest a little ole talk.

SOPHIA. A li'l ole work is what I want to see. [*To Ephraim*] An' I want to have a word with *you*!

ESSAYS, MEMORIES AND EXCUSES

CRICKET, LOVELY CRICKET: LONDON SW16 TO GUYANA AND BACK

My love affair with cricket began during the spring of 1973 in a London flat. As a nine-year-old, Sunday was the ultimate television day. I could admire the latest escapades of Barnaby The Bear, the animated antics of The Jackson 5, the further adventures of Catweazle, and gawp at University Challenge and feel elated if I understood a couple of the questions.

These events preceded the main business of the afternoon. This was to tune in to The Big Match, which featured football highlights from the previous day's action and was presented by Brian "The Voice of Football" Moore.

While preparing for the start of The Big Match, I took up my usual spot between the coffee-table and the television set. Without any warning, a figure approached from a darkened corner of the room and calmly switched the television over to BBC2. My dad was home on British Army leave, and therefore my usual Sunday television viewing was cruelly disturbed. He wanted to watch the cricket and despite my protests, he refused to change his mind.

However, after the first ten or so overs had been bowled, I was beginning slowly to appreciate what I was watching. I found myself spellbound by John Arlott's observant and humorous commentary, gift for language and that distinctive Hampshire accent. I began to follow the John Player League one-day games every Sunday with increasing enthusiasm. "Run-rates" and "maiden overs" became part of my ever-expanding cricket vocabulary.

I briefly supported Sussex in all of the major English county competitions. I can't remember why I made this decision. Perhaps I felt sorry for them when they were defeated in the 1973 Gillette Cup Final. However, when it came to supporting a national cricket team there was no choice. It had to be the West Indies.

I was born and brought up in England, but it never occurred to me to support the England cricket team. My parents were from Guyana and Barbados. I had often heard talk of Charlie Griffiths, Wes Hall, Everton Weekes, Ramadhin, Valentine and other "greats" during high-spirited, nostalgia-driven and occasionally drunken cricket debates. Cricket was always part of the conversation when grownup men gathered together in all the places we lived.

The first colour television arrived in our flat to coincide with the 1973 England v West Indies series. Therefore, I was able to watch the third test match – including the spectacle and tension of a bomb scare at Lord's. Spectators gathered in bewilderment in the outfield, while umpire Dickie Bird perched in the middle of the ground on the pitch-covers. This was followed by Gary Sobers from Barbados and Rohan Kanhai from Guyana each scoring a century. All live in magnificent colour.

I continued to rifle through books in public libraries to enhance my knowledge of the game. I indulged in regular banter with my classmates at primary schools who supported England during any England v West Indian test series. I always took huge run-ups to mimic the smooth, cultured but fiery bowling style of Michael Holding – whether I played for my primary school team, in public parks, streets or back yards.

During school summer holidays in England, I eagerly awaited the start of any test series. I would settle into position in front of the television at five to eleven, just before the start of the day's play. My pulse-rate would increase as the first notes of the Booker T and the MGs theme-tune piped up. If play was interrupted by rain, irritating news and weather broadcasts and unnecessary golf or tennis tournaments, I would storm around the flat in frustration. Thankfully, I could rely on uninterrupted ball-by-ball radio commentary, or at least radio cricket conversation if play was delayed or interrupted. I began to develop a habit of listening to the radio commentary and watching the television coverage with the volume turned down.

During summer months spent in the Caribbean, I would spend every day playing cricket with assorted relatives, friends and friends of friends. I was keen to prove that I was good enough to hold my own during any beach, street or yard cricket session.

I refused to give up my wicket easily and batted defensively. Although I was a West Indian fan, I admired the technique and dedication to occupying the crease adopted by Yorkshire and England's Geoffrey Boycott. In Barbados I was accused of "batting like an Englishman". This was something I was strangely proud of.

As a Caribbean lad growing up in England; the West Indian cricket team provided me with an enormous source of pride, and they regularly triumphed in matches against England. In Andy Roberts, Michael Holding and Malcolm Marshall, they had the most fearsome fast bowlers in the world. Viv Richards, Gordon Greenidge and Clive Lloyd (my all time number one cricket idol) were arguably the most exciting stroke-playing batsmen around.

The cricket team was filled with sportsmen who appeared to me as superstars. I was being presented with the opportunity to idolize people who came from countries where my family came from. Clive Lloyd had attended the same secondary school as my mother in Georgetown, Guyana. Rohan Kanhai and Alvin Kallicharran were from Port Mourant, Berbice. As a teenager I was thrilled to be shown around the pavilion at the Bourda cricket ground in Georgetown by my cousin.

Cricket was something that "we" were good at. Beating England at cricket gave me and other first and second-generation Caribbean cricket enthusiasts a chance to assume temporary superiority over our English friends, colleagues and enemies. Before the 1988 test series, Viv Richards outlined the responsibility of captaining a West Indian team on tour in England. "West Indians in England, bus drivers, guys who work on the Underground, some of them don't have a great life. Maybe their cricket team can give them a little bit of pride. When they're talking with English fellas they can say: Yeah, but did you see what we did to you at Lord's?"

I began comprehensive school in 1976 and gradually evolved into a reliable, if not always flamboyant, opening batsman. It was a month after the West Indies had beaten England 3–0 in that year's test series. The outstanding highlights were Viv Richards scoring 291 runs, Michael Holding taking 14 wickets, and the West Indies amassing 687 in the first innings at The Oval. The playing surface was parched and bare of grass due to that year's drought.

At school it always seemed as if cricket was a game struggling to maintain its respect among my peers. Football was considered to be the only sport worth paying any serious attention to. Only a handful of my peers at school were prepared to indulge in any serious conversation about cricket. I was always particularly disappointed when I attempted to initiate cricket conversation with other kids of Caribbean descent. When I succeeded, I was always delighted to find someone to share my passion.

However, I usually failed miserably with my efforts, as they thought it was weird to consider cricket a topic of meaningful conversation. Cricket was viewed as a game for the older generation. A "West Indian grandad's game", dull and associated with rum-sipping, stout-drinking, calypso, dominoes and the past.

Playing competitive cricket for a London comprehensive school was also fraught with considerable difficulties. We had no playing fields surrounding the school. For games lessons and competitive cricket games against local schools, we had to hire a pitch in a public park or get bussed to hired pitches in leafy Surrey.

We always seemed to be the poor relations against schools we competed against. Our kitbag looked like a collection of equipment purchased at a church-hall jumble sale, in comparison to the pristine equipment being paraded by our opponents. We were a little envious of our well-heeled, well-scrubbed and better-prepared Surrey opposition. Their teams always wore immaculate whites, while we dressed in a roughly assembled array of cream, light-brown, beige and yellow.

Victory was always sweeter against these sides. After a particularly narrow victory against a team in Surrey, our players invaded the playing area to celebrate with the batsmen who had struck the winning runs.

Mini pitch invasions often occurred during cricket matches in those days. Especially when West Indian fans were in the ground and a West Indian batsman had just completed a scintillating century. At cricket grounds, I regularly battled with other boys to pick up balls which crossed the boundary ropes for four. Then, we'd invade the playing area and throw the ball to the nearest fielder.

The Cheam school was not amused with our behaviour, and our over enthusiasm was punished. Our PE teacher/makeshift cricket coach was put under intense pressure to concede the game, due to our "unreasonable behaviour".

I continued to ply my trade as an opening batsman for school, Boys' Brigade and Scouts teams throughout the years, until the end of my period as a sixth-former.

My Stuart Surridge cricket bat was kept in good order. I continued scanning sports shops for a pair of Tony Grieg-style SP batting gloves (left-handed). I played West Indies v England games with my mate Nick and West Indies v Pakistan matches with my mate Shakil in their back yards.

The West Indies cricket team under the leadership of Clive Lloyd grew from strength to strength, and the 1980 series with England was, for me, a defining moment as an observer of West Indies cricket. The England v West Indies match at The Oval is where I first witnessed how powerful the feeling of victory against England at cricket could be. Cricket provided the ideal setting for thousands of West Indians to let off steam and express a sense of collectiveness.

Used beer cans were battered together to create a rhythmic noise. Music deriding England's South African-born captain, Tony Grieg, blared out from ghetto-blasting cassette players. Chicken, rice, salad, beer and rum were being consumed. Raw abuse and friendly banter was exchanged between West Indian and English supporters, and the regional, political and cultural differences between Bajans, Jamaicans, Trinidadians and Guyanese were temporarily put on hold.

Before the West Indies began beating England regularly, and before there was a large West Indian population in Britain, West Indian cricket was often damned with faint praise. Fallibility made West Indian cricketers "uninhibited" and "colourful". By the time I began to watch cricket on a regular basis, and particularly with Clive Lloyd as captain up to the mid-80s, carefree amateurism was replaced by hardened professionalism.

It seemed to symbolize a "coming of age" of Caribbean sporting competitiveness. West Indian national self-assertion on the cricket field also increased the self-esteem of British-based West Indians and their descendants.

However, supporting West Indian cricket could be a lonely job in years to come. The first generation of Caribbean migrants is slowly passing away, or living their dream of retiring "back home". The descendants that they've left behind have largely turned to football or basketball and left cricket behind. Overhyped and overexposed Premier League and Champions League football and American basketball produce the new heroes.

The production line of talent from the Caribbean, or of Caribbean descent, who represented England – including Roland Butcher, Mark Butcher, Norman Cowans, Devon Marshall and Mark Ramprakash – has sadly come to an end.

Within twenty years in England there will be very few West Indians roaring the team on from the stands. Ticket prices for test matches are becoming prohibitively expensive, and for the first three days of a match are difficult to obtain. Most of these seats are now booked months in advance.

The music, revelry, banter, flags and special atmosphere brought to English cricket grounds during the 70s and 80s, which increased in volume with West Indian success on the field, was thwarted by the cricket authorities. By the end of the 80s, horns, drums, whistles, flags, bells and klaxons were taboo.

I had my horn confiscated by a kill-joy security guard as I entered Lord's on the final day of the 2007 England v West Indies test. I picked it up from the guard's shed at the end of play, and was made to feel like a guilty school boy.

During recent West Indian tours to England, West Indian fans have been notable by their absence at grounds where they had previously turned up in large numbers. The disappointing performances by recent West Indian teams in England have been matched with a lack of atmosphere in the stands. Some of my England cricket-supporting friends long for the "carnival atmosphere" now absent from these grounds.

Contrast this with scenes witnessed during recent England cricket tours to the Caribbean. Thousands of English supporters join in with the passion, revelry, music, drinking and crowd participation during test matches. They're welcomed with opened arms by the vast majority of West Indian supporters and cricketing authorities. During recent matches in Barbados, there have been as many English Union Jack-clad cricket spectators as Bajan supporters in the ground.

Appreciating West Indian cricket is rooted in the sporting choices I made as a young boy in the 70s. I still support Leeds United and Glasgow Celtic football clubs and Wales at rugby union. I supported Belgium in *Jeux Sans Frontieres* on television because I liked their yellow outfits!

Those emotional moments watching epic performances, that particular Caribbean way of playing and appreciating the game, and the memory of commentaries by John Arlott, Jim Laker and Peter West will always propel me to The Oval, Lord's or Old Trafford to see the West Indies on tour. And to visit the new cricket stadiums in Guyana and St Lucia, and the revamped stadium in Barbados. Supporting West Indian cricket as a British Born Caribbean (BBC) isn't an easy job, but it's a job for life.

EDWARD BAUGH

JAMAICA CRICKET ASSOCIATION BANQUET
IN HONOUR OF ALLAN RAE

Allan's 80th birthday was September 30, and the event was originally scheduled for that day, but it had to be postponed until 11 November 2002.

Ladies and gentlemen: I intend to occupy the crease for a little while, and, since my model for this innings is Allan Rae, I intend to take my time. I shall not be hurried. I am sure Sir Everton will understand if I don't play an explosive Evertonian innings.

When I was trying to think what I might say this evening, I remembered that I had never looked into John Figueroa's book *West Indies in England: the Great Post-War Tours.* So I got hold of the book, and as soon as I opened it I knew that I had found the way to begin. For I found to my delight that, believe it or not, Figueroa's book begins with Allan Rae. What better timed an opening stroke could I play than by quoting Figueroa remembering Rae? (Incidentally, the rhyme – play/Rae – was not intentional.)

> On a sunny morning in August 1950 as I settled into my seat at the Oval, at the pavilion end, Allan Rae took up his position at third man on the boundary. He shouted across to me, "Hi John, just like Sabina Park." For he and I, in different ways, had grown up at Sabina, which looks up to the mountains, the Blue Mountains in our native island, Jamaica. He waved as he settled down to watch Hutton taking strike. Exclaimed a lively postwar blonde, as ever taking advantage of the sun, "Oh, he speaks English."
> Allan was in fine form. He had scored 109 in the first and only innings of the West Indies in that game. At Lord's, in the first Test which West Indies had won in England, he had scored 106. The young lady was also in excellent form, showing that difficult-to-understand English ignorance of people from "overseas"… But she had an eye, bless her, for a lively-looking young man much in the public eye.

Well, we don't have any lively postwar English blondes here this evening, and I should think we can do well enough without them, thank you, because we have our own lively, raven-haired, cricket-loving ladies. But it is our great good fortune, half a century after that sunny August morning, to be able to keep that "lively-looking young man" and the memory of his cricketing exploits in the public eye. And we give thanks for the fact that, although his feet and hands are not as lively as they once were, and he may not now be able to hold that steady, reassuring stance at the crease, we give thanks that, in spite of time and circumstance, he is still in the fine form of his character and spirit.

As for me, personally, it is *my* good fortune to have been given the privilege to speak this evening. It is like a reward and a fulfilment I could never have imagined. For on that August morning in 1950, I was a schoolboy, hunched in solitary, tense excitement by the short-wave radio in our drawing room, over there in Port Antonio – a boy who had never seen an inter-colonial match, as they were called then, let alone a Test match. How could I have dreamt, as I was lifted up in my imagination by the exploits of those heroes on those fabled fields, how could I have dreamt that half a century later I should be standing here, playing a part in honouring one of those heroes, and bearing witness, with some pride, that I in my small, passive way, as distant, invisible audience, was also part of that long-ago moment. And what all of this expresses for me now is the idea of the community of cricket, and the continuity of cricket, and all of this is for the love of cricket.

So it gives me particular pleasure to begin by quoting Figueroa on Rae, because it leads me into those general ideas about the community and continuity of cricket, and the love of cricket which informs that community and continuity, ideas which I'd like to reflect on this evening.

For my purposes now, it is important to note that John Figueroa was a friend of Allan's, and John was my friend, and I'd like to think that Allan will allow me to call him my friend, and I believe that John is well pleased to know, wherever he is, that I began my homage to Allan by quoting him. So there, in a small example, is the idea of the community of cricket, the fraternity of cricket – and I use that word, fraternity, not as gender-specific, but for want of a better word, and as including all genders, masculine, feminine and neuter. This community of cricket is a set of concentric or overlapping communities, all mutually supportive, all important. There are the players, who are, of course, central; and there are the fans, looking or listening; and there are the wordsmiths, who fashion the pen-pictures and the commentary which are an important part of the record, and of the total experience. And all of these communities have in common the one love of cricket.

And speaking of wordsmiths, let me share with you another sign and wonder that came to me as I was preparing this little innings. It came on the morning when it hit me that what I must speak about was the love of cricket. Just after I began to feel satisfied with my decision, and to feel satisfied that I had found my theme, I happened to take up the *Gleaner*. The article at the top of the sports page was Tony Becca's column "From the Boundary", and the instalment for that day was entitled "A Pledge for Cricket". It was a tribute to the late Laurie Williams, whose untimely death had shocked us, and whose funeral service was scheduled for that day. But the tribute, interestingly enough, was not an analysis of Williams' skill on the cricket field, or a recital of his averages. Tony acknowledged that Williams represented Jamaica and the West Indies well, "that he was good – so good that he contributed, with bat and ball, to Jamaica's successes during his time." But Tony wanted to emphasise a different point – that "one other reason why Williams made such an impact on people inside and outside the cricket fraternity" was that he:

> loved cricket, he respected the game, he played it with passion, he enjoyed it – so much so that wherever he played, at whatever level he played, he made others enjoy it, and even those who had only heard of him admired him for it… Fewer and fewer people are playing the game [today] because they love it, because they enjoy it, and that is what, *as far as* participation and the development of the skill are concerned is hurting the game… Today… it is all about money…

Imagine my further delight, then my even greater certainty, on reading that Tony Becca had asked me to speak, and now, without knowing it, he was confirming what I should speak about.

Yes, today it is all about money, and even in some sordid ways at times. Cricket has become work, and the thumping dailiness of it threatens to dull the appetite and blunt the joy of the fans and the players alike. It's a great thing when one loves one's job; but it's another thing when an avocation becomes just another job.

The morning after I wrote those last three sentences, I opened the *Sunday Gleaner* to find another piece of good luck, an Associated Press report from Colombo under the caption "Let's Enjoy Cricket". It was a report of a statement by Nasser Hussain, the England captain, "on the eve of England's match against India in the Champions Trophy limited overs tournament." Hussain is reported as saying that he has "been mourning… for a long, long time" about the fact that "the packed international schedule was forcing players to jump from one series to another, taking some pleasure out of playing cricket," and, we may add, out of watching and following cricket. He urges that we, and in particular the International Cricket Council, "must not forget that cricket's a game… It's not a business where you schedule as many games as possible, and suck the money out of the game." I concur, wholeheartedly. Nasser Hussain, Tony Becca, me – here is another instance of the community of cricket, the community of the love of cricket, articulating itself, spontaneously.

But let us not give over this evening to apprehension and regret. This is an evening of celebration. So let's get back to celebrating what we have known from the time before the mass-produced, media-machined game began to threaten to overwhelm us with numbness and numbers. Let's celebrate for a moment the true love of cricket as it has expressed itself through the community and continuity of cricket that have extended over time and space. And that will bring me back to Allan Rae. Don't worry, I haven't forgotten him; I haven't forgotten that *he* is what this evening is about. It's just that I've been trying to craft my innings carefully and patiently, as he used to do his.

In men like Allan Rae we have the embodiment of the community and continuity of cricket, the love and spirit of cricket. We remember and commend his prowess, because that is what brought him to attention in the first place. But I want to stress now that other tremendous part of his legacy to us, the spirit in which he played the game and in which he continues to be deeply involved in it.

It has been a spirit of absolute unforced commitment and responsibility, commitment and responsibility to the game, to the team, to the community of cricket. It is the spirit that made him, on that 1950 tour, change his style to suit the team, because, as he said, "We had enough stroke players." It was the spirit which combined with strong technique made R.C. Robertson-Glasgow praise his "adamantine skill and monumental solidity", and made John Arlott say of him, "[H]e was more reliable than any other batsman West Indies cricket has possessed in my time." It is the spirit behind what his heroic team-mate and friend Everton Weekes has described as "the type of contribution that does not go into the record books."

The reliability, the rocklike quality of the skill is something that has not exactly been a feature of West Indian batting for a long time now. I'd like to suggest too that, certainly in the case of Allan Rae, it was partly a matter of single-minded application to correct technique. Only the other day, in his garden, always ready to share what he has learned, he was explaining to me how one of the more promising of the young crop of West Indian batsmen continues to get himself out because he continues to turn his torso square to the ball when driving, with the result that he often plays across the line of flight and gets out leg before wicket. And Allan, being Allan, and fully involved in the lesson, got up out of his chair to demonstrate, the right way and the wrong way. And, with regard to fielding, he told me how his father, who had been coached by the famous English coach Hunter Humphries in 1925, had taught him that, when fielding in the slips, you should go down far enough that the backs of your hands are brushing the turf. I noticed that Allan didn't bother to go down the whole way, but he went far enough to make the point.

One feature of Allan's love of cricket that I should like particularly to notice is that for him cricket is not just a pleasure for the limbs and the eye and the reflexes, but it is quintessentially a challenge for the head, a thinking person's game. So he talks with relish of how Gerry Alexander, watching from behind the stumps as Hanif Mohammad made his mammoth 337 against the West Indies at Bridgetown, had figured out how to get Mohammed out, and, under Alexander's direction, Tom Dewdney as the bowler and Allan Rae as the fieldsman had executed the strategy, getting him out caught for ducks. Similarly, Allan talks with a sense of special achievement when he tells of having done an article on Headley in which he never once used the word cricketer to identify the great man, but made a point of calling him a great thinker. Then he will illustrate by explaining how Headley, bowling to Everton Weekes in a Jamaica-Barbados match, shrewdly laid the trap for Rae to run out Weekes, or how Headley carefully contrived to catch Clyde Walcott off his own bowling.

The great cricketing spirit that we recognise in Allan Rae *is* the spirit that keeps him focused always on the future, on what can be done for the youngsters in cricket, just as it is the spirit that *is* always ready to share his rich store of instructive cricket anecdotes. It is the spirit and the commitment that have caused him to live a life of unbroken service to cricket, first as player, then as administrator. He has told me that he thinks that his years of greatest satisfaction, after he stopped playing, were his years on the West Indies Cricket Board of Control, and, knowing him, we can be certain that it was not because they satisfied the lust for power that is said to afflict all men. What they satisfied was the spirit that accounted for his "unyielding stand against apartheid" – to quote this morning's *Gleaner* – when he was at the helm of the WICBC. What they satisfied was the spirit that accounts for the fact that he has never missed a Test match at Sabina Park since his playing days, and for the fact that every Saturday he still has lunch at Sabina with Esmond Kentish.

It is the spirit, too, that I am happy to meet whenever I run into him (but not in the cricket-pitch sense), as I have occasionally done these past few years, in the aisles of one of the supermarkets at Liguanea, and we stop for a little chat about cricket, and I wonder if the people who pass by us are aware of the importance I have momentarily acquired by association. On those occasions I am sure to get one or more choice items from Allan's inexhaustible treasure trove of cricket anecdotes. And the sense of humour and wit that accounts for that fund of anecdotes, always instructive, is a vital part of the spirit of cricket and the love of cricket which Allan embodies.

In that unforgettable August of 1950, when the name Allan Rae first stamped itself indelibly on my memory, I was fourteen years old and half his age. Since that time, I've been slowly catching him up, so that now, far from being twice my age, he is a mere fourteen years older than me. But, of course, I cannot catch him, least of all overtake him, and I shouldn't wish to try. For if George Headley, Ole Massa as Allan used to call him, once, when he was on 80, decided to stop scoring, so that young Rae, at the other end and on 85, could get his hundred out of the 20 runs allowable before the new ball was due to be taken, we say to our Ole Massa now, "Don't stop scoring. Play on, till stumps."

HILARY McD. BECKLES

HISTORY, THE KING, THE CROWN PRINCE AND I
(Published in the Sunday Sun *(Barbados) 24, 25 and 26 April 1994)*

Six months ago the University, for reasons still not altogether clear to many people, suggested that I could now use the title "Professor". Then someone placed the wretched idea in my head that a fete would be an appropriate instrument with which to represent the moment of weakness on the University's part. I am yet to meet a committed historian who is a fête man. I do not know why this is so. Perhaps we fear that if we abandon our senses while revelling, some historical event of seminal significance would come into being without proper documentation. Eric Williams wrote his history books while his nation went into social leave that is called carnival. As a young student I went to fetes with novels in my pocket just in case I "had" to read something.

I say all of this just to indicate that my counter proposal was simple, yet revolutionary in the context. I satisfied myself that "nothing" could be more pleasing than attending all matches during the upcoming Test tour. I supported my proposal with reference to being a "teacher" of cricket culture and that the cricket book in my head, which is crying out to be written, needed some assistance. In all honesty I could not say that I needed the rest since, as cultists, we all know that there is nothing more taxing upon the mind and soul than watching quality cricket. And so, I went off to Sabina Park, Amos Vale, Queen's Park, etc., etc. Kensington, I decided, would be the end of the line for me. This has nothing to do with being "home" or any such mindless sentiment. Rather, it was the end of the line because I could not take the weight of historical forces that had revealed themselves as England charged home to their first Test victory there since 1935 – supported by a massive cohort of 6,000 "domestic" supporters that had flown in specially for the match. Outnumbered, outplayed and out of pocket I was ready to retreat long before the hangman on the public announcement system indicated after our defeat by England that "union jacks are available two for ten dollars below the Three Ws stand".

My brother came in from Ohio, USA to watch Lara. US$2,000 is a fair investment to make on a statement from a younger brother in which it is indicated that the sum is quite modest with respect to the quality of the art likely to be seen. Lara flicked off the hip and the investment was written off as a bad debt; as pure and simple as the world inhabited by economists, accountants, and unaccountable governments. In spite of it all, and as one not afraid of the future on account of my unique mixture of naivety and Christian socialization, I suggested that he should go to Antigua for redress and compensation. I said that I could not make the trip, but that I had friends there who would look after him. There, I said, you would see what C.L.R. James meant when he indicated that the revolutionary spirit unleashed by Sobers will bear a sweet fruit for decades to come. We believers, of course, have become accustomed to the remarkable expressions of sinners when confronted with the naked declaration of our faith. He was taken to Sir Grantley Adams and that was that.

I really had no intentions of going to Antigua. Then I received an offer I could not refuse. I was called upon by my personal deity to do a small deed that sent my entire being into convulsions: "Professor Beckles, we, the Oval Action Committee, have decided to honour Viv Richards on Sunday night, and he would like you to come to Antigua in order to speak at the function. Viv is from our village, and he feels that you understand the circumstances and contours of his career. If you agree, all arrangements will be made." When I arrived in Antigua on the Friday morning my mind was filled with references to the fastest hundred Viv had played there. Notions of the "biggest" hundreds were not in the making. Hanging out with Viv was my only concern – in fact I had had enough field play and thirsted only for the cricket beyond the boundary.

Saturday morning I walked from my hotel to the ground, and arrived there about 9:45. Richie Richardson spotted me attempting to cross the road, picked me up in his Jeep and took me to the car park after which we entered the gates. He indicated that Lara would be vice captain for the match and I reflected on a discussion we had had along similar lines a year earlier. It had come to pass and I sensed the beginnings of a new era. Richie had to make arrangements for his young niece who was his companion for the day, and we parted company outside the Viv Richards Pavilion. As I approached the entry to this relaxed and unpretentious facility, Andy Roberts was standing there waiting. He presented me with a pass for the five days, and took me upstairs. I said good morning to David Holford, and he gave me the information requested. Walsh was captain, he had won the toss and obviously would bat, Simmons and Williams were in. I gave Gary a hug, shook the hands of Peter Short, Clyde Walcott, and settled down to watch the openers with young Dr McIntyre, my vice chancellor's son.

There is something about the spirit of the Antigua Recreation Grounds (ARG) that enhances high performance. I maintain that it is not the duppy wicket, but the welcoming spirit of a critical people that lifts the artist – if genuine – above and beyond self to a place where the reciprocity endemic to African theatre survives. After an expected ordinary prelude, Lara arrived at the wicket. No collars were turned up, and no gum was being chewed, but the intentions were identical as was the reaction of the crowd that has long learnt that there are ways to recognize false prophets other than placing them in fiery furnaces.

The ball is not coming on, and a second too soon can send you back to the

262

pavilion within the minute. Time for some is money, but for most it is the very essence of something greater – art and the glory thereof. Once, as a student, we invited C.L.R. James to address us on the state of the revolution in Angola and Mozambique. He was due to speak at 4:00 p.m. A snow storm that afternoon had trapped students in their dormitories. At 4:00 p.m. the audience consisted of just two students. We asked that the event be delayed for an hour. James refused and lectured to us two for two hours. At 6:00 p.m. five buses arrived with over 300 students. James looked at them and said that these students do not understand cricket and therefore are not fit to represent the people. Lara's timing was perfect. He did not go immediately into a boundaries gear, but the bat and pad methodology was in place as it should be, and the matter was settled. For the first time he looked the player that had risen above the flashes of brilliance; the sharp edges were rounded a little, but the instrument seemed more deadly. I have not seen such certainty of purpose, and display of control and command since Viv's 232 at Trent Bridge in 1976.

Watching a cricket match with Gary is not pleasurable. It reminded me somehow of my first lecture as a freshman student. Overwhelmed by the occasion, you can easily forget your own opinion. I asked, in a sheepish sort of way, my first question. "Gary, Lara seemed determined to do something extraordinary, would you agree?" "Well," Gary said, "we were a little disappointed with him in Barbados, and I told him so. I told him this morning that he must live his game, play it in his head first. I also told him that if he forgets flicking off the middle stump to mid-wicket from the rising ball they would never get him out, and that he should promise me to do just that." I certainly would not promise Gary anything. I couldn't live with the responsibility. You could feel the weight of his pledge to Gary during the first hundred; get over the ball before you cut, and push the good length rising ball to mid-on for a single. Mathematics is really quite simple once you know the relevant theorems, we were told. But simple things require complex analysis and teachers can never understand this matter.

After the first hundred, Lara took Fraser from outside the off-stump and deposited him at the mid-wicket fence. I told Gary that the Viv Richards in the "Boy" is clear. Sobers nodded. Said nothing. Next over, he got back and slapped the same gentleman straight down the wicket off a good length ball pitched about off and middle to the sight screen. Mid-off retreated. I said to Gary, this time with greater force of lung, "Now deny that that wasn't you out there!" Academics have not yet come to terms with clear explanations for these matters. To the question how are the varied elements that constitute the substructure of a cultural form consolidated and reproduced in the consciousness of progeny we have no convincing answer. The eye, technique and timing of Gary, the ideological contempt for foolishness of Viv, and the occasional display of Sir Frank's grace and elegance, were on show at the ARG and those gathered there, recently admitted to the Test fold, understood it. The first to achieve full emancipation in 1834, Antiguans are interesting people. The race is not for the swiftest!

Sunday night I spoke at Viv's function. My task was to place Viv within the context of the post-independence West Indies nationalist dispensation. Viv himself had said that for him cricket was always a highly politicized business. He wanted to bring certainty, mastery, and confidence in authority to a young nation seeking a secure place within an angry neo-imperialist world. The in-crowd at Lord's respected Gary's art, but feared Viv's politics. While speaking about Viv, I was very conscious that all within my audience could not wait to see whether Lara would "do it" the next morning. I had asked him how his body was coping with the stress and fatigue. He said that it was not a physical affair, but that his mental stamina was waning. That same Sunday night Gary spoke to him and offered him the keys to unlocking new sources of stamina. He told him then, and again at golf next morning, not to think of himself and the 45 runs, but to feel that West Indies needed 45 runs to win the match and that only he could score these runs. That is, keep the mind focused on the collective objective not the personal triumph. Lara told me that he went about the Monday morning task with that concept in mind, and that being vice captain made it easier to apply. It is important to understand this matter. The idea that supporting the "whole" motivates more than pleasing the "part" is critical to an understanding of cricket excellence. Geoff Boycott never understood this, and that is why selectors dropped him after scoring a "slow" double century that cost his team the game. When Richie spoke to my cricket class two years ago this was the basis of his thesis on leadership processes.

Monday morning proved difficult to negotiate. I was due back at Cave Hill to teach my cricket class. Wes Hall and Gary, I want to say, considered me rather unprofessional and "strange" for wishing to rush back to Cave Hill to teach cricket history when it was being made before me. Wes "is" a politician, and when Gary said that no "bird" in Antigua could pluck Brian, I made the phone call to Cave Hill and was told that my students had already indicated their unavailability for the class. All was well. I stayed because those who could read the future requested it. I ordered coffee, went downstairs, discussed the previous night's function with Viv, and prepared to see if Gary was reading things the way he had always done. As I sat down Lara gently placed Fraser's outswinger where a second slip could have been, beating Caddick at third man. My father always spoke about Sir Frank doing that sort of thing.

I should admit that when play began I was not yet convinced. I had been there at the Oval on 12 August 1976 when Viv "gave it away" at 291; I heard about Rowe's "collapsing" with exhaustion at Kensington. Reports said that dust got into the left eye of Gooch at 332, and I felt that only David Rudder's band which backed Gravey could help him with those 45 runs. How many believed Noah before the drizzle got heavier? There had been drizzles before, and a big boat was nothing to behold. Monday morning I was not on the Ark, but Gary would tell you that I was first to drown in the champagne when a long hop bowled by Lewis to a called-in field gave Lara 369. It was the final demonstration of technical brilliance and patience that characterized the innings.

Gary's playing golf with Lara at six o'clock Monday morning cannot be considered a minor detail. There are a number of issues to be considered here. The question of the "special" relationship between the two men is important. The Monday morning session was a deliberate expression of bonding on Gary's part designed to prepare Lara for the task ahead. When they returned to the hotel just after eight o'clock, the matter was settled between the two. This was clear to me. Lara was authorized and empowered. When he strolled to the wicket, then, two hours later, he was sent on a mission, and Gary's only apprehension was whether or not he would do as he was told.

I explained to Viv that morning that Lara had been put under "manners" by Gary from the beginning, and that the record of 365 would be adjusted. I went even further and told Prime Minister Lester Bird, that he would soon have two Test records in Antigua – the "fastest" and now the "biggest" hundred. He agreed and indicated that it was fitting that Viv and Gary were there to witness the event. I did not know then that Lester had been a fast bowler of sorts in his time, but he indicated to me that since Lara's bat had no edge when on the front foot, and that the wicket was too slow to produce one off the back foot, only a well disguised full toss could get him out. I do not quarrel with prime ministers in their countries. In fact, I do not quarrel with prime ministers in other people's countries.

At 351, Gary smiled and said that Lara's occasional display of nervousness was no problem, since the bowlers would be in an even greater state of psychological dislocation. I didn't think of the bowler's condition as relevant, but it was. The quality of the bowling attack deteriorated, as did the captain's field placing. Lara's edge through the slips off Caddick could have been fatal, but alas there was no slip and a diving Russell exaggerated the captain's vote of no confidence in the bowler. Russell got to his feet to the sound of an Antiguan version of "Ragga Ragga" to which Gravey was exposing his slip to 12,000 spellbound expectants. At 360, Sky Television removed Gary from our presence and positioned him at the fence for the entrance and the special embrace. Gary said, "Fellas, I will be back in a moment; a little matter to handle downstairs", and off he went to settle with Brian the matter in which his own hand had played so critical a role.

Desmond Haynes, meanwhile, had indicated that it was only "an act of God" that had prevented Lara from breaking the record in Australia. A batsman running himself out can hardly be considered an act of God; that he slipped, can be placed on the agenda for discussion. The wicket, someone said, was a duppy wicket. Well, we were 12 for 2, and duppy wickets can produce some pretty dumb shots. The first 50 runs was the slowest Lara had ever scored in Tests. That says a great deal. His second hundred was played along the carpet, that says even more. The wicket didn't kill the attack; it was the viciousness of Adams' and Lara's determination that blunted its edge. Chanderpaul's presence led to disillusionment on the bowlers' part. Lara reaped much of the rewards of his partners' efforts. It was a process of socialist redistribution and an affirmation of the higher productivity of collectivism.

We drank champagne, and we celebrated another stage in the rise of our cricket culture. I made reference to those who had gone before – Constantine, Headley, Sir Frank especially – and the king and I congratulated the new crown prince. Back at Cave Hill students in my cricket class confessed that it was the best seminar in the course so far. I did not argue, after all, circumstances had rendered my presence irrelevant to the process of history making. As a historian I have no problems in knowing my place, and understanding the occasional cruelty of historical forces. I did not intend to be there, but circumstances dictated otherwise. Now, who on earth can say that the professor is writing about things that he did not experience and therefore knows nothing about?

RETURN TO BOURDA

The India/Guyana match in March 1997 made me realise that it was in 1962, during another Indian tour, that I had last visited Bourda. On the second day of the match, I found a seat in what used to be called the South Stand, but now had been renamed after Rohan Kanhai. This name-change sent my head spinning, especially when I saw that other stands were named after Clive Lloyd and Lance Gibbs. My head spun faster when I also saw that the pavilion which, in 1962, was packed with white or near-white, colonial-upper-caste members with names like Wishart and Wight, was now almost completely dotted with black and brown faces.

It would be too much to claim that Lloyd, Gibbs and Kanhai, not to mention Kanhai's fellow denizen from Port Mourant, Cheddi Bharat Jagan, are entirely responsible for this transformation of the Georgetown Cricket Club (GCC) which has its home at Bourda; but these cricketers and Dr. Jagan undoubtedly had something to do with it. For this transformation was not due to any ordinary process of historical evolution: it was, to a large extent, the conscious handiwork of particular people. It seems, for example, when Kanhai first arrived from the outer darkness of Port Mourant to represent his country at Bourda, that the only accommodation he could find in Georgetown was the home of Badge Menzies, the GCC groundsman, who lived under the pavilion at Bourda. For GCC to name a stand after someone who formerly lodged under their pavilion is both ironic and symbolic, and it confirms the scale and speed of the transformation of the club. Irony and symbolism also strengthen the claim that the transformation of GCC is part of the nationwide process of social and political change engineered by many people, including cricketers and politicians, most notably by Dr. Jagan who spent his entire life in an attempt to dismantle, firstly, the feudalistic structure of colonial Guyana, and secondly, the global superstructure that holds poorer, Southern nations in a dependent relationship to wealthier nations in the North.

Other changes at GCC included additional stands that are larger and seemingly more comfortable, and a new press box that looked more like a dainty, oversized doll's house than an observation deck for manly contests of physical stamina, technical skill and psychological strategy. These changes evoked a mixture of nostalgia and patriotism that I came to relish as the day wore on. After all, it was no small thing to return to my native ground, the place where I first beheld the wonder of international cricket, after an absence of thirty-five years! My mind was rampant with memory: visions of Kanhai's dauntless audacity, Butcher's rhythmic punchiness, Gibbs's combative wizardry, and the inimitable artistry of Robert Julian Christiani who blended dance and poetry into a style of batsmanship that I have seen in no one else anywhere.

Now, as I watched, memories of these heroes gradually faded to be replaced by the spectacle of a new hero – Shivnarine Chanderpaul – the youth from Unity who kept India at bay while his even more youthful compatriots were being scattered like ninepins all around him. Three weeks before, I had seen Chanderpaul's historic 137 not out at Kensington Oval, Barbados, where he appeared to be threatened by purgatorial fire as he staggered through the final approaches to his maiden Test century. He stood motionless on 97 for the longest time, transfixed like a man about to meet his maker, until a stroke past mid-on opened the way to his coveted goal. Then, it truly looked as if the hounds of hell were after him; for I never saw a man run so fast for three paltry runs. The stroke was more push than drive, and like so much of Chanderpaul's batting, bespoke care, concentration and entertainment in classic rather than romantic vein. Chanderpaul is no Lara, just as Sir Frank Worrell was no Sir Everton Weekes. For all that, the reception of Chanderpaul's century at Kensington Oval probably did more for Caribbean integration than Lara's 375, Sobers's 365 or even Federation and CARICOM.

Guyana gushed with affection and pride as this native son, in this match, his first appearance in his native land since becoming a Test centurion, seemed to be coasting to his century with greater composure than he did at Kensington. Meanwhile, like forest fires which ignite spontaneously in hot sun, affection and pride soon sprouted an argument in my stand over the relative merits of Chanderpaul and Hooper as batsmen. As it happens, Chanderpaul's case was presented by a group of Indo-Guyanese, and Hooper's by Afro-Guyanese. A long row of empty Banks bottles beside the first group testified to the volume of beer that, in addition to affection and pride, fuelled the argument. Examples of each hero's merits were traded with mounting heat and decreasing cogency, since, as anyone familiar with West Indian cricket grounds will know, such arguments have less to do with intellectual exchange than with loudness, ribaldry and humour. Predictably, the argument ended as pointlessly as it began. But not before one Afro-Guyanese taunted his Indo counterpart: "Man, yuh doan support West Indies". To those who had ears to hear, this parting and seemingly irrelevant shot laid bare the underlying and, till then, unspoken racial logic of the whole argument. The Indo-Guyanese was stunned. He floundered for a moment in confusion, before catching himself to counter: "Man, I support Guyana". It was an admission of defeat; and the Afro-Guyanese ignored him with a suitably scornful sneer that confirmed his triumph.

Perhaps the changes that I had noticed earlier were more illusory than real, since this inconclusive argument made me recall a similar incident, during the Indian tour of 1962, when the overwhelming dominance of West Indies over India made it difficult for those Indo-Guyanese who supported India to argue their case convincingly. One ploy, when faced with Afro-Guyanese gloating over West Indian dominance, was the Indo-Guyanese riposte: "Man, is wha' yuh talking? When yuh all can sen' a team from Africa, den yuh can talk". Surprisingly, such hilarious ignorance effectively shut up many of the more timid Afro-Guyanese. It had evidently shut up one such man who found himself among a group of fellow Afro-Guyanese spectators whose jubilation over West Indian success was being effusively trumpeted. In the midst of their gloating, this man suddenly blurted out: "Well, me cyan talk yuh hear, till ahwee can sen' we own team from Africa!" Instant silence. The group's bubble of joy, confidence and dignity had been punctured. They could not make out whether this was sheer effrontery, gross treachery from one of their own, or the simple result of perverse indoctrination by rival Indo-Guyanese. They glared dumbfounded at the intruder until one of them, more out of pity than protest, upbraided him with: "Man, dat is de essence of shit!" Peals of uproarious laughter restored instant dignity to the group. "Is who out dey pon de field? Yuh eye good or wah?" The rhetorical force of such unanswerable logic utterly demolished the intruder who hung his head in remorseful silence. Had things really changed between 1962 and 1997! *Plus ça change...*

But things had indeed changed. I noticed several female Indo-Guyanese spectators, for instance, some with their families, others sitting by themselves. That didn't happen in 1962; and I was attracted by one woman of striking if unconventional beauty. She was brown skinned, full proportioned, and probably in her early thirties. She sat with her two sons, each about nine or ten years old, while her husband had moved off to drink with male buddies a few feet away. The woman had short, black hair which fell attractively around her neck. A squarish jaw and a dark mole on her right cheek added a touch of sensuality, while her short, wraparound denim skirt left less to the imagination than was healthy for the heartbeat of a middle-aged man. At teatime the woman uncovered a hamper and served her family delicious-smelling curried chicken wrapped in dhalpuri. I was devoured by lust – sexual and alimentary – as I stared in silence. Meanwhile, the erstwhile proponents of Chanderpaul and Hooper had also fallen strangely silent, whether because of similar lust or through delight – in Chanderpaul's escape from the purgatory of Kensington, I do not know. At any rate, this woman appeared to vindicate the transformation that had overtaken GCC and Guyana since 1962. For one thing, her presence as an Indo-Guyanese woman at Bourda was new; secondly, her beauty partly atoned for a circle of saman trees that had once bedecked Bourda with vanished splendour; and thirdly; the combination of her presence and beauty asserted the saving resilience of both her gender and nation in the midst of social and political change, much post-Independence folly, and grievous, national decline.

In 1939 Aimé Césaire of Martinique wrote a long poem, *Return to my Na-*

tive Land, that became a clarion call for decolonization, particularly among people from Africa and the African diaspora. "Aiee," cried Césaire, "for those who have explored nothing." This cry defied colonization and celebrated decolonization. My return to Bourda defied or celebrated nothing. But it acknowledges the role of cricket and politics in the decolonization of Guyana.

VILLAGE CRICKET

Village cricket in Trinidad – Cosmopolitan teams – Food, drink and boundary hits – We watch the umpire – Splendid fielding – When intercolonials play for their village – Six intercolonials beaten by two unknown batsmen – Derek Sealey's beginnings – Headley makes himself famous – George Gunn is followed about – Preparing to go to England as a professional – Aspects of the professional game.

That was wonderful summer! And yet – how glad I was to get back home, to feel every fibre of me responding to the old familiar smells and sights and sounds of Port of Spain! How glad, even after watching the cricket gods upon the heights of Olympus, to grin at the village children batting with terrifying earnestness with palm trees for wickets, or to cheer myself hoarse as I lay in the shade looking on at an inter-village struggle with bat and ball!

The average Trinidad village contains a few hundred people, mostly rather poor; labourers in the fields, carpenters, agricultural workers, the village teacher, perhaps two parsons (Roman Catholic and Anglican), Negroes mostly, a number of Indian labourers, some Chinese and Spaniards too.

The village cricket ground takes the place in social affairs occupied formerly in England by the village green. The ground is seldom more than half the proper size, the outfield is shaggy and bumpy, the wicket is hard – bare soil covered with a half-size bit of elderly matting with holes in it. On this the lads of the village practise every evening and on Sundays except when a match is being played.

The team is cosmopolitan, including Negroes, a fleet-footed Indian or two, and perhaps the son of a wealthy Chinese shopkeeper whose finances keep the side going. The Chinese may be the captain, or that post may be taken by the schoolmaster or some older Negro villager.

Matches are played mostly on Sunday afternoons, against other villages within a radius of ten miles or so. For the match they may borrow a full-length matting from a rich club in a nearby township; or, quite often, the visiting team takes its own half, and both halves are nailed down, full of patches, perhaps with a hole or two, but good enough for a fine, sporting game.

About one o'clock on a broiling Sunday afternoon two buses roll up beneath the palm trees, bringing the visiting team and its vociferous supporters. Later buses bring more onlookers, each with his own full-sized voice. The local villagers turn up in force, mostly men, but with an increasing sprinkling of women and girls, very brightly clad and very noisy. Drinks are going freely; there may be a village string band; there are usually some whistles and rattles.

The match starts about 2.30, invariably with a demon bowler. He really is fast, as fast as many a British county fast bowler, and very often with a savage off break. He can always find a hole or bump in the pitch, and wickets begin to fly early, and left-handed compliments, too. Every ball, every stroke, is received with yells of derision or encouragement; the atmosphere becomes electric; men field, bat and bowl as if for their very lives. The standard of the play is extraordinarily high. Seventy is a high score, and the batsman who makes 20 is considered to have borne himself gallantly. There are no appeals for bodyline, and none for light. If a ball bumps, the batsman is expected to flog it to the boundary, and if he is fool enough to hit it with his head instead of the bat, a leg bye is the most that is expected of it.

Each team has one or two real hitters. These are men of giant girth and enormous good nature. When they come to the wicket (since the capacities of each player are widely known and anyhow advertised by his admiring fans in attendance) the field opens right out. The first ball, however good, usually goes over the railway line, the next over the river or smack on to the roof of a house outside the ground. Very often the ball will be lost, and then both teams and the entire body of onlookers go to search for it. It is invariably found by a diminutive black boy who is loudly accused of having hidden it, replies shrilly in kind, and is carried shoulder-high back to the field.

There is an interval halfway through the afternoon, not to suck lemons but for solid food and mighty drinks. Then the other side goes in to bat. The umpire is closely watched by all spectators, advised, and, if he shows too much local zeal, warned of sundry blood-curdling dangers to his life. Every ball and every stroke, every bit of fielding and wicketkeeping, is photographically remembered by people who do not have newspapers, cinemas, greyhound racing and other vanities to distract their minds from the proper contemplation of the Great Game; and these things are talked of for months afterwards, the more outstanding performances being remembered and recalled in detail by all for many years. This is village cricket indeed, with the keenness that will one day soon turn out a team of world-beaters.

At night, after the match, there is dancing, more food, more drinks. Torches flare under the palms, or the great moon shines golden; there is warmth and companionship and simple happiness everywhere. Sometimes I wonder whether modern Western civilization, with all its mechanical gadgets and its blaring noises and wars and petrol-reeking smells and worries and nervous strains and the rush that gives people no time to be happy and no time to live, is really, after all, worth so much more than just a cricket match away there in a poor West Indies village.

The fielding in these village matches is sometimes up to crack British county standard. The batting is crude, but it gets the runs, and might do so even against fine bowling. Certainly, some of the swipers would knock the varnish off some famous bowlers I have met before they fell to the inevitable. Now and then, out there, you see the born cricketer, playing with a natural grace and style, forward and back, glancing them to leg, cutting, making strokes right out of the book; no one has taught him; probably he cannot read or write and will never have a chance to play big cricket or turn out for anything but his unknown village.

Sometimes one may see an intercolonial with a world-famous name, a man who has toured England or Australia, week-ending in his home village, turning out for the local team, and being treated with just as much hearty disrespect as anyone else, both by players and onlookers. The great man who has scored his century at Lord's or Sydney comes in, takes centre amid a shower of shouted humorous advice, and perhaps is bowled out for a duck by an Indian boy no one ten miles away has ever heard of; and no grey-haired newspaper critic of international celebrity can make such scathing comments as will follow from a thousand lusty throats!

I have myself been welted for three sixes from three successive balls in such a game. No use comforting oneself with the knowledge that on a full-size ground the swiper would have been out every ball. The game is being played here, and he has scored 18 off three balls, and the shouts have gone up above the palm-tops; I may bowl down an all-England side for a song next summer, but right here and now my name is mud and I know it, and only the roaring good nature of the occasion and much food and a couple of stout drinks will bring me back to normality again.

I remember one village match when six of us, all internationals, turned out. It was an all-day affair, a terrific affair; we were playing the pick of several villages and each man had dedicated his life to showing us up! Two unknown Negro batsmen settled at the wickets to do or die. Soon we who had begun in a spirit of fun were bowling all out. We could not move them. We sent up stuff that had worried Hobbs and Sutcliffe and turned Don Bradman green, and they rubbed their sweating hands and took deep breaths and knocked it flying over the treetops. Presently a boy we had picked up at random to help complete the side went on, and took 5 wickets for about 30 runs.

After that, so as not to disappoint our friends, we had to field as in a Test, run people out by "impossible" throws, take catches that nearly broke our necks (and hands!), and, in the second innings, bowl out the crack batsmen for nothing.

In some ways, intercolonial tournament matches are easier than these village games, because at least you do know what you will come up against. Though every now and again a new star rises and astonishes everyone.

Such a star rose in Barbados in 1929. Derek Sealey, a short, sturdy Negro, had played wicketkeeper for a village team, and was not reckoned to have much other ability. Then, at sixteen years old, he came in 1929 to Trinidad to play in the intercolonial matches. I was playing for Trinidad, and at the top of my form both with ball and bat; I had just scored my first intercolonial century, 131, establishing a Trinidad record and beating my father's record of 116 made 19 years previously. I had helped to bowl down most of the Barbados wickets when this young wicketkeeper came in, late in the innings, at a critical moment in the game. He played courageously and well, made quite a good score, and was proof against our best bowling.

Nobody except the bowlers on the field that day realized just how good this modest schoolboy was. But when the M.C.C. team arrived a few months later, with such bowlers as Wilfred Rhodes, Townsend, Voce and Calthorpe among them, and young Derek Sealey knocked up a level 100 against them for Barbados, and then went on to score 50 in a Test, it was obvious that he had a cricketing future.

During my visit to Jamaica, before I went on to Nelson, I saw another youngster who was later to make cricket history. Julian Cahn had brought a sort of miniature Test team from England to Jamaica, a very strong side indeed, and Small, Francis and I were invited to turn out in a match against them. Included in our side was George Headley, then eighteen years old and until the previous year quite unknown, as he had never before 1928 played in a first-class game.

In his first game against a visiting English XI, in 1928, young Headley knocked up a faultless 71, and in the third and last game he made 211 not out in one of the most stylish innings ever seen in West Indies cricket. Against Cahn's team I saw Headley knock up 44 on a very bad wicket. The thing that impressed me most was the way he treated Wilfred Rhodes' slows in the 1929-30 Tests. Rhodes at that time was still a name to conjure with; a year or two before he had bowled down an Australian Test team at the Oval for a ridiculous handful of runs and won the match almost by himself. Most batsmen covered up against him, taking no chances for many an over. Not so George Headley. He would run down the pitch to everything that was short of a length, and drive it clean over the bowler's head for a four or a six. He is one of the smallest of cricketers, and in those days was fairly slight also, and to see him do it made one laugh with sheer delight.

George Gunn, after beginning that tour quietly, at least in that respect, presently stole a leaf out of the youngster's book, and began running down the pitch to Achong, our new slow left-hander. Too much belabouring in first Tests will sometimes spoil a bowler's nerve almost for life, so I decided to intervene. I was fielding at slip in an early Test, and when Achong sent up the right ball I ran down behind George Gunn; he found the ball a little unexpected and played forward instead of driving it, and edged! I was already beyond the batting crease on his heels, and reached forward and gathered the ball from the side of the bat. George gave me an old-fashioned look and continued on his way to the pavilion; but young Achong's confidence went up several hundred per cent, and it is a matter of history now what a fine player he has become.

However, I am running a little ahead of my story. Before the M.C.C. came, I had a season to put in over in England as a professional, an adventure to which I looked forward with equal delight and uneasiness, for it was a very big new departure for me, and I naturally wondered how well I should stand up to requirements.

For there is a notable difference between playing as an amateur and facing batsman or bowler with the knowledge that a slip may cost you your job. In the modern county game, with captaincy possibilities, and international caps as rewards for brilliant amateur play, the tenseness is much the same for all the members of a team. But in the West Indies we have never played cricket quite like that; we have never forgotten that it is primarily a *game* for players and onlookers to enjoy, rather than a grim battle to be won at any cost of tedium and at the price of literally any stratagem not verbally forbidden in the rules – some of such stratagems being unpleasant ones. I do not for a moment suggest that county cricket is generally unscrupulous, though it is well known that the best batsman in some counties is the groundsman. But anyone who has taken part in Tests or trials for Tests is aware that the battle goes to the strong and the ruthless, that spectators may be bored to tears and nervous young players flogged into obscurity for life, that propaganda is not forgotten and that a cruel word that can unnerve a player on or off the field is not omitted. I have never been one to cry out for kid gloves, but I see no sense in pretending that they are always worn in cricket.

I had all these things in mind as I crossed the water once more for my first professional season in England.

A BIRTHDAY GIFT

The problem is that at a certain age it becomes difficult to buy birthday gifts for a boy. Fourteen years is probably when the trouble starts. My son's birthday is in three days' time. He will be fourteen. The challenge is to get something he needs and not something he might want, because at this age, what he wants would not be good for him. But he won't be forgiving and pretend that the gift is a good one even if he hates it. My son does not fake it well. He will try to smile and say, "I really don't know what I would do with this." And that will be that. I could buy him a CD, and I have done that, but I want to do something special, something that will connect us more powerfully, something that will change the world as we know it.

To the cynics among you I will say only one thing: he is my son, and why should this act of celebration not have a revolutionary impact on the universe? If everyone were to think so negatively, where would we be as a human race?

Several months ago, my son was talking about getting together with some of his friends to play cricket. They even formed a cricket club, but this was in the winter, and so they just talked – nothing was done. Today, three days before his birthday, he and his friends seem to have lost interest in the project. They are dealing with end of year exams, and the reality of summer heat has already set in here in South Carolina. The NBA playoffs are on, baseball is in full swing, and his friends are thinking about more pressing things. But the conjunction of a series of seemingly minor developments has made me think that perhaps I need to think along the lines of cricket for my son's birthday.

It is important to admit that the very idea of playing cricket in Columbia, South Carolina, is absurd. I have never seen a cricket game in Columbia – other than one in which I was playing. We had gone to a park with some of the kids from my son's middle school to have some fun. I took along a bat and a ball. We played cricket. They had a great time, as I recall. I certainly had a fantastic time walloping their balls all over the field. They were so impressed with my skills.

We moved to this state in 1992 from eastern Canada. There, I was playing with a cricket team – a Caribbean cricket team – in an amateur league during the small window of warm weather in the summer. The team was made up of students and residents of our town, Fredericton, who were all from the Caribbean. We played on uneven fields, rolling out our portable cricket matting to compete with teams of varied competence and experience. We travelled all across eastern Canada to play enjoyable, but decidedly skill-less matches. But we were playing cricket. That was the important thing. I was playing the game that I loved and had lived with in Jamaica.

But when we landed in the United States, in the small town of Sumter, I knew that my cricket days were over. I knew it so well that for a few months I would walk to then idle baseball stadium behind my university campus with a baseball bat and ball in hand, and practise hitting the ball, all by myself. I'd return home with a badly bruised wrist, and a terrible sense that this game was not going to replace my need for cricket. What I did not realise was that the loss of cricket would be thorough and would actually presage the demise of West Indian cricket as we once knew it. Many will recall that the decline of West Indian cricket did not begin until around 1993–95 – after our arrival in Sumter. We started to seem vulnerable, our respectability resting only on our one-day prowess. Much of this is a little vague to me. I lost track of the team. I lost track of their games. I lost track of what was happening with West Indian cricket, and once that happened, the powerful control and mental hold that I had on the team diminished.

What I am saying here, however, was not clear to me for quite some time. I did not know I had been holding the West Indian team together all those years, and that once I took my mind off the team – once, if you will, I took my eyes off the ball – the decline began. My neglect had tragic consequences. Batsmen would begin with great confidence, hitting the ball all over the place, and then they would lose focus and get out stupidly. Soon our teams were given to sudden collapses. Soon countries that did not even have a sensible Test team were beating us. Soon, our fast bowlers were being slaughtered. I heard rumours about this decline, and I felt some guilt, but I discovered too late that it was my fault.

I can understand the reader's scepticism, but I must explain that I was not a casual fan of West Indies cricket. I did not watch games just for entertainment. I watched games and listened to games as one who was actually out there playing. I could do this because I was a player of the game. I was a coach, I was a player and I could well have been a West Indian cricketer had I not been afflicted with a congenital disease of the cornea that at one point left me legally blind. When I was invited to try out in 1980 for the West Indies Youth Team at Sabina Park, I did not realise it then, but the fact that I could not see the four balls bowled to me by Patrick Patterson (yes, the one who would go on to play for the West Indies, that one) had nothing to do with his speed and fierceness, but entirely to do with the fact that I was suffering a serious problem with my eyesight. I had no problems hearing the whistling of the ball as it whizzed past me, or the thud of the ball in the keeper's gloves, or the giggle of the slip fielders at the spectacle of my bewilderment; but I just could not see the ball. I made fifteen runs thanks to Patterson's speed and by being able to guess, by the physical action of a bowler, generally where balls would go.

Yet throughout that humbling experience, my brain never stopped playing cricket, carrying each instant of the game in my head, controlling every step of the game. I spoke to myself while batting, while fielding, and while watching a game. It was a habit. I spoke to myself, spoke to the ball, spoke to the other players while I was coaching. They did not hear me speaking, but my words willed them to act in the way that I wanted them to act. That was my technique as a coach. This shaped how I listened to games on the radio, how I followed the game in general. This power did not work with non-West Indian players, however. It may have been a language issue.

I used this power to ensure the many victories of the West Indies from the mid Seventies, through the Eighties and until 1992. Then I became distracted. America built a force-field of forgetfulness around me, and I abandoned the West Indies cricket team to its tragic decline. In America, I could not concentrate on cricket. I was trying to understand baseball, trying to make sense of football, and I was actually enjoying and developing emotional relationships with basketball teams. In fact, during the 1995 NBA finals between the Houston Rockets and the Orlando Magic, I actually began to use my powers – well I tried. I calculated that since Hakeem Olajuwon was Nigerian and my father had been born in Nigeria (and I had been born in Ghana, a neighbour of Nigeria), I somehow had the right to exercise this brainpower on the game. As most of you know, despite Shaquille O'Neal's presence, I gave Houston a rare victory for a sixth-seeded team in the finals. I could not continue, though, after that. I felt dirty, felt like someone who had cheated on a game that had no geo-political relevance. America was making me a cheap, filthy prostitute, and that incident had a great impact on me, making me stop that kind of brain work altogether.

Today, May 21st 2008, I have come into the truth of my failing. The West Indies are to face Australia in the first test of a three-match series starting tomorrow morning, and I have started to pay attention to the series. The thing is, I came across the fact of the test by accident. I was getting ready to travel to Jamaica for the Calabash International Literary Festival that I programme each year, when someone asked me if I planned to arrive early to watch the test. The question hit me with such force and ferocity because the person was laughing. He was an old friend from my school days – a fast bowler who seemed to regard me as a better good luck charm than a cricketer. "Maybe you will bring us some luck," he said, chuckling. But he was also serious. I realised how desperate he was. At that moment, I did the math. I checked back to see when the West Indian decline began and I sat down filled with such sadness and regret when I realised that it was all my fault.

That is why I have decided to buy my son a cricket kit. I found a cricket store online. It, like most things cricket online, clearly caters to Indian customers, but for me it was like entering heaven. I could order tips, bats, seed guards, helmets, pads, stumps, bails, balls, everything! I could even find some of the famous brands that were the mantras of my younger faithful days, Gray Nicholls, SS Jumbo, Slazenger, and so forth.

My plan is simple. I am going to revive West Indies cricket. Yes. By this simple gesture of love for my son, I am going to ensure that first we win the series against Australia, one of the most consistently powerful teams in the world, and then begin the long march back to dominance.

How am I going to do this? By paying attention. I am going to start paying attention once again. I am going to pay attention because I am going to teach my son how to play, and that will mean that I will be thinking about cricket a great deal. I am going to teach him how to bowl properly and stop flinging the ball like a baseball pitcher. I am going to get him to call his friends and remind them that they have a cricket club to start. I am going to coach that club. I am going to organise that club. I am going to talk to my friends who live beside the golf course in my old neighbourhood and ask them to let the boys and me practise on the greens that are hidden from the main road. I am going to start a full-blown league in Columbia. I am going to start to dream cricket, think cricket, eat and sleep cricket. I am going to arrange my day to include an afternoon tea-interval – something I stopped doing so long ago. I am going to get an adult-sized bat, and then put a ball in a sock, and hang it on a string from the overhanging branch of the oak tree in our back yard, and I am going to spend two hours a day practising my stroke play and my concentration. The way I see it, the more I do that, the more I start to talk cricket, the greater the success of the West Indies team.

I am going to bring my cricket concentration to bear on everything in my life. When I am arguing with my wife, I will let that voice of calculation and concentration speak in my head, gauging her direction, anticipating her next ball, testing her capacity to handle my own strokes, and so on. I will start talking my way into having brilliant classes – in my head, of course. This will involve predicting the length of the next challenge – a bouncer aimed at my head, a yorker to slip under my guard – and how I will bat my way through the most testing questions, sometimes attacking, sometimes defending, or even stonewalling.

It may sound as if I am not really thinking about my son in all of this, but that would be unfair. It is true that I do not expect him to become a great player, but what I do know is that as a student of my skills, he will grow to be a better man for it. And I can't deny that a part of me holds the wild outlandish hope that perhaps what I am about to do is to train someone to be my successor.

For the next five days (Lord knows, I hope it lasts for five days!), I shall will the West Indies to win the test. And they will win that test, and then the second test and the third test and begin a new era of hegemony. Black people everywhere will thank me for this reminder of the potential of our people for domination. The West Indies team will return to the red, green and gold wristbands of past years, and will travel with the anthems of Bob Marley in their heads. This is no small revolution about to take place. I will sacrifice everything I have to ensure that it happens. I need no accolades, just one modest twenty-foot statue in front of Sabina Park of me, fully kitted in my whites, with index fingers pressed to my temples, my brows furrowed in deep thought, and the unmistakable aura of a man carrying the weight of a nation on his shoulders.

John Figueroa

WEST INDIES AND TEST CRICKET:
A SPECIAL CONTRIBUTION?

One is tempted to answer immediately with a strong affirmative. But in doing so one must be careful to avoid the usual generalisations. The West Indies teams have shown a certain élan which at times strongly contrasts with England teams which insist on "putting up the shutters" and playing it safe. But the matter is much more complicated than that.

Unfortunately it is hard to make the simplest statement without generalising. Yet generalisations can be so misleading, and they so easily lead to stereotypes: English batsmen are dull and over-careful: WI batsmen are enterprising and carefree. Denis Compton over-careful? Ted Dexter dull? And what of Botham? Allan Rae carefree? Haynes and Greenidge, at the Oval in 1988, carefree? Yet there is often a hint of truth in the stereotype – that is what makes it so dangerous.

On the whole, especially since the influence of Len Hutton as captain, England batting does tend to err on the side of "no cutting, no hooking". Trevor "Barnacle" Bailey is easily contrasted in the minds of some with the one and only L. N. Constantine. And as Learie was the West Indian best known to English fans for a long time, his penchant for hitting hard and for entertaining the crowds was what came to be associated with West Indies batting. But even in Learie's day there were players like F. R. Martin, first-class players who had a cautious approach to the game. Frank Martin opened the West Indies innings in the fifth Test, at Sydney, in 1931, saw his partner C. A. Roach go at 70, and took his bat out for 123 when his captain declared at 350 for 6. (Constantine made 0 in that innings, and Headley was lbw for 105.)

I and many others were brought up to be aware of over-generalisations and stereotypes. But many radio and TV broadcasters now don't seem to mind dealing in all kinds of stereotypes: "Italians don't have the temperament to win the World Cup"; "West Indians will drop their heads at the first sight of pressure". I can remember our Latin master in the fourth form pointing out how dangerous was the invitation given the reader, in the Aeneid, to judge all Greeks by the deviousness of one – "ab uno disce omnes". But my first practical experience, in sport, of the dangers and misleading character of accepted stereotypes was while covering the Olympic games in Rome in 1960.

Accepted wisdom then was that the black athletes (from the USA especially) must win all sprint races, whereas Anglo-Saxons and Scandinavians were the long-distance people. But it was a German who won the 100 metres and an Italian the 200, in the most conclusive manner, while an unknown Ethiopian, in the darkening Roman evening, lighted up the TV screens as he took over the marathon! Had "white" people's genes changed, or was the Ethiopian not really "black"? Of course, genes have little to do with it: but just try to convince your ordinary fan of this or your ordinary sports writer.

The thing is that when a group appears to play in a certain way, or to excel at a certain game, it is likely to have something to do with their genetic inheritance, but much more to do with their cultural experience, and most to do with the circumstances under which they most commonly play. The love of seam bowlers in English cricket has to do with green wickets being more common in England than anywhere else except perhaps New Zealand. But it also has to do with the old county cricket schedules in which it would have been silly for more than one player to bowl really fast week in and week out, and in which it was useful simply to hold an end quiet with seam bowling. Similarly there are now things about English batting which have much more to do with the plethora of one-day games in their regular schedule than anything else. It also tends to mean that there are not a few English bowlers who can give you a very sound ten or twelve overs, but who are not very penetrating and tend to fall off beyond the twelve-over spell – or to pull muscles and otherwise become injured.

Much of this is well illustrated by the black youngster in the Indiana library in the 1950s. He took out book after book on basketball, although he had been thought to be more or less illiterate. The intrigued librarian enquired of the young man the reason for this intense interest and study. "It's my way out," the young man answered, "it's my way out." Do you remember the old story about calling down a Yorkshire coal pit for a new fast bowler? Physical build and brawn are of course often involved, but so are the cultural and social conditions in which the athlete lives and has grown up. But in any case, why is it so easily forgotten that even within given "racial" groups physical characteristics vary widely? George Headley, neat and black and dancing, was very much more in build and movement like Don Bradman than Joel Garner. And Ted Dexter's movements were not exactly those of Sir Len Hutton; more like Sir Gary Sobers, shall we say?

Then there is the whole question of certain personal qualities, the origins of which we know little. Ian Botham, for example, like Constantine before him, had the gift of imposing himself on a game in such a way as to get the best – or nearly the best – of batsmen to hit long hops to square-leg's waiting hands. At Sabina Park when he came on to bowl in 1986 it took only one ball for a US colleague who was enjoying the hospitality of our commentary box to say: "I know nothing about cricket but this man is obviously going to impress his personality on the game." And he did.

But has West Indies made a special mark on the game? It certainly has the reputation, and has had it for some while, of flamboyance in batting, dangerous speed in bowling, briskness in the field, and a certain lack of consistency overall – what one of the most offensive writers on the game used to characterise as "calypso collapso". Perhaps he wrote before the England collapses of 1988. But he was certainly writing during the Ram–Val melting away of the England batting. The only thing that was right about the implication of his comment is that West Indies tend to go down, when they do, with all guns firing, whereas England's collapses give the impression of coming from over-cautiousness and the refusal to strike pale half-volleys to the boundary. After all, in 1950 Hutton was clean bowled by Val, *middle stump,* at Lord's, leaving the ball alone: in fact, shouldering arms!

These contrasting attitudes might be thought to reflect a difference in the two societies. But they might be concerned with quite other matters. In England, for instance, it is always worth holding on, except in the rarest of summers, because a brisk shower might be just around the corner. And one would look a fool to get out just before rain stopped play for half an hour or a few hours, or for the day! As a rule – but there are no iron laws about this kind of thing – when it rains in the West Inches the grounds become drenched, so if there is rain in the offing one had better make the runs now.

But a difference in attitude there is: Englishmen have been heard, and English women also, to rejoice because England had broken a losing spell by managing to draw a game. There is a quite common West Indies attitude which would consider this rather pettifogging. Their way of ending a dry spell would be to go for the win – and of course risk a loss in the effort. Clearly to some mentalities not to lose is more important than to win! And to a few wonderful people, decreasing in number every day, the style with which one plays is just as important as winning or losing. But this latter attitude is harder to maintain the greater the external prizes for winning, or excelling as man-of-the-match, become.

It is not only an inner moral habit which determines many of the general attitudes to playing games today; money is very much involved, as well as the possibilities of a greater fame which leads to being "marketable". This fame, fanned by the media and encouraged by advertisers and promoters, probably has more of an influence than even higher payment "by results".

But payment and the means of making a living have always played their part. George Headley did not go on one tour because the West Indies could not, or would not, pay him enough or pay his league club to release him. Learie went out to the West Indies to play against England on one occasion only because Sir Pelham Warner, who was born in Trinidad, wrote to the Board from England complaining that Learie was not selected to play. (They said they could not afford to pay him.) Sir "Plum", graduate of Queen's Royal College, Trinidad, had been supporting the idea that MCC should visit the West Indies. Why should he continue to do so when he knew that West Indies were not selecting their strongest team by leaving Constantine out?

In West Indies cricket one of the things that might have contributed from time to time to a less planned approach to the game, and to a more cavalier attitude at times, was that it was almost completely amateur, in the sense of being unwaged. One's living therefore did not depend entirely on one's performance. One had some other job – if one had a job at all!

It is not perhaps widely known that on some of the first West Indies tours players had to find their own passages. Learie's father, Lebrun, once was unable to join a tour he had been selected for because he had not enough to leave to keep the family going. He saw his "team-mates" onto the boat at Port of Spain, and, having bid them farewell, was about to head home. He was eventually whisked by fast launch to the disappearing ship when the necessary money was collected on the wharfside. It is said that one or two other players were selected precisely because they could not only play but could also pay! With this kind of history, plus island jealousies and mutual ignorance about each other, it could hardly be wondered that at times a certain instability and lack of cohesion was more than apparent.

The attitudes of teams so constructed, and accustomed to playing perhaps only on the weekends, could not compare with teams of regular professionals plus a few comparatively well-to-do amateurs – in the matters of strict discipline, concentration and sticking to a task that lasted three days, six days a week, for the better part of a summer. But what such teams could bring to the task was freshness, an appetite for the game, a willingness to concoct new solutions – to improvise.

And improvising, rather than recklessness, was the mark of Learie Constantine. It might look as if he were being cavalier when in fact he was intelligently trying to find a new solution. C. L. R. James gave an excellent example of this: when Learie was playing for Nelson he once found that the bowler was so controlling his line and length that it was impossible to score by piercing the off-side field. He considered and played forward and back, but to no avail. What he then did was to go outside his off stump and glide the ball just past his leg stump to the fine-leg boundary. He did this with a pendulum swing of the bat. When you think of it this was a most sensible thing to do; it was splendid improvisation. But it was not the acceptable thing to those calling themselves orthodox. I have been told by people who bowled long at Hammond that if you pitched up to him on any line he would attempt, often successfully, to drive you through the covers. And he was the very image of orthodoxy! But you could probably get him stumped with a googly just outside the leg stump! In fact C. B. Clarke dismissed him in just this fashion during the 1939 tour.

It is not that Learie's judgement was always faultless; and he had a generous, if exhibitionist, inclination to entertain the fans. This got him into trouble on occasion. Once in a big charity match in London I was at the other end when he was given out lbw very early in his innings. He was making one of his favourite shots: he would put his left toe down the wicket, just outside leg stump, and swing a perpendicular bat, starting in the direction of point and picking up the ball for a 6 over square-leg. The wicket this day was none too good, the ball did not come through as evenly as he expected, the umpire gave him out. He was livid – although I did not realise this until returning to the dressing-room at the luncheon break. But he had made the shot much too early in his knock, and he should have known that we were not playing with Test umpires.

This business of improvisation, of zest, of style, of stroking the ball rather than pushing or poking or prodding – these I would say tended to be the things that many West Indies batsmen brought to the game. But you must then resist the "explanation temptation", especially the physio-genetic explanation. Kanhai was sometimes as extravagant as Learie, and often more brilliant: the one of Indian heritage from Guyana, the other from Trinidad with African forebears. Stollmeyer was one of our most elegant and fluent of stroke-makers: he was from Trinidad and came from an originally Dutch planter family – his nephew now plays football for the USA! Ivan Barrow, a splendid square-cutter, in 1933 got WI's first Test century in England just before George Headley, and put on 200 with him for the second wicket in the process. He was from Jamaica, and a Jew. George himself, as is well known, was born in Panama, of African ancestry: his mother was from Jamaica, his father from Barbados, and he spent his early years in Panama and Cuba. His second name was Alphonso – not a common name in the Anglophone Caribbean.

Even the three Ws, from tiny Barbados (168 square miles), did not come exactly from the same stable socially. Everton Weekes probably would have led too hard a life to come to fame in cricket (and international bridge!) were it not for the fact that during the war he joined the Barbados forces. Frank Worrell went to school at Combermere, where for many years the famous West Indian writer and editor, Frank Collymore, taught and played cricket. But Combermere was not quite Harrison College, to which Clyde Walcott moved after a year there. Further, Walcott did not meet Everton Weekes until both of them went to Trinidad for trial matches in 1945, four years after Walcott had first played in Trinidad. All this, notice, in a place as small as Barbados – about which clearly generalisations could be dangerous!

As far as West Indies bowlers go: the first thing is to remind ourselves that fast bowlers first dominated the scene and have done so especially in the recent past. But one surely does not have constantly to remind the English press and fans of Ramadhin and Valentine – two people of different genetic inheritance! It is even more amazing that one has to point out that one of the few slow bowlers to be among the top wicket-takers in all Tests is Lance Gibbs of Guyana and the West Indies: 309 wickets at 29.09 in 79 Tests. May one note that Trueman played but 67 Tests.

But Ram and Val and Lance Gibbs were not the first or only ones. A list would have to contain C.R. ("Snuffle") Browne and O.C. (Tommy) Scott from the old days. At Old Trafford in 1928 Browne and Scott took 2 wickets each, as many as the total taken by the fast bowlers: Francis none, Constantine 1, and Griffith 3.

F.R. Martin was also an outstanding slow bowler, as were the Trinidadian Achong and the Jamaican left-hander Mudie. The latter took 3 for 40 at Sabina when West Indies defeated England by an innings and 161 runs in March 1935. And in 1939, in England, West Indies had two outstanding slow bowlers: J. H. Cameron, who had played for Cambridge, and C.B. (Bertie) Clarke, who was later to play county cricket and who might well have gone on the tour to India in 1948–49. In 1950, besides Ram and Val, there was also the "legger" with a good googly, "Boogles" Williams of Barbados. His figures in first-class matches on that tour were 301.2 overs, 856 runs, 31 wickets, at an average of 27.61. Compare these with Worrell's: 480.1-970-39-24.87. (He was a good batsman too: in Barbados he and Walcott shared a large partnership in which he got 185 and Walcott 120.) And, of course, even in the heyday of 1984 when West Indies swept the board, and when Marshall, Holding and Garner were dispensing their thunderbolts, there was a useful off-spinner on the team, Harper. He took 13 wickets in the five Tests, 6 of them for 57 runs in 28.4 overs at Old Trafford in the second innings.

But what of the fast bowlers, and the fact that for a while West Indies used four of them in harness? This gambit was much opposed by English critics who support the traditional – including the traditional "rights" of the chosen few under apartheid! I don't myself think that the success of the West Indies bowlers was mainly based on their speed, but on the fact that each one of them was so good. Never before did a batsman not feel relief at seeing off an opener and looking forward to "first change". The speed no doubt added to the tension, but a similar effect was had when Val and Ram were really in form: they kept coming at you, demanding full concentration all the while. The nearest thing I have seen to it was Lindwall, Miller, Johnston, Toshack – but the last named was not in any sense dangerous. He was mainly a negative bowler who had to be watched, but whose chief task was to keep an end sealed until the new ball, then available after 55 overs, was due.

I always said that, despite all the complaining – over the apparent destruction of the beauty of spin bowling, especially leg-spin – as soon as they found four good enough fast or medium-fast bowlers England would use them just as the West Indies had. And in the tour of the West Indies in 1989 that is exactly what England did: Angus Fraser, Devon Malcolm, Gladstone Small, Phil DeFreitas and the replacement Chris Lewis.

From the point of view of cricket, the main weakness in depending on one kind of bowling lies only in the fact that conditions can change suddenly and one might not have the necessary adaptability. Thus the decision to play Valentine instead of Dewdney at Lord's in 1957 was disastrous. Of the 20 wickets England took, only 1 fell to a slow bowler, Wardle. Bailey had 11 wickets in the game, Trueman 4, and Statham 4. England knew the Lord's wicket, and did not let aesthetics or tradition stop them from beating West Indies by an innings and 36 runs.

But Marshall, Garner and Holding were not only fast; they were exceptionally good bowlers. They along with Trueman have the best strike-rate among bowlers who have taken over 200 wickets in Tests. Marshall, has taken 1 wicket for roughly every forty-six balls bowled; Garner and Holding, one for every fifty balls! Andy Roberts had a strike-rate slightly inferior to these. If we add to these, say, Baptiste, or more recently Walsh and Ambrose and Benjamin, then what we have always is a foursome of excellent bowlers who are also fast. But I doubt that the situation would be much different if one could find on the same team four accurate and difficult-to-play slow bowlers. After all in 1950 some batsmen complained of the relentlessness of the bowling of Ram and Val. And some broadcasters complained that there was no time for comment, so quickly were overs being bowled – so relentless was the pressure!

It's the pressure that matters. But admittedly if to the difficulty of "reading" the bowling is added an element of physical pressure, then the batsman's difficulties increase. Modern slow bowlers tighten the screw by placing well-protected fielders very close to the bat. Is not the "bat/pad" catch now as common as the slip catch? Whether a certain field placing, or short-pitched balls, are fair is a matter that must be left to the umpires who are the sole judges of fair and unfair play. What has always amazed me is that England's pained whingeing and superior moral sentiments about short-pitched bowling have mainly taken place in England where, so far, English umpires – "the best in the world" – are indeed sole judges of fair and unfair play. Why have they not ruled in the fashion which would please the erstwhile cricket correspondent of *The Times*?

What the West Indies have contributed to cricket, particularly to English cricket, is not, as many letters to *The Times* suggest, nor as one of that paper's main correspondents is always saying, unfair fast bowling – I would abhor that.

What they have contributed is the refusal, to follow the tradition, loved by batsmen from all over the world, of allowing a breather after the first two bowlers have done their best, a sort of brief tea-break before getting on with the main business of getting runs and taking wickets – always, of course, within the spirit and letter of the law and always with a sense of style and aesthetic satisfaction. Farnes, Bowes and Voce were the only old-time English fast bowlers I had the pleasure of seeing in action. I heard all about Larwood and "have seen the film". I wonder if a foursome of Larwood, Voce – what a bowler!– Farnes and

Bowes would be any less effective, frightening and wonderful to watch than Holding, Roberts, Garner and Marshall!

But in an odd way, perhaps the greatest contribution which West Indies have made to the great game, again especially to English cricket, is the one started in 1950: that of showing to people ever so sure of themselves, and of their right to win, that the mighty can fall – even in their own territory. Good can come out of Nazareth! This is such an important point for both David and Goliath!

Whenever, alas, there is a world sporting event being broadcast by British commentators, one need listen for no more than five minutes to realise how many of the British, especially the English, like to suppose that any group they don't know, or which they think of as "Third World", or not out of the "top drawer", need not be taken too seriously, and would be happy to be patronised by them.

West Indies, by winning at Lord's in 1950, and subsequently keeping up the good work – though, of course, not always winning – made the very simple point so admirably put by the Caribbean poet Césaire:

> No race [and I would add nor group, nor country]
> holds the monopoly of beauty, of intelligence, of strength
> and there is a place for all at the rendezvous of victory.

It is a hard ideal to live up to, and one hopes that the West Indies and all their opponents on the field will always do so. This and aesthetic and somatic satisfaction is what the very essence of games should be, rather than their being promoted as the generators and sustainers of a virulent form of tribalism which is only seen for what it really is when the "hooligans" take to a logical conclusion all that they have been hearing on the radio and television about their own superiority and right to win, which generally is only frustrated by naive or cheating foreigners. You might wonder at the use of the word naive. I am only quoting what the television commentators called the Cameroons World Cup football team before they matched every move England could make.

And the word no doubt would have been used about West Indies cricket – or would it have been, "instinctive"? – before that day at Lord's made memorable by, among others,

> Those two little pals of mine
> Ramadhin and Valentine.

VILLAGE CRICKET

Village cricket matches were usually played on a Sunday afternoon and everybody attended them. We had our own cricket club, formed by the young men of the village. They represented all the different races who lived there and even my uncle, who was slightly lame, played for the club. Even though the temperature was in the nineties, they wore traditional dress consisting of flannels, blazer, white shirt, soft white plimsolls and cricket cap. The black blazers had S. C. C. – for Skeldon Cricket Club – in gold embroidery on the pockets. Brotherhood and belonging were the sentiments upon which the club was founded. No one talked of race and each unto his own. We were Skeldonians and proud of it. The tentacles of divide and rule had not yet appeared to entangle us. European overseers had no jurisdiction in our village.

When the club played cricket, the whole village played cricket. One match in particular comes back to me. The sun was "broiling" hot, and for some reason which I cannot recall, I left the house after all the others to attend the match. The village was like an enchanted garden; only the old were there, asleep on the verandahs. The silence was almost overpowering because even on Sundays children shouted across the yards to other children, or parents could be heard summoning their brood from some exploit among the mangroves or on the sand. Everyone had gone to the match and taken their voices with them. It was an important match. An invincible team had come up from Rosehall.

When I arrived, the visiting team from Rosehall were having a very hard time. They were falling like ninepins to the wizardry of our fast bowler, Bachan, a slightly-built, sociable, intelligent, Indian lad who could make the ball spin like a copper-coin. He had scored a number of successes and everyone was shouting and singing:

> *Constantine bowl you bodyline*
> *Bowl, bowl, bowl, you bodyline*

Then the visiting team made a stand and scored some sixes, and straight away some women from our village began to "cook them" in a pretend obeah cauldron. It was only a prank, but my Aunt Ella and her friend Myra Clark were pretty convincing obeah workers. They leaped and chanted round the pot, uttering magic words and shouting, "Out-for-nought-leh-e-out-for-nought!" to the delight of us all. By sheer coincidence the batsman was caught out, and the visitors took the prank seriously. Blows followed words and stumps were pulled, until the women stopped the distracting activity of casting spells. Everybody was in stitches because my aunt was harmless and full of fun. She offered to work obeah for the visitors. She picked up some grass and, whirling it into the wind, shouted, "Mek dem win!" in a deep guttural voice. The game was resumed when the captain of our team persuaded her to stop and enjoy "cakes and cool drinks" like everyone else. "Yes", agreed my aunt, "there's nothing like a full belly to mek the tongue feel sleepy."

Fresh enjoyment attached itself to whatever was happening. Every time a six was hit, a communal dance around the perimeter of the pitch followed. Every time someone was bowled or caught, gestures of protest were heard. "Sides" were changed in the fun. "Grease hand" was shouted when anybody dropped a catch. The children began a mini match on the sidelines, and some people became interested in that, so some of the exuberance was channelled away from the main match.

On the cricket field, the men took on new personalities, fashioning themselves on known Georgetown cricketers. During the week they did horrible, low-paid jobs in field or factory. But when it was time for cricket they became upstanding, proud men, committed to playing in the finest tradition of the game. They had all started to play cricket as soon as they could walk. Wherever the ground was flat enough, or a stick could be found to serve as bat, wherever a green, round fruit, or a piece of balata could be obtained to serve as ball, a game of bat and ball – which would develop into cricket – would start. Girls played too, but never with the same intensity as the boys.

Village cricket brought us all together. It was a time to forget the daily grind and to enjoy ourselves within the boundaries set by our own place, our own space, and within our own culture. The ball, a round object flying through the air, took on symbolic significance. Some saw it as destiny: they faced it squarely. Others took a halfhearted cut at it. Yet others turned it aside and watched its course along the grass.

THE JOYS OF CONJECTURE

I have not had any interest in cricket other than the backyard variety during childhood. The "history" that follows really began over my curiosity about the origin of the word "batman" which I first encountered as a young teenager reading tales about World War I. The personal orderly of an officer was called his "batman" an obviously un-military term. (not to be confused with BAT-MAN to whom I was introduced through comic books that arrived in Guyana with American military personnel in the 1940s in what was then British Guiana, but that is another tale). I was totally puzzled even after learning that officers were mainly from the aristocracy and upper class and therefore expected (demanded more likely) certain privileges.

The joys of reading are not to be denied and stray bits of information collected over a period can sometimes be put together to provide interesting and pleasing insights. Many years after encountering "batman" I learnt that social practices among the 19th century English aristocracy included weekend parties that could last for weeks – a certain disregard for the passage of time that would be easily understood by West Indians. Preparations by invitees to such parties meant loading carriages with family members, servants and all the paraphernalia required – food, clothing, cosmetics, dogs and games equipment. Daylight pastimes on garden lawns included the new game of cricket for men while ladies took delight in croquet. It did not take long for me to realize that no self-respecting aristocrat would even think of fetching his cricket gear – very rudimentary in those days – hence the appointment of a "batman". In bygone times going off to war always meant having someone to look after armour, weapons and uniforms. World War One's aristocrat warrior now needed his tea prepared so his batman had to join the army willing or not.

Aristocrats did no manual labour whatever – that's why they often wore whites. They would only be prepared to bat by recognizing the connection between a sword and the bat – often referred to as the "blade". The privilege – obligatory no doubt – of bowling was reserved for gardeners and off-duty footmen.

Encouraged by these thoughts I began a further examination of cricket. Here was a game that could last for days often without a definite conclusion and involving quite a bit of lawn space to play on. Time and space were treated in the same manner by aristocrats. They owned a great deal of both – along with servants – to treat as they wished.

An examination of today's cricket gear reveals interesting similarities between armour worn by aristocrats and batsmen. There is the "blade" of course, and the cricket hat has now been transformed to a "helmet" complete with a visor to protect the eyes from hostile action – fast bowling. There is the chest pad (breastplate), pads or shin guards (greaves), batting gloves (gauntlet). The batsman is a knight and for great deeds is indeed "knighted" by King or Queen. Bowlers are a forgotten lot – their origins are lower class.

Willow trees, a feature of 18th and 19th century English gardens, were made popular by the efforts of one Capability Brown who was in great demand. Great effort was made to make the gardens appear informal so as not to bear comparison with the formal gardens of the French with whom the English were not on speaking terms. The cultivated informality meant that trees had to be pruned and lawns kept in place just as cricket pitches today demand dedicated husbandry – no earthworms and just enough water to keep things under control. Pruning willow trees provided the best material for bats – hence "willow" along with "blade" for bats. The cutting off of heads, aristocrats and commoners – equality at last – was once a feature of English social history. "Cutting" and "slicing" the ball, all legitimate cricket terms therefore carry a disquieting association – bat as blade (aristocrat), ball as head (commoner).

As mentioned earlier, the commoner – gardener or footman – had to bowl. They could only employ an underarm style because to raise your hand in the presence of nobility was construed as a threatening action, a criminal offence. On their off-days the servants would visit the village to exchange gossip in the ale houses. News of the goings-on at the manor house created much interest. News about the new game cricket so fascinated them that they began to play it as well. There was one major difference. Bowling underarm was regarded as being too tame. They soon developed an overarm style that provided more excitement, not as much, of course, as football that could see entire villages as opposing teams.

One particular gardener liked the new action so much that he would practice it in a secluded corner of the garden. This clandestine activity was soon discovered by the lord of the manor who demanded an explanation. Much to the astonishment of the gardener he was immediately asked to bowl in that fashion during next batting practice. This created a problem. The Lord missed quite a few balls and retrieving them slowed things down. The solution was to bat in front of a small garden gate, a wicket gate which evolved into the three stumps we know today.

Ponds, a feature of gardens, were also home to ducks – swans too for those who could afford them. Hitting one of them with a stray ball eventually created the derisive "hitting a duck". Other such comments as "a duck egg" and "out for a duck" followed. One can only wonder what the ducks had to say about all this. "Hitting a six" would have probably come from the gaming table for playing dice. Another expression "bowled a maiden over" at first seems innocuous but on reflection one of the pastimes of off-duty knights was "bowling" village maidens over and this was recognized as a sign of prowess instead of oppression. Unlike the ducks, we certainly do not have to wonder what maidens thought of this.

In the past, being a member of the British Empire meant that statues of Queen Victoria were found in all colonies – and so were cricket pitches. In India, the "Jewel of the Crown", cricket was played between Indian aristocrats and their English counterparts in "whites", a colour that signified class in both societies. Aristocrats the world over have habits which make social life tolerable, so there was a mutual exchange of aristocratic games – India took up cricket and the English took up polo. It was the latter game that gave birth to the hard ball used in cricket. Relations became so tolerable that the English even began appropriating features of life in India that added more class to the game. Ornate pavilions feature in Indian gardens as a place to relax and enjoy refreshments. During cricket, tea and cucumber sandwiches were served. The latter being a marriage of convenience between India, the cucumber, and England, the sandwich. Both tea and cucumber are native to India. Pavilions, tea and cucumber sandwiches eventually became part of the cricket ritual wherever the game was introduced.

"Noblesse oblige" also became a feature of the game, gracious manners had to be observed, no quarrelling over whether or not one was out. The word and or gesture of the umpire was enough. Umpires have a long history, being originally associated with seeing that the rules of combat at knightly games were observed. Unseemly behaviour before one's peers could not be tolerated and more so seeing that commoners were usually present.

Being "sporting" is the present day observance of that behaviour. When bodyline bowling was first introduced there were outcries of unsporting tactics. This soon changed when winning the game took precedence over graciousness. This notwithstanding, it should be clear to all that the aristocratic origins of cricket, though forgotten, are still there to be recognized.

[This was actually the basis of a talk I gave at the University of Guyana in the 1970s. Ken Corsbie had heard it and actually broadcast it on the BBC overseas programme "Calling the West Indies". I was listening in and had a shock hearing the story and wondering how it got there. Ken later confessed that he had time left in the program he was producing and decided to include the story.]

C.L.R. JAMES

THE WINDOW
(from *Beyond a Boundary*)

Tunapuna at the beginning of this century was a small town of about 3,000 inhabitants, situated eight miles along the road from Port of Spain, the capital city of Trinidad. Like all towns and villages on the island, it possessed a recreation ground. Recreation meant cricket, for in those days, except for infrequent athletic sports meetings, cricket was the only game. Our house was superbly situated, exactly behind the wicket. A huge tree on one side and another house on the other limited the view of the ground, but an umpire could have stood at the bedroom window. By standing on a chair a small boy of six could watch practice every afternoon and matches on Saturdays – with matting one pitch could and often did serve for both practice and matches. From the chair also he could mount on to the windowsill and so stretch a groping hand for the books on the top of the wardrobe. Thus early the pattern of my life was set. The traffic on the road was heavy, there was no fence between the front yard and the street. I was an adventurous little boy and so my grandmother and my two aunts, with whom I lived for half the year, the rainy season, preferred me in the backyard or in the house where they could keep an eye on me. When I tired of playing in the yard I perched myself on the chair by the window. I doubt if for some years I knew what I was looking at in detail. But this watching from the window shaped one of my strongest early impressions of personality in society. His name was Matthew Bondman and he lived next door to us.

He was a young man already when I first remember him, medium height and size, and an awful character. He was generally dirty. He would not work. His eyes were fierce, his language was violent and his voice was loud. His lips curled back naturally and he intensified it by an almost perpetual snarl. My grandmother and my aunts detested him. He would often without shame walk up the main street barefooted, "with his planks on the ground"; as my grandmother would report. He did it often and my grandmother must have seen it hundreds of times, but she never failed to report it, as if she had suddenly seen the parson walking down the street barefooted. The whole Bondman family, except for the father, was unsatisfactory. It was from his mother that Matthew had inherited or absorbed his flair for language and invective. His sister Marie was quiet but bad, and despite all the circumlocutions, or perhaps because of them, which my aunts employed, I knew it had something to do with "men". But the two families were linked. They rented from us, they had lived there for a long time, and their irregularity of life exercised its fascination for my puritanical aunts. But that is not why I remember Matthew. For ne'er-do-well, in fact vicious character, as he was,

294

Matthew had one saving grace – Matthew could bat. More than that, Matthew, so crude and vulgar in every aspect of his life, with a bat in his hand was all grace and style. When he practised on an afternoon with the local club people stayed to watch and walked away when he was finished. He had one particular stroke that he played by going down low on one knee. It may have been a slash through the covers or a sweep to leg. But, whatever it was, whenever Matthew sank down and made it, a long, low "Ah!" came from many a spectator, and my own little soul thrilled with recognition and delight.

Matthew's career did not last long. He would not practise regularly, he would not pay his subscription to the club. They persevered with him, helping him out with flannels and white shoes for matches. I remember Razac, the Indian, watching him practise one day and shaking his head with deep regret: how could a man who could bat like that so waste his talent? Matthew dropped out early. But he was my first acquaintance with that *genus Britannicus,* a fine batsman, and the impact that he makes on all around him, non-cricketers and cricketers alike. The contrast between Matthew's pitiable existence as an individual and the attitude people had towards him filled my growing mind and has occupied me to this day. I came into personal contact with Matthew. His brother was my playmate and when we got in Matthew's way he glared and shouted at us in a most terrifying manner. My aunts were uncompromising in their judgments of him and yet my grandmother's oft-repeated verdict: "Good for nothing except to play cricket," did not seem right to me. How could an ability to play cricket atone in any sense for Matthew's abominable way of life? Particularly as my grandmother and my aunts were not in any way supporters or followers of the game.

My second landmark was not a person but a stroke, and the maker of it was Arthur Jones. He was a brownish Negro, a medium-sized man, who walked with quick steps and active shoulders. He had a pair of restless, aggressive eyes, talked quickly and even stammered a little. He wore a white cloth hat when batting, and he used to cut. How he used to cut! I have watched county cricket for weeks on end and seen whole Test matches without seeing one cut such as Jones used to make, and for years whenever I saw one I murmured to myself, "Arthur Jones!" The crowd was waiting for it, I at my window was waiting, and as soon as I began to play seriously I learnt that Arthur was waiting for it too. When the ball hit down outside the off-stump (and now, I think, even when it was straight) Jones lifted himself to his height, up went his bat and he brought it down across the ball as a woodsman puts his axe to a tree. I don't remember his raising the ball, most times it flew past point or between point and third slip, the crowd burst out in another shout and Jones's white cap sped between the wickets.

The years passed. I was in my teens at school, playing cricket, reading cricket, idolizing Thackeray, Burke and Shelley, when one day I came across the following about a great cricketer of the eighteenth century:

It was a study for Phidias to see Beldham rise to strike; the grandeur of the attitude, the settled composure of the look, the piercing lightning of the eye, the rapid glances of the bat, were electrical. Men's hearts throbbed within them, their cheeks turned pale and red. Michael Angelo should have painted him.

This was thrilling enough. I began to tingle.

Beldham was great in every hit, but his peculiar glory was the cut. Here he stood, with no man beside him, the laurel was all his own; it seemed like the cut of a racket. His wrist seemed to turn on springs of the finest steel. He took the ball, as Burke did the House of Commons, between wind and water – not a moment too soon or late. Beldham still survives...

By that time I had seen many fine cutters, one of them, W. St. Hill, never to this day surpassed. But the passage brought back Jones and childhood memories to my mind and anchored him there for good and all. Phidias, Michelangelo, Burke. Greek history had already introduced me to Phidias and the Parthenon; from engravings and reproductions I had already begun a lifelong worship of Michelangelo; and Burke, begun as a school chore, had rapidly become for me the most exciting master of prose in English – I knew already long passages of him by heart. There in the very centre of all this was William Beldham and his cut. I passed over the fact which I noted instantly that the phrase, "He hit the House between wind and water", had been used by Burke himself, about Charles Townshend in the speech on American taxation.

The matter was far from finished. Some time later I read a complicated description of the mechanism and timing of the cut by C. B. Fry, his warning that it was a most difficult stroke to master and that even in the hands of its greatest exponents there were periods when it would not work, "intermittent in its service", as he phrased it. But, he added, with some batsmen it was an absolutely natural stroke, and one saw beautiful cutting by batsmen who otherwise could hardly be called batsmen at all. When I read this I felt an overwhelming sense of justification. Child though I was, I had not been wrong about Jones. Batsman or not, he *was* one of those beautiful natural cutters. However, I said earlier that the second landmark in my cricketing life was a stroke – and I meant just that – one single stroke.

On an awful rainy day I was confined to my window, Tunapuna C. C. was batting and Jones was in his best form, that is to say, in nearly every over he was getting up on his toes and cutting away. But the wicket was wet and the visitors were canny. The offside boundary at one end was only forty yards away, a barbed-wire fence which separated the ground from the police station. Down came a short ball, up went Jones and lashed at it, there was the usual shout, a sudden silence and another shout, not so loud this time. Then from my window I saw Jones walking out and people began to walk away. He had been caught by point standing with his back to the barbed wire. I could not see it from my window and I asked and asked until I was told what had happened. I knew that something out of the ordinary had happened to us who were watching. We had been lifted to the heights and cast down into the depths in much less than a fraction of a second. Countless as are the times that this experience has been repeated, most often in the company of tens of thousands of people, I have never lost the zest of wondering at it and pondering over it.

It is only within very recent years that Matthew Bondman and the cutting of Arthur Jones ceased to be merely isolated memories and fell into place as starting points of a connected pattern. They only appear as starting points. In reality they were the end, the last stones put into place, of a pyramid whose base constantly widened, until it embraced those aspects of social relations, politics and art laid bare when the veil of the temple has been rent in twain as ours has been. Hegel says somewhere that the old man repeats the prayers he repeated as a child, but now with the experience of a lifetime. Here briefly are some of the experiences of a lifetime which have placed Matthew Bondman and Arthur Jones within a frame of reference that stretches east and west into the receding distance, back into the past and forward into the future.

My inheritance (you have already seen two, Puritanism and cricket) came from both sides of the family and a good case could be made out for predestination, including the position of the house in front of the recreation ground and the window exactly behind the wicket.

My father's father was an emigrant from one of the smaller islands, and probably landed with nothing. But he made his way, and as a mature man worked as a panboiler on a sugar estate, a responsible job involving the critical transition of the boiling cane-juice from liquid into sugar. It was a post in those days usually held by white men. This meant that my grandfather had raised himself above the mass of poverty, dirt, ignorance and vice which in those far-off days surrounded the islands of black lower middle-class respectability like a sea ever threatening to engulf them. I believe I understand pretty much how the average sixteenth-century Puritan in England felt amidst the decay which followed the dissolution of the monasteries, particularly in the small towns. The need for distance which my aunts felt for Matthew Bondman and his sister was compounded of self-defence and fear. My grandfather went to church every Sunday morning at eleven o'clock wearing in the broiling sun a frock-coat, striped trousers and top-hat, with his walking-stick in hand, surrounded by his family, the underwear of the women crackling with starch. Respectability was not an ideal, it was an armour. He fell grievously ill, the family fortunes declined and the children grew up in unending struggle not to sink below the level of the Sunday-morning top-hat and frock-coat.

My father took the obvious way out – teaching He did well and gained a place as a student in the Government Training College, his course comprising history, literature, geometry, algebra and education. Yet Cousin Nancy, who lived a few yards away, told many stories of her early days as a house-slave. She must have been in her twenties when slavery was abolished in 1834. My father got his diploma, but he soon married. My two aunts did sewing and needle-work, not much to go by, which made them primmer and sharper than ever, and it was with them that I spent many years of my childhood and youth.

Two doors down the street was Cousin Cudjoe, and a mighty man was he. He was a blacksmith, and very early in life I was allowed to go and watch him do his fascinating business, while he regaled me with stories of his past prowess at cricket and critical observations on Matthew, Jones and the Tunapuna C.C. He was quite black, with a professional chest and shoulders that were usually scantily covered as he worked his bellows or beat the iron on the forge. Cudjoe told me of his unusual career as a cricketer. He had been the only black man in a team of white men. Wherever these white men went to play he went with them. He was their wicketkeeper and their hitter – a term he used as one would say a fast bowler or an opening bat. When he was keeping he stood close to the wicket and his side needed no long-stop for either fast bowling or slow, which must have been quite an achievement in his day and time. But it was as a hitter that he fascinated me. Once Cudjoe played against a team with a famous fast bowler, and it seemed that one centre of interest in the match, if not the great centre, was what would happen when the great fast bowler met the great hitter. Before the fast bowler began his run he held the ball up and shook it at Cudjoe, and Cudjoe in turn held up his bat and shook it at the bowler. The fast bowler ran up and bowled and Cudjoe hit his first ball out of the world. It didn't seem to matter how many he made after that. The challenge and the hit which followed were enough. It was primitive, but as the battle between Hector and Achilles is primitive, and it should not be forgotten that American baseball is founded on the same principle.

At the time I did not understand the significance of Cudjoe, the black black-smith, being the only coloured man in a white team, that is to say, plantation owners and business or professional men or high government officials. "They took me everywhere they went – everywhere," he used to repeat. They probably had to pay for him and also to sponsor his presence when they played matches with other white men. Later I wondered what skill it was, or charm of manner, or both, which gave him that unique position. He was no sycophant. His eyes looked straight into yours, and an ironical smile played upon his lips as he talked, a handsome head on his splendid body. He was a gay lad, Cudjoe, but somehow my aunts did not disapprove of him as they did of Bondman. He was a blood relation, he smiled at them and made jokes and they laughed. But my enduring memory of Cudjoe is of an exciting and charming man in whose life cricket had played a great part.

My father too had been a cricketer in his time, playing on the same ground at which I looked from my window. He gave me a bat and ball on my fourth birthday and never afterwards was I without them both for long. But as I lived a great deal with my aunts away from home, and they did not play, it was to Cudjoe I went to bowl to me, or to sit in his blacksmith's shop holding my bat and ball and listening to his stories. When I did spend time with my parents my father told me about cricket and his own prowess. But now I was older and my interest became tinged with scepticism, chiefly because my mother often interrupted to say that whenever she went to see him play he was always caught in the long field for very little. What made matters worse, one day when I went to see him play he had a great hit and was caught at long-on for seven. I remembered the stroke and knew afterwards that he had lifted his head. Joe Small, the West Indian Test player, was one of the bowlers on the opposite side. However, I was to learn of my father's good cricket in a curious way. When I was about sixteen my school team went to Tunapuna to play a match on that same ground against some of the very men I used to watch as a boy, though by this time Arthur Jones had dropped out. I took wickets and played a good defensive innings. Mr. Warner, the warden, a brother of Sir Pelham's, sent for me to congratulate me on my bowling, and some spectators made quite a fuss over me for I was one of them and they had known me as a child wandering around the ground and asking questions.

Two or three of the older ones came up and said, "Your father used to hit the ball constantly into that dam over there," and they pointed to a old closed-up well behind the railway line. I was taken by surprise, for the dam was in the direction of extra-cover somewhat nearer to mid-off and a batsman who hit the ball there constantly was no mean stroke player. But as my father always said, the cares of a wife and family on a small income cut short his cricketing life, as it cut short the career of many a fine player who was quite up to intercolonial standard. I have known intercolonial cricketers who left the West Indies to go to the United States to better their position. Weekes, the left-hander who hit that daring century in the Oval Test in 1939, is one of a sizable list. And George Headley was only saved for cricket because, born in Panama and living in Jamaica, there was some confusion and delay about his papers when his parents in the United States sent for him. While the difficulties were being sorted out, an English team arrived in Jamaica and Headley batted so successfully that he gave up the idea of going to the United States to study a profession.

West Indian cricket has arrived at maturity because of two factors: the rise in the financial position of the coloured middle class and the high fees paid to players by the English leagues. Of this, the economic basis of West Indian cricket – big cricket, so to speak – I was constantly aware, and from early on. One afternoon I was, as usual, watching the Tunapuna C.C. practise when a man in a black suit walked by on his way to the railway station. He asked for a knock and, surprisingly, pads were handed to him, the batsman withdrew and the stranger went in. Up to that time I had never seen such batting. Though he had taken off his coat, he still wore his high collar, but he hit practically every ball, all over the place. Fast and slow, wherever they came, he had a stroke, and when he stopped and rushed off to catch his train he left a buzz of talk and admiration behind him. I went up to ask who he was and I was told his name was MacDonald Bailey, an old intercolonial player. Later my father told me that Bailey was a friend of his, a teacher, an intercolonial cricketer and a great all-round sportsman. But, as usual, a wife and family and a small income compelled him to give up the game. He is the father of the famous Olympic sprinter. Mr. Bailey at times visited my father and I observed him carefully, looking him up and down and all over so as to discover the secret of his athletic skill, a childish habit I have retained to this day.

Perhaps it was all because the family cottage was opposite to the recreation ground, or because we were in a British colony and, being active people, gravitated naturally towards sport. My brother never played any games to speak of, but as a young man he gave some clerical assistance to the secretary of the local Football Association. In time he became the secretary. He took Trinidad football teams all over the West Indies and he was invited to England by the Football Association to study football organization. I met him in the United States trying to arrange an American soccer team to visit Trinidad. In 1954 he brought the first team from the West Indies to play football in England, and before he left arranged for an English team to visit the West Indies. He has at last succeeded in organizing a West Indies Football Association, of which he is the first secretary.

Even Uncle Cuffie, my father's elder brother, who, like the old man from Bengal, never played cricket at all, was the hero of a family yarn. One day he travelled with an excursion to the other end of the island. Among the excursionists was the Tunapuna C.C., to play a match with Siparia C.C., while the rest of the visitors explored Siparia. Tunapuna was a man short and my father persuaded – nay, begged – Cuffie to fill the gap, and Cuffie reluctantly agreed. Siparia made forty-odd, not a bad score in those days, and Cuffie asked to have his innings first so that he could get out and go and enjoy himself away from the cricket field. Still wearing his braces and his high collar, he went in first, hit at every ball and by making some thirty runs not out won the match for his side by nine wickets. He quite ruined the game for the others. He had never even practised with the team before and never did afterwards.

The story of my elder aunt, Judith, ends this branch of my childhood days. She was the English Puritan incarnate, a tall, angular woman. She looked upon Matthew Bondman as a child of the devil. But if Matthew had been stricken with a loathsome disease she would have prayed for him and nursed him to the end, because it was her duty. She lost her husband early, but brought up her three children, pulled down the old cottage, replaced it with a modern one and whenever I went to see her fed me with that sumptuousness which the Trinidad Negroes have inherited from the old extravagant plantation owners. Her son grew to manhood, and though no active sportsman himself, once a year invited his friends from everywhere to Tunapuna where they played a festive cricket match. This, however, was merely a preliminary to a great spread which Judith always prepared. One year Judith worked as usual from early morning in preparation for the day, doing everything that was needed. The friends came, the match was played and then all trooped in to eat, hungry, noisy and happy. Judith was serving when suddenly she sat down, saying, "I am not feeling so well." She leaned her head on the table. When they bent over her to find out what was wrong she was dead. I would guess that she had been "not feeling so well" for days, but she was not one to let that turn her aside from doing what she had to do.

I heard the story of her death thousands of miles away. I know that it was the fitting crown to her life, that it signified something to me above all people, and, curiously enough, I thought it appropriate that her death should be so closely associated with a cricket match. Yet she had never taken any particular interest. She or my grandmother or another aunt would come in from the street and say, "Matthew made 55" or "Arthur Jones is still batting," but that was all. Periodically I pondered over it.

My grandfather on my mother's side, Josh Rudder, was also an immigrant, from Barbados, and also Protestant. I knew him well. He used to claim that he was the first coloured man to become an engine-driver on the Trinidad Government Railway. That was some seventy years ago. Before that the engineers were all white men, that is to say, men from England, and coloured men could rise no higher than fireman. But Josh had had a severe training. He came from Barbados at the age of sixteen, which must have been somewhere around 1868. He began as an apprentice in the shed where the new locomotives were assembled and the old ones repaired, and he learnt the business from the ground up. Then he would go out on odd jobs and later he became regular fireman on the engines between San Fernando and Princes Town. This proved to be a stroke of luck. His run was over a very difficult piece of track and when the white engine-driver retired, or more probably died suddenly, there arose the question of getting someone who understood its special difficulties. That was the type of circumstance in those days which gave the local coloured man his first opportunity, and Josh was appointed. He took his job seriously and, unless something had actually broken, whenever his engine stopped he'd refused to have it towed into the shed but went under and fixed it himself.

Josh was a card. In 1932 I went to say goodbye before I left for England. He was nearing eighty and we had lunch surrounded by the results of his latest marriage, some six or seven children ranging from sixteen years to about six. After lunch he put me through my paces. I had been writing cricket journalism in the newspapers for some years and had expressed some casual opinions, I believe, on the probable composition of the West Indies team to visit England in 1933. Josh expressed disagreement with my views and I took him lightly at first. But although in all probability he hadn't seen a cricket match for some thirty years, it soon turned out that he had read practically every article I had written and remembered them; and as he had read the other newspapers and also remembered those, I soon had to get down to it, as if I were at a selection-committee meeting. Apart from half a century, the only difference between us that afternoon was that in his place I would have had the quoted papers to hand, all marked up in pencil.

[...]

When I was ten I went to the Government secondary school, the Queen's Royal College, where opportunities for playing cricket and reading books were thrown wide open to me. When I was fifteen, the editor of the school magazine, a master, asked me to write something for it. Such was my fanaticism that I could find nothing better to write about than an account of an Oxford and Cambridge cricket match played nearly half a century before, the match in which Cobden for Cambridge dismissed three Oxford men in one over to win the match by two runs.

I retold it in my own words as if it were an experience of my own, which indeed it was. The choice was more logical than my next juvenile publication. At the end of term, during the English composition examination, I was very sleepy, probably from reading till the small hours the night before. I looked at the list of subjects, the usual stuff, "A Day in the Country", etc., etc., including, however, "The Novel as an Instrument of Reform". Through the thorough grounding in grammar given me by my father and my incessant reading, I could write a good school composition on anything, and from the time I was about eight my English composition papers usually had full marks, with once every three or four weeks a trifling mistake. I sat looking at the list, not knowing which to choose. Bored with the whole business, I finally wrote each subject on a piece of paper, rolled them, shook them together and picked out one. It was "The Novel as an Instrument of Reform". For me it seemed just a subject like any other. But perhaps I was wrong. Literature? Reform? I may have been stimulated. But I drew on my knowledge and my long-ingrained respect for truth and justice, and I must have done very well, for at the beginning of the following term the English master called me and surprised me by telling me that he proposed to print the "very fine" essay in the school magazine. Still more to my astonishment, when the magazine appeared I was constantly stopped in the street by old boys and the local literati, who congratulated me on what they called "this remarkable essay". I prudently kept the circumstances of its origin to myself.

As I say, those were the first two printed articles. Nearly forty years have passed, and very active and varied years they have been. In the course of them I have written a study of the French Revolution in San Domingo and a history of the Communist International. I went to the United States in 1938, stayed there for fifteen years and never saw a cricket match, though I used to read the results of Tests and county matches, which the *New* York *Times* publishes every day during the season. In 1940 came a crisis in my political life. I rejected the Trotskyist version of Marxism and set about to re-examine and reorganize my view of the world, which was (and remains) essentially a political one. It took more than ten years, but by 1952 I once more felt my feet on solid ground, and in consequence I planned a series of books. The first was published in 1953, a critical study of the writings of Herman Melville as a mirror of our age, and the second is this book on cricket. The first two themes. "The Novel as an Instrument of Reform" and "Cobden's Match", have reappeared in the same close connection after forty years. Only after I had chosen my themes did I recognize that I had completed a circle. I discovered that I had not arbitrarily or by accident worshipped at the shrine of John Bunyan and Aunt Judith, of W. G. Grace and Matthew Bondman, of *The Throne of the House of David* and *Vanity Fair.* They were a trinity, three in one and one in three, the Gospel according to St. Matthew, Matthew being the son of Thomas, otherwise called Arnold of Rugby.

PAUL KEENS-DOUGLAS

ME AN' CRICKET

Dedicated to the West Indies Test Players Honoured at the West Indies Cricket Board Commemorative Banquet, Jamaica, Sept. 18th, 1996.

Yu know, people always come to me an' say, "Paul Keens, is how come yu does write so much ting 'bout cricket, is like yu used to play plenty cricket when yu was ah boy?" I does only watch dem an' laugh, because up to now, even I can't tell why I does write so much 'bout cricket, because is ah game I never used to like at all, at all, when I was ah boy. Is only in recent years I grow to like cricket, an' from ah distance.

Yu see, in my day at school everybody had to play some kind ah game, whether yu one-foot, or bosey-back, it didn't matter, yu had to play. Games was supposed to build muscles an' give yu character. So from my first day at school, dey tell me ah have to choose de game of my choice. Ah tell dem ah don't mind takin' part in de marbles team, if dey had dat, because dat is one ting ah was good at. Dey tell me marbles, catchers, an' search de pack don't count. Ah had three choices, sports, football or cricket. So ah decide ah go' try out for all three to see which one ah could fit in.

Now yu have to understan' dat at de time ah was about twelve years old, four ah' ah half foot tall, weighin' 'bout fifty pounds, an' lookin' like ah half-ripe Lacatan banana. Yu also have to understan' dat in dose days, when yu fail exam yu didn't bound to leave school like now. Yu could ah stay on an' take it over, an' over, an' over, till yu pass. So my school had some hard-back old-men, wit' beard down to dey toe, who been failin' exam since dey born, an' still in school. An' all ah dem playin' cricket, kickin' football, runnin' race, an' generally havin' ah good time, while dey father wastin' school fees. An' is dem fellas I have to compete wit', poor little Lacatan me. Life was not fair.

Ah try for athletics. Now dey say ah was very good at "lime an spoon", "three-legged race", an' "wheelbarrow race", but when it come to hundred yards, two-twenty, an' four-forty, was tears. Is me an' all dem hardfoot old-men, an' all ah dem have on spikes, an' me barefoot. Yu ever get jook wit' ah spikes yet?

An' in dose days yu didn't have no coach to groom yu or encourage yu. Dey put yu out on de field an' tell yu play! kick! run! jump! an' if yu look good, yu get pick. Dat's why de West Indies produce so many natural players, yu had to be naturally good to get pick, nobody eh takin' yu aside an' train yu up. If yu good yu good, if yu eh good yu out, yu carryin' gears or yu fieldin' football behin' de goal-post, because we goal-post didn't have net neither, was bare post.

Ah decide ah better try out for de football team, not because ah had like

304

football too much, but because ah had like de jersey, an' only members of de team was allowed to wear de school jersey. Since den tings change, yu could buy yu jersey now, an' yu don't even have to know how to play football, muchless be on de team.

After one week of football practice, ah say not me an' football, is ah most unreasonable game. Eleven of you on ah team, an' everybody have to be runnin' up an' down at de same time, up an' down, up an' down, no rest whatsoever. An' men allowed to kick yu, an' cuff yu, jook yu in yu eye, stamp on yu foot, an' do all kinds of wicked tings to yu physiognomy, an' dey call dat sport.

Dey even allowed to lick yu down, dey call dat ah "tackle". If yu hear dem, "Tackle him!", nex' ting somebody brogues in yu back. In dose days wasn't football boots, was someting call "brogues" make out of leather dat hard like iron, wit' little wooden pegs underneath like iceskates. But de worse part, when rain fallin' dey still playin', in de mud, in yu nice, clean jersey. If yu see de jersey after, it nasty for days. Ah say to meself, football is ah primitive game. Dat's when all start to take ah interest in cricket, because everybody keep sayin' if how it's ah "gentleman's game!" An' de more I study de game, is de more ah say it suit my personality.

Ah mean, jus' like football, eleven of you on ah team. But unlike football, half de time yu off de field relaxin' in de shade, sippin' tea or snowcone, an' yu wearin' nice, clean, white clothes. When is time to bat, yu jus' walk out dey, swing de bat, make ah duck, an' in no time flat yu back in de shade eatin' roast corn. Now dat is what I call sport. An' if anybody kick yu, or even bounce yu too hard, or even look at yu "bad-eye", yu could complain to de umpire, an' is two of dem, not one like in Football, an' de umpire puttin' dem under real heavy manners. Now dat is ah civilised game. So ah decide to try out for de cricket team. But fate was against me, otherwise all now so I better dan Brian Lara.

In de first place our school didn't have too much money, so all de gears was de same size. We had one pair of battin' pads, an' we had to share dem. One man had on one side, an' de nex' man had on de other side. Dat is why it was so hard to get West Indians out LBW in de old days, because dey learn from early dat one-pad battin' had serious consequences for yu foot, Miss ah ball, an' LBW became BBW, "break-foot before wicket". Yu couldn't afford to pad-up ball neither. So yu had to learn to hit. When yu get out, de nex' man comin' in have to wait on you to take off yu pad to give it to him, before he could begin to bat. An' dat took time, because most times de pads didn't have straps an' yu had to tie dem wit' handkerchiefs.

When was my turn to bat, if yu see me, de pads so big it reachin' me all in me chest. It was hard to get me out LBW, because it was all of me before wicket. De nex' ting was de bat, same ting like de pad, one size, giant size. It take two men to carry out my bat for me. So when you see me wit' me one giant pad, an' me one-size giant bat in front of de wicket, ah look like all ice-cream can wit' ah hat.

Dey give me plenty advise on what to do, even people who passin' in de road used to shout out advice. Usually it was, "Mind dey bus' yu head!" Is only recently I get to believe dey had such ah ting as "placin' de ball!" My idea of cricket was to close yu eye an' VUP! hit de ball as hard an' as far as possible, den run for yu life. Because when dem fellas throwin' back in, dey never used at aim at de stumps, was at de batsman. Dey call dat intimidation. In de Civil Service dey call it "constructive dismissal".

Ah remember de first over ah ever bat. All pad up wit' me one pad, ah tell dem ah ready, an' ah put down de bat in what dey call de "forward defensive position". Is two ting dey had show me before ah go out to bat, "forward defensive", an' "backward defensive", "forward defensive" an' "backward defensive", because nobody thought dat ah would ever be able to hit de ball. If yu see me pose in de forward defensive position, ah stretch forward, bat an' pad together, toe pointin' down de wicket, head down, chin up. Yu know how hard it is to keep yu head down an' yu chin up? De captain shout out, "Yu lookin' good, but yu have to do dat after dey bowl de ball!" Man start to laugh. Ah settle down again. Ah see de bowler walk back wit' big, big steps, like he goin' for speed, den ah see him runnin' up, an' ah eh see nutten after dat, because ah close me eye. Ah feel de breeze when de ball pass, but ah wasn't studyin' de ball, I was studyin' de bat. Dat was de heaviest piece ah wood I ever lift up in me life. By de time ah get de bat up to swing it, ball done pass an' dey sendin' it back to de bowler. De captain shout out, "Keep yu eye on de ball!", all dis time I busy keepin' my eye on de bat.

Next ball ah play "backward defensive", if yu see pose. I didn't have me eye on de ball, but de ball had it eye on me. It fly up de bat handle an' knock of de shades ah had on. Yes, ah had on shades, ah black, black, black shades wit' ah red frame, used to sell for ah dollar-twenty-five. Fellas say de shades so black, dey wonder why I bother to close me eye. Ah say to meself, "Dis game gettin' dangerous!"

De third ball comin' up. Ah say to meself, "Ah go hit dis ball if it kill me!" De bowler run up an' bowl ah "hurry ball", he was gettin vex, because yu know how hard it is to out ah man who can't bat, dey does call it "unorthodox" battin'. Ah open one eye, lift up de bat wit' two hand, an' swing it wit' all me might. Ah make history, ah get catch by three man one time. De man in gully catch de ball, de wicketkeeper catch me hat, an' de umpire catch de bat. Dey say dat must be some kinda record, an' ah shoulda be in de Guinness Book of Records.

Is at dis point dat ah start considerin' football again, because if is one thing ah know ah could ah do good was run. Dis cricket ting of standin' up, an' gettin' hit wit' ball, didn't look too good. Ah say me an' cricket not goin' to see eye to eye at all. Ah didn't even try me hand at bowlin', because ah say if ah too weak to lift de bat, is no way ah could ah throw de ball down no wicket.

But ah had like to "field", because dey used to put me way-out on de long-on boundary. Out dere was nice. Yu could ah talk to spectators, watch de girls playin' nex'-door, buy sugar-cake, snowcone, doubles an' tings like dat, all dis while match goin' on. An' was extra nice, because very few balls ever used to make it down to long-on, I wasn't de only weak man on de team. So my cricket was to go in, close me eye, swing de bat, out quick, an' spend de rest of de game by long-on.

Until one Friday evenin', everyting goin' nice, I down by long-on enjoyin' life, havin' ah good time, when ah hear de whole team shout out, CATCH IT!" Some stupid batsman hit de ball down my way, an' he hit it hard too, an' it comin' through de air like ah bullet, to of all people, ME! Now let me tell yu someting, ah cricket-ball is not de nicest ting in de worl' to get hit by. Ah see de ball come towards me, an' de closer it get, de bigger it get. It comin' closer an' closer, an' it gettin' bigger an' bigger, an it lookin harder an' harder, an' everybody shoutin' "CATCH IT!"

But what inspire me de most, was de captain's kindly advice, he shout out at de top of he voice, "If you eh catch dat ball ah go' break yu foot!" Ah say today ah dead, an' ah put out me hand. Ah hear BLIP! an' de ball stick in me hand. Talk 'bout pain? Is like me whole hand catch fire. Me little finger bend right back an' say hello to me thumb. One fingernail decide to take ah holiday, it take off. Me mout' open in shock. Ah couldn't say boo! I was de most surprised man on de field. Ah catch de ball.

If you hear de crowd clap, ah was ah hero. Dey surround me. Dey say ah should play test cricket. Dey tell me ah have "potential", ah could be de nex' Sobers. Man start askin' for autograph. All dis time I askin' for ice.

Well to make ah long story short, ah get pick for de nex' match, me name at de top of de list. Was ah disaster. Ah out for duck. Ah bowl one over an' dey hit me for thirty-six. But worse of all, ah drop five catch. Dey say me hand like ah basket. Dey say ah couldn't even catch ah cold. Dey say go back to Grenada. Dey say ah sell-out to de nex' team. Dey say I is de worse cricketer God ever put on de face of de earth. Dey say ah should go to Convent an' take up netball. Yu tink is two ting dey say? Dose same people who tell me de week before dat I is de nex' Gary Sobers?

So ah decide to take in front before in front take me, ah decide to take early retirement, very early retirement, to quit while ah still ahead an' while ah still had me head, an' to try for de safest position in Cricket... Commentator. Yu don't have to do it, jus' talk 'bout it. But dat's another story. How is dat!?

LIKE WHEN SOMEBODY DEAD (2001)

I had never seen us lose a Test match live. I might have seen it on TV, heard it on radio; but to actually see us lose a Test match, see the stumps of the last man rocked back with the deadening sound of beaten lead, to hear the exhalation of a final communal sigh as the opposing bowler turns from his victorious leap and grabs a handful of stumps and know for certain that, yes, this is the end; this was the first time.

And it is not nice.

I was preparing to go on the day Walsh addressed the monumental task of taking his 500th Test wicket; but by the time I turn around twice, he had produced the deliveries to do it. No sense going that day.

Now, it is the last day, the final act. Two hundred to make and a day in which to make them.

Listening to the radio this week has made me aware that with one or two exceptions, West Indian commentators have a vocabulary less of appreciation than of censure. There is a sense of reproof and impatience that they inflict on West Indian players, making them more frequently the objects rather than the subjects of their constructions. But I listen, with some aggravation, hoping that the vibrations of such utterances do not reach the players, especially today.

On the radio, the bubbly Colin Croft, his mouth full of pebbles, is confidently predicting a West Indian victory. Brij Parasnath is saying Brian Lara is due for a big score, the others are making reasoned assessments. I get ready to go. We have a whole day. I can avoid the initial traffic and still see most of the play.

I am preparing to leave, when, Bam! Dinanath Ramnarine goes. Okay, so I will see Marlon Samuels bat. Baddam! Samuels goes. Lara enters. Okay, I will see Lara bat. I don't want to think of what that implies. Then boom! Chris Gayle is out. And as I turn around, Bam! Boodoom! Bodow! Lara is gone. Five wickets down, 51 on the board. What am I going to the Oval to see now?

"Lara out," I announce to the house. "Lara out!"

Nobody answers.

My daughter sees me spinning around.

"You not going?" she asks. "Go," as if she is slightly sorry for me.

We still have Ramnaresh Sarwan and Carl Hooper. On the radio, Croft confidently reaffirms his prediction, West Indies are going to win this match. It is what I want to hear. I put on my clothes and I leave the house. I park in the car park and get into the Oval.

Years ago when I was living Matura I had taken my family to the Oval. The children were small then, the Oval was packed and I had to find seats for five of us. It was terrible. Everywhere I saw a seat, a policeman told me to move on. But today there is room.

I find a seat on the cycle track and discover that next to me is Adolphe, an attorney-at-law in the US now, who I have known since my Rio Claro days. Between drinks and play he would remind me of those days when he played football for Hurricanes and I was writing my first novel and playing for Penetrators.

Hooper and Sarwan are batting. We have time. The crowd is thoughtful, hopeful, concerned. When a four is struck some fellars nearby race to the fence in mock display of invading the field, much like the runs footballers make nowadays when they score a goal. Otherwise the crowd is silent. With an edge of disappointment, Adolphe says to me, "You know when I watch this thing on TV in the US I see such excitement in the Trini Posse stand. Now here it seems so quiet."

Yes, the Trini Posse is quiet. I will reproach them later in a little postmortem with David Rudder. The crowd doesn't cheer up the players. It is the players that cheer up the crowd. But it wasn't as if I myself was making any big noise. I stop clapping when I notice that I am almost alone. Clapping suggests an appreciation of the play, whoever makes it. Cheering is more partisan.

We are in too precarious a position today to be anything but partisan. But our cheering is sporadic, drawn out of us only by the fruitful stroke.

Just when I think we are beginning to settle, the South African players gather in the middle for a puja, then the collapse begins.

First, Sarwan's hook that is neither hit over the fielder's head nor properly kept down, in the over before lunch. Next to me, one of Adolphe's party is vexed: "Three balls they put there for him to hit. They set him up."

Such a statement asks me to accept that the spectators are wiser and keener than the players. I would have preferred him to make Sarwan the subject. Sarwan took up the challenge. Unwisely, yes; but he took it up.

Then Ridley Jacobs is run out. When I played cricket, I used to feel that the throw from the fielder would miss the stumps and my speed would get me in. So I sympathise with Jacobs for losing out to a direct hit. But this is not Matura versus Recreation; this is Test cricket.

Nixon McLean comes in. If we get 20 runs from him that would be great. But McLean goes on the defensive, the crowd cheering. At this point, I feel that McLean should be hitting out. Cricket, like any other drama, is about making choices. Anything you do can work; anything you do can fail. McLean's choice fails.

BC Pires, who had joined me on the concrete, had been making the important point that the West Indies natural game is not wildness. It contains thought as well as adventure.

But now McLean is out, a soft out, edging to the wicketkeeper off Kallis, and I hear the wind squeeze out our hopes. Dillon's moment at the crease is a blur. As he leaves, I see on the off-and-on television screen, the images of the dancers and in my mind hear the theme song of T&T football, the American accented, "Go T&T, show them what you gat."

How can fellars from here be motivated by that? Imagine we playing the USA and this song is played. Why can't we just sing a tune which is honest, and which expresses the poetry of the more substantial we – "Give Praise Children"? "Dingolay"?

Courtney Walsh has come in. Someone reminds me that Walsh and Lara brought us home in Barbados or Jamaica. Well, Walsh is in now. Now Walsh is out.

How does it feel to lose a Test match? You would think we have had enough practice losing these last years to know. But it is not nice, this losing business. And I am not consoled by the idea that we were competitive. I am not consoled by Walsh's 500 Test wickets.

What does losing mean to the West Indies? What does losing mean to us? What do we feel is lost in the process of losing a Test match? The British used to say that losing a Test match was like losing a battleship. What is the equivalent to us?

In the Oval this afternoon, no West Indian is at ease. No one is philosophical. I sense with some satisfaction that we have begun to feel.

Later, at a party that might have celebrated our victory, had we been victorious, I got into a conversation with an educator and we talked about the need for an education rooted in the teaching of self-confidence.

The music in the background was morose, I felt, but nobody else seemed to mind it, so it played. Later it was changed to something more lively – from hymns to bongo songs, so to speak.

If we talked about the cricket it wasn't for long. We really didn't talk about politics either. We were taking it in, this loss, feeling it in silence, like somebody dead.

IAN MCDONALD

CRICKET'S MOST MEMORABLE OVER

I thought we would win the second one-day International against Australia decisively, if not comfortably, so I had planned to listen from 8 o'clock for 2 or 3 hours, then have a sleep, and listen again for a couple of hours at the end. The history of our contests against Australia should have taught me better. Like thousands, perhaps tens of thousands, of others I ended up listening every minute all the way though to the great climax. And I went on listening, after G.B.C. lost contact with Australia, to the replay of the last three balls bowled, to Dave Martin's classic folk song, "We Are The Champions", and to the people phoning in their excited views. The one I liked the best was the man who argued with what I thought was impeccable logic that since the series was 2 best out of 3 and we were the best in the 2 played so far therefore we were undoubtedly the winners. It all made up one more chapter to add to one's unforgettable sporting recollections.

It naturally brought back memories of the Test between West Indies and Australia which built up to that famous climax in Brisbane on December 14th, 1960. My heart always races when I recall that extraordinary event, undoubtedly the greatest match ever played in the greatest sport of all. That Brisbane Test was a "purer" tie than the tie in Melbourne in that all the available wickets on both sides fell and because of that and because it was a full five-day Test I give it pride of place – but we are privileged in one lifetime to have experienced two such games of glory.

Garner's last over at Melbourne will be fresh in your minds, but for my sake and yours too, can I recall again Wesley Hall's last over in the Brisbane tie. It is more than 23 years ago but I remember the night well, sitting around a bottle of Houstons Blue Label with four friends and pounding each other on the backs as each ball entered cricket history.

That most famous over began with Australia needing 6 to win, three wickets in hand, 8 balls to go, Hall bowling, Grout facing, Benaud at the other end. First ball of full length and good pace got up and hit Grout in the groin. Normally he would have crumpled, but Benaud was coming for the single so Grout forgot pain and ran. 5 runs to win, 7 balls to go. Hall bowled a bouncer, Benaud flashed, Alexander screamed his appeal with all the joy in the world. 5 runs to win, 2 wickets left, 6 balls to go, Meckiff coming slowly in. Hall bowled fast and straight as a bullet, and Meckiff blocked it in a tangle of arms and legs. 5 balls left, 5 runs to win. Next ball Hall bowled fast down the legside. Meckiff didn't even play a shot but the batsman ran one of the strangest runs seen in Test cricket – a run while the ball went to the wicketkeeper, with Alexander hurling the ball to Hall who turned and hurled it at the bowler's wicket but missed, and some West Indian hero threw himself full length and saved the overthrows. 4 runs to win, 2 wickets left, 4 balls to go. The next ball brought madness. Grout mishit and the ball spooned up high, high over mid-wicket. Kanhai positioned himself right under it to make the easy catch. But Hall in a frenzy of resolve charged across, jumped all over Kanhai, and dropped the catch! 1 run scored, so 3 runs were needed, 2 wickets to fall, 3 balls to go. Hall must have heard the good Lord saying, "You asked for the ordinary miracles, not stupid ones!", as he walked back in disgrace. Worrell came over and calmed him, encouraged him. Hall came roaring in again. Meckiff swung and the ball sailed away to square-leg where there was no fieldsman – a sure boundary and the match won, except that Conrad Hunte sprinted to burst his heart and saved the ball on the boundary-edge and turned and threw and 90 yards away found Alexander's gloves poised over the wicket and Grout, diving headlong for the crease, was run out going for the winning third run. The score was now tied. 2 balls to go, 1 run to win, 1 wicket to fall. Hall, fingering the cross on his chest as he started his run, bowled his heart out to Kline. Kline hit to leg. Twelve yards away, Joe Solomon, cool as ice in that crucible, from completely side-on to the wicket, swooped one-handed and threw as he picked up and broke the one stump visible to him. The greatest cricket match of all time was over. In the whole history of sport it is unlikely that there has been any period of ten minutes so highly charged with drama and emotion as that last over bowled by Wes Hall in the tied Test at Brisbane.

I have said many times that cricket is the greatest of all games. This is not simply because above all other games it requires a combination of all the skills – batting, bowling, catching, throwing, running – and use of all the physical talents – quick eye, sharp reflexes, speed of foot, dexterity, strength and stamina. It is also the greatest game of all because, at its best, it contains drama as good as the finest theatre, plots as complex and intriguing as in well-written novels, and beauty of performance at times as piercing as a painting or a poem. In other words, at its best, cricket is an art as well as a game. As at Brisbane, so at Melbourne last weekend, there was high drama on display, not just simple sport and the players all were heroes, with one or two villains, and not just ordinary sportsmen. It was a day of passion and for a while a cricket ground, as sometimes happens, became an amphitheatre for a performance fit for Gods.

And now the Australians will be with us very soon. After that match in Melbourne the omens are good for a great series. The stage is set. It seems we can look forward to play that will fill the days with something more than ordinary sport.

ALFRED H. MENDES

FROM THE AUTOBIOGRAPHY OF ALFRED H. MENDES

I have said that field games – cricket, football, tennis [*sic*] – are nothing to me. And yet, cricket is in a class by itself – not as a game but rather as what it symbolizes and what it means, at least to me. Created by the English, I believe during the earlier years of the building of their empire it was fashioned in the image of the Englishman, quite naturally: his high civilization, his slow and deliberate pace, his anxiety to appear fair at all times, his dignity, the too aesthetic accent and artificial timbre of voice nurtured in his ancient universities of Oxford and Cambridge, his sense of order and discipline: all of these characteristics are reflected in the game, and, it seems to me, much more too. I cannot be sure of how conscious he was that cricket was destined to be his ally, his "public relations officer", so to speak, in the protracted struggle of empire-building: Maybe he simply stumbled into perceiving its disarming value. Be that as it may, every green field in the British Caribbean colonies, in the vast subcontinent of India, in the Anglo-Saxon extensions of Australia and New Zealand saw, *pari-passu* with the growing colossus, black boys and men, brown boys and men with sticks for wickets and improvised bats, clad for the most part in rags, and white boys and men with immaculate impedimenta, revelling in the game and learning its multitude of fine points fast. If national temperament is taken into account – the ebullience of the Negro alongside the dignity of the Englishman, the obsequiousness of the Indian alongside the silent self-assurance of the Englishman – then certainly these black and brown boys playing cricket looked like a contradiction in terms. But not at all, for the Negro at once proceeded to impose *his* personality upon the game, *his* subtle version of its spirit, and this was vividly illustrated when teams from England played Test Matches against black West Indians. I am not trying to animadvert against the game. After all, it has perhaps served an historical purpose (to the benefit of the English, let it be said) in that it has certainly exercised a restraining influence over the colonial masses against a too premature and impetuous, and thus bloody, attempt at destroying something that, by the evidence of all history, was inexorably moving towards destroying itself.

The English themselves were so charmed with and impressed by this black transformation of their national game that their queen first of all knighted Learie Constantine, the brilliant exponent of West Indian cricket; and, not satisfied with this, later elevated him to the House of Lords, that extraordinary anachronism in the modern world, as Lord Constantine of Maraval, fully rigged out in the ermine of the ancient institution – an honour, so far as I am aware, never conferred upon an English cricketer.

Note that the new peer no longer needed the identification of his first name: the prefix "Lord" was in effect deification. When I contemplate this diabolical astuteness of the English ruling class, I am overawed by the magic of a game which requires little intelligence for outstanding performance in it, playing the role, no matter how imperceptibly, of a buffer cushioning the impact of an imperialism in full marching order.

EDGAR MITTELHOLZER

EXTRACT FROM A SWARTHY BOY

For cricket I could not build up any kind of enthusiasm. I found it too slow and laborious – that is, however, when it was played according to the rules. In the backyard at "Westbourne Villa", we played a rough-and-ready version in which the idea was that the fielders competed among themselves to win a spell of batting. If you managed to grab the ball when the batsman swiped it, or if it missed the wicket and you were at long stop, or even wicketkeeper, you became bowler and sent down a scorcher. If somebody else caught the batsman out, however, he it was who went in to bat, not you the bowler. It was a purely cut-throat business. I enjoyed this kind of cricket immensely. It was exciting and highly competitive. We all enjoyed it – until the ball crashed through a window and ended up on the floor of the dentist's surgery. That generally brought the afternoon's play to an abrupt conclusion.

TEST

The First Day

At Waterloo and Trafalgar Square the Underground train begins to fill. Young men in tweed jackets, carrying mackintoshes and holdalls. Older men in City black, carrying umbrellas. At every station the crowd grows. Whole families now, equipped as for a rainy camping weekend. And more than a sprinkling of West Indians. At Baker Street we are like a rush-hour train. It is eleven o'clock on a Thursday morning and we are travelling north. The train empties at St John's Wood. Buy your return ticket now, the boards say. We will regret that we didn't. Later. Now we are in too much of a hurry. We pass the souvenir sellers, the man selling the West Indian newspaper, the white-coated newspaper vendors. The newspaper posters. What billing these cricket writers get!

Then inside. It is wet. Play has not begun. A Barbadian in a blue suit, a tall man standing behind the sightscreen, has lost his brother in the crowd, and is worried. He has been in London for four years and a half. He has the bearing of a student. But: "I works. In transport." The groundsmen in vivid green lounge against the wicket-covers. Someone rushes out to them with a plate of what looks like cakes. There is applause. Few people have eaten before such a large appreciative audience. Presently, though, there is action. The covers are removed, the groundsmen retreat into obscurity, and the rites begin.

Trueman bowling to Conrad Hunte. Four, through the slips. Four, to midwicket. Four, past gully. Never has a Test opened like this. A Jamaican whispers: "I think Worrell made the right decision." A little later: "It's all right now. I feel we getting on top." The bowling tightens. The batsmen are on the defensive, often in trouble.

"I think Conrad Hunte taking this Moral Rearmament a little too seriously. He don't want to hit the ball because the leather come from an animal."

A chance.

The Jamaican says: "If England have to win, they can't win now."

I puzzle over this. Then he leans back and whispers again: "England can't win now. *If* they have to win."

Lunch. In front of the Tavern the middle-class West Indians. For them too this is a reunion.

"...and, boy, I had to leave Grenada because politics were making it too hot for me."

"What, they have politics in Grenada?"

Laughter.

"You are lucky to be seeing me here today, let me tell you. The only thing in which I remain West Indian is cricket. Only thing."

"...and when they come here, they don't even change."

"Change? Them?"

Elsewhere:

"I hear the economic situation not too good in Trinidad these days."

"All those damn strikes. You know our West Indian labour. Money, money. And if you say 'work', they strike."

But the cricket ever returns.

"I don't know why they pick McMorris in place of Carew. You can't have two sheet-anchors as opening batsmen. Carew would have made 16. Sixteen and out. But he wouldn't have let the bowling get on top as it is now. I feel it have a lil politics in McMorris pick, you know."

After lunch, McMorris leg before to Trueman.

"Man, I can't say I sorry. Poke, poke."

Hunte goes. And, 65 runs later, Sobers.

"It isn't a healthy score, is it?"

"My dear girl, I didn't know you followed cricket."

"Man, how you could help it at home? In Barbados. And with all my brothers. It didn't look like this, though, this morning. Thirteen in the first over."

"But that's cricket."

A cracking drive, picked up almost on the boundary.

"Two runs only for that. So near and so far."

"But that's life."

"Man, you're a philosopher. It must be that advanced age of yours you've been telling me about."

"Come, come, my dear. It isn't polite to agree with me. But seriously, what you doing up here?"

"Studying, as they say. Interior decorating. It's a hard country, boy. I came here to make money." Chuckle.

"You should have gone somewhere else."

In a doorway of the Tavern:

"If Collie Smith didn't dead, that boy Solomon wouldn'ta get pick, you know."

"If Collie Smith didn't dead."

"He used to jump out and hit Statham for six and thing, you know."

"I not so sure that Worrell make the right decision."

"Boy, I don't know. I had a look through binoculars. It breaking up already, you know. You didn't see the umpire stop Dexter running across the pitch?"

"Which one is Solomon? They look like twins."

"Solomon have the cap. And Kanhai a lil fatter."

"But how a man could get fat, eh, playing all this cricket?"

"Not getting *fat*. Just putting on a lil *weight*."

"O Christ! He out! Kanhai."

Afterwards, Mrs Worrell in a party at the back of the pavilion:

"Did you enjoy the cricket, Mrs Worrell?"

"All except Frank's duck."

"A captain's privilege."

The Second Day

McMorris, the West Indian opening batsman whose failure yesterday was so widely discussed by his compatriots around the ground, was this morning practising at the nets. To him, bowling, Sobers and Valentine. Beyond the stands, the match proper continues, Solomon and Murray batting, according to the transistors. But around the nets there is this group that prefers nearness to cricketers. McMorris is struck on the pads. "How's that?" Sobers calls. "Out! Out!" the West Indians behind the nets shout, and raise their fingers. McMorris turns. "You don't out down the line in England." Two Jamaicans, wearing the brimless porkpie hats recently come into fashion among West Indian workers in England, lean on each other's shoulders and stand, swaying, directly behind the stumps.

"Mac, boy," one says, "I cyan't tell you how I feel it yesterday when they out you. I feel it, man. Tell me, you sleep well last night? I couldn't sleep, boy."

McMorris snicks one into the slips from Valentine. Then he hooks one from Sobers. It is his favourite shot.

"I wait for those," he tells us.

A Jamaican sucks his teeth. "Tcha! Him didn't bat like that yesterday." And walks away.

The West Indian wickets in the meantime fall. Enter Wesley Hall. Trueman and he are old antagonists, and the West Indians buzz good-humouredly. During this encounter the larger interest of the match recedes. Hall drives Trueman straight back for four, the final humiliation of the fast bowler. Trueman gets his own back by hitting Hall on the ankle, and Hall clowningly exaggerates his distress. The middle-class West Indians in the Tavern are not so impressed.

"It's too un-hostile, man, to coin a word. You don't win Test matches with that attitude."

West Indies all out for 301.

And England immediately in trouble. At ten past one Dexter comes in to face a score of 20 for 1. Twenty for one, lunch nearly due, and Griffith gets another wicket. A Jamaican, drunk on more than the bitter he is holding, talks of divine justice: Griffith's previous ball had been no-balled.

"You know, we going to see the West Indies bat again today."

"But I want them to make some runs, though. I don't want it to be a walk-over."

"Yes, man. I want to see some cricket on Monday."

But then Dexter. Tall, commanding, incapable of error or gracelessness. Every shot, whatever its result, finished, decisive. Dexter hooking: the ball seeming momentarily *arrested* by the bat before being redirected. Dexter simplifying: an illusion of time, even against these very fast bowlers.

"If they going to make runs, I want to see Dexter make them."

"It would be nice. But I don't want him to stay too long. Barrington could stay there till kingdom come. But Dexter does score too damn fast. He could demoralise any side in half an hour. Look, they scoring now at the rate of six runs an over."

"How you would captain the side? Take off Griffith?"

Sobers comes on. And Dexter, unbelievably, goes. West Indian interest subsides.

"I trying to sell a lil insurance these days, boy. You could sell to Barbadians. Once they over here and they start putting aside the couple of pounds every week, you could sell to them. But don't talk to the Jamaicans."

"I know. They pay three weeks' premiums, and they want to borrow three hundred pounds."

In the Tavern:

"You know what's wrong with our West Indians? No damn discipline. Look at this business this morning. That Hall and Trueman nonsense. Kya-kya, very funny. But that is not the way the Aussies win Tests. I tell you, what we need is *conscription*. Put every one of the idlers in the army. Give them discipline."

The score mounts. Worrell puts himself on. He wants to destroy this partnership between Parks and Titmus before the end of play. There is determination in his run, his delivery. It transmits itself to the West Indian crowd, the West Indian team. And, sad for Parks, who had shown some strokes, Worrell gets his wicket. Trueman enters. But Hall is damaged. There can be no revenge for the morning's humiliation. And matters are now too serious for clowning anyway.

West Indies 301. England 244 for 7.

Afterwards, Mrs Worrell in her party.

"You can still bowl, then, Mrs Worrell. You can still bowl."

"Frank willed that, didn't he, Mrs Worrell?"

"Both of us willed it."

"So, Mrs Worrell, the old man can still bowl."

"Old man? You are referring to my father or my husband?"

The Third Day

Lord's Ground Full, the boards said at St John's Wood station, and there was two-way traffic on Wellington Road. No one practising at the nets today. And

319

Trueman and Titmus still batting. Hall, recovered this morning, wins his duel with Trueman by clean bowling him. But England is by no means finished. Shackleton is correct and unnervous against Hall and Griffith, Titmus regularly steals a run at the end of the over.

Titmus won't get 50; England won't make 300, won't make 301. These are the bets being made in the free seats, West Indian against West Indian. Lord's has restrained them: in the West Indies they will gamble on who will field the next ball, how many runs will be scored in the over. For them a cricket match is an unceasing drama.

Titmus gets his 50. All over the free stands money changes hands. Then England are all out for 297. More money changes hands. It has worked out fairly. Those who backed Titmus for 50 backed England for 300.

Anxiety now, as the West Indians come out for the second innings. With the scores so even, the match is beginning all over again. "I feel we losing a wicket before lunch. And I feel that it not going to be McMorris, but Hunte. I don't know, I just have this feeling." Hunte hits a six off a bad ball from Trueman, and alarms the West Indians. "Trueman vex too bad now." What opens so brightly can't end well. So it turns out. Hunte is caught by Cowdrey off Shackleton. And in comes Kanhai, at twenty past one, with ten minutes to lunch, and the score 15 for 1. How does a batsman feel at such a time?

I inquire. And, as there are few self-respecting West Indians who are not in touch with someone who is in touch with the cricketers, I am rewarded. I hear that Kanhai, before he goes in to bat, sits silent and moody, "tensing himself up". As soon as the first West Indian wicket falls he puts on his gloves and, without a word, goes out.

Now, however, as he appears running down the pavilion steps, bat in one hand, the other hand lifted and slightly crooked, all his tenseness, if tenseness there ever was, has disappeared. There is nothing in that elegant figure to suggest nervousness. And when he does bat he gives an impression of instant confidence.

The crowd stirs just before the luncheon break. There is movement in the stands. Trueman is bowling his last over. McMorris is out! Caught Cowdrey again. McMorris has made his last effective appearance in this match. He goes in, they all go in. Lunch.

For West Indians it is an anxious interval. Will Worrell send in Sobers after lunch? Or Butcher? Or Solomon, the steady? It is Butcher; the batting order remains unchanged. Butcher and Kanhai take the score to 50. Thereafter there is a slowing up. Kanhai is subdued, unnatural, overcautious. It isn't the West Indians' day. Kanhai is caught in the slips, by Cowdrey again. Just as no one runs down the pavilion steps more jauntily, no one walks back more sadly. His bat is a useless implement; he peels off his gloves as though stripping himself of an undeserved badge. Gloves flapping, he walks back, head bowed. This is not the manner of Sobers. Sobers never walks so fast as when he is dismissed. It is part of his personality, almost part of the grace of his play. And this walk back is something we will soon see.

84 for four.

"You hear the latest from British Guiana?"

"What, the strike still on?"

"Things really bad out there."

"Man, go away, eh. We facing defeat, and you want to talk politics."

It looks like defeat. Some West Indians in the free seats withdraw from the game altogether and sit on the grass near the nets, talking over private problems, pints of bitter between their feet. No need to ask, from the shouts immediately after tea, what has happened. Applause; no hands thrown up in the air; the West Indians standing still. Silence. Fresh applause, polite, English. This has only one meaning: another wicket.

The English turn slightly partisan. A green-coated Lord's employee, a cushion-seller, says to a West Indian: "Things not going well now?" The West Indian shrugs, and concentrates on Solomon, small, red-capped, brisk, walking back to the pavilion.

"I can sell you a good seat," the man says. "I am quite comfortable, thank you," the West Indian says. He isn't. Soon he moves and joins a group of other West Indians standing just behind the sightscreen.

Enter Worrell.

"If only we make 150 we back in the game. Only 150."

And, incredibly, in the slow hour after tea, this happens. Butcher and Worrell remain, and, remaining, grow more aggressive.

The latest of the Worrell late cuts.

"The old man still sweet to watch, you know."

The old man is Worrell, nearly 39.

The 50 partnership.

"How much more for the old lady?" The old lady is Butcher's century, due soon. And it comes, with two fours. A West Indian jumps on some eminence behind the sightscreen and dances, holding aloft a pint of bitter. Mackintoshes are thrown up in the air; arms are raised and held in massive V-signs. Two men do an impromptu jive.

"Wait until they get 200. Then you going to hear noise."

The noise comes. It comes again, to mark the 100 partnership. Butcher, elegant, watchful, becomes attacking, even wild.

"That is Mr Butcher! That is Mr Basil Fitzpatrick Butcher!"

And in the end the score is 214 for five.

"Boy, things was bad. Real bad. 104 for five."

"I didn't say nothing, but, boy, I nearly faint when Solomon out."

In the Tavern:

"This is historic. This is the first time a West Indian team has fought back. The first time."

"But, man, where did you get to, man? I was looking for a shoulder to lean on, and when I look for you, you gone."

Many had in fact sought comfort in privacy. Many had joined the plebeian West Indians, to draw comfort from their shouting. But now assurance returns.

"I know that Frank has got everything staked on winning this match, let me tell you. And you know what's going to happen afterwards? At Edgbaston they are going to beat Trueman into the ground. Finish him off for the season."

Behind the pavilion, the autograph hunters, and some West Indians.

"That girl only want to see Butcher. She would die for Butcher tonight."

"I just want to see the great Garry and the great Rohan." Garry is Sobers, Rohan is Kanhai. These batsmen failed today. But they remain great. West Indies 301 and 214 for five. England 297.

The Fourth Day

After the weekend tension, farce. We are scarcely settled when the five remaining West Indian wickets fall, for 15 runs. England, as if infected, quickly lose their two opening batsmen. Hall is bowling from the pavilion end, and his long run is accompanied by a sighing cheer which reaches its climax at the moment of delivery. Pity the English batsmen. Even at Lord's, where they might have thought they were safest, they now have to face an audience which is hostile.

And Dexter is out! Dexter, of the mighty strokes, out before lunch! Three for 31.

Outside the Tavern:

"I just meet Harold. Lance Gibbs send a message."

How often, in these West Indian matches, conspiratorial word is sent straight from the players to their friends!

"Lance say," the messenger whispers, "the wicket taking spin. He say it going to be all over by teatime."

Odd, too, how the West Indians have influenced the English spectators. There, on one of the Tavern benches, something like a shouting match has gone on all morning between an English supporter and a West Indian.

"The only man who could save all-you is Graveney. And all-you ain't even pick him. You didn't see him there Thursday, standing up just next to the tea-stand in jacket and tie, with a mackintosh thrown over his arm? Why they don't pick the man? You know what? They must think Graveney is a black man."

Simultaneously: "Well, if Macmillan resigns I vote Socialist next election. And – I am a Tory." The speaker is English (such distinctions are now necessary), thin, very young, with spectacles and a tweed jacket. "And," he repeats, as though with self-awe, "I am a Tory."

In spite of that message from Lance Gibbs, Barrington and Cowdrey appear to be in no trouble.

"This is just what I was afraid of. You saw how Cowdrey played that ball? If they let him get set, the match is lost."

When Cowdrey is struck on the arm by a fast rising ball from Hall, the ground is stilled. Cowdrey retires. Hall is chastened. So too are the West Indian spectators. Close comes in. And almost immediately Barrington carts Lance Gibbs for two sixes.

"Who was the man who brought that message from Lance Gibbs?"

"Rohan Kanhai did send a message, too, remember? He was going to get a century on Saturday."

Where has Barrington got these strokes from? This aggression? And Close, why is he so stubborn? The minutes pass, the score climbs. "These West Indian cricketers have some mighty names, eh? *Wesley* Hall. *Garfield* Sobers. *Rohan* Kanhai."

"What about McMorris? What is his name?" A chuckle, choking speech. "Easton."

Nothing about McMorris, while this match lasts, can be taken seriously.

Now there are appeals for light, and the cricket stops. The Queen arrives. She is in light pink. The players reappear in blazers, the English in dark blue, the West Indians in maroon. They line up outside the pavilion gate, and hands are shaken, to a polite clapping which is as removed from the tension of the match as these courtly, bowing figures are removed from the cricketers we have been watching for four days.

With Barrington and Close settled in, and the score at the end of play 116 for three, the match has once more swung in England's favour. Rain. The crowd waits for further play, but despairingly, and it seems that the game has been destroyed by the weather.

The Fifth Day

And so it continued to seem today. Rain held up play for more than three hours, and the crowd was small. But what a day for the 7,000 who went! Barrington, the hero of England's first innings, out at 130, when England needed 104 to win. Parks out at 138. Then Titmus, the stayer, came in, and after tea it seemed that England, needing only 31 runs with five wickets in hand, was safely home. The match was ending in anticlimax. But one shot – May's cover-drive off Ramadhin at Edgbaston in 1957 – can change a match. And one ball. That ball now comes. Titmus is caught off Hall by – McMorris. And, next ball, Trueman goes. Only Close now remains for England, with 31 runs to get, and the clock advancing to six. Every ball holds drama. Every run narrows the gap. Hall bowls untiringly from the pavilion end. Will his strength never give out? Will Worrell have to bring on the slower bowlers – Sobers, himself or even

Gibbs, whose message had reached us yesterday? Miraculously to some, shat-
teringly to others, it is Close who cracks. Seventy his personal score, an English victory only 15 runs away. Close pays for the adventuring which until then
had brought him such reward. He is out, caught behind the wicket. However,
the runs trickle in. And when, two balls before the end, Shackleton is run out
any finish is still possible. Two fours will do the trick. Or a four and a two. Or
a mighty swipe for six. Or a wicket. Cowdrey comes in, his injured left arm
bandaged. And this is the ridiculous public-school heroism of cricket: a man
with a bandaged arm saving his side, yet without having to face a ball. It is the
peculiar *style* of cricket, and its improbable appreciation links these dissimilar
people – English and West Indian.

Day after day I have left Lord's emotionally drained. What other game could
have stretched hope and anxiety over six days? A slow game, but there were
moments when it was torment to watch, when I joined those others, equally
exhausted, sitting on the grass behind the stands. And what other game can
leave so little sense of triumph or defeat? The anguish and joy of a cricket match
last only while the match lasts. Close was marvellous. But it didn't seem so to
me while he was in. Frustration denied generosity. But now admiration is pure.
This has been a match of heroes, and there have been heroes on both sides.
Close, Barrington, Titmus, Shackleton, Trueman, Dexter. Butcher, Worrell,
Hall, Griffith, Kanhai, Solomon. Cricket a team game? Teams play, and one
team is to be willed to victory. But it is the individual who remains in the
memory, he who has purged the emotions by delight and fear.

PHILIP NANTON

NIGHT CRICKET AT CARLTON CLUB, BARBADOS

The lines of silent vehicles suggest Sunday mornings with their owners all in church. The cars are strung along the road. They poke their bonnets out of side streets and stand in unused driveways. They take up most of the pavement, tracing a path to the cricket ground, pushing pedestrians into the road.

The route to the ground is up a side street. At the end of the street a wall begins. It is topped with razor wire; where there are holes in the wall they have been patched with galvanized sheeting. From a distance you can hear the gathered crowd. They clap, sigh and intone in unison. You join a line and follow the wall. The queue of people, heads bowed from the sudden bright light of the entrance, shuffle forward, constantly passing into the ground. At first the way in seems to be through a small hut, but it turns out to be an alcove open at both ends. In the middle a man and a woman sit collecting money filling a big biscuit tin. Heavies stand around in fluorescent waistcoats, proud to serve a good cause.

At the end of the hut, just before you can join the throng, another server, more committed, intones – "Only two dollars, get one now". A kind of specialist muezzin, what he really conveys is "Come to cricket. Cricket is great". On a table in front of him are large cardboard boxes full of programmes. Most people pay their two dollars and buy one. They are left over from three years ago. No matter. In the middle is a folded sheet, the night's order of service, the list of teams, from Walsh to Browne and Browne to Williams; "Past and Present West Indies v Barbados, Under the Patronage of the Prime Minister" (there in spirit), "Attractive Door Prizes To Be Won. The Children of Barbados And The Eastern Caribbean Thank You".

The stand is bright and full. Adults sit in pews, lie in the dark outfield, or they move around the bar greeting friends, buying drinks – "You want, what?" ... "Don't spill that"... "It's precious"... "Take this"... Children spread themselves around the edge of the ground twitching restlessly like cherubim everywhere, always in flight. If they get too excited or encroach beyond an imaginary line, adults admonish them and they move back, reluctantly. After each over there is music; old scores blast out to feed the faithful. In the light, moths trace patterns in the sky against the black background of the night. Most eyes face forward. Ahead of them the vision of a bright green pitch glows like a promised land.

In the middle of the park bats twirl; leather hits wood; runs, like souls, are sometimes saved. People erupt from their seats, shout, sit, mutter. Glove knocks glove. Generators whirr. Eventually, rain stops play. Refreshed, the congregation, some a little more upright than others, head for home. Forever and ever. Amen.

WEST INDIAN CRICKET

As a small boy I used to go to the ground of the Georgetown Cricket Club, Bourda, to watch British Guiana play intercolonial games with other colonies, and to watch the Georgetown Cricket Club play club matches in the local leagues. Intercolonial games started at eleven-thirty, but I was always there at ten. I used to like to sit all alone in one corner of the stand, and just look at the great empty ground, only the groundsman and his crew of small boys working on the pitch, and a couple of white-coated waiters wandering around, clearly visible from the ground outside as they went about their respective duties in the members' pavilion. There would have been rain recently. In British Guiana it is always raining, or has just rained, or clearly it is about to rain, and the telephone in the pavilion would be going constantly as members rang up to ask what sort of condition the ground was in, what time the barman thought play would start, had so and so got there yet, and so on and so forth.

As time went by people would begin trickling into the ground, and by quarter to eleven there was always a smattering of the cricketers present, taking a preliminary practice, where any and everybody was allowed to gather round and field or bowl, and scatter madly as someone put his weight behind a straight drive. Then the captains, mighty men, would walk out to inspect the pitch, the coin would be tossed, and the game would start. The ground would as yet be not more than half full, as most people would be working, and for an hour and a half, until one o'clock and the luncheon break, we would concentrate on the cricket, not missing a ball, and discuss the finer points with the gravity and learning of professors.

But during the lunch-break the shops would close (all business places close half-day when a big cricket match is going on) and people would just flood into the ground. By three every available place would be taken, all in shirt sleeves and pretty dresses, for women are just as keen cricketing fans in the West Indies as men, and there in the broiling sun this capacity crowd would sit day after day as long as the match continued.

But sitting and just watching cricket was never any fun for a West Indian crowd. It had to feel that it was getting into the game itself. Barracking is one method of accomplishing this, but usually there is little to barrack about in an intercolonial game. The handclap when a batsman is nearing his fifty or hundred is another. This can be very unnerving. When a batsman is about 97 the entire crowd starts clapping slowly as the bowler starts his run up. Should the necessary runs not be scored the clapping dies away sadly, to recommence as the bowler starts another ball. But should the batsman step in and punch a boundary, everyone leaps up and shrieks his delight!

When all is said and done, however, there is nothing that a West Indian spectator enjoys so much as betting on the game. By this I do not mean to imply that we have bookies and that large sums of money change hands on the results of a match. This may happen, but is generally and rightly condemned. But the small bet, a few shillings, sometimes even a dollar (four-and-twopence) on the most unlikely occurrences, or on anything at all, keeps everyone in a combative, and happy, mood. Men bet on whether a batsman will score off the coming ball, on whether the bowler will bowl a full toss, on whether a wicket will fall in the over, on whether such-and-such a batsman will make ten. I have even heard two old cronies betting on whether the umpire would give a nine-ball over by mistake, which, incidentally, in that particular game he never did.

And this betting is not confined to the big games. At any cricket match there will always be someone anxious to bet on some crazy thing, and there will always be someone anxious to take him. Perhaps the most prophetic bet I ever heard made was at the start of a first division club match between Georgetown and the East Indian Cricket Club. Georgetown were the stronger team, including several first-class cricketers, and on this occasion they won the toss and had first use of a splendid pitch. There was nothing in the East Indian opening attack to alarm the batsmen, and everyone was quite sure that Georgetown would enjoy a great day. As the opening pair came out the betting started. The two batsmen were Alan Outridge and A. B. de Caires. Outridge was a splendid all-round cricketer who had represented British Guiana and was a very useful bat. De Caires was one of a cricket-playing brotherhood, one of whom, Frank, had played for the West Indies in test cricket. He was a good solid batsman, who in this match actually scored a century. As they neared the pitch, someone near me turned to a friend and said: "I'll bet you two bob that Outridge makes a duck." It was taken, naturally. Outridge faced the opening bowler, and to one of the very first balls, before he had scored, essayed a square cut and placed the ball in the hands of gully. The side went on to make considerably more than 400, but this particular spectator, who was, remarkably enough, a Georgetown supporter, had certainly put the evil eye on Outridge.

A GRAND CRICKET MATCH
(from *A Life in Guyana*, vol 1.)

A grand cricket match was arranged for Boxing Day 1918 in the hospital yard, the only fairly flat ground in the undulating hills of Arakaka. The ground was on a slight slope of hard red clay. The morgue, or, dead house, formed the long stop at one end of the wicket whilst the blacksmith's shop served a similar purpose at the other. Most of the outfield on one side of the pitch was occupied by the drying ground for the hospital laundry. Though the linen was removed during the match, the drying wires, at the height of the human neck, remained a very serious hazard for players.

On this occasion the Arakaka Civil Service Cricket Club, composed of the warden's boat-hands, public works labourers and the local police contingent, was matched against Ho-a-Shoo's Cricket Club, composed of that firm's clerks and the public at large. The former had a new captain in the form of P.C. Smartt, one of the crack players in the B.G. Churchman's Union Cricket Club in Georgetown. His batting did not show up very well on this wicket, but his bowling was the best and the fastest seen in Arakaka for many a year.

To anyone accustomed to well conducted cricket at one of the big Georgetown clubs, this match would be highly entertaining. In the first place, hardly two players were garbed alike beyond the fact that about half of them wore white drill pants, the combined teams sporting only a single pair of flannels. Then, the hats! Green felt homburgs, slouchy caps, a Panama and wide-a-wake felts, all were in evidence. As varied was the footgear. The police, of course, all wore their service dogs, the white canvas tennis shoes that in this country are supposed to be the certain badge of a detective. Swell brown boots, more commonplace black ones and alpargatas were in evidence. It being a festive occasion, no one dreamed of appearing in their usual footwear as supplied by Dame Nature. The majority, of course, were full blooded Negroes with a slight sprinkling of mulattos. Ho-a-Shoo's team was made up of Chinese and black clerks and boat-hands. I was the only white man present.

Phang and I occupied chairs of honour outside the nurses' quarters behind which we had to run for shelter at every alternate change of over, we being in close and direct range of leg drives from the nearer wicket. On these occasions we would keep our persons carefully round the corner of the building, with just a nose and an eye exposed to watch the play. The government smithy, in direct line with the pitch, about eighty feet from the end, filled the triple role of grandstand, bandstand and scorer's booth. Here the Arakaka "second class" band consisting of flutes, triangle and bass drum, as distinguished from the regular "first class" band, now disbanded on the dispersal of its members through the decline in the local gold industry, sat on benches formed of planks set on empty barrels. In front and all round the musicians were packed, like sardines in a tin, what appeared to be the entire remaining population of Arakaka. Among them were a couple of the ubiquitous cake and mauby ladies with their trays of refreshments, whilst outside the smithy, beneath the mango tree, a group of naked Caribs stood or squatted as they watched the ball play, as they termed cricket.

One of Ho-a-Shoo's players was a Chinese lad of fourteen or fifteen who was up from Queen's College on his Christmas holidays. The little fellow was somewhat nervous at playing with adults but, nevertheless, stood up pluckily to Smartt's fast bowling. Suddenly one of the spectators, a gold digger, sitting under a tree and evidently somewhat high, shouted out, "Bump he, Smartt, or you never get the boy out". By a coincidence the very next ball bounced up and caught the youth on the chin. He was escorted to the adjacent hospital for first aid and returned with a prominent bump but for the time being nothing more was heard of the matter.

Towards the end of the match there was a commotion in the stand and big Gordon, the overseer, went to investigate. It appeared that one of Ho-a-Shoo's boys, waiting his turn to bat, was giving an exhibition of hip contortions to the accompaniment of the music when, accidentally, he bumped into a black lady known as Lady Webber. A most notorious character, she wanted to start a fight then and there and Gordon called on Captain Sealy, a rural constable, to eject both parties from the compound.

Losing one of their players under these circumstances roused the ire of Ho-a-Shoo's team and for a moment it looked as though there would be a general melee, but fortunately saner counsels prevailed and the match came to an end satisfactory to Ho-a-Shoo's team, who won by several wickets.

As the crowd began to disperse, a large piece of rock suddenly descended on the corrugated iron roof of the police station with great noise. The Chinese lad who had been injured during the match was seen wending his way from the scene. Six or seven policemen came out and held every person in the vicinity, leading them back to the station where the old Corporal began catechising them individually as to who had been guilty of the assault. Everyone swore he was innocent and knew nothing about it until a young black boy admitted having seen the Chinese boy throw it. The latter was sent for and admitted quite frankly to being the culprit, adding that he had not intended to hit the station roof, but the head of Policeman Smartt who had with malice and forethought hit him on the chin with the ball. The Corporal gave him a long lecture on the error of his ways and sent him away.

CHRIS SEARLE

LARA'S INNINGS: A CARIBBEAN MOMENT (1995)

I tole him over an' over
agen: watch de ball, man, watch
de ball like it hook to you eye

when you first goes in an' you doan know de pitch.
Uh doan mean to poke
but you jes got to watch what you doin;

this isn't no time for playin'
the fool nor makin' no sport; this is cricket!

Kamau Brathwaite: Islands[1]

On 18 APRIL 1994 at St John's, Antigua, Brian Lara, a young Trinidadian cricketer, knelt and kissed its Caribbean earth, and his people rejoiced.

He had gone beyond the furthest boundary, scoring 375, more runs in a single innings of an international match than any previous player, with a powerful one-footed pull that crashed the ball against the legside boundary fence. The man whose score he had surpassed, the Barbadian Gary Sobers, walked out to the centre of the ground and embraced him. Antiguans and other Caribbean people watching the drama engulfed and feted him and his young Indo-Guyanese batting partner, Shivnarine Chanderpaul. The Antiguan police, called out to control them, guarded Lara like a 'national treasure',[2] while join-ing in the celebrations of a scattered nation finding its centre. For this nation, Lara's kneeling to the earth was more than an act of patriotism: it was a sacred moment. The team of the old colonial power, defeated by Lara's strength, crea-tivity and epic concentration, stood around the Antiguan field and beheld.

The team of the Caribbean, watching from their pavilion, marvelled and celebrated: from Jamaica and Guyana, from Barbados, Antigua and Trinidad. Also, there was wicketkeeper Junior Murray, the first Grenadian to be part of a West Indies test side. In the midst of this joy, the words of Lara's late country-man, C.L.R. James, from *Beyond a Boundary* blew in the sea breezes across the Antigua Recreation Ground: "What do they know of cricket who only cricket know? West Indians crowding to tests bring with them the whole past history and future hopes of the islands."[3] For Brian Lara had done more than all the imperial ritual re-enactments of Columbus's 1492 landfall upon the Americas, staged across the region two years before, could ever accomplish. He had touched the collective Caribbean brain and heart of a dispersed people and fuelled their unity and hope. As the Barbadian Brathwaite had written over two decades before, the spectacle of cricket had provoked a sudden new regional pride and confidence – as it had done at Lord's in 1950 or after the "Blackwash" of England in 1980:

> All over do groun' fellers shakin' hands wid each other
> as if was they wheelin' de willow
> as if was them had the power.4

The context

More needs to be said about the particular context of this moment in the Caribbean. The young black Englishman, Chris Lewis, who had bowled the ball to which Lara had swivelled and then pulled decisively to the legside boundary for his record score, was himself from an Afro-Guyanese family of the diaspora. One of Lewis's team-mates, Mark Ramprakash, was a Londoner whose father is Indo-Guyanese. Watching from the English dressing-room, and foolishly omitted from the team by the English selectors, was a man born in Jamaica whose family emigrated to Sheffield in Yorkshire – Devon Malcolm. According to the great Jamaican fast bowler, Michael Holding (now retired and writing in the regional cricket journal), Malcolm was the one English bowler who had threatened Lara's ascendancy in a previous test match encounter, exposing a 'delectable flaw' in Lara's failure to deal with the sheer pace and 'line of attack' of rising balls coming in towards his body.[5] Thus, the Caribbean was unequivocally a part of English cricket, too. Like the English health and transport systems, it could not function effectively without the essential Caribbean contribution. Lara's achievement had also been integrally linked to the diaspora: it was something much more than a routine meeting of two sporting nations; it transcended a historically-charged confrontation between the ex-colonisers and the decolonised. Now the Caribbean was on both sides.

This truth was exemplified most forcibly during England's final test match against South Africa (now readmitted into international cricket after the end of formal apartheid) in August 1994. Along with Devon Malcolm's match-winning bowling of nine wickets for fifty-seven runs in the second innings, which, in Malcolm's own words, "made history", of the still all-white South African team, nineteen of the twenty South African wickets fell to bowlers of Caribbean origin. In the October 1994 issue of *Wisden's Cricket Monthly*, normally a staunchly establishment journal, a poem called "Irresistible", written by one Paul Weston, was published. Referring to the `whipped-up cream of Devon', the poet ingeniously contrived the following verse:

> For every Bok who took a lick
> Was rendered copiously sick,

Their faces whiter than their shirts
Struck down by Malcolm's just desserts.

Such admiration from the white sports media was unusual for a black cricketer who, as Stephen Brenkly of the *Independent on Sunday* had put it, "had been written off more times than he had been written up" and who, at a function at Buckingham Palace in 1991 when both the West Indian and England teams had been invited, had been asked by the Duke of Edinburgh himself, "Why are you wearing an England blazer?"

In *Beyond a Boundary*, James had written of the pioneer English cricketer, W.G. Grace, that he "was strong with the strength of men who are filling a social need." If only the old agitator could have seen Lara's innings and experienced its impact within Trinidad and across the Caribbean! As Lara returned to Piarco airport in his home island on the night after the test match ended, a huge crowd awaited him. Prime Minister Patrick Manning called it a "redletter night" and the next day was designated "National Achievement Day", with all schools having a holiday and Lara traversing the two-island state in a motorcade. President of Trinidad and Tobago Noor Hassanali presented him with the Trinity Cross, the highest national honour. An elated prime minister also announced that he could have a house of his choice, and a street in Independence Square, Port of Spain, was renamed "Brian Lara Boulevard". Lara, like James a boy from a small settlement in the hinterland, was presented with the keys to the city by the mayor of Port of Spain. And all this in a country that has often been slow to give public recognition to its own great national figures, such as its writers James and Selvon. In these scenes of festivity, Lara travelled side by side with his team-mate, Chanderpaul, making a tableau of Afro-Caribbean and Indo-Caribbean unity against the communalism that has often plagued political progress in Trinidad and Guyana. It was a felicitous public expression of James' assertion in *Beyond a Boundary*: "The cricketer needs to be returned to the community."

And this community was a regional and international one wherein the shout of Maurice Bishop could be heard: "One Caribbean!" The Barbadian daily paper *Nation* printed on its front page a photograph of Sobers with an affectionate arm around Lara's shoulders, and wrote in its editorial: "In years to come, Caribbean people of this period will refer to the events of yesterday at the Antigua Recreation Ground with great relish and pride. The distinction of being the scorer of the highest individual number of runs in a test match was transferred from the shoulders of our own Sir Garfield Sobers and now rests on the shoulders of our own Brian Lara."[6] In Jamaica, Tony Becca, cricket correspondent of the *Gleaner*, wrote: "When, years from now, the fans talk about the highest individual innings of all time… they will remember the strokes that glittered in the Antiguan sunshine. What will keep flashing in the mind's eye forever were the drives and cuts, the hooks and pulls of Lara, strokes which sparkled like diamonds and which will also last forever."[7] The Antiguan socialist and cricket enthusiast, Tim Hector, wrote in the *Outlet*:

> What an event Lara's innings was – the acuity of mind, the athleticism, the economy of movement and motion, using the bat for his brushwork, a bat commonly used by boy and girl. Boy and girl in the Caribbean, and maybe well beyond, will be lifted to new heights, for Lara is the beginning of something new.[8]

Island and race, nationality and gender suddenly fused in these words of a Caribbean morning, and cricket was their spur. And the words followed the diaspora. The most commonly published photograph of the Antiguan events across the world where cricket is played was of Lara kissing the pitch. "Sealed with a kiss" headlined the London *Daily Mail*, and Australia's *Adelaide Advertiser* declared, "Lara's greatness sealed with a kiss". In Canada, the *Toronto Star* highlighted the innings, and even across the USA, where cricket is a relative rarity, Caribbean migrants and exiles could read about Lara in *Newsweek* or *Sports Illustrated* and watch the news of his achievement on the CNN cable network. In England, even that habitual peddler of sporting racism, the *Sun*, suddenly and uncharacteristically changed from vulgarity to a more sophisticated, even poetic, mode:

> ...he shattered one of the oldest and most majestic records in sport, he made the world stand still. He temporarily cleared troubled minds of war and want, of conflict and poverty, prejudice and greed. He deals in numbers beyond the imagination, the comprehension and reach of almost every batsman who has lived... Go and see him, watch a genius at work.[9]

It was as if Lara's batting had also transfixed what Bishop used to call the "saltfish" establishment press of the Caribbean, as well as strangely affecting the tabloid mammoths of the old seat of empire.

Other more authentic voices across the Caribbean and through its diaspora communities were raised in praise of Lara. Writing to the *Caribbean Cricket Quarterly* and island newspapers were cricket-loving letter-writers from across the region, from Dominica to Montego Bay, from New Amsterdam in Guyana to Belize. Many of these correspondents praised Lara as an example to Caribbean youth, as a role model in a region sinking deeper into US cultural influences and a drugs ethos. From Edwin Scott in Penal, Trinidad, came typical sentiments:

> What impressed me most about Brian Lara's great innings in Antigua was not his strokes or his concentration. What I found very revealing was the tributes he paid to those who helped him in his career and how he made special mention of his parents and his family.
>
> A lot of young sportsmen tend to get very swell-headed and self-centred when they achieve not a quarter of what Lara has. He is an example to all our youth, not only in the way he bats but the way he conducts himself.[10]

Filling the need

Yet in more than a cricketing sense, Lara's innings – all 768 minutes of it – had come with a deep breath of relief across the Caribbean. Starting to bat from what Barbadian cricket writer Tony Cozier called a "base of potential crisis",[11] he had rescued the West Indies' first innings in Antigua after the loss of two early wickets – while facing the aftermath of the previous test match which had been lost in Barbados. This was but the microcosm on the cricket field of a more general social crisis, for there were wider and deeper sloughs that the Caribbean people and their progressive spirit had been mired in over the previous decade. The revolutionary defeats and setbacks suffered in Grenada and Nicaragua, the tightening squeeze of the US upon Cuba, the collapse of the Left in Jamaica and its weakening in Trinidad were all lodged within the consciousness of the region. And, in Lara's homeland, the violent and futile lunge at power in 1990 by the Jamaat-al-Muslimeen sect had followed months of humiliating exposures of rampant corruption at the government level, in the shape of the Tesoro scandals.[12] The Trinidadian soca artiste, David Rudder, had satirised such sordid depths in his "Panama", singing of those who made their dishonest thousands and then moved elsewhere to spend and benefit from them:

> Dem rich Trinidadians show me
> Dis whole El Dorado ting
> Dey say dey living here like lords
> But den dey gone to live there like kings
> As dey get a little money in dey pocket...[13]

It had been ten years of US domination, through IMF and World Bank structural adjustment packages and attacks on local dependent economies, as well as cultural offensives through religious evangelism, tourism, food, music and information. And there was also what Tim Hector called 'the increasing influence of Americanised sport in the region'.[14]

Rudder had seen this loss of strength directly manifested in cricket. In his calypso, "Rally round the West Indies", he had related it to externally organised attempts to confuse and divide Caribbean people by insularity, "conflict and confusion" – as well as the making of new "restrictions and laws" to undermine directly the West Indies' cricketing strengths, particularly the efficacy and power of its squad of fast bowlers. Yet, even in 1988, he could point forward to a cultural breakthrough through cricket, remembering James:

> in the end we shall prevail
> this is not just cricket...
> This thing goes
> Beyond the boundaries

and could even anticipate the new era of Lara and the devastating Antiguan fast bowler, Curtly Ambrose, another destroyer of English cricket hopes in the Caribbean in 1994:

> Pretty soon runs will flow again like water
> Bringing so much joy
> To each and every son and daughter
> So we going to rise again like a raging fire
> As the sun shines
> You know we got to take it higher!

When James wrote that "if and when society regenerates itself, cricket will do the same", he gave an implicit message to the Caribbean people: watch your cricket, study it too, for it will tell you where you are and where you could go. This is not a fiction – so integral is cricket to the national spirit of the English-speaking Caribbean. It gives the one enduring image of unity and aspiration, as well as inter-island cooperation. It is also an emblem, almost an icon, across Caribbean life that has been rendered even more powerful by the spectacular contribution of Lara. When the Barbadian government came to present an official gift to the first legitimate president of South Africa, Nelson Mandela, upon his inauguration in May 1994, it was an oil-painting depicting Sobers driving a cricket ball. Even the baseball-loving Fidel Castro became involved in the cricket life of Cuba's sister islands in April 1994, during a visit to Barbados for a UN conference on sustainable development for small island states. *Caribbean Cricket Quarterly* described this bizarre yet unifying event in its region's cultural history:

> As his entourage drove past a ground in the Holder's Hill district on his way to the Sandy Lane Hotel where he was staying, Castro ordered his car's driver to stop. He got out, an aide went onto the field to speak to the umpires and it was agreed that the famous and unexpected guest could have the chance of playing the game for himself. Play in the Barbados Cricket League match between St John the Baptist and Police was temporarily halted. Castro, in military uniform, faced and missed three balls from a Police bowler and bowled a couple of deliveries before thanking his hosts and taking his leave.[15]

Inventiveness and concentration

If there were two particular qualities that marked Lara's innings in Antigua directing the Trinidadian's speed of wrist and hand, they were confidence and concentration.[16] During the 1993 tour of Australia, Lara had scored 277 at Sydney and caused Sobers to change his mind about whether his record score could ever be passed. There were few batsmen playing, he had declared, "with the necessary depth of concentration to stay at the crease for ten hours or more and aim for a score of 300 plus".[17] After watching Lara bat at Sydney, he thought again. For Lara, and particularly for his mother, confidence was not a problem. Pearl Lara saw her son's innings as ordained, as a gift of God, and remained utterly unsurprised by his achievement, declaring that she knew it would happen from when he was a boy. Lara himself had remained composed all through his time at the wicket, building his score consciously, fifty by fifty, his confidence being expressed in the way that he described his reaction to the ball that gave him his record-breaking boundary. Recalling Lewis's bowling approach to him, he said: "The minute I saw him running in to bowl that ball, the energy I saw him putting in – I kind of predicted it was going to be short. I latched on to it pretty early and got it away."[18] As for concentration, Michael Holding compared Lara with the great Caribbean batsman of the previous decade, Viv Richards of Antigua. Whereas "Lara still manages to keep his concentration no matter what his score, and never seems to become distracted", Holding sees Richards' genius as more adventurous and less disciplined: "After he had been out in the middle for a few hours doing as he pleased, he would start looking to do something different and lose his wicket through carelessness."[19]

These two, often counterbalancing, approaches to Caribbean cricket have also formed a dialectic for decades. They fascinated James, who knew that studying the way a people played their cricket meant that "much, much more than cricket is at stake". His friend, collaborator and great Trinidadian all-rounder, Learie Constantine, personified the creative genius of the Caribbean and its cricket in the years between the two world wars. Utterly inventive in his approach to batting, he made brilliant strokes with "no premeditated idea" of making them, and thus continued a tradition in Trinidad begun by Wilton St Hill who, to the cricket-loving people of his island, was "our boy" in the way that Lara is today. According to James, St Hill would "invent" a stroke on the spot – like Rohan Kanhai and his falling-down pull of the 1960s – and Constantine added that this "slender boy flashed his wrists and the ball flew to the boundary faster than sound".[20] Yet in international cricket, St Hill failed sadly and Constantine, despite his snatches of brilliance, never scored a century in a test match and could not sustain his domination over the bowling for long periods. James knew that with such erratic cricketing talent the Caribbean was "still in the flower garden of the gay, spontaneous, tropical West Indians". And, he added wryly, "we need some astringent spray". That came initially with the concentrated and disciplined batting of the Jamaican George Headley during the 1930s, and was followed by the "Three Ws" – Weekes, Worrell and Walcott – in the 1950s, by Sobers and Kanhai in the 1960s, and Greenidge, Lloyd, Richards and Haynes in the '70s and '80s. But the apotheosis of Caribbean batting stamina, as well as creative confidence in the fierce pulling, hooking, powerful cuts and drives, has come with the 375 runs in Antigua of Brian Lara. His innings provides an image of relentless application and will, of concentration and colossal physical and mental effort. "I believe every great batsman is a special organism," pronounced James, and Lara has become a living symbol of dedicated striving, fused with a virtually peerless technique, that will serve towards countering the self-critical fear in the Caribbean – made, for example, by the Barbadian cricket spectator in Brathwaite's "Rites". This is the fear that continued in the wake of the murder of Walter Rodney, the self-devouring collapse of the Grenada Revolution after so much promise and achievement, and the violent fiasco in Port of Spain's Red House in July 1990 when the Muslimeen attempted their futile coup:

> when things goin' good, you cahn touch
> we, but leh murder start
> an' ol man, you cahn fine a man to hole up de side... [21]

Lara and Caribbean hope

Writing in the *Outlet*, Tim Hector invested Lara's innings with the heraldry of a profound hope and optimism. He recalled the all-round brilliance of Sobers and his 365 against Pakistan in Jamaica in 1958 as a product of the Caribbean federal and liberating impulse of the time – which gave birth to the short-lived West Indian Federation, the Cuban Revolution of 1959 and the cultural flowering of Naipaul, Wilson Harris and Lamming in literature and the Mighty Sparrow in calypso. And he pointed towards a new era signalled by Lara's achievement:

> I would want to think that Lara's innings put behind us the conditionalities of the IMF with its structural adjustment that has structured Caribbean people out of their own economy and history. They will return centre stage after Lara because Caribbean history can be divided into BL (Before Lara) and AL (After Lara). After Lara, there will come in this part of the world a new creative impulse, rejecting the Ramboisation of life and living which now plagues our cracking or crumbling economies.[22]

Optimism indeed, but not groundless optimism, for these are the thoughts of a tireless Caribbean activist, a veteran doer who knows well his people and his culture. Those who do not know cricket and its beckonings and symbols may well say to themselves or each other, "What is all this?" But, as James wrote and Hector knows, others, like Frank Worrell, the first regular black captain of the West Indies, have "cleared the way with bat and ball" for the struggling people of the Caribbean, and new cricketing generations will do likewise in completely new contexts. The key to Hector's hope lies in James's assertion that "the cricketer needs to be returned to the community" – for there are many alternative forces waiting to consume such talent as that of Lara and the temptations of big money are enormous and potentially corrupting, as Caribbean cricket already knows well. They destroyed the previous West Indies triple centurion, the Jamaican Lawrence Rowe, who became a Caribbean hero after his innings of 302 against England in Barbados in 1974. Rowe took the repugnant step of leading a cricket tour to South Africa and promoting apartheid by breaching the sporting boycott of the racist regime. Now Brian Lara is the hottest potential acquisition in world cricket, and companies across the Caribbean and beyond are thrusting to sponsor him and milk his achievement. His prodigious batting exploits while playing English county cricket for Warwickshire during the summer of 1994, including the highest ever individual first-class cricket score (501 made against Durham at Edgbaston in June 1994), have made him even more of a prize for multinational corporations. Early contracts promoting Coca-Cola and "501" jeans presage one potentially dangerous direction – the ordinary people of the Caribbean and its diaspora, their hopes and aspirations, stand on another road and they have claimed Lara as their own. He is "their boy" and his bat strikes for their future.

But the temptations towards a multifaceted exploitation of Lara's achievement, in a US-dominated carnival of profit and graft, are only too real and enticing for those in the comprador economies of the Caribbean. It is a true test match for cricket, as well as for Lara. For if sport, particularly a sport so integral to the regional psyche as cricket is to the Caribbean, is to remain, as James saw it, both a spur and reflector, and not a deflector, of political and social reality, it must stay close to the people, to the community of those who love it and play it on recreation grounds and pitches improvised from pastures in villages all through the English-speaking Caribbean, to those who have transformed it from the imperial game and made it their own. If not, it becomes for that same community what Learie Constantine once wrote it could be, "a hasheesh... a drug in their poverty-stricken and toiling lives"[23] – not the mirror which James saw into, but a clouded glass that reveals only cultural theft and the oppression of the new imperialism of the north.

A place in the world
As Lara played his innings in Antigua, another pathmaking Trinidadian died on their island. This was Sam Selvon, novelist, playwright and short story writer, of whom James said, "He has an ear for the West Indian language, the West Indian speech that is finer than anything that I have ever heard."[24] In the 1950s, Selvon's writing, in particular his recreation of the ordinary speech of Trinidadians at home and as arrivants in London, had broken through the imposed, "correct" and often lifeless version of English spoken and vindicated by the coloniser and his education system. The real world of Trinidad's people and their creole tongue – its images, its wit and tenderness, its beauty, energy and irrepressible national spirit – burst through in the narrative of Selvon's works: *A Brighter Sun* (1952), *The Lonely Londoners* (1956) and *Ways of Sunlight* (1957). Like Lara's cricket, his writing was made in the bloodstream of

the Caribbean, in the villages "behin' God back" like Cantaro, near Santa Cruz, Trinidad, Lara's own birthplace. As one of Selvon's characters expounds in his play *Highway in the Sun*:

> Whatever it is, what do you expect to happen in this half-dead village? One day just like another. Is only in England and America big things does happen.[25]

But every village has its cricket pitch, has its young people that can be other Brian Laras. That is what Selvon teaches us, and James too – the boy who formed his politics watching village cricketers like Matthew Bondman and Arthur Jones through his parents' bedroom window, cutting and driving on the recreation ground outside – that everywhere there is excellence and power in the ordinary, in the community of humans, in the languages that they speak and in their bodies which they move for work, pleasure and achievement. It had been the working-class Australians of town and outback who had adopted Donald Bradman as "their boy" and their living anti-colonial symbol after his record-breaking scores of the early 1930s. Like the cricket lovers of Antigua who ran onto the pitch in a passionate embrace as Lara kissed the ground in April 1994, sealing what T.S. Eliot once described as "the intersection of a time-less moment",[26] so thousands of working people in London, like my father, also fled from work and risked a sacking to see Len Hutton, a shy 21-year-old batsman from a Yorkshire village, score the final runs to overcome Bradman's record score at the Oval in the summer of 1938, on the threshold of war against Hitler, and then to see Bradman, with the same 'grace and consideration'[27] as Gary Sobers, shake Hutton's hand in the middle of the pitch.

But back to Selvon, for his death upon one Caribbean island coincided with a massive blast of life upon another. The Trinidadian novelist, Earl Lovelace, another beautiful user of his people's language as expressed in *The Dragon can't Dance* or *The Wine of Astonishment*, who helped to clear the trail blazed by Selvon, takes up the narrative:

> Sam had talked almost in a voice of bewildered hurt of what he was seeing in Trinidad. Something had gone dreadfully wrong. And that is why I believe it must have given him great pleasure and renewed hope that at his passing the young batsman Lara was playing his historic innings in Antigua. I don't think it's out of place to claim that as a stone in the monument for a man whose work was one of the earliest expressions of the West Indian's unconditional self-con-fidence and demands for a place in the world.[28]

For that is what Brian Lara's success truly signified, like Selvon's liberation of language, Bishop's and Rodney's struggles or James's lifetime of luminous insights, an "unconditional self-confidence and demand for a place in the world". And those who will follow and emulate Lara's innings must strive to transform his moment into their era.

Endnotes

1. Edward Brathwaite, 'Rites' from *The Arrivants: a New World Trilogy* (London: 1973)
2. Ian McDonald, writing in *Caribbean Cricket Quarterly* (Barbados, July 1994)
3. This and other quotations from C.L.R. James come from *Beyond a Boundary*, re-published in 1994 by Serpent's Tail, London.
4. Brathwaite, op.cit.
5. See *Caribbean Cricket Quarterly*, op.cit.
6. *Nation*, Barbados (19 April 1994)
7. *Daily Gleaner*, Jamaica (19 April 1994)
8. See article by Tim Hector in *Lara: 375* (Barbados: 1994)
9. *Sun* (19 April 1994)
10. *Caribbean Cricket Quarterly*, op.cit.
11. Ibid.
12. See Chris Searle, "The Muslimeen insurrection in Trinidad" in *Race and Class* (Vol. 33, no. 2, 1991)
13. See booklet with David Rudder's lyrics with compact disc, *Haiti* (London, 1988)
14. *Caribbean Cricket Quarterly*, op.cit.
15. Ibid.
16. Qualities that the Hampshire captain, Mark Nicholas, had seen as an expression of Lara's "outstanding cricketing brain".
17. *Lara: 375*, op.cit.
18. See Reds Perreira's interview with Brian Lara in ibid.
19. *Caribbean Cricket Quarterly,* op.cit.
20. Quoted in C.L.R. James, op.cit.
21. Brathwaite, op.cit.
22. Tim Hector in *Lara: 375* op.cit.
23. Learie Constantine, *Cricket Crackers* (London: undated)
24. C.L.R. James in an unpublished interview with Chris Searle (London, 1983)
25. Sam Selvon, *Highway in the Sun* (Leeds: 1991)
26. T.S. Eliot, "Little Gidding" from *Four Quartets* (London, 1959)
27. Ian McDonald, op.cit.
28. From an article by Jeremy Taylor, "Play it again, Sam". BWee *Caribbean Beat* (Trinidad, 1994)

DEREK WALCOTT

LEAVING SCHOOL

"Sometimes an ancient and infinitesimal detail will come away like a whole headland; and sometimes a complete layer of my past will vanish without a trace."   Tristes Tropiques

I had given up sport early. In first or second form. Because I had been christened a prodigy, I couldn't endure failure, except it was so ridiculous that it looked like self-sacrifice. I had been considered a promising, conventional off-break bowler, but "conventional" had no promise in it. All those promises were a long way behind me, all those angry urgent cries to leave the life of a young silverfish and get out in the sun, and in the swim.

"Walcott, man!" Man was the cry, whatever your age. "Get out there and give Abercromby a point, boy!" Once Walcott had tried. Pale, sallow, big-headed, the blue heart of his house emblazoned on his singlet, the blue stripe of his house running down the seam of his shorts, flailing away towards the tape. Then how come fathead Simmons, who he was sure was bound to come last, put up a desperate final burst for Abercromby (his own house) to save himself? Also, what was the point of the wicketkeeper when some full toss, meant by an ambitious stylist to be swept to leg, just missed my Adam's apple by a gulp? I was so furious that I stretched out flat behind the stumps, playing dead until the team collected around me, then rose, threw off the gloves and left. Abercromby had to look elsewhere for points: in essays, and in conduct. In addition to the Black Book, where canings were noted, and the Detention Book for minor crimes, the Brothers had introduced the Alpha book for academics. I concentrated on getting points for Abercromby there.

P.F. WARNER

CRICKET IN THE WEST INDIES (1897)

English elevens nowadays go over to all parts of the world to play the great national game, and meet good cricketers, moreover, in the most unexpected places. The West Indies, however, is comparatively a new field, and as I had the pleasure and privilege of being a member of the team which lately visited the islands, I have ventured to think – and the Editor agrees with me – that a brief article about our experiences might be of interest.

Cricket in the West Indies attains a far higher standard than people in England imagine. Especially is this so in bowling and fielding, a high level of excellence being attained in these departments of the game. The native's of the islands are very fine natural cricketers, being possessed of supple wrists and shoulders, and able to throw a long distance. Perhaps the two best bowlers we met during the tour were natives, viz. Woods and Cumberbatch, while Constantine is a capital bat and wicketkeeper. The amount of interest taken in the game in the West Indies is extraordinary. During our visit the community seem to have gone cricket mad. On our way to the grounds we were continually greeted with shouts of "Success! Success! England for ever!" and I am not sure that they did not imagine that we were the best eleven England could put into the field. Lord Hawke was a special source of wonder; the people never seemed to understand a "live lord" playing cricket. "Steady, my lord!" was a frequent cry from the ropes. In Trinidad, Cumberbatch, the great native bowler, was offered five dollars by the Attorney-General of the island if he dismissed Lord Hawke for a duck. "Very well, sir, it shall be done" was the reply of the local hero, and sure enough Lord Hawke's middle stump was seen reclining on the ground before the Yorkshire captain could claim a single run! When we were meeting the Queen's Park Cricket Club in Trinidad, the home team had an uphill game to play, and "Courage, Queen's Park!" was a not unusual cry. At Barbados we met a most amusing person called "Britannia Bill". He was a staunch supporter of Lord Hawke's team, and carried with him a Union Jack which he waved enthusiastically whenever the fortunes of the match varied in our favour. When we were leaving Barbados for British Guiana a successful member of the team was greeted on the wharf by this same gentleman with the following remark: "That you may never get out in Demerara is the wish of Britannia Bill." The cricketer in question was so pleased that he promptly gave him a shilling. St. Vincent, too, was most amusing, many of the batsmen paying very little attention to the decisions of the umpire. As a member of the side very aptly put it, "the centre ash had to be absolutely felled" before a batsman would think of retiring without a protest. A somewhat amusing story is told of the Oxford captain, G. R. Bardswell. When he went in for his second innings he expressed his intention of remaining at the wickets for the rest of the day, as he felt in such good form. He ordered a whisky-and-soda to be ready for him at 5.30 (the time for drawing stumps), but alas for the uncertainty of the great game, he only received one ball, and that proved his last. "What a funny game cricket is!" was his only remark as he left the wickets. In this match, too, Lord Hawke was unfortunate enough to get a duck in his first innings, being bowled by Layne, a black man, amidst a scene of indescribable excitement. When Lord Hawke went in for his second innings the bowler was exhorted by the crowd to "give the lord a duck," but this time the Yorkshire captain made no mistake, and put together an excellent fifty-one, including two hits for six each. In Trinidad I was lucky enough to get a century, but in the next island we played (Grenada) I only made four, and on my way back to the pavilion was greeted with shouts of "Where is your hundred, sir?" The cricket grounds attain a very fair level of excellence, and in Trinidad, Barbados, Antigua, and Demerara we had really splendid wickets, though in Barbados and Trinidad the ball showed a distinct inclination to jump a bit. In our second match at Barbados we had a most exciting finish – we eventually proved successful by four wickets just on the stroke of time. H. D. G. Leveson-Gower and myself happened to make a very useful stand at a critical point, and we were encouraged by the natives shouting "You are little men, but you play well." As regards the climate, we all concluded that it had been much maligned. We kept in the best of health out there (though more than one of the team had a little fever on the ship coming home), and the sun though very hot is by no means injurious if ordinary precautions are taken. White sun-hats, and a handkerchief round the neck, are nearly always worn when playing. Trinidad and Demerara are undoubtedly the hottest, but Barbados is a splendid climate, as a pleasant sea breeze is always blowing.

As to which was the best eleven we encountered opinions differ – some thinking Barbados, while others prefer the Trinidad representatives. For my own part I consider Trinidad the best side, their bowling being especially strong. Woods and Cumberbatch, the two Trinidad bowlers, are really excellent, and quite good enough to play for any English county. Woods bowls fast right-hand with rather a low and swinging action, and every now and again breaks the ball back considerably from the off. Cumberbatch is right-hand rather over medium, and varies his pace well. The fielding all round is A1, while the batting is very fair, D'Ade being much the best. Barbados possess undoubtedly the finest batting side in the West Indies, every man in the team being capable of making a good score, and in Clifford Goodman they possess a fine bowler. Goodman stands 6 ft. 3 in., and brings the ball down from a great height. He is over medium pace, and, keeping an excellent length, gets considerable work on the ball from the off side. Against Mr. Priestley's eleven he met with astonishing success, and Mr. A. E. Stoddart, the famous Middlesex batsman, has a very high opinion of his abilities. On anything like a sticky wicket he is almost unplayable, as he makes the ball get up very straight from the pitch. Demerara did not show their best form against us, but they undoubtedly have several excellent cricketers. In estimating the respective merits of Trinidad, Barbados, and Demerara, it must be borne in mind that Trinidad played natives (black men), while Barbados and Demerara did not. In the Intercolonial Cup, which is played for every other year between the three above-mentioned places, black men are excluded, and Trinidad, thus deprived of her two great bowlers, is by no means so good as either of her opponents. In the smaller islands, such as Grenada, St. Vincent, Antigua, St. Kitts, St. Lucia, black men are always played. As a matter of fact, it would be impossible in these islands to raise a side without them, but Barbados and Demerara have strenuously set themselves against this policy.

With the attitude taken up by Barbados and Demerara I cannot agree. These black men add considerably to the strength of a side, their inclusion makes the game more popular locally, and tends to instil a great and universal enthusiasm among all classes of the population. Their inclusion, too, would enable the smaller islands to compete for the Intercolonial Cup, although I believe that the absence of these islands is mostly due to difficulty in the way of communication. The visit of a West Indian team to England within the next two or three years is by no means improbable, and there can be little doubt that a capital side could be got together if the black men were included. Without them it would be absurd to attempt to play the first-class counties, and a West Indian combination would derive no benefit whatever from playing against the second-class. The team should not arrive in England until June, so as to avoid the cold winds of early summer, which the black men of the team would naturally feel keenly. The team would be composed of nine or ten gentlemen and four or five professionals. To expect the team to beat Yorkshire or Surrey would be too much, but that they would make a good fight against the other counties I have little doubt. Of course, in expressing these views on the merits of the West Indian cricketers, it must be remembered that I am basing my statements on the fact that I saw them on their own grounds, and under climatic conditions quite different from those of the Old Country. Light, different wickets, and surroundings must no doubt be taken into consideration, but still I think the attempt would be well worth trying. A missed catch in the West Indies is very rare. Especially is this so with the black men. Their throwing is splendid, nearly all the cricketers we met being able to throw well, and many of them considerably over a hundred yards. The black men of any West Indian eleven that might visit England would doubtless prove a great attraction with the cricket-loving public, and I am sure that Goodman, Woods, Cumberbatch, and others would command the respect of the best of English batsmen. In conclusion, I should like to say that Englishmen have the most erroneous ideas about the West Indies. They imagine them as the home of the centipede, the snake, and a thousand other terrors. For myself, I never saw any of these terrible things, with the exception of a snake in the wilds of British Guiana, and that was dead. Hotel accommodation is rapidly improving all over the West Indies, and in some places is quite excellent. Electric light, tramways, telephones, &c., are everywhere in use. The hospitality of the people is unbounded, and, everywhere meeting with the same cordial reception, we had the most delightful of times. That an English team will visit the West Indies every two years may be taken as certain, and the members of these future teams ought most certainly to enjoy themselves. Assuredly Lord Hawke's eleven took away with them most pleasant memories of the islands and the many charming people they met there.

Notes on Contributors

John Agard (Guyana, b. 1949) is a poet, performer, anthologist who came to Britain in 1977. He won the Casa de las Américas Prize in 1982 for *Man to Pan*, and a Paul Hamlyn Award in 1997. His books include five collections from Bloodaxe, including *From the Devil's Pulpit* – which won the Guyana Prize – *Alternative Anthem: Selected Poems* (2009) and most recently, *Clever Backbone*.

Joan Anim-Addo (Grenada) is the Director of the Centre for Caribbean Studies and Professor of Caribbean Literature and Culture at Goldsmiths, University of London. She is the Chair of the Caribbean Women Writers Alliance and founder-editor of *Mango Season*. She has published two collections of poetry, *Haunted by History* and *Janie Cricketing Lady* (Mango, 2006).

Michael Anthony (Trinidad, b. 1932) grew up in Trinidad but migrated to Britain in the mid-1950s. He established his reputation as a novelist with *The Games Were Coming* in 1963, *The Year in San Fernando* and *Green Days by the River*. He returned to Trinidad in the early 1970s and has subsequently published many more novels and collections of stories, as well as several popular history and travel books.

Colin Babb (UK, b. 1965) is a freelance journalist and broadcaster who has worked extensively with the BBC World Service. He has an MA in Caribbean Studies from the University of Warwick, and has family connections in Guyana and Barbados. He has written and made radio programmes on various Caribbean topics over many years.

Edward Baugh (Jamaica, b. 1936) is Professor Emeritus of English at the University of the West Indies, Mona. A fine poet, he has published *Tales from the Rainforest* and, in 2000, *It Was The Singing*. As a distinguished critic his work includes: *Derek Walcott* (2006) in the CUP series on African and Caribbean writers , and *Frank Collymore: A Biography* (Ian Randle Publishers, 2009)

Deryck M. Bernard (Guyana, 1950-2008) was an academic and teacher who was at one time Dean of the Faculty of Arts at the University of Guyana. He also had a political career in Guyana and served for some time as Minister of Education. He published a collection of short stories, *Going Home*, in 2002.

Hilary McD. Beckles (Barbados, b. 1955) is a distinguished historian with many academic publications. He has been Principal of the Cave Hill Campus of the University of the West Indies since 2002. A keen cricketer and 'student of the game' he was instrumental in establishing the C.L.R. James Centre for Cricket

Research and he has published several volumes on the social history of cricket in the West Indian, including *A Spirit of Dominance: Cricket and Nationalism in the West Indies* and *A Nation Imagined: First West Indies Test Cricket Team*. He has also written a play, *Scobie,* based on the life of Garfield Sobers.

James Berry (Jamaica, b. 1924) migrated to Britain in 1948, where he established a reputation as a poet and short story writer. In 1976 he edited *Bluefoot Traveller*, and *News from Babylon*, the first anthologies of what he described as WestIndian-British poetry. His own poetry is collected in such volumes as *Chain of Days, Hot Earth, Cold Earth, Windrush Songs* and *A Story I Am In* (Bloodaxe Books, 2011).

Frank Birbalsingh (Guyana, b. 1938) is a literary scholar and university teacher. He lectured at York University in Toronto for more than 30 years, and published several important anthologies and works of criticism related to Indo-Caribbean literature and culture, including *From Pillar to Post: The Indo Caribbean Diaspora*. He has also written extensively on West Indian cricket, including *The Rise of West Indian Cricket: From Colony to Nation*,

Roger Bonair-Agard (Trinidad & Tobago) teaches at Fordham University and is co-founder and Artistic Director of the LouderARTS Project in New York City. He has published three collections of poetry, most recently *Gully* (Peepal Tree, 2010). A Cave Canem fellow, he splits his time between Chicago and Brooklyn.

Kamau Brathwaite (Barbados, b. 1930) is one of the great poets of the Caribbean, an important historian, cultural critic, editor and teacher. After working for many years at UWI in Jamaica, he is currently Professor of Comparative Literature at New York University. His reputation was founded on the epic vision of his first trilogy, *The Arrivants* (1973). His more recent work challenges literary convention in all sorts of ways, from the monumental *Barabajan Poems* (1994) to *Born to Slow Horses* – which won the 2006 International Griffin Poetry Prize – and *Elegguas* published in 2010.

Jean 'Binta' Breeze (Jamaica, b. 1957) studied at the Jamaican School of Drama with Michael Smith and Oku Onuora in the 1970s, where she began to write poetry – performing and recording first in Kingston then in London. She has worked as a director and scriptwriter for theatre, television and film and performed throughout the world. Her poetry collections include *Ryddim Ravings* (1988) and *Third World Girl: Selected Poems* (Bloodaxe, 2011). She has published a collection of stories, *On the Edge of an Island* (1997) and issued several recordings of her work including *Tracks* with the Dennis Bovell Dub Band and *Riding On De Riddym: selected spoken works* (57 Productions).

Lloyd W. Brown (Jamaica) was Professor of Comparative Literature at the University of Southern California before his retirement. He has written a book on Jane Austen's fiction, edited a collection of essays, *The Black Writer in Africa and the Americas* (1973) and wrote the pioneering study, *West Indian Poetry* (1978). His poetry, first published in the collection, *Duppies* (Peepal Tree, 1996) attests to the continuing power of Jamaican memory in his life.

Stewart Brown (UK, b. 1951) taught secondary school in St. Ann's Bay, Jamaica between 1972-74 and edited the 'little' literary magazine *Now*. Since 1988 he has lectured at the Centre of West African Studies, University of Birmingham, where he is Reader in Caribbean Literature. He has edited several anthologies of African and Caribbean writing and edited critical studies of Martin Carter, Kamau Brathwaite and Derek Walcott. In 2007 he published a collection of essays on poetry, *Tourist, Traveller, Troublemaker*. His most recent collection of poems is *Elsewhere: New and Selected poems*, (Peepal Tree, 2000).

Faustin Charles (Trinidad b. 1944) had published three important collections of poetry, including *Crabtrack* (1969) before the recent publication of his substantial new and selected poems *Children of the Morning* (Peepal Tree 2008). He has published two adult novels, *Signposts of the Jumbie* and *The Black Magic Man of Brixton*. More recently he has built a successful career as a writer for children. His book *The Selfish Crocodile* has now sold over 100,000 copies.

Merle Collins (Grenada, b. 1950) was born in Aruba to Grenadian parents who later returned to Grenada. She grew up on the island and studied at the UWI in Jamaica. After graduating in 1972, she returned to Grenada, where she worked in education. She was deeply involved in the Grenadian revolution but left for Britain in 1983. She teaches at the University of Maryland. Her poetry includes *Because the Dawn Breaks*, *Rotten Pomerack* and *Lady in a Boat*. She has published two novels, *Angel* and *The Colour of Forgetting*, and two collections of short stories, *Rain Darling* and *The Ladies Are Upstairs* (2011).

Learie Constantine (Trinidad, 1901-1971) was a great cricketing all rounder, who made his debut for the West Indies in 1928. The following year he began his Lancashire League career with Nelson. In 1930 he played a major role in the first West Indies test match victory and later he was part of the 1934-35 team that achieved the first series win against England. He was a Wisden Cricketer of the Year in 1940. He wrote several books about cricket, and a book on race relations in the UK in the 1950s: *Colour Bar*. Later, he became a barrister, served as Trinidad's first High Commissioner in London, a Governor of the BBC and a member of the House of Lords in 1969, as Baron Constantine of Nelson and Maraval.

Cyril Dabydeen (Guyana b. 1945) has published many collections of poetry and short stories, and several novels. He edited *A Shapely Fire: Changing the Literary Landscape* and *Another Way to Dance: Contemporary Asian Poetry in Canada and the U.S.* His work has been widely anthologized, including in the *Oxford Book of Caribbean Poetry*. He was appointed Poet Laureate of the City of Ottawa for several years and in 2010 received a Lifetime Achievement Award for Excellence (Guyana Council of Canadians). His recent publications include *Unanimous Night*, a collection of poetry and a novel *Drums of My Flesh*.

David Dabydeen (Guyana b. 1955) is the author of six novels, three collections of poetry and several works of non-fiction and criticism. *Slave Song* won the Commonwealth Poetry Prize and his first novel, *The Intended*, won the Guyana Prize for Literature. He is Professor at the Centre for Caribbean Studies at the University of Warwick. He co-edited *The Oxford Companion to Black British History*. His novel, *Molly & the Muslim Stick* (which won the Guyana Prize), was published in 2008, when he was also awarded the Anthony Sabga Award for Caribbean Literature. He is currently Guyana's Ambassador to China.

Fred D'Aguiar (Guyana, b. 1960) was born in London, but grew up in Guyana until he was 12, returning to England in 1972. Poet, novelist and playwright, he established his reputation in the UK with the poems of *Mama Dot* (1985); his novel, *The Longest Memory* (1994) won the Whitbread First Novel Award. He has subsequently spent much of his time in the USA, where he taught at the University of Miami for several years and is currently the Gloria D. Smith Professor of Africana Studies at Virginia Tech. His most recent poetry collection, *Continental Shelf*, was shortlisted for the 2009 T. S. Eliot Prize.

Kwame Dawes (Jamaica, b. 1962) was born in Ghana but grew up Jamaica. He has also lived in Britain, Canada and currently the USA. After many years at the University of South Carolina, he is now Glenna Luschei Editor of *Prairie Schooner* and a Chancellor's Professor of English at the University of Nebraska. He has been the programming director of the Calabash International Literary Festival, in Jamaica, and is the associate poetry editor at Peepal Tree Press. He is the author of fifteen books of poetry, of which *Wheels* (2011) is the most recent, and works of fiction, non-fiction and drama that include *Natural Mysticism*, *Bob Marley: Lyrical Genius*, and *A Far Cry From Plymouth Rock: A Personal Narrative*. He has edited several anthologies including *Wheel and Come Again* and *Red*.

Neville Dawes (Jamaica, b. 1926) was born in Nigeria of Jamaican parents, but grew up in rural Jamaica. He studied for an MA at Oxford and later taught in Jamaica, Ghana and Guyana. He published a collection of poems, *Sepia* and two novels, *The Last Enchantment* and *Interim*. His *Prolegomena to West Indian Lit-*

erature was an influential critical intervention in the debates around Caribbean Literature in the independence period. He was Director of the Institute of Jamaica and established its short-lived but important publishing programme.

Raywat Deonandan (b. Guyana 1967) is a scientist, author and journalist. He is currently an Assistant Professor in the Faculty of Health Sciences at the University of Ottawa. He published two books of fiction, a collection of short stories *Sweet Like Saltwater* (1999), which won a Guyana Prize and a novel, *Divine Elemental* (2003). He remains active in the arts and presently sits on the Board of Directors of Harbourfront Centre.

Ann Marie Dewar (Monserrat) is the principal of the St Augustine Primary School and active in the arts and culture of Montserrat.

Ian Diefenthaller (Trinidad b. 1962) grew up around San Fernando and was schooled at Pointe à Pierre. He trained as an architect and was awarded his PhD by the University of Birmingham. He has written widely on West Indian and West Indian British poetry and is the author of *Snow on Sugarcane* (2009) and *Crossed Suns*, (2009) a collection of poems. He established Cane Arrow Press in 2009, to promote West Indian British poetry and republish the poetry of Trinidad and Tobago.

J.D. Douglas (Curaçao/St Lucia, b. 1956) came to England from St. Lucia in 1968. He studied economics at the University of Essex and the University of Wales. He is a playwright, author of *Toussaint* and *The Life of Muhammed Ali*, and a collection of poems, *Caribbean Man's Blues*.

Garfield Ellis (Jamaica b. 1960) graduated as a marine pilot from the Jamaica Maritime Institute and completed his MFA at the University of Miami, as a James Michener Fellow. Author of five books of fiction, he has twice won the prestigious Jamaican literature award, the Una Marson Prize, for his first collection of short stories, *Flaming Hearts* (1997) and for his novel, *Till I'm Laid to Rest* (2010). He has taught writing at Nova University and the University College of the Caribbean.

J.B. Emtage (Barbados). There is not much biographical material to be found about Emtage, although it seems he was writing from the 1930s to the 1990s! In his seminal study *The West Indian Novel and its Background*, Kenneth Ramchand describes Emtage as "a West Indian of the old planter type."

Howard Fergus (Montserrat, b. 1937) has served Montserrat in a variety of roles, as Chief Education Officer, Acting Permanent Secretary, and from 1975, Speaker of the Montserrat Legislative Council and De Facto Deputy Governor from 1976. Since 1974 he has been the Extra-Mural Resident Tutor of University of the West Indies, Montserrat. He was awarded a CBE in 1995 and knighted in 2001. His poetry collections include *Cotton Rhymes*; *Green Innocence* (1978), *Lara Rains & Colonial Rights* (1998), *Volcano Song: poems of an island in agony* (2000) and *Volcano Verses* (2003).

John Figueroa (Jamaica, 1920 -1999) was the first Jamaican appointed to a chair at the University College of the West Indies in Jamaica. He finished his teaching career as Professor of Humanities in Puerto Rico. While in Britain in the 1950s he worked with the BBC radio programme 'Caribbean Voices' and later edited *Caribbean Voices*, the first comprehensive collection of West Indian poetry. His own work is found in *Blue Mountain Peak: Poetry & Prose* (1944), *Love Leaps Here* (1962) and *The Chase* (Peepal Tree, 1991). He published widely on cricket.

Delores Gauntlett (Jamaica, b. 1949) was born in St. Ann. Her first full collection, *Freeing Her Hands To Clap,* was awarded a National Book Development Council prize. Her poems have won prizes in *The Observer* Literary Arts annual competitions. She published *The Watertank Revisited*, in 2005. Her work has appeared in many anthologies, magazines and newspapers, including the special edition of *Obsidian – Catch Afire: New Jamaican Writing*.

Beryl Gilroy (Guyana 1924-2001) grew up in Skeldon village, Berbice. She worked as a school teacher in Guyana until 1951 when she was selected to attend university in the U K. She became probably the first Black headteacher in the UK, an experience recorded in *Black Teacher* (1976). She wrote the pioneering children's series *Nippers*. Her first novel, *Frangipani House* was published in 1986, followed by seven other titles. Her last novel, *The Green Grass Tango* was published in 2001. She was awarded an Honorary Doctorate by the University of London and an Honorary Fellowship by the Institute of Education for her writing and pioneering work as a psychotherapist.

Cecil Gray (Trinidad, b. 1923) was born and lived all his working life in Trinidad. He taught for many years at the University of the West Indies, training secondary teachers. His important anthologies for schools helped shape the literary taste of a generation of Caribbean students. In 1976 he was awarded the Medal of Merit, Class One, Gold, by the Trinidadian Government for his service in education and culture. Since his retirement in 1988 and his move to Canada he has published several collections of poetry, including *The Woolgatherer*, *Lillian's Songs*, *Leaving the Dark*, *Plumed Palms* and *Careenage*.

Stanley Greaves (Guyana b. 1934) was part of the Working People's Art Class in Georgetown in the 1950s. He studied at Newcastle College of Art and was head of the Division of Creative Arts at the University of Guyana for several years. He left Guyana in the 1980s and was resident in Barbados until 2007. He is one of the Caribbean's most distinguished artists with major exhibitions in the UK and Europe as well as throughout the Caribbean. He is also an accomplished poet; his *Horizons* (2002) won a Guyana Prize, another, *The Poems Man*, (2009) celebrated his long creative friendship with the great Guyanese poet Martin Carter. Since 2008 he has lived in the USA.

A.L. Hendriks (Jamaica, 1922-1992) was a broadcaster and media executive, as well as a much-travelled poet who finally settled in the UK. He published eight collections of poems over the years, including *Madonna of the Unknown Nation* (1974) and *To Speak Simply: Selected Poems 1961-86* (1988). He co-edited, with Cedric Lindo, the *Jamaica Independence Anthology*.

Bernard Heydorn (Guyana, b. 1945) grew up in Georgetown and New Amsterdam. He taught at St. Joseph's High School in Georgetown and was Research Fellow at UWI St. Augustine, Trinidad. He has both scientific and literary publications. He is an educator, novelist, essayist, humorist, poet, and newspaper columnist, and received the Wordsworth McAndrew Award for his outstanding contribution to Guyana's Culture and Heritage. His publications include *Walk Good Guyana Boy (1994)* and *Unlit Roads* (2000)

Carl Jackson (Barbados) attended Providence Boys' and Boys' Foundation Schools. Later he studied at the Ryerson Polytechnical Institute in Toronto. He has worked as a career diplomat and currently works in Barbados as a communications consultant. His first novel, *East Wind in Paradise* (New Beacon, 1981) was one of the first political thrillers to emerge in Caribbean writing. His second novel, *Nor the Battle to the Strong* , was published by Peepal Tree in 1997.

C.L.R. James (Trinidad, 1901-1989) was perhaps the Caribbean's first true 'man of letters'. As well as being a prolific writer on cricket he was an historian, cultural commentator, literary critic, political theorist, philosopher and a novelist. His most celebrated works include his campaigning political essay *The Case for West Indian Self-Government* (1933), his novel, *Minty Alley* (1936), his historical study of the Haitian revolution, *The Black Jacobins* (1938) and, of course, *Beyond a Boundary* (1963) his autobiographical social history of cricket in Trinidad and beyond. In 2006 his writings on cricket were collected in the volume *A Majestic Innings: Writings on Cricket*.

Errol John (Trinidad, 1924–1988) was an actor and playwright. He was a founder member of the Whitehall Theatre Group in Trinidad before migrating to England in 1951 where he continued to work in the theatre. He landed several small TV and film roles, and then a major role in *A Man from the*

Sun (1955). In 1958 his play *Moon on a Rainbow Shawl* won the best new playwright award from *The Observer;* in 1969 he wrote *The Exiles* for the BBC's *Wednesday Play* series. Through the sixties and seventies he worked in the US film industry, playing minor roles in films.

Linton Kwesi Johnson (Jamaica/UK, b. 1952) was born in Chapelton, Jamaica, and came to Britain in his teens. A radical activist, journalist, broadcaster, record producer, as well as a poet and musician, he has published several collections of poetry and many records and CDs of his work. His most substantial collection of poems is *Mi Revalueshanary Fren: Selected Poems* (2002) and his recent work on disc includes *LKJ a capella live* (1995), an unaccompanied reading of a selection of his best known poems, and *More Time* (1998). In 2005 he was awarded a Musgrave medal by the Institute of Jamaica, for eminence in the field of poetry.

Paul Keens Douglas (Trinidad & Tobago, b. 1942) is one of the great storytellers of the Caribbean, a poet and performer who has captivated audiences all across the region and beyond. Born in Trinidad, he spent his early childhood in Grenada. He was a pioneer of the use of creole and folk story traditions in contemporary Caribbean literature. He has published ten collections of his stories and poems since 1975, as well as many CDs and at least three DVDs. His many awards include a silver Humming Bird Medal and the Zora Neale Hurston-Folklore Award.

Anthony Kellman (Barbados b. 1955) was educated at Combermere School and UWI in Barbados. In 1987 he left for the USA where he studied for an MFA in Creative Writing at Louisiana State University. In 1989 he moved to Augusta State University, Georgia, where he is now a professor of English and creative writing. In 1990 Peepal Tree published his third collection of poetry, *Watercourse*. His first novel, *The Coral Rooms,* followed in 1994. He has published several other books of poetry, including *Limestone* (2008) – an epic poem about Barbados – and a second novel, *The Houses of Alphonso*, in 2004.

Ismith Khan (Trinidad, 1925-2002) attended Queen's Royal College in Port of Spain and later worked as a reporter on the *Trinidad Guardian*. He left Trinidad in the 1950s to study at Michigan State and Johns Hopkins Universities. He published three novels, *The Jumbie Bird (1961), The Obeah Man* (1964), and *The Crucifixion (1987)*. His short stories are collected in *A Day in the Country* (1994). He lived in New York until his death in 2002.

Roi Kwabena (Trinidad, 1956-2008) was an historian, poet, drummer and cultural activist. In the mid-1990s he served as a senator in the Parliament of Trinidad and Tobago. He then made Birmingham, England, his permanent base and was appointed its sixth Poet Laureate in 2001. As a cultural ambassador, he both performed widely and hosted numerous readings by writers and actively promoted literature development. His publications include the poetry collection *Whether or Not* (2001) and his performance style is perhaps best represented on the audio CD *Y24K* (2000).

George Lamming (Barbados, b. 1927) left the Caribbean for England in 1950 and this experience informs the essays in *The Pleasures of Exile*. His novels have become classics of West Indian literature, including *In the Castle of My Skin* (1953), *The Emigrants* (1954), *Season of Adventure* (1960) and *Water with Berries* (1971). He is recognised as one of the Caribbean's most important thinkers on the issues of political and cultural independence. He has been a visiting professor at the Universities of Texas at Austin and Pennsylvania. He is now mostly resident in Barbados.

Earl Lovelace (Trinidad & Tobago, b. 1935) was born in the village of Toco. He worked for a time as a forest ranger and in the Department of Forestry. He studied in the USA at Howard University and on Johns Hopkins writing programme. His first novel, *While Gods Are Falling*, was published in 1965, followed by *The Schoolmaster, The Dragon Can't Dance, The Wine of Astonishment,* and *Salt,* which won the Commonwealth Writers Prize in 1997. His latest novel *Is Just a Movie* was published in 2011. He is one of the few major Caribbean writers who, except for brief periods, has never left the region. He taught for many years at the University of the West Indies in Trinidad.

Glenville Lovell (Barbados) toured the globe as a dancer before he became a writer. He is the author of four novels, several short stories and a number of prizewinning plays. He published his first novel, *Fire in the Canes*, in 1995, followed by *Song of Night* in 1998. In *Too Beautiful To Die* and *Love and Death in Brooklyn* he entered the crime/thriller genre. He won the 2002 Frank Collymore Literary Award for his play *Mango Ripe! Mango Sweet!* and in 2008, his play *Going for Love* played to packed houses at CARIFESTA X in Guyana.

E. A. Markham (Montserrat 1939-2008) grew up in rural Montserrat, then settled in Britain in the mid 1950s. Poet, critic, novelist, dramatist and editor, he published many collections of poems, including *A Rough Climate* (2002), *Human Rights: Selected Poems 1970-1982* (1984) and the posthumous collection *Looking Out, Looking In: New and Selected Poems* in 2010. He also edited the *Penguin Book of Caribbean Short Stories* (1992) and the poetry anthology *Hinterland* (1989). He ran the Creative Writing department at Sheffield Hallam University for ten years until retiring in 2005, when he moved to Paris. He also published novels, collections of short stories, a travel book and the autobiographical *Against the Grain: A 1950s Memoir* (Peepal Tree Press).

Ian McDonald (Trinidad/Guyana b. 1933) grew up in Trinidad, read History at Cambridge and has lived in Guyana since 1955. A poet, novelist, essayist and editor, he was also a senior executive in the Guyana Sugar Corporation for many years. His novel *The Hummingbird Tree*, (1969) was recently made into a BBC TV film. He edited the Guyanese literary journal, *Kyk-over-al* for more than a decade and in 1998 he was awarded an honorary Doctorate by the University of the West Indies for his contribution to West Indian literature. His poetry is widely anthologised and he has published several collections in recent years, including *Essequibo* (1992), which won the Guyana Prize, as did *From Silence to Silence* (2002). His early work is collected in *Jaffo the Calypsonian* (1994). His *Selected Poems* was shortlisted for the 2009 Royal Society of Literature Ondaatje Prize.

Earl McKenzie (Jamaica b. 1943) grew up in rural Jamaica and studied at Mico Teachers College. He obtained an MFA and a Ph D from the University of British Columbia. In Jamaica he taught in several high schools and at Church Teachers College. He lectured in Philosophy at the UWI, Mona. His poetry collections include *Against Linearity* (1993) *The Almond Leaf* and *A Poet's House* (both 2008). His fiction includes the novel, *A Boy Named Ossie: A Jamaican Childhood* (1991) and *Two Roads to Mount Joyful & Other Stories* (1992). He published a critical study *Philosophy in the West Indian Novel* in 2009.

Mark McWatt (Guyana, b. 1947) recently retired as Professor of West Indian literature at UWI, Cave Hill. He has published three collections of poetry, *Interiors* (1989) which won the Commonwealth Poetry Prize, The *Language of Eldorado* (1994) which won the Guyana Prize and most recently *The Journey to Le Repentir*, which won the Guyana Prize and Caribbean Award for Poetry. His collection of stories, *Suspended Sentences*, won the Commonwealth Literature Prize for best first book in 2006. As a critic he has published widely in journals on many aspects of Caribbean literature and is joint editor of the *Oxford Book of Caribbean Verse* (2005).

Alfred H. Mendes (Trinidad, 1897-1991) was of Portuguese creole background and a key member of the Beacon Group of writers in Trinidad in the 1930s, along with C. L. R. James and Ralph de Boissiere. Highly regarded as a writer of short stories and for two novels, *Pitch Lake* (1934) and *Black Fauns* (1935), he was made an honorary D. Litt. by the University of the West Indies in 1972 for his contribution to the development of West Indian literature.

Edgar Mittelholzer (Guyana, 1909-1965) began writing in 1929 and despite constant rejection letters persisted to become the West Indies first professional writer. In 1937 he self-published *Creole Chips* and sold it from door to door. His *Corentyne Thunder* was published in 1941. He moved to Trinidad and then

Barbados; in 1948 he left for England with the manuscript of *A Morning at The Office*, published in 1950. Between 1951 and 1965 he had published a further twenty-one novels and two works of non-fiction, including his autobiographical, *A Swarthy Boy*. He died by his own hand in 1965, a suicide by fire predicted in several of his novels.

Kei Miller (b. Jamaica, 1978) read English at the University of the West Indies and completed an MA in Creative Writing at Manchester Metropolitan University. His first collection of short fiction, *The Fear of Stones*, was short-listed in 2007 for the Commonwealth Writers First Book Prize. His poetry collections include, *Kingdom of Empty Bellies* (2006), *There Is an Anger That Moves* (2007) and the much praised *A Light Song of Light* (2010). He is the editor of *New Caribbean Poetry: An Anthology* (2007). He has published two novels, *The Same Earth* in 2008 and *The Last Warner Woman* in 2010. He currently teaches Creative Writing at the University of Glasgow.

Egbert Moore (Lord Beginner) (Trinidad & Tobago, 1904-1980) had established a reputation as an accomplished calypsonian in Trinidad, part of the "Old Brigade" that recorded and toured in New York, before he emigrated to the UK on the *Empire Windrush*, in 1948. His best known work is "Victory Calypso" (which includes the line we have borrowed as the title of this anthology) composed following the West Indies victory against England at Lord's in 1950, which inspired Beginner and fellow calypsonian Lord Kitchener to lead a spontaneous musical march from the ground to Piccadilly Circus, followed by dancing spectators. He had a successful recording career in London in the 1950s.

Moses Nagamootoo (Guyana) was born in Whim Village on the Corentyne. He has worked as a teacher, a journalist and in the law. He was for many years an activist member of the PPP and from 1992 to 1999 was a member of the Guyanese parliament and for some time held the portfolio of Minister of Information. His *Hendree's Cure: Scenes from Madrasi Life in a New World* (2000), is a work of documentary fiction, drawing on memories of the world of his youth.

V. S. Naipaul (Trinidad, b. 1932) was born in Chaguanas, Trinidad, in 1932. He was educated at Queen's Royal College, and, after winning a government scholarship, in England at University College, Oxford. He worked briefly for the BBC as a writer and editor for the 'Caribbean Voices' programme. Since then he has lived as a writer, publishing many novels, collections of essays, stories and documentary travel narratives. Perhaps still best known in the Caribbean for *A House for Mr Biswas* (1961), V. S. Naipaul was knighted in 1989. He was awarded the David Cohen British Literature Prize by the Arts Council of England in 1993 and the Nobel Prize for Literature in 2001.

Philip Nanton (St. Vincent, b. 1947) is a sociologist by training but has 'another life' as a freelance writer, poet, dramatist, filmmaker and producer of radio-documentaries. He lectured at the University of Birmingham in the UK for many years but relocated to Barbados in 1999 where he held various positions at UWI and at St. George's University, Grenada. His recent publications include editing a commemoration of the life and work of Frank Collymore, *Remembering the Sea*, and the spoken word cd *Island Voices from St. Christopher & the Barracudas*, a sequence of dramatic monologues which he both wrote and performed.

Christopher Nicole (Guyana b. 1930) spent his childhood in Georgetown, where he studied at Queen's College and later at Harrison College in Barbados. He initially worked in banking but in 1957 he moved to the Channel Islands and has since published over 200 novels and non-fiction books – many of them written under pseudonyms. His *Amyot* trilogy, *Caribee*, *Ratoon* and *Shadows in the Jungle* are set in Guyana.

Grace Nichols (Guyana, b. 1950) is a novelist, children's author and poet. She has lived in Britain since 1977. Her first book of poems, *i is a long memoried woman* (1983) won the Commonwealth Literature Prize. She also published *The Fat Black Woman's Poems* (1984) and *Lazy Thoughts of a Lazy Woman* (1989). Her collection, *Sunris* won the 1996 Guyana Prize for Poetry. Her novel, *Whole of a Morning Sky* (1986) is based on her remembered childhood in Guyana. In 2000 she received a Cholmondeley Award from the Society of Authors. Her most recent books are *I Have Crossed an Ocean: Selected Poems* and *Picasso, I Want My Face Back*, both published in 2010.

Eileen Ormsby Cooper (Jamaica) was a regular contributor to the BBC *Caribbean Voices* programme between 1948-1954, with both short stories and poems. Whether her poem 'Cosmopolitan' is autobiographical cannot be determined, but it may offer the closest to a biographical clue we have found: 'Is there no hope that I shall find repose?/None! For within my veins there mingling flows/The blood of many races of mankind,/Fighting within a single human frame...'

Ivor Osbourne (Jamaica) has published three novels, *The Mercenary* (1977), *Mango Season* (1979) and *Prodigal* (1986). His books contain no biographical details.

Sasenarine Persaud (Guyana, b. 1958) left Guyana for Canada in his early twenties. He has published two novels, seven collections of poems, including, *A Surf of Sparrows* (1996) *The Hungry Sailor* (2000) and *A Writer Like You* (2002) and several published essays. The title story of his *Canada Geese and Apple*

Chatney, (TSAR, 1999) is included in *The Oxford Book of Caribbean Short Stories*. He received the 1999 Arthur Schomburg Award for his pioneering of Yogic Realism and outstanding achievement as a writer. His most recent collection of poems, *In a Boston Night*, (2008) was short listed for the Guyana Prize in 2010. He now lives in Miami.

Rajandaye Ramkissoon-Chen (Trinidad, 1936-2009) was a Fellow and Life Member of the Royal College of Obstetricians and Gynaecologists of London. In 2003, she was awarded the Trinidad and Tobago National Chaconia Gold Award for her meritorious service in the field of Medicine. She wrote short stories and poetry and published widely in journals and anthologies. Her short story "Josiah's Escape" won the Longman Trinidad Short Story Contest in 1966. She published four volumes of poetry: *Ancestry, Mirror Eye, Many Sides of Red*, and *Meenachi*.

Eric Roach (Trinidad and Tobago, 1915-1974) was a poet, playwright, teacher and journalist who stayed almost all his life in Tobago. He struggled to make a career as a writer but refused offers of university scholarships which would have taken him abroad. Disillusioned by the struggle, the lack of tangible success and the direction he saw West Indian literature taking, he committed suicide in 1974. Although his poems were published in journals and anthologies across the region, there was no collection of Roach's poems until 1992 when his collected poems were published as *The Flowering Rock: Collected Poems 1938-1974* by Peepal Tree Press. He was awarded the Trinidad and Tobago National Hummingbird Gold Medal, posthumously in 1974.

Vincent Roth (Australia/Guyana 1889-1967) joined his father, Dr Walter Roth, who had taken up the post of Government Medical Officer in the North West District of British Guiana in 1907. After a brief spell as a newspaper reporter, Vincent Roth joined the Lands and Mines Department, for which he worked as a surveyor and Warden/Magistrate for the next twenty-five years. In 1964 he left Guyana for Barbados, where he began to write his memoirs. His journals are published by Peepal Tree in two volumes as *Vincent Roth, A Life in Guyana: Volume 1: A Young Man's Journey 1889-1922; Volume 2: The Later Years: 1922-1936*.

Krishna A. Samaroo (Trinidad & Tobago, b. 1954) holds a B.A. and an M.A. in English from the University of the West Indies. Since 1979 he has been a teacher of English in San Fernando. He has written works for the stage which were regularly produced and performed by the Nowtime Players. A first collection of poetry *Tentacles & Tendrils*, was published in 1985 and a long narrative poem, *Song of a Barefoot Soul*, was published in 2000. His work has been awarded several prizes in national literary competitions.

G. K. Sammy (Trinidad & Tobago) is an environmental engineer by profession, and an elder at the Maracas Valley Presbyterian Church. His poems and stories have been published in Trinidad and are available online at georgieboy53.tripod.com

Chris Searle (UK, b. 1944) has been an activist-intellectual and educationalist his whole adult life. A longtime English teacher and sometime head-teacher in East London, Grenada, Mozambique and Sheffield, he has written many books on education, one of which, *The Forsaken Lover: White Words and Black People*, won the Martin Luther King Award in 1972. He teaches at Goldsmiths' College, University of London, and still plays weekend cricket in the Derbyshire League, opening the batting, occasionally bowling and almost always fielding at third man. As a youth he opened the bowling for English schools.

Sam Selvon (Trinidad & Tobago, 1923-1994) was born in San Fernando where he attended Naparima College. From 1940-1945 he was a wireless operator with the Royal Naval Reserve. From 1945-1950, he worked for the *Trinidad Guardian* as a reporter, edited its literary page and began writing stories and descriptive pieces. In 1950 he left Trinidad for the UK where he established himself as a writer with *A Brighter Sun* (1952). Ten further novels followed, including *The Lonely Londoners* (1956), *Ways of Sunlight* (1957), and *Moses Migrating (1983)*. In 1978 he left the UK for Canada where he lived until his death in 1994, on a return trip to Trinidad.

Bruce St. John (Barbados 1923-1995) was a multi-talented figure who trained as a classical singer, and took a diploma in physical education before he became Senior Lecturer in Spanish at the UWI in Barbados. A man of the theatre, he was one of the region's wittiest writers, his poetry exploring the voices and characters of Barbados in ways that anticipate the concerns and strategies of a later generation of West Indian writers. His poetry collections include *Bruce St. John at Kairi House* (1975), *Joyce & Eros and Varia* (1976) and *Bumbatuk 1* (1982). His work is included in several regional anthologies.

Derek Walcott (St. Lucia, b. 1930) won the Nobel Prize for Literature in 1992. He studied at the University College of the West Indies in Jamaica before moving to Trinidad in 1953, where he became a theatre and art critic, and wrote poetry and plays which established his reputation. He founded the Trinidad Theatre Workshop in 1959, and has since divided his time between Trinidad, St. Lucia and the USA, where he taught Literature and Creative Writing at Boston University for many years. He is an honorary member of the American Academy and the Institute of Arts and Letters. His latest poetry collection is *White Egrets* (2010), won the 2010 T. S. Eliot Prize.

William Walcott (Canada) teaches Sociology and Humanities at the Humber Institute of Technology and Advanced Learning in Toronto, Canada. He is interested in using sociolinguistics to analyse racism in large urban centres, as well as studying the sociological challenges associated with changes to high level international cricket.

P. F. Warner (Trinidad/UK, 1873-1963) came from an old planter family. His brother Aucher Warner not only captained the first combined West Indies side in the West Indies during the 1896-97 season but also led the first West Indian touring side to England in 1900. When he was thirteen 'Plum' was sent to school in England. He played first-class cricket for Middlesex and fifteen Test matches for England, captaining in ten of them. In 1897 he returned to the West Indies with Lord Hawke's side, a tour which is recounted in the report he wrote that we have included in the anthology. He did once play for the touring West Indies side, against Leicestershire, making 113. He had a distinguished career as a cricket administrator and was a prolific writer on cricket.

Milton Vishnu Williams (Guyana, b. 1936) was born on a sugar estate. His first poems appeared in *Kyk-Over-Al* and a small collection, *Pray For Rain*, appeared in 1958. By 1960 he was in Britain, living at first in London and then moving by a strange process of chance to Newcastle where he lived until 1984. In 1979 he published a small collection, *Sources of Agony*, and in 1986 Peepal Tree collected his poems in *Years of Fighting Exile: Collected Poems 1955-1985*.

Sylvia Wynter (Jamaica, b. 1928) was born in Cuba, but grew up and was educated in Jamaica. A series of scholarships took her to the Universities of London and Madrid. She wrote for the BBC's Caribbean Voices as well as for its then Third Programme, for which she created and adapted radio dramas. Her novel, *The Hills of Hebron*, was published in 1962. In that same year she returned to Jamaica where she joined the faculty of the University of the West Indies and became a foundational voice in the project of decolonisation. In 1977 she took up a post at Stanford University where she is still a Professor Emeritus.

Benjamin Zephaniah (UK/Jamaica, b. 1958) is an oral poet, novelist, playwright, children's writer and reggae artist. Born in Birmingham, he grew up in Jamaica and in Handsworth. After a somewhat misspent youth, he turned from crime to music and poetry. He has produced numerous recordings, including *Dub Ranting* (1982) and *Naked* (2004). He has published several books of poems, including *City Psalms* (1992), and *Too Black Too Strong* (2001). He has also published several novels for younger readers. He has received honorary doctorates from several English universities.

SOURCES AND ACKNOWLEDGEMENTS

We are grateful to the following firms and individuals who have granted permission to reprint original and copyrighted material. Every effort has been made to contact all copyright holders prior to printing, although this has not always been possible. The publishers would be pleased to rectify any omissions or errors brought to their notice at the earliest opportunity.

John Agard: 'The Devil at Lords', *From the Devil's Pulpit*, (Newcastle: Bloodaxe Books, 1997), p. 31; and 'What More Can One Ask of Cricket?', from *We Brits* (Newcastle: Bloodaxe Books, 2006), p. 17; reprinted by permission of the publisher; 'Prospero Caliban Cricket' from *New Writing 2*, ed. by Bradbury and Motion (Minerva, 1993) and 'Professor David Dabydeen at the Crease' (unpublished, 2009), reprinted by permission of the author.

Joan Anim-Addo: 'Thoughts from a Cricket Orphan' from *Haunted By History* (London: Mango Publishing, 1998), pp. 51-52; 'Take a Peep at the Crowd' and 'She Cousin From Trinidad', *Janie: Cricketing Lady* (London: Mango Publishing, 2006) p. 39 , p. 15; all reprinted by permission of Mango Publishing.

Michael Anthony: 'Cricket in the Road' from *Sandra Street and Other Stories* (London: Heinemann, 1973), pp. 16-19; reprinted by permission of Pearson Education.

Colin Babb: 'Cricket, Lovely Cricket: London SW16 to Guyana and Back' first published in *IC3: The Penguin Book of New Black British Writing in Britain*, ed. by Courttia Newland and Kadija Sesay (Penguin, 2000), revised for this collection and published by permission of the author.

Edward Baugh: 'The Pulpit Eulogists of Frank Worrell' and 'View from the George Headley Stand, Sabina', used with permission of Sandberry Press, from *It Was the Singing*, 2000; 'Speech in Honour of Allan Rae', published by permission of the author.

Hilary McD. Beckles: 'History, the King, the Crown Prince and I', *Sunday Sun* (Barbados) 24, 25 and 26 April 1994

Deryck M. Bernard: story 'Bourda' from *Going Home and Other Tales from Guyana* (London: Macmillan Caribbean, 2002), pp. 15-20, reprinted by permission of the publisher

James Berry: 'Fast Bowler' from *Hot Earth, Cold Earth* (Newcastle: Bloodaxe, 1997), pp. 95-96; reprinted by permission of the publisher.

Frank Birbalsingh: 'Return to Bourda' from *Guyana and the Caribbean*, ed. by Frank Birbalsingh (Chichester: Dido Press, 2004), reprinted by permission of the author.

Roger Bonair-Agard: 'Gully' ; 'To Mimic Magic' (Leeds: Peepal Tree Press, 2010) p. 25, pp. 55-58; reprinted by permission of the publisher.

Kamau Brathwaite: 'Rites' from *Islands* (London: OUP, 1973), pp. 40-46; reprinted by permission of the publisher.

Jean Binta Breeze: 'Song for Lara' from *On the Edge of the Island* (Newcastle: Bloodaxe, 1997) pp. 67-69, and 'on cricket, sex and housework' from *The Arrival of Brighteye* (Newcastle: Bloodaxe, 2000), p. 50; reprinted by permission of the publisher.

Lloyd W. Brown: 'Cricket Grounds, Plymouth' from *Duppies* (Leeds: Peepal Tree, 1996) p. 36-37; reprinted by permission of the publisher.

Stewart Brown: 'Test Match Sabina Park' from *Zinder* (Poetry Wales Press, 1986); 'Counter Commentary at Kensington Oval' from *Elsewhere: New and Selected Poems* (Leeds: Peepal Tree, 1999), pp. 14-16; reprinted by permission of the publisher

Faustin Charles: 'Viv' and 'Cricket's in My Blood' from *Selected Poems* (Leeds: Peepal Tree, 2006), p. 105, 107

Merle Collins: 'Quality Time' from *Lady in a Boat* (Leeds: Peepal Tree, 2003), pp. 13-14

Learie Constantine: 'Village Cricket in Trinidad' from *Cricket in the Sun* (London: Stanley Paul, 1943), pp. 32-36

Eileen Ormsby Cooper: 'Cricket in the Blood' broadcast on 'Caribbean Voices', BBC Colonial Service (1 July 1951)

Cyril Dabydeen: 'Faster they Come' from *North of the Equator* (Vancouver: Beach Holm, 2001), pp. 19-26; reprinted by permission of the publisher

David Dabydeen: 'For Rohan Babulal Kanhai' from *Coolie Odyssey* (London: Hansib, 1988), p. 25; reprinted by permission of the author

Fred D'Aguiar: extract from 'Guyanese Days' from *Mama Dot* (London: Chatto & Windus, 1985), pp. 46-47; reprinted by permission of the author

Kwame Dawes: 'Alado Seanadra' from *Progeny of Air* (Leeds: Peepal Tree, 1994), pp. 21-22; reprinted by permission of the publisher; 'A Birthday Gift', unpublished, by permission of the author

Neville Dawes: extract from *Interim* (Kingston: Institute of Jamaica, 1978), pp. 53-54; reprinted by permission of Kwame Dawes for the Estate of Neville Dawes

Rayhat Deonandan: 'King Rice' from *Sweet Like Saltwater* (Toronto: TSAR, 1999), pp. 16-20; reprinted by permission of the publisher

Ann Marie Dewar: 'Cricket (A-We Jim)' from *La Montee, La Sabida, Ascent*, Poetry Chapbook Series 3, ed. by Bruce St. John (Cave Hill: UWI Press, 1985), pp. 12-13; reprinted by permission of Howard Fergus and the author

Ian Dieffenthaller: 'Weather Report' (unpublished, 2009), published by permission of the author

J.D. Douglas: 'I'm a West Indian in Britain' from *Caribbean Man's Blues* (London: Akira Press, 1985), p. 12

Garfield Ellis: two chapters (pp. 9-21) from *Such As I Have*, copyright © Garfield Ellis 2003, reprinted by permission of Macmillan Education

J. B. Emtage: extracts from *Brown Sugar: A Vestigial Tale* (London: Collins, 1966), pp. 15-17, pp. 25-30

Howard Fergus: 'Lara Reach' and 'Short of a Century' from *Lara Reigns and Colonial Rites* (Leeds: Peepal Tree, 1998), p. 10, 17; 'Conquest' from *Volcano Verses* (Leeds: Peepal Tree, 2003), pp. 59-60; reprinted by permission of the publisher

Delores Gauntlett: 'Cricket Boundaries' first published in *The Caribbean Writer* 10 (1997), reprinted by permission of the author.

John Figueroa: 'West Indies and Test Cricket: A Special Contribution?' from *West Indies in England: The Great Post-War Tours* (London: The Kingswood Press, 1991), reprinted by permission of Esther Figueroa for the Estate of John Figueroa

Beryl Gilroy: 'Village Cricket' from *Sunlight on Sweet Water* (Leeds: Peepal Tree, 1994), pp. 101-104; reprinted by permission of the publisher

Cecil Gray: 'Sonny Ramadhin' from *The Woolgatherer* (Leeds: Peepal Tree, 1994), p. 105; 'Practice' from *Only the Waves* (Toronto: Lilibel, 2005), p. 20; 'Still Driving' from *Lilian's Songs* (Toronto: Lilibel, 1996), p. 46; reprinted by permission of the author.

Stanley Greaves: 'The Joys of Conjecture' (from an unpublished talk delivered at the University of Guyana in the 1970s), published by permission of the author.

A.L. Hendriks: 'Their Mouths But Not Their Hearts' from *Madonna of the Unknown Nation* (London: Workshop Press. 1974), p. 53; reprinted in *To Speak Simply: Selected Poems, 1961-1986* (Frome: Hippopotamus Press, 1986); reprinted by permission of the publisher

Bernard Heydorn: 'Cricket lovely Cricket' from *Walk Good Guyana Boy* (Ontario: Learning Improvement Centre, 1994), p. 179-185.

Carl Jackson: 'The Professional' (unpublished) by permission of the author.

C.L.R. James: 'The Window' from *Beyond a Boundary* (London: Hutchinson, 1963), pp. 13-23, 299-300; 'Driving the Ball is a Tradition in the West Indies' from *The Cricketer* (1968), reprinted by permission of Professor Robert Hill for the Estate of C.L.R. James.

Errol John: extract from *Moon on a Rainbow Shawl* (London: Faber, 1958), pp. 60-63; reprinted by permission of the publisher.

Linton Kwesi Johnson: 'Reggae fi Dada' from *Tings and Times* (Newcastle: Bloodaxe Books, 1991), pp. 34-36; reprinted by permission of LKJ Music Publishers Ltd.

Paul Keens-Douglas: 'Tanti at de Oval' from *Tanti at De Oval: Selected Works of Paul Keens-Douglas Vol.1* (Trinidad: Keensdee, 1992), pp. 35-41; reprinted by permission of the publisher.

Anthony Kellman: extract from *The Houses of Alphonso* (Leeds: Peepal Tree, 1986), pp. 182-183; reprinted by permission of the publisher.

Ismith Khan: 'The Red Ball' from *A Day in the Country* (Leeds: Peepal Tree, 1994), pp. 7-17

Roi Kwabena: 'all part of a day's play' from *Whether or Not* (Birmingham: Raka Press, 2000), reprinted by permission of the author.

George Lamming: extract from *In the Castle of My Skin* (London: Michael Joseph, 1953), pp. 98-99, and extract from *The Emigrants* (Michael Joseph, 1954), p. 66; reprinted by permission of the author.

Earl Lovelace: extract from *Salt* (London: Faber & Faber, 1996), pp. 29-33; reprinted by permission of the publisher; extracts from 'Victory and the Blight' from *A Brief Conversion* (Oxford: Heinemann, 1988), pp. 133-141; 'Like When Somebody Dead' from *Growing in the Dark: Selected Essays* (Trinidad: Lexicon, 2003), pp. 89-91, and 'Franklyn Batting' from *Is Just a Movie* (London: Faber, 2011), pp. 86-91; reprinted by permission of Capel & Land, on behalf of Earl Lovelace.

Glenville Lovell: extract from *Song of Night* (London: Soho Press, 1998), reprinted by permission of the author.

E.A. Markham: 'Part V: On Another Field, an Ally: A West Indian Batsman Talks Us Towards the Century' from *Towards the End of a Century* (London: Anvil Press Poetry, 1989), pp. 16-17; reprinted by permission of the publisher.

Ian McDonald: 'Test Match' from *Mercy Ward* (Calstock: Peterloo Poets, 1988), p. 31; reprinted by permission of the publisher; 'Massa Day Done' from *Between Silence and Silence* (Leeds: Peepal Tree, 2003), pp. 87-88 ; extract from *The Hummingbird Tree* (London: Heinemann, 1969), pp. 57-60; 'Cricket's Most Memorable Over' (first published in *Stabroek News*), all reprinted by permission of the author.

Earl McKenzie: 'Cricket Season' from *A Boy Named Ossie: A Jamaican Childhood* (London: Heinemann, 1991), pp. 19-24; reprinted by permission of the author.

Alfred H. Mendes: extract from *The Autobiography of Alfred H. Mendes*, ed. by Michèle Levy (Mona, Kingston: UWI Press, 2002), pp. 34-35;reprinted by permission of the publisher

Kei Miller: 'Drink & Die' from *Kingdom of Empty Bellies* (Coventry: Heaventree Press, 2006), pp. 83-84; reprinted by permission of the publisher

Edgar Mittelholzer: extract from *A Morning at the Office* (London: Hogarth Press, 1950), pp. 232-233; and extract from *A Swarthy Boy* (London: Putnam, 1963), p. 130;both reissued by Peepal Tree, 2009

Rooplall Monar: 'Cookman' from *High House and Radio* (Leeds: Peepal Tree, 1994), pp. 163-174

Egbert Moore (Lord Beginner): 'Victory Calypso, Lord's 1950', reprinted from A Breathless Hush: The M.C.C. Anthology of Cricket Verse (London: Methuen, 2007), pp. 228-229

Moses Nagamootoo: extract from *Hendree's Cure* (Leeds: Peepal Tree, 2000), pp. 92-94

V.S. Naipaul: extract from 'Hat' from *Miguel Street* (London: Penguin, 1959), pp. 154-156 and 'The Test' from *Summer Days: Writers on Cricket*, ed. by McDonald Meyer (Eyre Methuen, 1981), reprinted by permission of Aitken Alexander Associates on behalf of the author

Philip Nanton: 'Night Cricket at Carlton Club, Barbados', published by permission of the author

Grace Nichols: 'Test Match High Mass' from *Picasso, I Want My Face Back*, (Newcastle: Bloodaxe Books, 2009), p. 27

Christopher Nicole: 'Introduction' from *West Indian Cricket* (London: Phoenix Sports Books, 1957), reprinted by permission of the author

Ivor Osbourne: extract from *Prodigal* (London, Antillian Paperbacks, 1986), pp. 78-80

Sasenarine Persaud: 'Call Him the Babu' first published in *The Caribbean Writer* 10 (1996), reprinted by permission of the author

Rajandaye Ramkissoon-Chen: 'On Lara's 375' from *Ancestry* (London: Hansib Caribbean, 1997), pp. 101-102; reprinted by permission of the author

Eric Roach: 'To Learie' first published in *The Trinidad Guardian* (19 Jan 1939), reprinted in *The Flowering Rock: Collected Poems 1938-1974*, 2nd ed. (Peepal Tree, 2012)

Vincent Roth: extract from *A Life in Guyana, Vol. 1* (Leeds: Peepal Tree, 2004), pp. 239-240

Krishna A. Samaroo: 'A Cricketing Gesture' from *Crossing Water: Contemporary poetry of the English Speaking Caribbean*, ed. by Anthony Kellman (New York: Greenfield Review Press, 1992), p. 185

G.K. Sammy: 'Cricket in the Road' from <http://georgieboy53.tripod.com/id7.html>, reprinted by permission of the author

Chris Searle, 'Lara's Innings', from Pitch of Life: Writings on Cricket (Manchester: The Parrs Wood Press, 2001), pp. 35-48

Sam Selvon: 'The Cricket Match' from *Ways of Sunlight* (London: MacGibbon & Kee, 1957), pp. 161-166; reprinted by permission of Mrs Althea Selvon for the Estate of Sam Selvon

Bruce St. John: 'Cricket' from *Bumbatuk 1* (Bridgetown: Cedar Press, 1982), p. 17-19

Derek Walcott: extract from 'Leaving School' from *The London Magazine* (1965), reprinted by permission of Farrar, Strauss & Giroux on behalf of Derek Walcott

INDEX OF PROPER NAMES
Author contributions in bold

Achong, Ellis (Puss), 274, 286

Adams, Grantley, 262

Adams, J.C. (Jimmie), 266

Agard, John, 20, 24, **37-39**, 347

Alexander, Gerry, 259, 311, 312

Allen, George, 79

Ambrose, Curtly, 16, 287, 335

Anim Addo, Joan, 22, **40-42**, 347

Anthony, Michael, **123-125**

Arlott, John, 251, 255, 258

Arnold, Matthew, 303

Babb, Colin, 30, **251-255**, 347

Bailey, McDonald, 300

Bailey, Trevor, 281, 287

Baptiste, Eldine, 287

Bardswell, G.R., 343

Barrington, K.F. (Kenny), 319, 323, 324

Barrow, Ivan, 285

Baugh, Edward, 27, **43**, **256-260**, 347

Becca, Tony, 257-258, 332

Beckles, Hilary McD., 16-17, 261-266, 347

Bedser, Alec, 103

Beginner, Lord (Egbert Moore), 26, 32, **103-104**, 357

Beldham, William, 296

Benaud, Richie, 14, 310

Benjamin, Kenny, 287

Bernard, Deryck M., **126-130**, 347

Berry, James, **45-46**, 348

Best, Carlyle, 113

Birbalsingh, Frank, 33, **267-270**, 348

Bird, Harold Dennis (Dicky), 37, 251

Bird, Lester, 265

Bishop, Maurice, 332, 333, 339

Bonair-Agard, Roger, 25, **47-51**, 348

Bondman, Matthew, 23, 294-295, 297, 300, 303, 339

Booker T and the MGs, 252

Botham, Ian, 281, 282

Bowes, W.E. (Bill), 287

Boycott, Geoffrey, 25, 51, 131, 252, 264

Bradman, Donald, 97, 273, 282, 339

Brathwaite, Kamau, 19, 21, 28-29, **52-57**, 330, 331, 337, 348

Breeze, Jean Binta, 22, 348

Brenkly, Stephen, 332

Brodsky, Joseph, 18

Brown, Capability, 292

Brown, Lloyd, **61-62**, 349

Brown, Stewart, **19-34**, **63-65**, 349

Browne, C.R. (Snuffle), 286

Bunyan, John, 303

Burke, Edmund, 295, 296

Burnham, Forbes, 212

Butcher, Basil, 267, 320, 321, 322, 324

Butcher, Mark, 255

Butcher, Roland, 255

Caddick, Andrew, 264, 265

Cahn, Julian, 274

Calthorpe, Hon F.S.G., 274

Cameron, J.H., 286

Carew, M.C. (Joey), 317

Castro, Fidel, 335

Césaire, Aimé, 269-270, 288

Challenor, George, 16, 67, 179

Chanderpaul, Shivnarine, 16, 23, 33, 109, 266, 268, 269, 330, 332

Charles, Faustin, **66-67**, 349

Christiani, Robert J., 103, 268

Cipriani, André, 42

Clarke, C.B. (Bertie), 179, 284, 286

Close, D.B. (Brian), 323, 324

Collins, Merle, 22, **68-69**, 349

Collymore, Frank, 285

Compton, Dennis, 281

Constantine, Learie, 16, 21, 25, 31, 32, 42, 67, 110, 131, 171, 245, 266, **271-275**, 281, 282, 283, 284-285, 286, 289, 313, 336, 338, 349

Constantine, Lebrun, 274, 284, 342

Cornelius, Lloyd, 128

Corsbie, Ken, 293

Cowans, Norman, 255

Cowdrey, Colin, 320, 323, 324

Cozier, Tony, 334
Croft, Colin, 308
Cudjoe, Cousin (of C.L.R. James), 298, 299
Cumberbatch, A.B., 342, 344
D'Ade, L.S., 343
D'Aguiar, Fred, **71**, 350
D'Aguiar, Peter, 213
Dabydeen, Cyril, 25, **131-136**, 350
Dabydeen, David, 26-27, 39, **70, 350**
Davidson, Alan, 131
Dawes, Kwame, 24, **72-73, 276-280**, 350
Dawes, Neville, **137**, 350
de Caires, A.B., 327
de Caires, Frank, 327
DeFreitas, Philip, 286
Deonandan, Rayhat, **138-140**, 351
Dewar, Ann Marie, **74-75**, 351
Dewdney, Tom, 259, 287
Dexter, E.R. (Ted), 281, 282, 317, 318, 319, 322, 324
Dieffenthaller, Ian, **76**, 351
Douglas, J.D., 30, **77**, 351
Dujon, Jeffrey (Jeff), 113
Edinburgh, Duke of, 332
Eliot, T.S., 339
Ellis, Garfield, **141-151**, 351
Emtage, J.B., **152-155**, 351
Evans, Godfrey, 210
Farnes, Kenneth, 287
Fergus, Howard, **78-80**, 351
Ferguson, Wilfred, 13
Figueroa, John, 256, 257, **281-288**, 352
Francis, George, 245, 286
Fraser, Angus, 263, 286
Fraser, Babsie, 85
Fredericks, Roy, 16
Fry, C.B., 296
Funk, Ray, 34
Garner, Joel, 282, 286, 287, 288, 311
Gauntlett, Delores, **82**, 352
Gavaskar, Sunil, 131
Gayle, Chris, 23, 76, 308
Gibbs, Lance, 16, 77, 130, 267, 285, 322, 323, 324

Gilroy, Beryl, **289-290**, 352
Goddard, John, 103
Gomes, Larry, 112
Gomez, G.E. (Gerry), 104, 216
Gooch, Graham, 264
Goodman, Clifford, 343, 344
Grace, W.G., 12, 37, 38, 303, 332
Graveney, Tom, 322
Gray, Cecil, 26, **83-85**, 352
Gray, Tony, 113
Greaves, Stanley, 20, **291-293**, 352
Greenidge, Gordon, 16, 97, 113, 252, 281, 338
Greig, Tony, 254
Griffiths, Charlie, 16, 77, 131, 210, 251, 318, 319, 320, 324
Griffiths, Herman, 286
Grout, Wallie, 210, 311, 312
Gunn, George, 274
Hall, Wesley, 16, 25, 77, 97, 129, 131, 189, 210, 251, 264, 311, 312, 318, 319, 320, 322, 323, 324
Hammond, Walter, 284
Harbin, Len, 216, 217
Harper, Roger, 286
Harrigan, Major A.E. (Bertie), 12
Harris, Wilson, 337
Harvey, Neil, 131
Hassanali, Noor, 332
Hawke, Lord, 32, 342, 343, 345
Hawke, Neil, 127
Haynes, Desmond, 113, 265, 281, 336
Headley, George, 16, 97, 131, 179, 217, 259, 260, 266, 274, 281, 282, 283, 285, 299, 336
Hector, Tim, 333, 334, 337
Hegel, G.W.F., 297
Hendriks, A.L., **86**, 353
Heydorn, Bernard, 23, **156-160**, 353
Hobbs, Jack, 273
Holding, Michael, 16, 25, 48-51, 97, 113, 131, 251, 252, 253, 286, 287, 288, 331, 336
Holford, David, 262
Hooper, Carl, 23, 102, 268, 269, 308, 309
Hopkins, Gerard Manley, 13, 18

Humphries, Hunter, 259
Hunte, Conrad, 204, 312, 316, 317, 320
Hussain, Nasser, 258
Hutton, Len, 256, 281, 282, 283, 339
Jackson, Carl, **161-169**, 353
Jacobs, Ridley, 309
Jagan, Cheddi, 106, 212, 267
James (father of C.L.R.), 298-299
James, C.L.R., 14, 15, 16, 21, 23, 31, 32, 77, 262, 263, 284, **294-303**, 330, 332, 334, 335, 336, 337, 339, 353
Jenkins, R.O. (Roly), 104
John, Errol, 25, **245-247**, 353
John, George, 16, 245
Johnson, Linton Kwesi, 22, **87-89**, 354
Johnson, Tyrell, 217
Johnston, W.A. (Bill), 286
Jones, Arthur, 295, 296-297, 339
Kallicharan, Alvin, 252
Kallis, Jacques, 310
Kanhai, Rohan, 16, 26-27, 39, 70, 77, 80, 97, 106-107, 127, 131, 210, 251, 252, 267, 285, 312, 317, 318, 320, 322, 323, 324, 336
Keens Douglas, Paul, 28, **90-95, 304-307**, 354
Kellman, Anthony, **170**, 354
Kentish, Esmond, 260
Khan, Imran, 131
Khan, Ismith 26, **171-177**, 354
Kipling, Rudyard, 86
Kline, Lindsay, 312
Kwabena, Roi, **96**, 354
Laker, Jim, 56-57, 255
Lamming, George, **178, 179**, 337, 355
Lara, Brian, 16, 23, 33, 58-60, 78, 108-109, 131, 261-266, 268, 308, 330-340
Larwood, Harold, 287
Layne, F., 343
Lee, Brett, 131
Leveson-Gower, H.D.G., 343
Lewis, Chris, 265, 286, 331, 336
Lillee, Dennis, 16
Lindwall, Ray, 131, 286
Lloyd, Clive, 16, 77, 80, 97, 131, 207, 252, 254, 267, 336

Lovelace, Earl, 23-24, **180-182, 183-185, 186-188, 308-310**, 339, 355
Lovell, Glenville, **189-190**, 355
MacMillan, Harold, 322
Mahmood, Fazal, 204
Malcolm, Devon, 64-65, 255, 286, 331-332
Mandela, Nelson, 335
Manning, Patrick, 332
Markham, E.A., 30, **97-98**, 355
Marley, Bob, 279
Marshall, Malcolm, 97, 112, 252, 286, 287, 288
Martin, Dave, 311
Martin, F.R. (Frank), 281, 286
Martindale, E.A. (Manny) 67, 179
Martin-Jenkins, Christopher, 64
May, Peter, 131, 323
McDonald, Ian, **11-18**, 19, 25, **99-100, 191-194, 311-312, 340**, 356
McKenzie, Earl, 23, **195-198**, 356
McLean, Nixon, 309
McMorris, Easton, 316, 317, 318, 320, 323
McWatt, Mark, **199-207**, 356
Meckiff, Ian, 311, 312
Melville, Herman, 303
Mendes, Alfred, 20-21, **313-314**, 356
Menzies, Badge, 267
Michael Angelo [sic], 296
Miller, Kei, **102**, 357
Miller, Keith, 286
Milton, John, 86
Mittelholzer, Edgar, **208**, 315, 356
Mohammed, Hanif, 259
Monar, Rooplall, **209-213**
Montgomery, Field-Marshall, 80
Moore, Brian, 251
Moore, Egbert (Lord Beginner, **103-104**, 357
Mudie, George, 286
Murray, D.L. (Deryck), 318
Murray, Junior, 330
Nagamootoo, Moses, 20, 214-215, 357
Naipaul, V.S., 19, 28-29, **216-217, 316-324**, 337, 357

Nanton, Philip, **325**, 358
Nicholas, Mark, 340
Nichols, Grace, **105**, 358
Nicole, Christopher, **326-327**, 358
Nurse, Seymour, 128, 129
O'Neal, Shaquille, 278
Olajuwon, Hakeem, 278
Ollivierre, Charles Augustus, 67
Ormsby Cooper, Eileen, 22, **218-222**, 358
Osbourne, Ivor, **223-234**, 358
Outridge, Alan, 327
Parks, J.M. (Jim), 319, 323
Patterson, Orlando, 24
Patterson, Patrick, 113, 277
Persaud, Sasenarine, **106-107**, 358
Phidias, 296
Pires, B.C., 309
Rae, Allan, 16, 103, 256-260, 281
Ramadhin, Sonny, 16, 26, 67, 83, 103-104, 251, 283, 285, 286, 287, 288, 323
Ramkissoon-Chen, Rajandaye, 33, **108-109**, 359
Ramnarine, Dinanath, 308
Ramprakash, Mark, 255, 331
Rhodes, Wilfred, 274
Richards, I.V.A (Viv), 16, 64-65, 66, 80, 95, 97, 99-100, 112, 131, 207, 252, 253, 262, 263-264, 336
Richardson, Richie, 113, 262, 264
Ring, Doug, 80
Roach, C.A. (Clifford), 179, 281
Roach, Eric, **110**, 359
Roberts, Andy, 77, 131, 252, 262, 287, 288
Robertson-Glasgow, R.C., 259
Rodney, Walter, 337, 339
Rohlehr, Gordon, 33
Roth, Vincent, 32, **328-329**, 359
Rowe, Lawrence (Yagga), 63, 264, 337-338
Rudder, David, 264, 309, 334-335
Russell, R.C. (Jack), 265
Samaroo, Krishna A., **111**, 359
Sammy, G.K., **112-113**, 360
Samuels, Marlon, 308

Sandys, Duncan, 212
Sarwan, Ramnaresh, 308, 309
Scott, Dennis, 26
Scott, Edwin, 333
Scott, O.C. (Tommy), 286
Sealey, Derek, 179, 273-274
Searle, Chris, **330-340**, 360
Selvon, Samuel, 29-30, **225-228**, 332, 338-339, 360
Shackleton, Derek, 320, 324
Shelley, Percy Bysshe, 295
Simmons, P.V., 262
Simpson, Robert (Bobbie), 129, 131
Small, Gladstone, 65, 286
Small, Joe, 299
Smith, O.G. (Collie), 317
Sobers, Garfield (Garry), 16, 77, 80, 97, 129-130, 131, 170, 202, 204, 205, 206, 210, 251, 262, 263-266, 268, 282, 307, 317, 318, 319, 320, 321, 323, 330, 332, 335, 336, 337
Solomon, Joe, 16, 312, 317, 318, 321, 324
Sparrow, Mighty, 337
St. Hill, Wilton, 296, 336
St. John, Bruce, **114-116**, 360
Stanford, Allen, 19
Statham, Brian, 131, 287, 317
Stoddart, A.E., 344
Stollmeyer, Jeffrey, 16, 103, 217, 285
Sutcliffe, Herbert, 273
Tawney, R.H., 17
Tendulkar, Sachin, 131
Thackeray, William, 295
Thompson, Jeff, 16, 131
Titmus, F.J. (Fred), 319, 320, 323, 324
Toshack, E.R., 286
Townsend, L, 274
Trueman, F.S. (Fred), 131, 160, 285, 287, 316, 317, 318, 319, 320, 322, 324
Valentine, Alf, 16, 26, 67, 103-104, 251, 283, 285, 286, 286, 287, 288, 318
Voce, W. (Bill), 274, 287
Walcott, Clyde, 28, 55-57, 104, 204, 205, 206, 260, 262, 285, 286, 336
Walcott, Derek, 18, 20, **341**, 360

Walcott, William, **117-118**, 361
Walsh, Courtney, 16, 113, 262, 287, 308, 310
Wardle, Johnny, 28, 54-55, 103, 287
Warner, P.F. (Plum), 32, 67, 283, 299, **342-345**, 361
Washbrook, Cyril, 104
Weekes, Everton, 54, 251, 256, 258, 259, 268, 285, 336
Weekes, K.H. (Bam-Bam), 299
West, Peter, 255
Westall, Claire, 34
Weston, Paul, 331
Williams, C.B. (Boogles), 286
Williams, Eric, 261
Williams, Laurie, 257-258
Williams, Milton Vishnu, **119**, 361
Williams, S.C., 262
Winkler, Anthony, 23, **229-236,**
Woods, J., 343, 344
Worrell, Frank (Tae), 13, 14, 18, 27, 43, 53, 67, 77, 80, 207, 266, 268, 285, 286, 312, 317, 318, 319, 320, 321, 323, 336, 337
Wynter, Sylvia, 22, **237-242**, 361
Yardley, Norman, 103, 104
Yeats, W.B., 17
Zephaniah, Benjamin, 30-31, **120**, 361

Roger Bonair-Agard, *Gully*
ISBN: 9781845231583; pp. 96; Pub. 2010; Price: £8.99

'One need not be fluent in the language of cricket to enjoy the swift, percussive rhythms of Roger Bonair-Agard's second opus calypso. He has refined his line, composed a pulse upon which he conjures, with a sort of astonishing and tender obligation, the fantasies and pathos of adolescence as well as the complexities of mature reflection. These are love poems for Trinidad and America, love poems for their histories, which are tragic, hilarious, wistful and unfinished.'
– Patrick Rosal

'Roger Bonair-Agard is a poet of blue lightning and white hot passions—even if the the subject (or metaphor) is the game of cricket. Gully means a lot of things, but in Bonair-Agard's masterful, musical hands, the word means a lot more!'
– Thomas Lux

'In *Gully*, Roger Bonair-Agard presents the phenomena of muscle memory with such wit and lyricism that the body comes alive. The reader finds his or her own limbs twitching in response to the poems' infectious groove. [...] and the aftershocks of history are revealed under that lens in all their vivid contradiction and verve.'
– Gregory Pardlo

Howard Fergus, *Lara Rains & Colonial Rites*
ISBN:9780948833953; pp: 88; pub. 1998; price: £7.99

Howard Fergus's poems explore the nature of living on Montserrat, a 'two-be-three island/hard like rock', vulnerable to the forces of nature and still 'this British corridor'. He writes honestly and observantly about these contingencies, finding in them metaphors for experiences which are universal.

Beyond Montserrat, Fergus looks for a wider Caribbean unity, but finds it only in cricket (and crime). Cricket, indeed, provides a major focus for his sense of the ironies of Caribbean history: that through a white-flannelled colonial rite with its roots in an imperial sense of Englishness, the West Indies has found its only true political framework and the means, explored in the sequence of poems celebrating Brian Lara's feats of 1994, to overturn symbolically the centuries of enslavement and colonialism.

All Peepal Tree titles are available from the website
www.peepaltreepress.com
with a money back guarantee, secure credit card ordering
and fast delivery throughout the world at cost or less.